YIDDISH WOMEN WRITERS

The Exile Book of Anthology Series, Number Six

YIDDISH WOMEN WRITERS

THE EXILE BOOK OF ANTHOLOGY SERIES, NUMBER SIX

Edited by Frieda Johles Forman

Translated by the Toronto Yiddish Translation Group:
Sam Blatt, Sarah Faerman, Vivian Felsen, Frieda Johles Forman,
Shirley Kumove, Sylvia Lustgarten, Goldie Morgentaler,
Alisa Poskanzer, and Ida Wynberg.

EXILE editions

singular fiction, poetry, nonfiction, translation, drama, and graphic books

Library and Archives Canada Cataloguing in Publication

The exile book of Yiddish women writers / edited by Frieda Johles Forman ; translated by Sam Blatt ... [et al.].

"The exile book of...anthology series, number six." "The Toronto Yiddish Translation Group." Includes bibliographical references. Text in English. Includes glossary of Yiddish words with English translations.

ISBN 978-1-55096-311-3

1. Short stories, Canadian (Yiddish)--Women authors--Translations into English. 2. Canadian fiction (Yiddish)--20th century--Translations into English. 3. Canadian literature (Yiddish)--20th century--Translations into English. 4. Short stories, Yiddish--Women authors--Translations into English. 5. Yiddish fiction--20th century--Translations into English. 6. Yiddish literature--Translations into English. 7. Jewish women--Literary collections. I. Forman, Frieda II. Blatt, Sam III. Toronto Yiddish Translation Group IV. Title: Yiddish women writers.
PS8331.Y53E95 2013 C839'.1301089287 C2013-900675-3

Second Printing 2022
Text and cover design by Michael Callaghan. Typeset in Fairfield, Hellas Fun, Perpetua Tilting, Optima and Zapf Dingbat fonts at Moons of Jupiter Studios
Published by Exile Editions Ltd ~ www.ExileEditions.com
144483 Southgate Road 14 – GD, Holstein, Ontario, N0G 2A0
Printed and Bound in Canada by Gauvin

We gratefully acknowledge the Canada Council for the Arts, the Government of Canada, the Ontario Arts Council, and the Ontario Creates for their support toward our publishing activities.

Canadian sales representation: The Canadian Manda Group, 664 Annette Street, Toronto ON M6S 2C8 www.mandagroup.com 416 516 0911

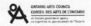

North American and international distribution, and U.S. sales: Independent Publishers Group, 814 North Franklin Street, Chicago IL 60610 www.ipgbook.com toll free: 1 800 888 4741

to the memory of

Chava Rosenfarb

(1923-2011)

and

Miriam Waddington

(1917-2004)

CONTENTS

INTRODUCTION

Less than five percent of thousands of volumes of Yiddish literature have been translated into English. Tragically, Yiddish – the marker of a rich and diverse culture and history spanning centuries and continents – is no longer the *lingua franca* of the Jewish people. Before the Holocaust, eleven million people spoke, read, and/or wrote in that language. Now, in our era, translation is the only viable medium to ferry Yiddish literary history to contemporary readers. While we bemoan the diminution of Yiddish as a spoken language, we are heartened by the enthusiasm with which its literary translations have been received. Yiddish has lost its centre but the margins are strong and can offer us a glimpse into that civilization.

Of the Yiddish literature that has been carried over into English, only a very small proportion of the works by women has been translated, belying their earlier significant appearance in newspapers, journals, and books in Europe, North and South America, and Israel. *The Exile Book of Yiddish Women Writers* will rectify the impression that Yiddish women writers did not exist, did not contribute to Yiddish literature. This collection brings to light not only women's hidden writings but also Canada's unique role in the development of Yiddish literature in the original mother tongue, *mame loshn*, and in translation.

Translation is a political act. Who gets the visa to the other language, to the other country is decided by the powerful – and they are not women writers. Yiddish literature in translation was until recently a single-sex creation, disregarding, dismissing the participation of the other half of humanity. It is only now, when feminists noted the absence of translated works by women, that the project of reclaiming these silenced voices has begun.

The range of prose – not only one genre – is our focus, to show the diversity of literary responses and cultural coherence. During the first half of the twentieth century, women writers were widely published and respected for their contribution to Yiddish literature. In the following decades, however, as Yiddish culture receded after the Second World War, their works were lost to contemporary North American readership. The major anthologies of Yiddish prose in translation concentrated on male writers and excluded not only fiction by women, but their memoirs and diaries as well. These works were consigned to oblivion. However distinctive North American Jewish literature by women may be, it carries with it only a faint echo of the rich, complex, often tragic past. The link broken with earlier generations of women over time and place remains a vague memory.

Montreal was and is second only to New York in the range, influence, and hospitality to Yiddish literature. In historical and contemporary contexts, the Canadian Yiddish community played a significant role not only through its sizeable literary production and talent, but with its open door to writers. The national Yiddish daily, *Der Keneder Adler* (*The Jewish Daily Eagle*) printed in Montreal, serialized women's stories over seven decades of the twentieth century, often providing them with their first introduction to a large and loyal readership. Miriam Waddington's essay "Mrs. Maza's Salon" expresses the communality and solidity of Montreal Yiddish literary society through the prism of one of its beloved writers, Ida Maze.

Montreal is also a centrepiece for Chayele Grober's "To the Great Wide World." It is here that she finds friendship, support, and affirmation for her calling as one of the pioneer actors in the first Jewish theatre, Habimah. Grober's memoir portrays the idealism and sacrifice attending this enterprise after the Russian revolution.

Our collection spans time and place of Jewish life: from the early part of the twentieth century to the last decades, from the small towns and cities of Eastern Europe to Israel and North America. Themes range from traditional life in the *shtetl* to emigration and the Holocaust; from intellectual journeys, family conflicts, political and religious battles to first generation American life.

Shtetl (small town) Jewish life is the backdrop and often foreground of much Yiddish literature, and women's writings also draw upon that world, but from women's perspectives. Rokhl Brokhes, in her time an acclaimed and widely read writer, was fierce in her portrayal of lives besieged by poverty in all its manifestations. In her short story "The Neighbour," unrelieved grief encloses a family, infiltrating every fibre of life as they witness the death of the young mother. "The Shop," serialized in the 1920s in the distinguished journal *Di Zukunft*, portrays an embittered young man whose scholarly life is sacrificed on the altar of commerce by his family's need to survive. In Brokhes' work, even in her children's stories, there is not the romantic transcendence of the poverty we sometimes find in sentimentalized depictions of the *shtetl.*

In "Aunt Mindl, Uncle Yoyne, and Meir Yontef," Mirl Erdberg Shatan joins realism and the surreal in a series of folkloric anecdotes centred on her aunt Mindl. With vivid details, the author evokes her small town in Poland in the early twentieth century: its class and social structure, relationships between Jews and Gentiles, family ties, and the specifics of women's lives. "The Bagel Baker," Erdberg Shatan's gentle description of a day in the life of a baker in a *shtetl* at the beginning of the twentieth century, allows us a glance at a life of abject poverty and little hope where humane values nevertheless still prevail.

"Miltchin," an extract from Dora Schulner's autobiographical novel of the same name, depicts the political turmoil in Russia during and following the revolution. Against a background of contradictory forces of corruption and idealism, Dora and her four children begin their journey to join husband and father in America.

Sheindl Franzus-Garfinkle's "Rokhl and the World of Ideas," excerpted from the novel *Rokhl*, is a work that is fully immersed in the wide expanse of twentieth-century thought. In it we confront modernity as it impinges on family life, educational changes, gender relations; where political movements, socialism, the Bund and women's equality collide with strongly held traditional values. Hearts as well as heads are engaged in the serious debates of the period, be they between Rokhl and her mother or between the courting couple.

"Chana's Sheep and Cattle," extracted from Shira Gorshman's autobiographical novel by the same name, takes place against a background of early collective life in the Crimea, a world seldom seen in Yiddish literature and certainly not from a woman's perspective. In Chana we find the revolutionary par excellence: headstrong, true to her principles, who brings the personal to the political, including her tender relationship to the animals in her care.

Known primarily for her poetry, Ida Maze was revered for her commitment to the Yiddish literary community of Montreal. In her autobiographical novel, *Denah*, the young heroine struggles to comprehend the tumultuous changes in her world: Revolution is in the air and young idealists abandon religion and home for political activism.

Beginning in the mid-twentieth century, the Holocaust became a recurring theme in Yiddish literature. One hesitates to introduce a gendered perspective into the discussion, but women's individual experiences need to be heard – even during those catastrophic times. This group of Holocaust narratives comprises distinct voices as well as diverse genres: personal knowledge and empathic expression.

Lili Berger's "Jewish Children on the Aryan Side" documents attempts by Jewish parents to save their children during the Holocaust, and it provides some insight into the motivation of a widowed Polish schoolteacher who becomes one of the "righteous gentiles." "The Teacher Zaminski and His Pupil Rifkele," Lili Berger's multilayered story extends in time and place from pre-World War II Poland to a post-Holocaust DP camp. Religious faith lost and regained is at the heart of this complex narration.

Sarah Hamer-Jacklyn's "The Holy Mothers" is a woman-centred narrative of spiritual and psychic resistance during the Holocaust. Antithetical aspects of reality, between an underground hiding place and a celestial, paradisiacal dream, are intertwined in the lives of a group of mothers.

The generative author Blume Lempel creates a unique ethos of magic realism surrounding the Holocaust in her story, "The Sprite." Her depiction of a small Eastern European town inhabited by Jews and Gentiles, forest animals, and wandering spirits does not prepare the reader for the shocking ending.

"Shadows" gives us a glimpse into the lives of Holocaust survivors living in the city of Lodz shortly after the war. A highly respected author, a survivor herself, Rachel Korn stages each scene in dramatic format with vignettes revealing hidden pasts and uncertain futures. The story leaves us questioning the very term "survivor."

In "A Cottage in the Laurentians," Chava Rosenfarb, one of the most important Yiddish writers of the second half of the twentieth century and the recipient of numerous prestigious awards, weaves together two thematic threads: the devastation wrought by the Holocaust on the afterlives of Holocaust survivors, and the way in which those tragic events affect the dynamics of one particular marriage. The story also addresses the use of art and literature as a balm against the sufferings of the past.

The stories set in the new world, be it the State of Israel or North America, reflect profound changes in character and disposition unimaginable in former lives. "The Tenth Is Born in Mishkenot" is the story of the tribulations faced by immigrant Jews in the Yemenite quarter of Mishkenot in Jerusalem. The profound clash of cultures – modernity and tradition – often sacrificing women's lives, makes this deceptively innocent tale a haunting document. Rikudah Potash is that rare Israeli writer who wrote in Yiddish, not about the destroyed world of the *shtetl,* but about *Mizrakhi* Jews from Turkey, Salonika, and Bukhara among whom she lived in Jerusalem. "The Little Messiah" is one of Potash's folkloric stories, which lures us into a world where much is understood and explained by dreams and religious faith. The birth of a son is such an occasion.

A spiritual literary sister of Fanny Hurst, best-selling Jewish American author of the 1920 and 1930s, Sarah Hamer-Jacklyn makes the move from *shtetl* setting to the fictional world of American soil with verve and versatility. "She Found an Audience" touches on the concerns and artistic aspirations preoccupying three young women in New York. She develops her story with psychological insight into her characters and with dramatic rhythm drawn from her days in the Yiddish theatre.

"In a Museum" is a romance set in New York City written in the popular magazine style of the day, the early to mid-century decades, years of intense efforts at Americanization. Despite its new world context, the story retains and articulates values reminiscent of the *shtetl,* such as respect for scholarly traits. Hamer-Jacklyn is a fascinating writer who is able to capture authentic sounds and language spanning cultures, time, and place.

The "Afterword" pays special tribute to the Canadian content of the anthology and includes one Yiddish piece and two written in English. In *Entwined Branches: Essays and Poems (Geflecht fun tsvaygn),* Miriam Krant pays homage to poets, many of whom are Canadian, by focusing on their lives and works. She was ahead of her time by opening up the literary world to women, by taking their work seriously. Due to space restrictions, we have included only one of her essays, "On Mirl Erdberg Shatan"; other pieces reviewed the works of Ida Maze, Esther Segal, and Rikudah Potash, among others.

"Love and Translation," Goldie Morgentaler's tribute to her mother Chava Rosenfarb, speaks for itself and to all readers.

As the years pass, and with them the generations of Yiddish Canadian writers Miriam Waddington so vividly depicts in "Mrs. Maza's Salon," we can only be grateful to the geniuses who understood the necessity of safeguarding this precious legacy.

A few words about our Yiddish translating group: We all grew up where Yiddish was the daily language at home, and for some, our schooling included a formal Yiddish education in the celebrated Folks Shule. A commitment to Yiddish in all its aspects drew us together.

Our choice to concentrate on reading women writers was based on a number of considerations. For some, it was a feminist project: to retrieve lost, silenced voices. For others, it satisfied a curiosity to read unfamiliar literature, and still for others to hear once again their mothers' voices in *mame loshn*, mother tongue. Some of our members had already participated as editor and translators in the creation of *Found Treasures: Stories by Yiddish Women Writers*, the first anthology on the subject in the world. For others it was a new experience they took on with zeal and dedication, discovering in the process unknown talents that drew upon their past history and predicted a restorative future.

In researching our material, we benefited from the pioneering work of *Found Treasures*, which taught us to look everywhere: in books, journals, archives, and private collections. We read countless stories, focusing on Canadian writers whose talent and scope deserved greater exposure than it had received to date.

The social component of our work deserves mentioning: we not only enjoyed the Yiddish words and sounds around the table, we also took pleasure in the companionability of our group, fully aware that we were in all likelihood the last generation to bring to the task our ancestors' voices. Throughout the years we met, occasional interruptions notwithstanding, and maintained our direction, inspired by the knowledge that we were reclaiming a Yiddish literature that now included the other half of humanity, never seen by Anglophone readers.

The entry of Richard Teleky into the life of our group brought us renewed energy, and we soon referred to him in Yiddish as our *meylets yoysher,* an honorific meaning advocate, intercessor. A former editor who had worked with Miriam Waddington and a number of other women writers, Richard shared with us the belief that silenced voices of all cultures must be heard, and to that end he took the book from possibility to actuality. His editorial and scholarly gifts were bestowed upon us in the wisdom, encouragement, and dedication he brought to the entire project.

We hope *The Exile Book of Yiddish Women Writers* will bring us out of exile and inspire a new generation of readers, writers, and translators to discover the riches of our mothers' words.

Frieda Johles Forman
February 2013

THE STORIES

THE TEACHER ZAMINSKI AND HIS PUPIL RIFKELE

Lili Berger

Whether or not Zaminski was a teacher by profession, no one knew and no one thought to inquire. Whether he had students in the city where he lived was of no concern to the Jews in the *shtetl.* For them it was enough that under his tutelage a servant girl, who had never so much as held a pen in her hand or lifted the cover of a book, had learned to write a proper letter and read almost fluently. It was sufficient to establish his pedagogical prowess.

Sheyne Broche had told the women that the teacher Zaminski had performed a miracle for the servant girl at the dry goods store who looked older than her years. Since childhood, her hand had trembled from hard work whenever she tried to put pen to paper. Evenings, after she finished her work, he taught her to write smoothly without a tremor. In short, his reputation as a teacher was indeed illustrious.

There were mothers who quietly lamented the fact that the teacher spent only three months each summer at his *dacha* in their *shtetl.* As soon as his vacation was over, he disappeared. While some were sorry to see him leave, others thanked God to be rid of an apostate; none more than Rifkele's father, Reb Abraham, the most prominent Hasid in the *shtetl.*

And what a tiny *shtetl* it was, tucked away and as big as a yawn. Scoffers would joke that its one long street, without even a name, stretched out like a noodle. But make no mistake: that was not the whole *shtetl*. Scattered behind the long row of houses and huts were other Jewish houses and huts. At one time it had boasted a prayer house, a bathhouse, a *heder*, and even special living quarters for the rabbi.

Behind the *shtetl* were fields and meadows, and beyond the meadows flowed the majestic Bug River. Across from the nameless main street was the highway, and behind it a ramp, and to the right of the ramp, the great forest. The small forest began on the other side, to the right of the "sands" where the *shtetl* ended.

And what relevance, you might ask, has all this to the teacher Zaminski? The fact is that the teacher loved forests. And since he had lodgings with a distant relative in a house in the middle of the long nameless street, he had to walk some distance through the town along the highway to reach the forest.

This in itself would not have been a problem for the *shtetl*'s inhabitants. The problem was that the teacher did not wear a hat, and he walked among the Jews bare-headed. When pious Jews, especially women, saw him, they made a wish that his head would shrivel, that heretic. If Abraham, the Gerer Hasid, saw his bare head up close, or from afar, he did not curse, Heaven forbid, but turned away and quietly entreated God to take pity on the sinner.

Reb Abraham did not derive much satisfaction from any of his six sons. He had sent them all to the famous *yeshiva* in Lomzhe. The second oldest son had even graduated from the *yeshiva* and received ordination as a rabbi. Great was the father's sorrow when that son chose a different direction. The best evidence was found concealed in the boys' bedroom – Maimonides' *Guide for the Perplexed* – which the father threw at once into the burning oven. He guessed that this unholy object had been brought into the house and hidden by none other than

Aaron, who had been the first to complete his *yeshiva* studies. Of the ten children, not one of the sons followed their pious father's path, although all were observant Jews. Instead, when it came to the strict observance of Judaism, the only one to follow in the father's footsteps was a girl, the second oldest daughter, Rifkele. And who could tell what would become of her when she grew up? She was overly absorbed in religious books not intended for women, thought Reb Abraham.

Indeed, Rifkele was as strictly devout as her father. On the Sabbath or on holidays, from the age of six, she carried the prayer book to the women's section of the synagogue for her mother. But by the age of ten Rifkele was no longer allowed to perform this function. She was now prohibited from carrying anything on the Sabbath. She would wrap her handkerchief around her wrist so as not to commit a sin by carrying it in the pocket of her Sabbath dress. Once, however, she unintentionally committed a sin. One Saturday in summer, while with her girlfriends in the forest, she had unwittingly stepped on a dry twig with her heavy shoe, and broke it in pieces. Rifkele knew that a sin required atonement. The penance she chose was to put the middle finger of her right hand into her mouth and bite it so hard that her eyes welled up with tears. When her friends brought her home injured, her pious mother yelled at her as she bandaged the finger. Her father, the silent one, smiled to himself. On the other hand, her widowed maternal grandfather, an opponent of Hasidism, gave her a kiss on the forehead and let her know that God would not have considered her transgression a sin because she had not done it deliberately. Rifkele was his favourite, and he often said to his daughter that it was a shame, a shame that Rifkele was not born a boy. She would have grown up to be a rabbi, and perhaps a great rebbe. To which his daughter answered: "You know what I say, father? It's enough that my husband is only interested in Godly matters. I was not happy that he wanted to make our sons into nothing but benchwarmers. And as far as the girl is concerned, she can serve God in her own way."

And indeed, Rifkele served God in her own way. By the age of ten she had read the *Tsena-Urena* several times, and had not neglected a single one of the other religious books written for women. And she had even studied the *Tanakh* with her grandfather without her father's knowledge. Her mother also hired a teacher for the girls.

There was no Jewish school in their small town. There was a Christian school, but it was two or three kilometres away. Once in a while a Jewish teacher would appear. When the teacher Zaminski arrived, Rifkele was in her thirteenth year and almost an autodidact. Her religious belief went hand in hand with her thirst for learning. Her mother secretly sent a message with Rifkele to the teacher Zaminski, which Rifkele delivered word for word: "My mother sent me to ask you whether you would give daily lessons to her daughter Rifkele who will bring her younger sister along with her. My mother asks that the lessons begin at eight o'clock in the morning."

The teacher listened to the entire message and asked why it had to be exactly at eight o'clock in the morning.

"Because my father is in the prayer house at that time..." and Rifkele stammered. She suddenly remembered something else and added: "My mother will send you the payment for the lessons. Just tell me the amount."

A deal was struck, and the lessons began the next day.

The early morning lessons went very smoothly. Rifkele was a conscientious pupil who absorbed every word her teacher uttered. When it came to writing, she blushed because she used her left hand, although at home she tried to get used to writing with the right hand, but only scribbles appeared. Despite this, the teacher constantly praised her progress. Her mother was happy, most of all with Rifkele's newly acquired knowledge of arithmetic, which would make her useful in business dealings. The only complaint she had about Rifkele was that she woke up her younger sister, who was somewhat lazy. When Rifkele was ready to go, the little one was still asleep. "Leave the child alone," she said. "She'll come a little later. She can find her own way."

But wanting to protect the reputation of her younger sister, Rifkele sought and found a solution. With a mouth full of water she sprayed the child's face. The sleepy little sister woke with a start. When the mother saw what had happened, she shouted: "What are you doing? It is a real sin to do this to a child!"

When Rifkele heard that she was committing a sin, she almost put her finger in her mouth, but remembered that her mother had forbidden it. "Mother, who is going to say the morning prayer with her, if I'm not here?"

"Someone else will say it with her. Don't be God's Cossack!"

Rifkele, however, made up for it that night. When they both were lying in their beds, their hands washed, Rifkele recited the evening prayer with her younger sister so fervently that the little sister fell asleep immediately.

Often, when her father sat until late at night in the small adjacent room, bent over his *Gemore,* chanting quietly to himself, Rifkele listened attentively. She enjoyed the musical murmuring. But when he hunched over his book of Psalms, quietly singing the words "Happy is the man that hath not walked in the counsel of the wicked," Rifkele silently repeated the words with the same melody until she had memorized all the verses of the Psalms that particularly appealed to her.

The summer vacation was coming to an end. The teacher suggested an extra lesson on Friday, a day when no lessons were scheduled. Perhaps he wanted to prolong the final week with an extra school day, or more likely he foresaw that on a Friday morning the younger sister would not attend, and he could feel less constrained. The extra class was devoted to natural science. Where the rain came from, how clouds formed in the sky, why rain was transformed into snow in the winter, and similar wonders of nature he had already explained in detail. In the extra Friday class he vividly depicted for Rifkele how and why the earth we inhabit turned continuously on its axis, and other secrets of the universe. Finally he asked her, "Do these things interest you?"

"Why not? I want to know everything. After all, I'm already a big girl. In six months I'll be thirteen, I'll be an adult. By then I should like to know everything there is to know."

"Well, if you would like to know everything, I'll give you something to read."

He took a small book out of a drawer. On the cover in large letters were the words NATURAL SCIENCE. "Put it in your satchel and don't show it to anyone! Don't let anyone see you reading it, and bring it back to me on Sunday."

"Can't I show it to my mother and my grandfather?"

"No! Not to anyone! Do you understand? Promise me."

"Yes, I promise. I will read it and return it to you."

On Saturday, after lunch, Rifkele disappeared. No one knew where she was. Her grandfather, who always came to Rifkele's defense, calmly reassured everyone that she must have walked to the forest where all the other young people went on Saturdays. Her mother resented the fact that Rifkele had not told them that she was going out. This time her father's silence indicated that he was displeased with her behaviour. It was understood that Rifkele had gone with her friends to the large forest.

In fact, Rifkele was in the attic. She had hurriedly eaten her lunch, crept out of the house through the back door to the porch, and climbed up the ladder to the attic. Amid boxes filled with Passover dishes, she took the thin volume from her Sabbath dress, sat down on a box, and began reading. It was not easy for her to decipher the difficult introduction. But she had already climbed up to the attic and, more importantly, she had promised her teacher to read the whole book. Therefore, she made an effort to read it a second time. The second time it was much easier. But the clearer the words became, the heavier they weighed on her heart. Her head was in a state of confusion.

Later, her worried mother scolded her: "Where did you disappear to? We looked for you everywhere."

"I went to get some fresh air in the yard. I lay down in the grass and fell asleep. I was…I was exhausted…"

"Yes, you're worn out," her mother observed. "You want to grasp everything. You're always peering into your notebooks, your schoolbooks, your religious books. You look as though today is not even the Sabbath."

Indeed, that Saturday Rifkele walked around in a daze. She decided to skip the prayer she recited every Saturday evening with her mother – God of Abraham, Isaac and Jacob – so that her mother would not notice how disturbed she was. Immediately after *havdalah* she pulled out the day-bed in her bedroom, made it herself, and lay down. Her uneasy mother put her hand on her daughter's forehead and repeated her diagnosis: "Exhausted, worn out. I'll take care of you, my little girl. Your lessons are tiring you out. Thank God that they're coming to an end." She said this quietly so that only Rifkele could hear her, but Rifkele was absorbed in own thoughts.

Sunday morning Rifkele got up earlier than usual, walking on tiptoe so as not to wake her sister. Her mother was busy in her shop. Rifkele forced herself to eat the bowl of cornmeal that her mother cooked for her breakfast every day. She put on a happy expression so that no one would become suspicious. Today she would be able to argue with her teacher alone, without anyone watching.

"I brought your book back," she said, catching her breath. "I hid it so that no one could see it."

"So, are you happy you read the book?"

She started to stammer, her head dropped, and she spoke more quietly than usual. "It turns out that the world created itself…nothing else…no one else…all by itself…"

"And you don't like that?"

"What about 'In the beginning God created the heavens and the earth'?" She said the words in one breath, almost choking, as though stifling a sob.

"Rifkele, the Five Books of Moses are very interesting and beautifully written. We can learn many wise things from them. But they were written many thousands of years ago. In those days people thought differently. They wrote differently."

"Was God also different than He is today?"

"That, I don't know… When you grow up and have much more knowledge and experience, perhaps you'll be able to better comprehend… You're tired today, you don't look well. And I have something else I must attend to. Tomorrow we'll have a longer session… Go home before your little sister comes. Maybe you can meet her on the way and take her home."

These were the last days of the summer vacation. The teacher Zaminski regretted that whole episode. What was the point? Did he want to make a freethinker out of a religious girl? She probably wouldn't come to the last few lessons. But she did come. She even brought her younger sister. However, she was no longer the same Rifkele. Her happy eyes were clouded by sadness.

Eighteen years passed.

Rifkele, now Rifke Firmol, was late for lunch in the cafeteria for the so-called "displaced persons" – survivors of the deportations who were unwilling to return to their destroyed homes. Rifke sat alone in the dining room thinking about how long she would have to remain in this accursed German land. Under no circumstances would she return to Poland. The Germans had murdered her entire family. Should she wait until the American Joint Distribution Committee located her mother's brother and his family in Montreal? She could only give the Committee their names, but not their address. Should she apply to the local Joint office and ask for assistance to travel to Paris? She had already bothered them enough. They would probably advise her again to be patient and wait for an answer from Canada. You were supposed to exhaust all your family connections first. But it wouldn't hurt to apply to the Joint again. They say that the more you pester them, the faster they find a solution.

She was so lost in thought that she didn't hear the door open. Suddenly she felt two eyes biting into her from a distance. She lifted her head to see an elderly man, his face covered with scars. She shivered. The man smiled at her broadly, slowly approached her round table, and nodded his head in greeting. His appearance, his head covered with a black hat, aroused in her both fear and pity.

"Are you Rifke Firmol?"

"Yes, but how do you know my name?"

"I saw your name while searching the lists in the Joint."

"Who are you to be interested in my name?"

"My name is Zaminski."

"Zaminski?" she asked in amazement.

On his face was a strange smile, both bitter and ironic.

"You once had a teacher called Zaminski. Don't you remember?"

"So what if I had a teacher called Zaminski?"

"It's me, your former teacher."

"Mama!" she cried in astonishment, the way they did in her *shtetl* when something extraordinary was happening.

"What happened to you? You're unrecognizable."

"The same happened to me as happened to you, except that maybe I received too many beatings."

Rifke looked at him, trying unsuccessfully to find a trace of her handsome former teacher. "Take off your hat. Why are you wearing a black hat in such blazing heat?"

"I wear a hat because I'm a Jew. A real Jew wears a hat."

She suddenly had the desire to make him feel more at ease. "Teacher, you're not going home?"

"I have no home, and no one left."

"Then we're in the same boat. Where are you planning to go?"

"With God's help, I hope to go to America. They promised it would be very soon. And you, where will you go?"

"I had hoped to go to relatives in Canada, but I don't have their address. They're searching for them by their family name, but who knows whether anything will come of it. I would rather go to Paris, and I've already talked to the Joint about it. But as you can see, I no longer count on any help from God. In our greatest hour of need He didn't help us, even when little children were being tortured and murdered." Her pain was mixed with sarcasm.

For a few moments Zaminski smiled discreetly, as though he understood that this was aimed at him. Then he answered calmly, like a teacher providing an explanation: "When great misfortunes befall them, people change. Sometimes they find God and become committed Jews. During my four-year ordeal, like other fugitives, I had the opportunity to observe such spiritual transformations."

"And I, teacher, am also a committed Jew, as you call yourself. However, you were once my teacher, and you planted a seed in my mind. The seed slowly took root and, in the circumstances that you just mentioned, the roots sprouted."

Zaminski was taken aback. He stood deep in thought. Then he gently took her hand and raised it toward his dry lips. He nodded his goodbye, with nothing more to say. He stopped at the door for a while, then turned, and in a friendly voice let his former student know that they would see each other again.

"Yes, teacher, we will see each other again," Rifke Firmol answered with a smile.

Translation by Vivian Felsen

JEWISH CHILDREN ON THE ARYAN SIDE

Lili Berger

First the "girl" was brought to the village schoolteacher Katerina Kubak. Then a few weeks later came the "boy." The nine-year-old girl was pensive, she moved quietly, and her eyes were filled with sadness. Occasionally she tugged at her dress with her right hand, as if to lengthen it. When she talked, she seemed to gag a little, as though she were forcing the words out of her throat. Her words came out mangled, like those of a chronic stutterer. Katerina, a veteran teacher, tried to rid the child of her bad habits. Since she had undertaken to hide the child, she would have to take every precaution to ensure that things went smoothly.

That was the summer of 1944. Katerina Kubak was free of her school responsibilities. A widow, she had too much time to think, and to dwell upon the tragedy that had befallen her. Only a few months before, the Germans had shot her only son and both adult grandsons. That her son had committed a crime by visiting – more than once – the forest where Russian parachutists had landed, she could understand. Why the Germans had killed both boys, eighteen-year-old Kazkhik and twenty-year-old Yurik, she could not fathom. It had happened about twenty kilometres from her village, so there was no one to tell her exactly what had occurred. People were afraid to talk, and some avoided her altogether. The only information she could obtain was that they had "taken care" of her daughter-in-law by deporting her. Who knows where they sent her, or whether she would even survive.

The teacher was consumed with anger and hatred toward the Germans. There was nothing she would not do to avenge the murder of her only son and her two grandsons who, during summer vacations, had brought so much happiness into her lonely widow's life. To repay the Germans for the suffering they had caused her, she was prepared to face any danger.

Thus, when people from the city came to ask her to take in an unfortunate child, an orphan, she did not think twice. They only hinted at the child's past, but they let Katerina know that the child had a birth certificate. It was all explained more with gestures than words. They did not have to elaborate. Katerina surmised more than she was told. She understood that she would have to be constantly vigilant, on guard not just against the hated Germans but her own neighbours, and even the village children, her pupils, who occasionally came to play in the schoolyard. She knew it would not be easy. But had it been easy for her son to risk his life?

The girl was delivered by an "aunt." Behind a locked door and closed windows. she whispered with the old teacher for some time before disappearing. Little Kristina had blonde hair, two small pigtails, and wore a dark blue dress that reached well below her knees. From her pale and troubled face her downcast eyes looked around with suspicion. A few garbled words rolled out of her mouth.

Despite her short life, the girl had a long, unusual biography. A year before, the eight-year-old Kristina had been a boy called Yurik. In the Lemberg ghetto, Yurik and his parents had been lucky enough to avoid the roundups and deportations by going into hiding. On one occasion, Yurik had escaped a roundup by crouching for an entire day in a doghouse in the corner of the small garden where the family had once kept their dog. Since dogs were not permitted in the ghetto, the empty doghouse became Yurik's hideout until his father, a dentist, finished digging a bunker in the cellar. Then, one grey dawn, all three of them – father, mother, and son – surreptitiously left the ghetto. They lived on the Aryan side with Aryan papers.

The Aryan papers, however, did not protect Yurik's father for very long. A former patient spotted him and informed the Germans. Yurik's father did not surrender easily to the Gestapo. He argued with them: no, he was not a Jew, the man had mistaken him for someone else. He was a Ukrainian, a pure Aryan, as attested to by his documents. But the Gestapo agents required other evidence of his Aryan identity, and sent him to one of their doctors who found the sign of his Jewishness on his body.

Yurik's mother was lost in confusion. For so long they had managed to survive all their ordeals and afflictions. Had they escaped every danger, survived all the roundups, and become "free," only to fall into the hands of the Germans? How was she to protect her child from the sign of the Jew on his body? She had heard how children in the courtyard had pulled down the trousers of a hidden child to see whether he was Jewish. It would have been much easier to protect her child had he been a girl. Then an idea came to her. She now had to obtain new Aryan papers and look for another place to live, as the place they were in now was no longer safe. Perhaps the informant had been spying on them. Since everything had to be changed, why not move into a new hiding place with a girl?

Having obtained new papers, she dressed Yurik like a girl, let his hair grow, tied it into small pigtails, and gave him a girl's name, the name on the Aryan birth certificate. It was not easy for the small Kristina to repeat her new name. Even harder for her was speaking in the feminine form. Yurik's mother worked hard to teach the eight-year-old boy how to be a girl. But for a girl it was enough to have an Aryan birth certificate, in particular if the child had "the right appearance." What luck amid all this bad luck for a Jewish child to have blonde hair! Blonde hair and fair skin would not reveal the fact that the Aryanism had been bought. The appropriate appearance and reincarnation as a girl would save the life of this child who was living under a death sentence.

This is what her mother had tried to explain to Kristina, but the newly minted girl had already understood that she had no alternative but to become accustomed to being a girl. Although a year had now passed, when she spoke Polish in the feminine form it sounded like she was stuttering. The children that came to the schoolyard called her "the stutterer." Sometimes she tugged at her dress with her right hand, as though she had something to hide underneath. No matter how many times the old Katerina quietly reproached her, explaining that she must behave like the other children, Kristina could not forget that she was not like the others – she was a boy disguised as a girl. Among the children, she felt like a lost lamb in a strange flock. In the tree-lined garden around the village school she sought the most remote, inconspicuous corner to sit cross-legged, covering her knees with her long dress, sadly and enviously watching the village children at play. The children gave her a new nickname. They began calling her the stuttering nun. But they did not harm her. How could they hurt a nun, even if she stuttered? Yet, although they left her alone, she still suffered. She suffered because the Germans had shot her father, because her mother had left the house one day and never returned, because she, Kristina, wanted to be a boy, but because of the Germans and the new birth certificate she had to be a girl. How could she play with the other children when she did not know what had happened to her mother? How could she be like the other children when she was so unhappy? Her profound sadness continued unabated until the day that the village teacher brought home Janek.

Janek was a seven-year-old boy with a shaven head, brown eyes, a long face, and two beauty marks. His tight trousers revealed the roundness of his limbs, despite his thinness. His dark grey shirt, buttoned to the neck, made him look older than his age. Janek also spoke very little, but whatever he said, he said clearly. He did not avoid Kristina or the other children. On the contrary, he liked their company, although he made friends not with the boys but with the girls, with whom he felt more comfortable. He listened to their stories and secrets; he laughed at their jokes. The boys made fun of him, calling him a mama's boy. It did not bother him. He was also quite content to have Kristina as his best friend. She was, after all, Pani Katerina's foster child just as he was. Kristina also felt more at home since Janek's arrival. When she was with him, her tongue moved more easily, and she stuttered less. When she spoke to him, it was easier for her to use the feminine forms. She stopped going off alone to a corner. She became livelier. Her sadness gave way to childish joy.

The two children got along well, although they kept their secrets deep inside, revealing nothing to each other. Why, you might ask, had a girl been reincarnated as the boy Janek? Her mother, before her arrest and deportation, had exhausted her limited resources to procure a Christian birth certificate for her eight-year-old daughter. After a long search, she was offered the birth certificate of a seven-year-old Christian boy who had died. To change the birth certificate was impossible. She had no choice but to make her daughter into a boy. The little girl was a lively, gifted child. She quickly became accustomed to living in the skin of a boy in order to survive.

The older Kristina and the younger Janek were both the Pani Katerina's foster children. It made no difference that Kristina had been there longer. Janek, the newcomer, was more at home in Pani Katerina's house. Janek also immediately began helping Katerina with the household chores. When Katerina peeled potatoes, Janek did the same. When Katerina cleaned the house, the boy helped her, while the girl did not know what to do with herself. When Janek saw Katerina's large doll on her bed, he wanted to comb her hair and dress her up. As the old teacher watched her two foster children, her heavy heart felt lighter at the thought that she was able to fool all those who were collaborating with the Germans, and especially that she was able to deceive the Germans themselves. Was she not playing a trick on them by taking in both children, by keeping their secrets, by rescuing them from their claws?

To keep the secrets of the children from one another, Katerina shared her room with Kristina, while for Janek she prepared a bed in her spotless kitchen. She braided Kristina's hair every day. As Kristina's hair grew, her braids grew longer, but Katerina kept Janek's hair closely cropped, to make him look more like a boy.

The summer sped by. The German armies moved eastward. The village of B., where Katerina Kubak was a teacher, became a corridor for German military personnel. The peasants remained in their huts, afraid to show their faces. The head of the village had to find places to billet the Germans. He soon came snooping around Katerina's house. A shadow of fear fell over her peaceful home as danger began spreading its dark wings. That night, Katerina Kubak put the children to bed early, hung a lock on the door, and went to seek help.

One cloudy afternoon, a nun in her long black habit and a large, white winged wimple arrived at the house. She said little, having no time to lose. Silently, she stuffed two folded birth certificates into the deep pocket of her robe. Taking the children by the hand, she led them out without saying a word. Kristina and Janek did not ask where they were going. Like hunted animals, they felt the net spreading out around them, and realized the need to flee the deadly dangers that lurked all around. Silently, they kept up with the hurried steps of the nun. A new anxiety gnawed at their hearts – concern for Katerina Kubak. Who would protect her now? What would become of her?

They arrived at the convent as night fell. Exhausted by the journey, and by their fear, the children fell asleep at once. The next morning, Kristina and Janek met at the breakfast table but did not recognize each other. Kristina was dressed in trousers, her hair cut short. Janek had again become a girl, wearing Kristina's long dress.

In the convent it was no longer necessary to live in disguise. However, Yurik and Balbina had to pretend they were deaf and mute until they became reacquainted with their true identities.

Translation by Vivian Felsen

THE NEIGHBOUR

Rokhl Brokhes

Our neighbour is ill with consumption.

Her apartment is a small one. From two small rooms, two windows look out onto the courtyard. The beds are never made, the walls are not wiped down, the floor is never swept, the dishes unwashed, and everywhere, things scattered and out of place. The children are always crying and needy – they want something, something is lacking. They aren't washed, aren't dressed. They are always clinging to their mother, pulling at her, pushing her and getting tangled under her feet. They make her already-difficult movement even more so. Her black dress droops over her feet and hampers her steps.

When she goes out, her head is covered in an old, worn, grey scarf, dropped low over her forehead. Only her eyes are visible – large, deeply sunken, wild with a sick fire, and a dark yellow spot in the middle of her pale, long nose. She can't stand for long, and has to sit down on the log lying in the yard. But her children attack her and whimper, and tear and poke at her. They are heartless, these little children…what do they want from her? Why don't they give her a rest? However, one can't be angry with them…they are so little, so pale and forlorn, it's heartbreaking – the little orphans. Today, tomorrow, their mother will be dead. She is already spent.

The children don't laugh, don't play. The younger little girl – about three years old – her face is always smudged with tears.

She is always distressed, always demanding. Seldom is she quiet – and then distracted. Her dark little eyes open wide, look away, seeing something, anticipating something bitter and frightening…

Their father is seldom seen at home, he is busy the whole day. He's a clerk at a counter somewhere and only comes home at night. He is still a young man though, youth grown old. He has a blond beard, hairy, neglected…and he is remote.

When the neighbours speak with the sick woman, they choose soft, light words; they don't mention life and death. They shudder, wary of catching "it" from her, and quietly back away…and when they see her, they are filled with pity. All joy is stifled, and a terrifying thought surfaces: death.

On *shabbes* or *yontef*, the sick woman rests, as it were, and her husband takes time with the children. Then they tear at him and cry and demand, and do not let him breathe…what do they want from him? He is so weary, so strained, so desperate…but the children are little ones, tiny; they understand nothing…though they want something, need something.

She is still trying to cure herself. Medicine bottles fill up a whole window sill. Though apparently, the husband-wife understand by now there is no remedy. They no longer look for help…abandoned, unhappy, and silent.

One never sees them talking to each other, amusing each other. Their father is not there…it's as if they are done talking. The most important issue has already been dealt with… Yes, they are alive…but what kind of life is it? They are alive, waiting only for death. The next day may bring them death. Maybe not today, but tomorrow… In the evenings, a dark cloud descends, and it seems that death steals into the dark yard. One can see him standing – a black, frightening mass, bent low over the entrance to the house. There, he pulls away for only a few moments… He pulls away, and the ailing woman dies choking on a slow, horrible cough.

The coughing… She coughs quietly now…but often, wearily. A trembling moves through her body as she coughs. One wonders what will eventually be the end. Although one already knows what the end will be. Although the end is already known, one resists, fears. Although one wants it…wants it to be over already, quickly, get it over with, it is drawn out, unbearable. Healthy people are annoyed by it…become impatient… are filled with a heavy, evil expectancy. It overwhelms the soul…and one wants it over and done with… Healthy people want to live, and fear and tremble at the thought of death… They would sacrifice thousands of others…as long as it is not they, themselves.

In the evening, when the husband arrives, the house is lit by two lamps, one hangs in the middle of the ceiling in a smoky glass. It looks sadly from top to bottom, as though worried… the other one sits by the oven, flickering. The young man is cooking something for supper… His sad figure, bent over the oven, stands preoccupied and somehow removed. The sick woman is also sad…searching the room…touching things around her…as though cleaning up. The children are now quiet…exchanging secrets or napping. The fear of death is at the head of the table, sitting on the sofa, present in all corners. The fear of death dominates.

On a cold, raw autumn morning, the neighbours found out that the woman had died. How, when and why, all of them asked; and, one at a time, they entered the house to take a look.

In the first room, the body was lying on the floor, long and laid out. A few candles were burning around it, and a few old Jews were reciting prayers. On the side, a young man busied himself and took charge. At a table, the women, watching over the dead person, were stitching white linen shrouds...quietly, with an atonal hum of prayers...

The husband was not seen anywhere. Whoever entered glanced around looking for him. In the other small room, behind a curtain, the two children, half-dressed, were sitting on a bed. Their faces were even more besmirched than usual. They were quietly leafing through a large, illustrated book. The little boy explained a few of the illustrations, pointing with his finger. The little girl was trying to follow, while at the same time, sighing deeply and heavily. The other bed, standing nearby, was messy, rumpled. Apparently, the dead woman had been removed from there. The coat that she had pulled over herself yesterday was still hanging on the wall next to the bed. Everyone who came into the room glanced at the empty bed. A neighbour was sitting in the room near the children, an older man, Azriel the goldsmith; and two or three women from the neighbourhood; also a rather tall young woman, a stranger, unfamiliar. Azriel was talking to the women, but he mainly deferred to the young lady.

"I tell you, I am terrified, when I remember. As you can see, I am not strong... It was midday already. I heard knocking on the wall. Thank God I already understood that all was not well here. How could I not understand? I came running in, and right here on this bed, they were both sitting – he and she – dressed in nothing but underwear. She had attached herself to him with her arms about him, and would not let go. Her hair was uncombed, undone, and hanging down. Her eyes were wide open, unblinking. And her face, deathly. And he was speaking, incoherently, speaking without words...he was saying something, but I couldn't understand. His face was exactly like hers – without a drop of blood, almost dead – as white as his shirt...and he was speaking...and I didn't understand... Finally

I heard him, and he was asking me to get a doctor quickly. However, I saw that she was already dead. I told him that she was already dead. One should say a prayer for her soul…and he wanted to say something…but his face was distorted, and his jaw was trembling…

"'Get a doctor!' he screamed, even though he saw for himself that she was already gone.

"I said to him, 'Lay her down on the bed.' But he stared at me, whispered something… What terror, what dread. Her hair, disheveled, was hanging around him…and the dead woman's arms were still clasped around him…I had no idea…such a very young person…"

"Where is he?" an old woman asked quietly. Everyone spoke softly. There were no hosts present, and no one had the impertinence to speak loudly.

"Where?" Azriel repeated again with a sour face. "Where?"

"With a friend of his, somewhere. Apparently he became ill, and stayed there. Probably there were good people there, and they didn't let him leave—"

"Who," asked the other old woman, "is the young man who helped out, who was dealing with household matters?"

"That's actually where he is," said Azriel. "That one, that same one is his good friend, who works in the same office that he does."

"Poor, wretched thing…" said another woman.

"What are you talking about?" Azriel turned to the young woman. "This little girl slept next to her dead mother…when we put the dead woman back on the bed here… Come to think of it…the little girl was sleeping, clinging to her mother, not knowing anything. How terrible…how frightening…"

"There are no complainants, there is no Judge…" said the first woman, and she wiped her eyes. "They don't even understand their grief…my little birds…" she referred to the children. But at that moment, the children started to quarrel. The little boy pulled the book closer to him, and his little sister also wanted it for herself.

"You are the older one," chided the old woman. "You should let her have it."

The little boy let go, but with a complaint. He wanted to have the small book over there, the one lying on the small table next to the little mirror, the overturned mirror…

Behind the empty bed was a small table with many dusty little objects, and next to that, a small picture album, red velvet with a bronze little lock.

"No, you can't have that," said the old woman, and gestured with her finger to her nose.

The little boy frowned, ready to cry. Someone else picked up the album and handed it over to him. He cheered up. "Now, I will look at it." The little girl dropped hers and wanted to join him.

"We will look at our mother…" said the little girl.

Everyone shuddered and turned to the children. The little boy turned the thick pages and showed everyone the pictures…

Azriel sighed, "Still a youth, such a young person." They looked on.

Here, she is with him…both together. Her face is round and youthful, energy and life reflected in her eyes. Tender limbs, lovely…his shoulder lightly touches hers…a smile brushes the corners of her lips…and he stares earnestly, with a faraway look, a happy, loving expression…to the future.

Another photograph: a little girl, about eight years old, with a childish, wonderstruck, charming little face…together with a father, with a mother, and a little brother…

Translation by Ida Wynberg

THE SHOP

Rokhl Brokhes

The shop was the fifth from the right, the third from the left – exactly the third opposite from the vivid-coloured gate of the Church.

As a young man the father had worked with lumber products and was never much at home. The mother, neglected and frail, was busy with housekeeping and raising the children, and the shop stood empty and locked for many years. When the father came home for the holidays, the moment he crossed the threshold, all kinds of conversation filled the house.

"A shop, our shop, stands empty, stands locked, and I wander around with strangers. If I were to make my living in my own shop, in my own city, in my home, at my table, next to my wife and children, I would live like a normal human being. I would have both the respect of the people around me, and myself as well. Now, I live like the perpetual *yeshiva* boy, who, each day, has another landlady, sits at another table..."

His father was a fretful man, an ailing man. When he spoke, his words seemed to be stretched tight by needles. Always someone was to blame. His tone was thus cross, irritable.

"Khaskl," mother pleaded, "I am telling you, we don't need a shop. I am a simple woman, in weak health, and I don't understand business. Think about it, if you open the shop, you'll have to quit your job. God knows what will happen then."

"If business takes off and opening the shop actually provides us with a living," said Father, "then I will, indeed happily, quit my job and be grateful to God, for my job has become a burden. I have no strength for this wandering life. If it doesn't work out, God forbid, I will still be left with my job. We'll be able to sell the merchandise, and put the lock back on the door."

And so, the shop was opened. Father gathered up his meagre savings, which amounted to about six hundred rubles, and set off to buy, little by little, all kinds of products – some dry goods, some dishes, some writing materials, and some groceries.

The shop was wide and deep. The shelves were only half-filled. One wall was almost completely empty, but the father hoped that for a trial it would be enough, until the business took off. Afterwards, he would get credit, and things would become more orderly.

Father went off. The sister took over the household chores, and the mother took her place in the shop.

At that time, Velvl was a student in *cheder*. When he came to his mother in the shop asking for money for *cheder*, she had no time: here she had to deal with a client who needed an invoice, here a customer who needed a receipt, here a customer for whom she had to weigh or measure something.

The mother could not manage alone in the shop, so the elder sister, Bayle, had to help her. Thus the housekeeping was neglected. The children did not get their dinners, and were not looked after. And when the father returned, he studied the books and discovered that the business was losing money, because the mother was not cut out to be a shopkeeper. She would lend money where she shouldn't, and she sold merchandise below its price.

If the shop was his only hope to get out of his bitter existence, he realized that he needed to let go of his job and run the shop himself.

"Remember, Khaskl," the mother nagged, "we will be left without food. The store will be our undoing. God only knows what this business will bring us to, us and our children."

The father did not have a good opinion of the mother's common sense – once she started to talk she would go on for an hour.

"Before your foolish imagination takes you too far," the father started, "bite your tongue. Or, better yet, go to the shed and milk the cow, or take a broom and sweep the house."

Father became a homebody. Velvl now had someone to go to synagogue with, someone to solicit for him the honour of a *Torah* reading, someone with whom to sit in the *sukkah*, or share the cushioned seat at the head of the *Pesach* table. However, along with the father's staying at home, came poverty. As time went on, mother's *shabbes challah* became smaller, the candles thinner, the dinners leaner. It was as if all of life had turned into a strange puzzle. Mother called Father a *shlemazl*, a persistently unlucky man. Since he'd opened the shop he brought the poverty home. The father called the mother a fool, because she did not understand that the reason they were poor was because he quit his job, and he quit his job because he opened the shop. And the mother complained that had he not opened the shop, he would not have had to quit his job.

Velvl could not decide which of them was right. He might have been angry at his father, but the man was not in good health. When he spoke, he started to cough noisily and painfully. He might have found fault with his mother, but as she argued she cried with bitter tears.

Velvl was an only son. Three younger brothers had died before they could utter a word. And his father, out of his last earnings, had paid tuition so that Velvl could study as was proper for a respectable son. Velvl had a good head. His teachers were proud of him. Even the priest's son – his non-Jewish teacher – praised him and always gave him a book to read.

The father would often repeat, "Look here, if the shop had succeeded the way I hoped, Velvl would grow up to be a man of learning. I would not have torn him away from his studies."

And the mother spoke with bitterness, "You see, if not for the shop, if you had not taken your place in the shop, you would have been able to send him away to be educated. And now, because of the shop, God only knows what will become of him."

He was not needed in the shop. It was enough that the father, mother, and sister, all three of them dejected, worried, waited, and watched throughout the week for a customer from the Cloister-Garden. When the father spotted Velvl, he said, "You might at least try to come into the shop once in a while. The whole household is miserable, and you walk around like a prince with your book."

"Come into the shop and give your father a break," the mother softly pleaded with her only son. "Your father is a sick man, worn out by worry. He would, at least, get an hour's rest."

"What do you think of our delicate child!" his sister pounced on him as soon as she saw him. "I stand watch in the shop from morning to night, and he avoids Tenth Street altogether."

And Velvl did indeed rush by Tenth Street in order to avoid the shop. Far beyond the city, he chose the wide meadows and white roads. But even when he got there, he would see from far away, from up high, the silvery tip of the church tower. Directly across the street there would have been the long row of shops: the third from the left side, the fifth from the right, the large hole with a red hanging chintz cloth.

It was as if he was looking at everyone from a distance. The small, slender Jew with a sparse grey beard, with the sickly face, looking at mother, a softly moving woman, neglected, with frightened, mournful eyes, at the sister, angry, quarrelsome. All of them were silently standing or sitting, each in his own corner, angry and distraught, each resentful of the other.

And when he, Velvl, occasionally came to see them, he stood there like a stranger. If he was not suffering his sister's laughter, it would be his father's anger. If it was not his father's outcry, he had to endure his mother's tears. He would always tear himself away feeling resentful, and persecuted.

His father died when Velvl was eighteen years old – he died still a young man – forty-five or forty-six. He died unexpectedly on a frosty winter evening, in the shop, sitting with his head resting on his arms on the edge of the counter, his eyes open like a window blind, a fixed, rigid gaze.

It was evening and the hanging lamp was burning with a low flame. The cold shelves with a bit of merchandise spread out, tearfully looked at the lonely dying gasp. It was quiet. A wind was blowing the red piece of chintz from the door, as if talking to someone, calling to someone.

Velvl was the first to arrive and was the first to see the dead, accusing glance striking him in the heart like the tip of a sharp knife.

"Close the shop, let there be an end." During the *shiva* week he wandered around the house in his socks, complaining and holding his head. The shop had sucked his father's marrow out of his bones, drop by drop.

"He was taken from the world before his time," the sister cried.

And his mother added, "It will drive us all from this world before our time."

However, when the *shiva* week was over, they picked themselves up from the floor, washed up, put on shoes, and did what was needed. The sister, as was her habit, took the key from where it hung on the wall, and went to open the shop. The mother wandered around the house for a while as if looking for something, moaned, and quietly sobbed. And then, she followed the sister.

Only Velvl was left to ponder the great concern: what is to be done now?

The shop! Was there ever a moment in his life when he imagined himself a shopkeeper? In as much as he detested shopkeeping and the shop, could he put himself in that same place where his father endured the most difficult moments, where he uttered his deathbed groan?

Late that evening, his mother and sister came from the shop silent, disconsolate, as though bringing with them his father's staring gaze. Velvl saw that look several times in the movement of these two helpless women.

Looking into his heart, he asked himself, was he not really to blame? Was he not to blame for his father, lonely and forgotten, his early death, on that cold winter's day? Could he not have sympathized with his father's bitter mood, and said something to lighten it? And *will* he not be to blame when his mother – broken, aged – will sit freezing in the shop, on a frosty, cold morning, looking out with the same helpless expression for a customer?

Guilty, guilty, but what is he to do? How is he to do it, he asked himself, and tortured himself through the long, sleepless winter night and, when the morning came, he went along with the others into the shop. He squeezed himself into a corner somewhere, and quietly observed his sister serving whoever was there whatever the customer wanted. He looked and reflected. He looked at every piece of fabric, every glass on the shelf. He looked and examined every thing individually. It was as if he were searching for his father's glance on every object.

He was overcome with worry, despair, pain. He was counting and recounting each knot in a thread, each grape in a wooden crate, he was searching, scraping, looking for the secret to selling, to shopkeeping.

He would establish the shop for them so that they would make a living, and then he himself would go away, far into the world, and forget about that black hole which buried his early years.

The tailor sewed a short cotton tunic from grey, coarse cloth for him. He put on a hat with ear flaps, tall boots, found two new sources of money to pay bribes, and with a long list in hand, he traveled into the city to buy merchandise. After he arrived with several cases and packages of merchandise, he himself painted the shop. He repaired the stoop, tore down the old, rotten yellowish fabric on the door, and replaced it with a gaudy red one. He laid out the new merchandise on the shelves – new and fashionable, not yet seen in their town, and he became a shopkeeper.

"Look at Velvl now," the other shopkeepers mused amongst themselves. "He seemed such a quiet one, but what a clever creature he is. Who would have thought it? We didn't expect it at all." "A quiet one is always a thief," another shopkeeper remarked. "A man preoccupied – who knows what he is thinking to himself?"

"We just never thought it of him, never thought it of him," people said with amazement.

And Velvl himself wondered. He did not recognize himself. He had always been shy, silent, closed off within himself. Now as he worked in the shop, he found a word to say to each customer, a clever comment, and a caustic word for his neighbour, the merchant who regretted having started with him. He became more lively, more social, more open. His whole character was transformed. His face, which had always been delicate and soft, became darker and fuller, his hands stronger and tougher, his eye more open and plain. He could look at a customer and guess what to offer him. His language became more hurried and blunt.

Not only his mother regarded him with respect, but also his sister no longer quarreled with him, but let him do what he wanted.

When they sat in the shop, they watched him quietly: how deftly he straightened out a tangled thread, how neatly he laid out the dishes in their rows, how he overturned each sack after another.

It was hard to recognize Velvl. And also the shop was not the same. A lucky thing – the door didn't close. And when someone left, someone else appeared. Velvl was ready, quickly switched from one to the other, from the ribbons that he had just shown a young lady, to the smelly wagon grease which he had to measure out for a gentile, or to the barrel where he picked out a herring with his bony fingers.

More than once, the mother said tearfully, "It was not your father's fate to live and be proud. If only he could see our shop today, he would come alive with joy." And the mother's sigh was then followed by Velvl's own deep sigh.

This shop claimed the life of his father, as well as his own best and youngest years. He was the last to return home – exhausted and cold – in the winter, soaked from sweat and dust in the summer. Then he turned to the collection of books he had on his desk. There were books to study, books to read – they were obtained from the large cities. He could not tear himself away from them till late at night, and often till the light of day.

He had his own ideas which he had not shared with anyone else, not confided to anyone. As he lay exhausted in his bed, his eyes wide open, he saw himself in happy times when he would tear himself away from his small town to go to another city where his thirst for knowledge would also be satisfied, where he would no longer have to look at the detested shop. As his reflections and longings crossed his mind, his young body was suffused with fresh energy, and thus he could rise for an early morning in the shop, where he greeted his customers smiling.

Every morning, like clockwork, he took the keys from their hook on the wall, and every evening he put them back in place. Often the days would go slowly, the time would crawl. But often he would not even notice the passing of time when a customer had his attention. When he was not in the shop, people would wait for him.

On a winter day he would warm his hands on the hot coal stove. In the summer he would refresh himself with ice water. Summer days were long, and he disposed of them. Winter nights were long, lonely, desolate, and he pressed them on, one by one. Crowding one another, the years flew by – uniform, repetitious, cyclical. He became broader in the shoulders, more relaxed, and a dark-yellow mustache appeared on his lip. His older sister got married. His younger sister spent hours in front of a mirror and dressed herself up like a bride. It was almost time for him to leave, although he had not yet decided when. The days came one after another, and to break through the habitual order was as difficult as it had been to construct.

Each day at the same time, his mother took his place, and he went home to eat his lunch. More than once along the way, he would remember that he needed to stop off and collect a long neglected debt, or that he needed to pick up some merchandise at the post office, or, on one occasion, get a loan from someone. His mother would complain softly to a customer, "My Velvele will probably eat a cold lunch today also, as you see, he is absorbed in the shop with his whole heart and soul."

Once, at the beginning of a spring day, instead of crossing over the puddles on little wooden bridges, he had to step on rotten pieces of wood lying on the city streets. He was walking home at the regular time to eat his lunch. The air was pleasant, warm. He was preoccupied, his hands in his pockets, his head lowered, his shoulders raised. Someone came up to him and called out with enthusiasm, "Velvl, what a timely encounter, you've saved me a lot of effort. I am not eager to walk the muddy roads. The fact that I have met you is a good sign."

Velvl raised his head and found himself looking at a familiar face – a good friend of his mother's.

"The delay, Velvele, is actually because of you. You can ask for whatever dowry you wish, whatever value you decide, we won't haggle with you. They want you there, both the father-in-law and the bride are eager. If you want you will become a partner in their shop, or you will take them as partners in your shop. Whatever you wish."

The man was talking gibberish. Velvl regarded him with an expression of indifference. However, after a minute, when the man started to speak again, he suddenly understood. He felt a strange thud in his chest, and a deep red colour washed over his face. No instant reply sprang to his lips in answer to the matchmaker. He merely pushed him away with his arm, wanting only to be on his way.

However, the matchmaker caught him by the sleeve, and with the same sweetness of tone and brave persistence, he said: "Don't berate yourself, Velvele, for thinking of a glass of schnapps. You're no doubt on your way home to have some dinner. I will accompany you, and we will have a chat there. Your mother is already bursting with pride since her enemy Leyke Manyas will be her in-law, and Peshke will be her daughter-in-law. This is not the first time they have argued about it. But, among business people, it is not a big deal."

By now Velvl had found the answer, and he spoke firmly and abruptly in a decisive voice, "Your efforts, my friend, are wasted. You can't talk to me about marriage. I am leaving soon." And before the man had time to reply, Velvl raised his shoulders, and was gone.

He didn't go home where his food was waiting for him. He also didn't return to the shop. He took the pathway downhill, behind the old bathhouse. He hurried, his head lowered, his shoulders hunched.

Down from the slope stretched a long road, well trod by horses, wheels, and people walking. In some places the ground was already bare, in others it was covered with a thin green brush. The distant sky was filled with little grey-white clouds. They swarmed in, as though rushing by, passing through, while blending at the same time. In the distance, the silver spire of the church was visible. There, on the opposite side of the street, in that lonely row, under those low hanging roofs, were the shops – the third one from the left, the fifth one from the right – broad, widely open like the open mouth of a wild animal wanting to swallow him. That's where his mother was sitting, calm, confident. No doubt she was boasting about her only son, who took over the shop, boasting about his cleverness, dreaming about the rich in-laws, and glowing with pride.

"No!" he shouted in rage and desperation. He would not return to them again! Enough! The best years of his life, the youngest years, he had sacrificed. What more do they want? And tears of disappointment began to tumble down his face.

There, at the top of the hill, the whole town could be seen, all those established homes, all those projecting roofs. The marketplace was visible: people walking, fingering the produce in the wagons, searching and talking. They haggled and made deals. Velvl felt the most intense disgust for them, the worst hostility.

He longed to carve out a stick and to set out over this long road, and never look back.

When he arrived home, his mother had already returned from the shop.

"Where were you?" she asked him. "No doubt you ended up in some village. The whole world is preparing for the holiday, and I was left alone in the shop, not knowing what to do first."

Velvl quickly darted to his room, tired, and lay down on his bed. His mother followed him. "What's the matter with you?" Her eyes, as always, were tearful and fearful. "Why don't you tell me where you've been?"

Velvl answered brusquely, "You have to know everything – where I was. Tomorrow I am going away from here, then you won't know how I am getting along."

"For merchandise?" she asked.

"For *Torah*," he answered her in kind.

"What are you talking about?" She did not understand.

"I said," he cut in and answered angrily, "that's enough already. It's time for me to begin doing something for myself. I've spent enough time here with your troubles."

"What do you mean, Velvele, God is with you 'for yourself' alone? I don't understand what you're talking about. Our shop, thank God, is now one of the best in the market. Leyke Manyas sends a matchmaker and is dying for you."

Angrily, Velvl sprang up quickly and banged the table, knocking down all the books resting there. Pale and angry, he cried out, "For the few days remaining, I don't want to hear that word *marriage*. Otherwise, I'll run away this minute."

This was the first time in her life that his mother witnessed such anger from him, and she was left standing pallid, in horror, totally immobilized, not even a twitch of the eyebrow.

"They want to make a merchant out of me, forever a shopkeeper! They don't want to know what's in my soul! I would rather dig ditches, chop wood, than be a shopkeeper!"

He ran around the house at length, upset and angry, and kept talking. His mother stood silent and listened to it all.

Because of this fact alone, that his father died in this cursed shop, he should never have set foot in it. As long as he can remember, he has been crying about the shop, everyone is crying, and she, his mother, was also crying. He remembers her tears. If that is what he became, a shopkeeper, it was only because of their need to make a living. And now, they must run it themselves. And he would leave. He had his own dreams and ways.

He began preparing for his departure. His mother couldn't hold him back, not even until after the holidays, not even for the big fair taking place in a couple of weeks. He was determined to leave, and no entreaties helped. The whole time he was preparing to leave, he didn't set foot in the shop. He didn't want to look at it. However, once the day of departure had been set, he came into the shop for a day and gave his mother and his younger sister advice, and told them how to sell the merchandise, and he promised that he would help them with suggestions or solutions, in any way he could.

An acquaintance came into the shop, Reb Eyliyahu, before whom the mother had shed a mountain of bitter tears. He came to buy snuff, and also to criticize Velvl.

"You are an impudent lad, a smart aleck," he said. "If your father were alive, you would not be going to a strange city and leaving everything here in shambles. Your father had been over half the world, and barely made it home. He sat down in this shop, which at that time was barely a *sukkah,* a temporary shelter. Do you remember, there were merely two plates, and five pieces of calico lying there?"

"And sitting here all alone, he died," Velvl cut in on the old man.

"You are a smart aleck. Before you became a shopkeeper, you were a fine young man. You studied in *cheder*. I used to love you. You don't realize that when you're destined to die, you die. If you are destined to fall, you will fall in the middle of the street, and surrender your soul back to God. And your father died in his shop, near his bed. You are your mother's only son, so you get whatever you want. With me you wouldn't get what you want, because I understand that it's not right for you to abandon the shop and tear yourself away. It's crazy, anyone will tell you, it's crazy."

"Listen to him, my son, and understand what a wise friend is telling you," his mother said tearfully.

Velvl didn't answer. This was the last day he was going to be with them. Soon, there would be an end to all these discussions.

In the middle of the night, in a small-town linen buggy, he drove away from his home, drove past a large, deep, muddy road, through the market, to a narrow street, past the pitiful shops. Quietly, on someone's small porch, the night watchman was knocking. People were standing outside, the large locks hanging on the iron front doors.

In that row, the fifth from the right side, the third from the left, was standing the shop, with its now widened door closed. That was the void that consumed his young years. Not so long ago, it seems, on that dark, cold evening, a crowd of noisy people carried his father out from that same dark hole. Now also, people were furtively chasing him, like black shadows, silently running after him with flaming torches in hand.

He arrived at the town where he used to come to buy merchandise. He picked that town because it was large and beautiful, and he had friends, and he hoped to find out from them where to find work.

The first of his friends, a rich storekeeper, who had always greeted him with fatherly affection, now looked at him with suspicion. Velvl told him that this time he didn't come as a buyer with a list, but as a person looking for a job, only enough work to survive. He didn't want to work full-time, because he wanted to study.

"Young man," said his friend, with eyes narrowed, "Tell me the truth. How big is your debt?"

Velvl was incensed.

What's the idea? Who dared insult him in such an ugly way? He came here to live independently. The shop was his mother's.

But the shopkeeper didn't believe him, and shook his head.

A second shopkeeper greeted him the same way, a third, a fourth – no one understood his madness to give up his own shop and go looking in a strange city for whatever work was available. One of them said there must be something more there, and Velvl was making a fool of himself. Another said Velvl was indeed a fool.

Velvl rented a room, bought books, and sat for days over them. He hired a good teacher, and waited for a job to materialize. Meanwhile he studied and read.

He had nice new clothing. His hands became soft. His cheeks became smooth again, and fair, and his movements once more reserved and quiet. His new friends, at first shy, now grew to love him. In this strange city he began to feel at home and at ease, and life became more gracious for him. He often wanted to shout out a toast, his chest puffed out, his voice unreserved: "To life and to laughter!"

The city was large and beautiful. There were things to see, to look at, everything was new to him. And he didn't notice the days passing. The books he read were so interesting that he didn't notice the nights passing.

However, often as he talked with someone, he would suddenly break off sighing. Often, in the midst of his greatest delight in a book, he would get up and pace around his room. It was not just these long letters – precisely two a week – which he received from his mother, or the long lists she sent him, that kept him attached to his home, to the detested shop.

He had a wild thought which didn't let him rest. It pounded in his head like a hammer. Did he have the right to sit here and do nothing while his aging mother sat in the shop working for him? Why the ten rubles that she would send him from time to time, even though he didn't want them? Though he walked around with the paper note, not wanting to exchange it, he would eventually have to, and live on it, because he had no job yet, no earnings. His friends considered him a rich man. No one went out of his way for him, or looked out for him, or said, with tearful eyes and a quivering voice, that he is a poor boy, who doesn't have two kopeks of his own. They would smile at him and doubt him because his clothes were cleanly washed and his handkerchiefs were trimmed with lace, and the tea he drank was the best. In almost every letter, his mother would enclose some kind of gift: handkerchiefs, white collars, some nuts, a pound of honey cake. "I don't buy it for myself, my son, so you, in a strange place, will surely not buy it. Eat it in good health, and I will send you more." His mother's letters were long: how a certain fabric did sell, while another one lay there and no one wanted to touch it. One shopkeeper found a good bargain, a rare occurrence, and customers would trip over his doorstep. Since he left, their income had diminished, because she was very ill with grief and worry beyond her strength. She barely managed to stay on her feet. Her daughter was of no use. In fact, she dragged out of the shop whatever she could – a piece of wood, a collar – and she was not practical. "Look, look, my dear son, learn what you need and come home. It will be as it was once, not like today. The shop without you is without a manager, even the walls are in mourning, don't waste time."

Long letters, he read them holding his breath, and then he hid them away. But the familiar style would echo in his ears, and the crooked letters would reappear on certain pages of the book that he was reading. Late in the evening, pictures would materialize before his eyes, strange, frightening.

He would see an old, bent-over figure sitting at the entrance of the shop, frozen, with eyes anxious, helpless. He saw other eyes, also frozen, blind, but with hard, accusing looks. He saw them, those glances, lost, expressing something – that was during those long sleepless nights. And on nights that he did sleep, he had dreams that he was standing in the shop weighing coarse salt on the wooden scale, or laying out the red flowered calico for women, or he was looking for something on the shelves, and couldn't find it.

He was walking with a tall, thin young woman with dark hair and a pale face. Pressed to his arm, she was talking earnestly, she was upset.

"Don't you understand that for me, it's easier to have my wedding with my parents – I'm only asking for a small thing. Tell my father that you are a shopkeeper, that you have a shop in a city, that you are not so poor. He will consult the local shopkeepers, and he will believe them."

His head was spinning from her warm breath, and her imploring tone, soaked with tears. It evoked in him a gentle tenderness. But he firmly tore away.

"Anything you want, but not that. You say that it needs only to be said. I know that. I will not return to the city, and I would throw myself in the river rather than become a shopkeeper again. But to improve my situation through a lie. Whatever that shop touched in my life, it brought tragedy. A shop! It's not a shop at all. It's a wide, deep pit – a grave. There my father lies buried, and with him the harmony between my parents, and my youth, and my sister's youth."

She interrupted him, her voice trembling with tears. "I don't need your shop, I don't want your town. I just want our wedding to be sooner, together with you. I won't wait for a better time. You find it hard to make it easier for me by making a small concession." She was tired; she sat down on a small chair, near somebody's house. He was standing nearby, pensive, lightly leaning on his cane.

It was evening; one side of the sky was low, painted in red-yellow sunset colours. The other side was deep, white, cheerful. Somewhere far away, sounds spread out one by one. The scent of blooming apple blossoms wafted in from a neighbour's garden, and a light breeze blew white down, clean and soft, into the air. Velvl was standing bent over his cane, and his large blue eyes were wide, open, immersed in thought, into himself, and she, who was more precious than his own life, was sitting nearby. Her tear-stained young face filled him with sorrow and worry, and her dark eyes were coated with shining, distressing tears. He wanted to be even closer to her, press her head to his breast, and comfort and console her. Everything around was so soft, so balanced. He wanted to wipe her tears and tell her that everything would be better. Good fortune would be theirs. Their love would provide increasing happiness. He came up to her and sat down on the bench.

"Freydele," he uttered, soft and earnest. His words were gracious, but they suddenly caught in his throat. His spirit broke, pulled and painfully recoiled.

The shop. A picture emerged before his eyes: the dusty small town, the market in the middle, the narrow church street, the row of shops – low, hidden under the low hanging roof, with wide door openings, pasted with pieces of calico, with pelts, and belts, and on the stools, the shopkeepers, some tired and sleepy, some angry and preoccupied, some exchanging "the last word."

To forget all this, not to think, forget everything that is so substantial, forget with her together, greet the good fortune to come, somehow endure the bad.

It was again a summer's evening – open windows, fluttering curtains, lamp lights flickering. People were sitting around the white covered tables, relatives of the bride, a large family; from his side, only his mother and two acquaintances, local shopkeepers. The mother was wearing her small-town hairpiece, with two large strands of pearls on her throat – one her own, the other borrowed. She was shy, sitting not far from the table, clutching her white handkerchief in her hand and talking to the bride's two aunts. Their conversation was being followed by two uncles, earnest and amiable – leaning on their chairs.

"Good people have always told me," said the mother, "he is an only son. He will always have his way. His leaving was so strange, but it turns out that he was leaving to find his destiny.

"The shop," the mother said, "is an orphan without him. If a child comes in, he says without Velvl here, there is nothing to buy. If a gentile from the village comes in and Velvl is not there, he can't decide on a fabric. If he comes back, the shop will revive and I will also live." Now happy, the mother added, "He will surely come back."

Velvl heard his mother's words from a distance. He wanted to cry out spitefully to her, and to them all, and even the girl in the white satin jacket, that he would never be a shopkeeper. He wanted to reveal the truth: that he presented himself to be shopkeeper to fool his father-in-law. That's what Freydl told them all. He had as much to do with the shop as he had with the next world. Freydl wanted it that way. Freydl lied to them. There she stands, upset, afraid to meet his eye.

A guest is sitting speaking about business, specifically about shopkeeping, and particularly about small-town shopkeeping. A shopkeeper is sitting at the window, the same one who took Velvl for a fool because he had come here "to find a position."

"Go home," he had advised him then. "I am not impressed that you have become a teacher. That is a very small accomplishment." Now he is praising Velvl to the father-in-law.

"A wonderful expert, I've never seen such a skilful young man. I hadn't noticed at all. Never mind he appears to be so quiet, but he has a good head, and he's gifted, a sensitive boy."

"If you could only see him buying fabric," the bride's father beams with pride. "A good match. In these times, finding a match for a child is a supreme act of creation, and here 'the goat is fed, yet all the hay remains.'"

The daughter has what she wants and the match is a good one.

"I don't care," he said to a friend. "So, it's not a great big store, but a small shop – it doesn't matter. The main point is that the young man is a talented shopkeeper. With money you can make it into a big store. I prefer small-town life – it's more peaceful, simpler, healthier. My whole life I've envied the small-town merchant. You have your own home, a nice garden, and your head is clear."

Not only did Velvl see the shop standing there, but others had envisioned it also. It was situated at the head of the street, took up the largest lot. The people were pleased with it – they drank wine, ate cake, and broke pottery. They liked it. There was a clatter of chairs, a clanging of wine goblets. They delighted in it, they wished him *mazel tov*. They praised him, and wished him well. Velvl felt he was dreaming – a strange, heavy dream. The large lamps and candelabras had gone out. Instead of walls with pictures hanging, he saw plain, rough boarding thrown together. And the people – instead of clamouring joyfully, were crying in fear, scurrying back and forth, not knowing what to do first. Under his holiday suit, on his bare skin, he felt the touch of an icy hand.

Velvl and Freydl were living in an attic room, having quarrelled with everyone, hiding from everyone. His father-in-law and mother-in-law considered him cruel for letting his young wife suffer. He had only two or three students. He didn't want to go home. In her letters his mother had asked him to come back, but he had become so used to her letters he was no longer much disturbed by them. All his thoughts now centred on Freydl. She was close to giving birth and he didn't know how to make her more comfortable. She didn't complain to him, but he constantly looked for hidden tears. He now avoided friends. The world had lost its attraction for him. He wandered the streets like a stranger, indifferent. And if he noticed one of his former friends he would cross the street, or hide in a courtyard.

"Freydele," he said one gloomy evening, "if you want, we can go home to my mother. She loves you very much. She will care for you and treat you like the apple of her eye. We have a big house, good milk, fresh air. You'll recuperate and then we will return."

"We will go if you want," said Freydl. "Why not, we can come back at any time."

"Of course we will come back. The road is always open."

He had not been home for three years. It was time to find out how his mother and sister were managing. They would not remain there for long. It was only a few weeks before Passover. He imagined sitting with his old mother at the *seder*, how happy she would be. Then it would take Freydl a few weeks to get her strength back. Maybe a month, no more, before they would be able to bring the baby back. He could already sense the relief he would feel upon their return. But perhaps not Freydl? No, she would also.

"You have no idea, Freydele," he said, "what a muddy little town it is. You are too refined for me to keep you there long. You can't imagine the memories that place evokes in me but, Freydele, only for a short while. Agreed, Freydele?"

"Yes, yes, for a short time," she answered him.

He was grateful to her. How she suffered because of him, so quietly, at such a time. Silently, they prepared for their journey.

He was so tired, he had experienced so many humiliations and insults in the last while, knocking on strangers' doors, looking for work so that Freydl would not feel powerless in dealing with her parents' anger.

"Freydele, Freydele," he said quietly, as he watched her search for something in the room, her body heavy, and he felt hot tears running down his face.

They arrived in town in the middle of the night. It was dark, and a light rain was falling. They took the same road he had taken three years earlier. The wagon driver recognized Velvl and chatted with him, giving him the town's latest news – who had built a house, who had fallen into poverty, who died, and who got married. He heard names he knew, but also names he had forgotten. As they drove through old familiar streets, he saw where his old school had stood, and where once there was an apple orchard. Soon they would reach the narrow street, with the Church garden; soon the familiar row of shops, closed now, quiet, their locks hanging on the outside iron bars.

A night watchman, sad and shabby, was banging somewhere in a corner. A gloomy emptiness began to gnaw at Velvl's heart.

"You see, Freydl," he said, "Here are the shops on the right, see the fifth one, that's ours."

Freydl struggled to see out of the buggy, but the driver urged the horses on, and the wheels splashed her with mud. She saw nothing.

They arrived at an old, wide house, with the porch falling apart. His mother woke from sleep, wearing an old dress, tears in her eyes, her voice dry and melancholy…

"Barely lived to see you again," she said. "My little birds, just managed to call you back into the nest."

Velvl threw himself at the first chair in the house and placed it in front of the fireplace, which his mother had just lit. He looked around, considering all the gloomy furniture, neglected, dusty, old, and familiar. There was the door of his small bedroom, where he dreamt and endured much. Now, his mother tells him, she stores dried mushrooms and onions there for the winter.

"Why do I need such a big house? I am one person, alone. A small corner is enough for me. I am not strong enough for this shopkeeping. Now that you have come, children, I will be happier, since I have lived to see my Velvl's child…"

Mother scrambled over the cases, made some tea, and prepared a table of freshly made dishes and her own baking. Her heart told her that the children would arrive suddenly, so she had prepared. Her heart always alerted her. Her heart was a clock. It informed her, it advised her. And now they have arrived. Tomorrow at dawn, while they are still sleeping, she will run to tell her daughters. They happen to live close by. The younger one was actually doing well in her studies. She was being supported by her father-in-law and mother-in-law. The older one, Beyle, suffered, poor girl. Her husband was a big problem, he failed at whatever he tried. She herself was actually a skilful person, but what's the use, if there was nothing to put her skills to. She had three little ones, but there was no food.

"And besides," Mother added a moment later, "she is a malicious woman. You know our Beyle, with her mouth. When she hears me coming, she would devour me. She wants me to give her the shop, send me away, and in her hands the shop will become as it once was with you."

"Well, why not?" said Velvl. "It's possible. It would be easier for you. You wouldn't need to struggle so hard, and you would be with your grandchildren."

"Is that right?" Mother heated up. "And you, what do you plan to do? How long do you plan to play around? You're a father already, thank God!"

"I won't be here long anyway, maybe a month."

Mother wouldn't talk about it. They were her dearest guests, and now was not the time to discuss such issues. She sat down next to Freydl, put her arm around her, and looked at her with great affection.

"Wait it out, my daughter. You won't regret coming to your mother-in-law. This is all Velvl's inheritance, from his father, as it should be in this world, and it's time he became a *mentsh.*"

Velvl, tired out from the trip, paid little attention to his mother's words. He lay down where his mother had made the bed, but couldn't sleep, because he saw before his eyes the old and worn again. Not that long ago things were like this. Not so long ago, his father walked around the house, talking, debating about opening the shop. Right over here his mother sat when his father called her a fool because business was bad, and Mother cried long, bitter tears. She didn't wipe them, she didn't notice. And on this same little sofa on which he now lay, his father lay, hoarse, sick – on a market day. His mother boiled rock candy in hot water for him. It was also on this little sofa that they had brought him that night from the shop and laid him down – dead. And then, in the other room, he was laid out on the floor, surrounded by candles, with men reading Psalms over him. Here above this room Velvl paced during that difficult week of mourning, his lapel torn, his heart broken.

In the morning, while they were still lying in bed, the sisters arrived, also the brothers-in-law. They were excited, they bustled and shouted. Even before lunch, some friends arrived, and then acquaintances, and then neighbours from the street, to welcome and find out how they had lived for the past three years. Could they join them for dinner?

They also came to the shop. The mother had hurried earlier and happily announced: "I have visitors, precious visitors, long awaited." Everyone looked at Velvl and Freydl, and smiled.

"Look, he's the same Velvl, but he's wearing a small white collar, his face is pale, he has a thin neck."

In the shop he sat down behind the counter, Freydl on a stool, and the mother greeted people at the door, and again announced: "My Velvele has come home, my Velvele and my Freydele."

And all the other shopkeepers and acquaintances came in and welcomed them and marvelled at them.

"Not all these people are good friends," Velvl said to Freydl softly. "They are all enemies. They study you and find your weakness. Don't believe the sweet talk." He looked at Freydl's modern big-city coat, and her refined, gentle appearance, and felt his heart tighten in sympathy – what is she doing here in this filthy town, among these small-town shopkeepers, with their old-fashioned, outmoded style of clothing.

Not for long, not for long, he comforted himself.

An old lady came into the shop, asked for something, but didn't find what she wanted. Another one entered and also couldn't find what she needed. And a third came and bickered over the price.

"Look at me, children, I worked so hard," the mother complained. "Yet, in these three years the shop has deteriorated completely." On one side, a beam had moved, a shelf broke off and wound up in a corner somewhere, cobwebs and dust covered everything. An old barrel was standing empty and falling apart. From somewhere, spices spilled, and the strong, sweet smell mixed with sawdust and dead mice. Freydl clutched a white handkerchief to her nose, and Velvl was thrown into a coughing spell.

Freydl gave birth to a boy. She was healthy and lay in bed, pale, calm, and pensive. The baby was swaddled and sleeping. Velvl was sitting nearby, bent over, thinking. Everything was finished now. Life would begin anew, peacefully and with renewed energy.

"Yes, Freydele," he said, with a smile of devotion. "When you get well, we will leave, we will go back."

Freydl smiled back at him. She looked around to make sure nobody was there, and cautiously, without words, pulled his head toward her and kissed him. Pleased, she pointed at the baby.

It was evening. On the windows, the flowerpots that had withered in the winter were coming back into flower. They became greener, ripe, emitting a fragrant scent. Mother left a young hired girl to look after the shop, and treading softly, began to prepare all kinds of dishes for her daughter-in-law. Velvl felt light-hearted, so good that all his cares melted away.

He imagined himself still a young boy, on a Friday evening, he had finished with *cheder*, and his mother served him a bowl of cooked plums with a large egg cookie.

"Your in-laws have arrived, your in-laws have arrived!" Mother, still in her old dress, ran to greet them. Velvl woke up flustered, didn't know what to do.

"Father and mother, father and mother," Freydl also began to whimper.

Her father was tall, stout, with a black but already greying beard. Her mother was a little round woman, with a thin voice and short arms. They brought with them baskets and packages with good things for the *bris*, the circumcision, and all kinds of gifts for the newborn grandson – shirts and trousers. For their daughter, they brought pretty dresses; for their son-in-law, a new hat; for his mother, a silk shawl; and more and more gifts... They asked questions and talked until late at night, telling stories about everything and everyone. It was the kind of *bris* that would give the whole town something to talk about. In addition to the good things – the wines and the honey cake – that the in-laws brought, Velvl's mother brought whatever she could from the shop. She cooked and she fried and served the whole crowd. The child was named Khaskl, after Velvl's father, and he was carried around like a treasure.

The in-laws stayed for a whole week. Velvl lived as if he were at a fair – fancy warm dinners each day, and guests.

"The house is a big one," said the father-in-law, "but old. It needs renovation. My opinion," he said to Velvl, "you need to redo the rooms. Build a large one for yourself, with lots of light, and from this room, you can make two. You need to make new windows. The frames are falling apart from just a touch. As for the porch, you need a new one. You could kill yourself stepping on this one. You need to fence the yard. What do you want with your neighbour's goats and pigs rummaging around?"

"There are craftsmen here, Velvl – lumber, Velvl. For a small price, you can make it like new. You need to build up the shop. Which shelf is it that's rotten? Throw it out! Knock out another window, it will be brighter."

Freydl's father was a practical man. He hated to postpone for long what had to be done now. That same week he found a carpenter and a painter, and got together with them. He negotiated with them, and contracted them to get to work.

"Why didn't you ask me whether I want to stay?" said Velvl.

"What could you possibly not want here?"

"But, I am going away from here. Freydl, we're leaving."

But the father gave his daughter a sharp glance, and said, "Where do you want to go? What do you lack here? You are no longer responsible only for yourself. You have a child. The child needs fresh milk and clean air, and a clean little room for his cradle."

"What did you leave behind?" he asked Velvl. "What kind of good fortune is waiting for you? What don't you have here? Haven't you suffered enough there?"

"Stay, Velvele, stay Freydele!" his mother swooped down on them. "Freydele, my child, tell me why you want to leave me, why? I will return Freydele's dowry, I don't want to rob her."

"Let her have a place, let her child have his corner," said her father. "Ask anyone in town whether I'm right or not." And even before the in-laws had left, the tradesmen arrived with saws and hammers to break and to build.

Outside, the weather was already warm. The sky was clear, as though it had been washed – deep and open over the entire world. Little chirping birds, like little black dots, rose high above. All the houses on the other side of the street were awash with rays of sunshine. Velvl was sitting on the porch watching the workmen. He felt as though they were digging his grave. His heart was crying, silent, lonely, and uneasy.

The mother was in the shop. Freydl had quietly put the child to sleep. The hired servant girl was doing the laundry, singing while she worked. Across the street, a neighbour, a teacher, was studying with *cheder* students, his voice was loud and clear and carried over the street through the open window. Two little boys were moving a small cart, one pulling, the other pushing, both tired and sweating. Each was working hard. Everything was alive, everything in its place. The white tablecloth lay on the table. Mother's Sabbath candlesticks were standing, scrubbed shiny. The old wall clock was wound. The flowerpots were blooming, watered, and fragrant.

What was the celebration here? Who had won out here? Whose stature was enhanced? His heart was asking.

It was evening, the tradesmen had dispersed, and the white paint chips on the black earth reflected the light from the open window. Freydl came out on the porch and sat down quietly near him. Her face was pale, the jacket draped over her body was crumpled. All of her movements had become broader, older, and distended.

"Velvl." She spoke quietly but earnestly. "You are upset, I understand. It's difficult for you to be here. Go away, go away alone. For you it will be greener there, without me, without the child. I will remain until the baby grows up."

"Go where?" he asked, and his voice was choked and hushed. "What will I go to if you remain here? And what will you be left with?"

Freydl was silent for a while. Then she shook her head, and squeezing her hands, she said, "You ask to what you will go.

What do I know? Maybe you will find something. I will be here with your mother."

Velvl caught his breath as though he had swallowed something. Something wafted through the cool air – a word, or a hidden misery. He suddenly jumped down from the porch, caught his shoe on a loose board, and almost fell. His steps were quick and firm over the quiet street.

When he turned and looked behind him, he saw Freydl's white jacket reflected in the light from the window. He remained standing, watching, for a long time. In the darkness of night she was like a white speck, lost, unfamiliar. No doubt she was now crying with those hidden tears, the tears which he was always expecting. It was because of them that his heart was torn, and he was even more ill-fated. Just one year ago, and where did they go, those beautiful, sensitive dreams. All at once, that white speck was erased, and his eyes filled with biting salty tears.

As he sat on the porch late at night, he recalled that years ago when he became a shopkeeper, he thought it would only be for a while. Everyone was sleeping, the fire was extinguished and the whole town had become a black, indistinguishable mass. To become a shopkeeper, not for his mother and sisters as it was then, but for himself alone now – Freydl and the baby – that was the same as for he himself. If he became a shopkeeper, it would be forever, final, like the nails driven into the boards for a new coffin, final – forever.

So what was he to do, he asked himself in the dark glow of the night. Should I leave them here? With whom should I leave them? Should I become a shopkeeper for them, a shopkeeper forever?

When they had unpacked the new merchandise from the large crates that his father-in-law had sent, Bayle, the sister, came and wrangled, complained that she should also be included as a partner. The shop was as much hers as Velvl's. She had also put in a lot of work in the past. While Velvl was running around as a schoolboy, she was already working in the shop, arguing with that gentile, or that customer, as any of them.

"We are going to do bloody battle for that shop," she complained. But Velvl didn't answer. Wordlessly, he heard her out, her curses, and her denial of having profited from her efforts. Their mother sided with him. Who ever heard of a daughter taking over a son's inheritance?

And when the shop was made ready, repaired and painted, whitewashed, the merchandise organized the way it should be...the sister came again and argued and cried, and cursed. The neighbouring merchants listened and were amused.

He put on his old shopkeeper clothes, which his mother had put away in a box, and began to run the shop. However, one couldn't compare him to the Velvl that used to be, the difference was so great. Once well-disposed and full of enthusiasm toward customers, he now stood slothful, silent, his face averted, his lips tightly pursed. His eyes never smiled; once bright blue, they became grey and dry. People thought he resembled his father more. He stayed late in the shop because he didn't want to go home. No longer did he have his friendly little room with its many books, and youthful dreams. They had been absorbed into the building somewhere. The walls merged into other rooms. No more "dear little room," no more special corner – erased – washed away.

He no longer rushed out of town, to the deep valleys, the distant overgrown fields, green and fragrant. Their beauty no longer beckoned him.

His little son, pale, with a round and hairy little head, and lively blue eyes, spoke and laughed wordlessly with everyone. Only Velvl stood silent in front of his carriage. He felt responsible, ashamed, and unhappy. His face was bitter, sad, and he would quickly walk away, so as not to make the baby cry.

He was a peaceful child, healthy, didn't disturb anyone. Freydl put on a wide apron and an old dress, and came to the shop. Her glistening black hair was covered with a scarf. The apron diminished her height, and she looked like the wife of a typical shopkeeper. She also knew how to hang onto the sleeve of a customer, haggle with him and promote the value of the product.

"I want to be a shopkeeper," she said the first time she came into the shop. "You will be able to leave later, and I want to make it easier for you." This very same thought had already entered his mind, but this time it went deeper. He turned away from her, gazed at the fence of the Cloister garden, as tears – peculiar, large, womanly tears – flowed down his face.

They were all quiet in the shop. Both spoke with the customers, but between the two of them, not a word was exchanged. It was so tense, so difficult, the mother sighed and cracked her knuckles. Freydl would pull her wrap tight and become quiet. Velvl felt an odd coldness and withering in his heart.

At night, when he came home, Freydl would wait for him, sad and longing, but she got no loving word from him. He came from the shop at the end of a long day, and any soft or endearing sentiments in his heart had dried up.

Freydl no longer concealed her tears from him. He saw them in the middle of the night, during the day while, eating and even when she nursed the baby. Tears were a common sight in the house now. Velvl saw them often. Once, in this same spot, his mother's bed had stood, covered with a stitched red blanket. Today, Freydl's bed was there, covered with a white, ironed bedspread. Today the mother, with silent tears, poured out her heart to Freydl.

The shop was running well again. The shelves were groaning under the weight of merchandise. The cash box, with the tricky leaf lock, was full of money earned, yet nobody was happy. The mother couldn't bear her daughter's struggle, and she regretted not having Velvl include her in the partnership. She now sided with Bayle. If her own brother wouldn't help her, who then? If the shop is doing well, there would be enough for everybody. Why shouldn't Bayle have a share, a very small share? She would surely work hard to contribute. She was right when she said she had played a part. Velvl was just a mere child, while she was here dealing with things. She did everything for his sake, from sewing his little shirts, to bringing him marmalade tarts in school. And now, he was not even moved by her children's struggle.

Velvl should take Bayle in as a partner. She was in a position to claim the whole business, but Freydl wouldn't allow it. She didn't want Bayle here.

"I certainly heard enough from her for that half year. My health was affected, life isn't so sweet that we should deliberately try to make it bitter. I don't want, I don't want her here with me."

And from Velvl, "What do you mean 'you don't want'? Regardless of what you don't want, do we have to ask you about everything? Are you the opinion *zogerin,* the official spokesperson here?"

"If you take Bayle into the shop," said Freydl, "I am leaving. I am taking my child and leaving."

"Where will you go," the mother argued. "Where to?"

Freydl burst into tears.

She would go wherever possible, only not to remain here. They have spoiled her whole life, embittered her existence, her youth, and now they were chasing her away… Bad enough they had made her a shopkeeper in this filthy town, Velvl was now having the last word.

"We made you a shopkeeper? Who made you a shopkeeper? Try to remember. Maybe you should try to remember that you made me a shopkeeper, you and your father."

"I am the person in charge here," the mother became incensed. "What I want, I will do!"

"In charge of my father's contribution?" from Freydl.

"Your father is boss here? We'll pay him off, we'll repay him his daughter's dowry, and he will cease to be boss over the shop. Do you hear? I am hardly here already. Do you mean to chase me out? Her father is 'boss' here," Mother protested.

It was a dark autumn evening. A heavy rain was falling. No stranger heard their battle. Only the light of the hanging lamp was seen from the window, and it illuminated a large, dense puddle of mud outside. The rain made the quagmire even greater.

The next day it was still raining. A cloudy rawness lay on them. Everyone was still sleepy, but they got up before Velvl. The servant girl needed to bake bread today, and the mother got up to supervise. Freydl was busy with the baby who was cutting teeth and was restless – he bit his mother's finger.

"Eight o'clock. It's raining. There isn't even any business, but Velvl, get up," said his mother. "We need to open the shop."

He was lying in bed in his white nightdress, on white cushions, his eyes half open. He looked young now, no more than his twenty-five years. His dark hair was silky, suiting him like a pretty frame to his white forehead and his bare throat. A light pink colour played on his cheeks.

"Velvl, we have to open the shop. Get up." The mother's voice was, as always, soft, sorrowful. She couldn't hide the emotion from yesterday's arguments. As he got up, Velvl was irritated and quarrelsome. His cup of tea was already on the table, but he didn't drink it. He reached for the keys on the wall and headed for the door. For a moment he stopped and looked at Freydl, sitting at the table with the baby. She also looked at him and waited for something. Her eyes were tired, with black circles around them. He said nothing and walked away.

It was quiet in the streets. Large raindrops were chasing each other and falling noisily. He walked, indifferent to his path, his keys clinking, his feet padding in the water.

In the row of shops, one or two were open. The rest were closed and locked. He unlocked the door and went in. It was dark inside, and oddly still.

The rain was still coming down, but people were running to the market to behold the sight of him hanging. But even those rushing were too late. He was lowered from the gallows. His head was resting on a sack of salt, which had been tossed there. His face was covered by a dark piece of calico. His feet were awkwardly splayed in large, muddy boots.

Translation by Ida Wynberg

ROKHL AND THE WORLD OF IDEAS

Sheindl Franzus-Garfinkle

It was the end of summer, 1916. In the Ukrainian town of B., far from the battlefields, people had grown as accustomed to war as dogs to iron chains; on some the mark of suffering lingered, others feasted on the fat bone and prospered.

A large crowd had gathered in Leah Frank's parlour because word had gotten out that two prominent merchants would be visitors in her home. They were said to be timber merchants hoping to export a couple of wagonloads of grain. Manufacturers' agents also wanted to be included. "It doesn't hurt to have one's ear to the ground – to hear what's going on in the world. And Leah's deals could succeed even with garbage. She'd buy anything, and with her good luck there was always a profit."

Just as the gracious Leah (strings of pearls under her substantial chins) opened the door to the merchants, Chaya, her maid, entered from the kitchen. "Mistress, I won't allow you any business deals now. As it is, the food will be tasteless, it's been moved on and off the grate a hundred times. They've waited so long, they can chat a little longer, until you've eaten."

The merchants laughed. "Leah, she's almost more mistress than you are. How long has she been supervising you this way?" "So! What else would you expect?" another remarked. "After all, Leah's Rokhl was raised in her arms."

Leah guessed immediately what had brought the merchants: they were itching for something. She, on the other hand, had her own headaches. But since they were asking, she was ready to make a killing.

When the talk of business was finished, no one wanted to leave. Somebody then mentioned that the town's new gymnasium would be completed that year.

Rokhl knew there would only be five grades, but the principal had said she was ready for the seventh. So she wanted to go to Odessa. Leah was opposed, and argued with her.

"Don't forget, dear daughter, that – health permitting – you'll turn seventeen this winter. It's enough that the gymnasium stole Issar from his home and that Chayim graduated a madman as a result of book learning. Other mothers keep their children by their side, and that's that. Not me. No good tutors in the village? Then immediately the boys are sent to town. For Chayim, only God himself would do – for him only Motel, the great Hebraist. Money was no object. So he became – my troubles on my enemies' heads – a vegetarian! Nothing helped, neither kindness nor harshness. So I set him up in a business, a well-stocked shop. Next he hankered after farming. He fled to Argentina, then Palestine, and returned weak-eyed and without his trousers. I opened yet another store for him, but he just stood there in the doorway like an outsider. The business could go up in flames but he remained lost in his Esperanto books. He thinks we're not decent enough to the gentiles, nothing will do but to share all we own with them. Usually you chase after customers but they came on their own to Chayim. They sniffed out his honest weights – and word got around."

"Honesty is the best policy!" Rokhl said triumphantly. "Education brings these results."

Her mother grimaced. "Like a pea sticks to the wall – there's absolutely no connection. This much I know for sure – if I hadn't sent Issar off to study, he'd still be at home. A fifteen-year-old boy who convinced himself that he couldn't study in Russia. Only America suited him. Now he's there working like a dog. See what comes of your enlightenment! There are enough over-educated imbeciles without you."

Rokhl was as stubborn as her brothers. She wouldn't listen and wanted to hear nothing more. She was going away to study with or without her mother's permission.

"So then, go-o-o! And may you be among the wise ones. When we need a sack repaired, we'll go from door to door and the response will be: 'Move along! A doctor lives here.' Chayim believes the servants should also study. But how would he feel if Chaya were to study and there'd be no one to serve up a fluffy pancake the way he likes it? But go! Do as you wish! I no longer understand anything. I moved to the city because of you, but that didn't help either. So go your way!"

Rokhl stood with head bowed, weighing pity for her mother's despair against her own passion for learning. To no avail. Her books, clothing, and sundries already packed, she stood at an open window. The clear air seemed to meet her boldly and proudly, flowing right through her: "There, far away, after you've acquired culture and knowledge, you too will become as independent as I am, with the power to inspire and delight."

Vifchik, the coachman, called in, "Well, Madam Frank, is your young lady ready yet? Hurry! She'll miss the train!"

Leah's head throbbed. How could she convince Rokhl not to go? Nowadays, one needed a course on how to speak to one's own children. In her parents' home, a shout of "I say no!" and ten children were left trembling, none daring to make a sound.

"Daughter, do you know what? Here, take three years' tuition, spend it freely on the most expensive, most exquisite clothing. At least you'll have done something practical. These are war years, and a suitable match won't wait for you to complete your studies."

Aunt Eni and other rich relatives, even the wise and learned merchant Reb Yisroel, took it upon themselves to warn that a young woman overly immersed in books wouldn't easily find a suitable groom, and often remains an old maid.

Though they thought they were right, Rokhl was tormented. Resentment gnawed at her. A woman's place was so insignificant, so marginal: a woman was an appendage.

She'd already been in Odessa for two months, but Rokhl gave little thought to meeting new acquaintances. She sensed a vague tumult around her, a muted struggle; in that atmosphere she searched for answers.

Several times, a blond young man had seated himself next to her in the library and taken notes from a variety of books.

One day, on their way home, their eyes met. They both smiled, and removing his hat, Gustav Feldman greeted her. "I believe books have already introduced us and that I may take the liberty of addressing you."

He was somewhat above medium height, tanned, with mild blue eyes that attested to a right-thinking nature. She was pleased with his greeting. "I think so, too," she responded.

After that day they often walked together from the library to Rokhl's residence.

Several times he stopped by to call on her. One Saturday he suggested the cinema Urania, where a professor usually spoke about the films. Rokhl accompanied him happily. He pleased her: a cultured, intelligent, and serious young man. But under no circumstances would she let him pay for her.

Gustav bore brutal scars from the days when tsarist hooligans drove homeless Polish Jews from the war front. He ached and raged against the oppressors of his people. To Rokhl he said: "The Jewish youth in Polish villages are more serious and more idealistic. Here in Odessa I collided with a vast emptiness. But eventually I did succeed in finding informed and sensible young men who needed only to be set on the right path."

She always listened to his wise words with great interest. Would her Lilliputian soul ever achieve such heights?

One evening, Rokhl accompanied Gustav to the home of an acquaintance. At their entrance, noisy conversation resolved into a joyous "Gustav! Feldman! Gustav!"

Gustav introduced Rokhl. Then, turning to a student, he said: "This is the person."

Ziskind, the student, responded by offering Rokhl both hands. "One to Miss Frank and one to Rokhl."

Rokhl was confused: why should the usually tactful Gustav have introduced her so strangely? And this prankster with the pleasant face, was he having fun at her expense? Nevertheless, her eyes softened, and she too offered both hands.

From a corner of the room Gustav was heard. "Comrades, I'm very pleased to see new friends at our classes each time. We Bundists mustn't be concerned because we're few in number. We're a party, not a club. Each group must strive to increase its awareness – that's the greatest strength of our political struggle. One brief, well-written pamphlet can reach millions. We must send out our call to brothers and sisters throughout the world."

The word "Bundist" was foreign to Rokhl. What exactly was it? She listened further and laughed at her own ignorance. Of course! They were socialists! Gustav's flowing speech evoked such beautiful ideals. All of his writing at the library was in preparation for these lectures. How masterfully he spoke about the French Revolution! What detail! What extraordinary powers of expression! "… Pyramids of injustice arising from generations' long enslavement – at the hands of lords, aristocrats, tsars, and capitalists." He could even draw on examples from before history began.

A girl asked how to explain our constant turning back to ancient ideas.

"According to Bern," said Gustav, "we feel spiritually close to the Greeks because they also had their early and middle periods. We must understand that every thinker has the right to consider his own period as the new age. That's why their ideals and views are sometimes compared to our own."

Nachman, a short young man of about twenty, with shabby clothes and a gymnast's hat pushed back on his head, said, in a voice full of conviction, "Oddly enough, primitive societies were often more spiritual than our own."

Ziskind jumped up so impetuously Rokhl could almost feel a breeze passing by. "Recently, when I had occasion to be in a village near Odessa, I asked a peasant if he was interested in what's in the newspapers. He looked at me intensely and said, 'I've heard their lies more than once. Our tsar reports on how far back we've pushed the enemy and of their losses; our enemy reports the exact same thing.' Shrugging indifferently, he continued: 'From all the conscripts in our village, not one has returned. Come with me, I'll take you to my neighbours. In the first house you'll meet a middle-aged woman; suffering has turned her into an old grandmother. Her eyes have lost their light since receiving the box with the few things that her son asked be sent to his mother after his death. Not a person, not a thing remains alive for her. In the second house, the agitated voice of a younger woman will come at you. Just listen to how her voice struggles with sorrow – unless you've come with good news from her young man. Open another door: wretched children wrap themselves around you like worms. Papa, Papa! wails through the house. The mother has gone to find bread, who knows by what means.'"

A debate followed as to whether war could be prevented.

Rokhl was stirred. What superior beings! How beautiful their reasoning! They criticize one another without bitterness. How dedicated they are: they're prepared to sacrifice themselves for the sake of humanity.

It was past one o'clock when Gustav accompanied Rokhl home. He was so deep in thought it seemed he'd forgotten all about her. Suddenly he said, "Rokhl, do you want to attend our Tuesday lectures?"

"Oh yes! I wish it were Tuesday already. I've been completely removed from social issues, I've simply never given thought to questions of society. I'm less interested in anti-theological arguments – I've heard enough of these from my middle brother, he's a vegetarian. Everyone in your group has the gift of teaching the essence of an idea while standing on one foot. With your help I may yet become a bit of a scholar myself," Rokhl said, laughing.

Never before so spirited, Gustav grabbed the belt of her coat. "Let's run to your courtyard."

The road applauded under their feet. But, unexpectedly, Gustav stopped Rokhl and whispered earnestly, "On the other side of the street, you see those two officers? Stare at them so they'll turn their faces to you – it's urgent."

She did as he asked, and for a minute felt numb. Both officers turned their heads toward her, as if on order, and smiled with their drunken, swollen faces.

Gustav, unnoticed, took the opportunity to fix the lines of their faces in his memory, then quickly pulled Rokhl away with him.

She was astounded. "What is it, a hallucination or a prank?" she asked.

"I don't know myself!" Gustav shrugged his left shoulder and a thought seemed to spring from his forehead. "Ay, your eyes really have a compelling power."

She turned her face toward him with her singular signature, but Gustav pulled down the brim of her hat, and said, "It's not smart to put your nose into everything."

Rokhl burst into laughter. "You frightened me. I thought you'd seen my class chaperone and concealed me from her. When I first heard that she's been stalking about like a cat for twenty years, I gave a hoot, and our class continued without disruption. Then, ten times more devout, I put my gymnasium hat to bed at nine o'clock and didn't return to my residence before daybreak – the guard-boy will be a witness."

Gustav merrily placed his hand on his heart: "I swear by the 'friend of Reason' not to tell."

Gustav's Tuesday lectures, and the discussions they generated, greatly excited Rokhl. The contrast to her psychology teacher reading his entire lecture from a book angered her. He concluded with: "However absurd one's speech may be, it's nevertheless true that each word is related to the next."

One student added: "In my babbling there's no connection between one word and the next." Their teacher smiled easily, forgetting that it was a student who spoke. Rokhl pushed her chair back so loudly that everyone turned around. He alone heard nothing, saw nothing. No wonder the gymnasium left her dissatisfied. They weren't taught to live productive lives, and certainly not to understand human suffering.

She felt cheated because of the fraud the teacher had committed against his students. His high forehead and delicate hands spoke of his four degrees. Yet he didn't deem it necessary to provide his own interpretation for such an important paragraph. He, who had been an elected deputy! Was his mind consumed with higher things? High enough to neglect his teaching responsibility? Well hardly!

She was determined to read philosophy, and borrowed a volume of Kant from the library. Impatiently, she hurried home, glad that everyone would be out because the weather was so pleasant.

From the very first page, profound ideas captured her curiosity. She read every paragraph two and three times. Her blood rushed feverishly, whip driven. Here, human reason was above everything else; here, man was no more than a speck of dust in nature's mystery. She closed her book with a heavy heart: she couldn't comprehend it. She would ask Gustav when he came.

"Yes, I used to study philosophy with my colleagues in Poland. Why do you ask? Why do you want to clutter your head with philosophy?"

She felt belittled by his question, her courage drained. Gustav must have understood that such lofty ideas were not meant for her limited intelligence.

Gustav noticed her sudden sadness. His eyes burned with self-reproach. "See how destructive the accepted attitudes toward women are. That's the poison we must eradicate, and the sooner the better. My question to you implied that I doubted women's competence. Not so. I've long been convinced that she's the equal of man and must occupy an equal place in society."

But Rokhl was grieved and deeply disappointed. His attempt to sweeten bitter truth was in vain. She presented her interpretation of certain memorable passages to him. "You see," she said, "because of Kant's profundity I feel even more insignificant. I'm in a total fog."

Gustav smiled, and she was certain he was laughing at her. Adding to her pain, she continued: "It seemed to me just now that he'd already solved the problem – hit the bull's eye! Then, suddenly, he jumped back again. Or perhaps he jumped forward. Man and world go up and down with him like a seesaw. First, man is high above the world, he becomes the receiver and the creator, everything dependent on his pure reason! Then, suddenly, the world springs aside and man is deposed with a crash. To the point of confusion. Then the world becomes a side issue, man's logical reason barely, barely understanding it."

Rokhl drew a deep breath, as though she'd just moved a boulder. But the pressure and the pain lingered. Gustav took her head in both hands.

"Ay, Rokhl, Rokhl, you don't know what a modest girl you are, what a beautiful and honest thinker you are. I'll come by every Saturday evening and we'll read philosophy together."

His offer was very dear to her. Perhaps with his help she'd begin to understand. But no! He had hugged her as he would a young child. That meant: Don't stick your nose where you shouldn't.

Translation by Frieda Johles Forman

CHANA'S SHEEP AND CATTLE

Shira Gorshman

Day in, day out, Chana was gripped with a constant fretting. There simply was never a day she wasn't comparing all that surrounds her here with the surroundings from which she was torn, thanks to Mendel Elkind. Now she understood very well that he was blind and he couldn't foresee the future. She understood, also, that not only was he blind, but that he was deeply selfish. It's possible, she thought, that it was entirely due to his spitefulness towards Ben Gurion that Mendel wanted to prove what a great commune he would establish in the Crimea with lefties from the core group on the Kibbutz. Her soul was embittered.

Now, day after day in the last month of summer, 1930, she rides her horse, sprinkling salt on the parched grass of the lime-encrusted Crimean steppes. That was her idea – the cattle, with their bristly tongues, would be more likely to pasture in the wilted yellow grasses that resembled unraveled straw mats. Chana did not guide him; the bridle lay across his neck. Occasionally, when the horse changed his stride, she quietly let fall from her lips, "Boruch, Boruch, it's true, you're very clever, but – no joking around – be a *mentsh.*" Boruch – which is how Chana called her horse – immediately altered his stride to a soft, calming gait. Chana stroked his warm throat with her small, work-worn hand, and again gathered a fistful of salt from the sack, again spreading it, so that the miserable grass should be a little tastier.

Quiet, open, illuminated as far as the horizon, lay the expanses of the vast steppes. A distorted echo returned Chana's song to her. She was singing a melody, no words, but it was clear that this was a lament about herself and about all who were torn from Palestine, thanks to Mendel Elkind. In her deep, melodic voice she sang out her wordless melody. Boruch's ears quivered, and a thin, mild neighing escaped from his throat, as though sympathizing with the complaint of his beloved rider. Yes, his beloved rider. Chana treated Boruch almost as an equal, never raising her voice to him. Never the whip, never a stick when riding. That morning, when she led Boruch into his stall, she said to Shimkeh: "See what royalty I brought? So I ask of you kindly, do not allow even the chairman to ride him. His name is Boruch and he's my horse."

"What do you mean 'your horse'? In the commune, nobody owns anything, and we all own everything" – Shimkeh attempted to simplify the issue. But Chana interrupted: "Do me a favour, don't clarify what we all know. Don't forget what I told you! From today on I'm in charge not only of the cattle and sheep, but luckily, I have a horse too, and I'm asking of you that what is said between us should remain between us. Yesterday I expressed a few words about our sorry situation, so Tsiporke Brill said to me: 'What here doesn't please you? Internationalism is always better than stinky nationalism.' So I'm telling you, remember that we're not in Palestine. Our closest neighbour is the secret police."

Some time had passed since the discussion that morning.

Chana watched as Boruch's thin ears wrinkled, she listened to his tender neighing, removed her fist from the wide-mouthed sack, and momentarily forgot what to do. As before, the bridle was lying across Boruch's neck. Chana was singing. Her bare, cracked soles, with tiny beads of dried blood around the splits in the skin, rose and dropped as the horse's stomach rolled with each strong, young breath. By Chana's estimation, the horse's age, judging by his teeth, wasn't more than four years. Chana was twenty-three. So, she calculated that according to a horse's lifespan and a person's given years, she and he were the same age. She also had solid grounds for considering him her peer, but more of that later. By the time the Crimean sun was overhead and hot enough to singe, both salt-sacks were emptied and draped over Chana's shoulders. She had "measured" a good few hectares with Boruch, and he knew that he now had to head toward the ravine near the town of Dsjabahai. Carefully, he lowered himself from the edge of the gully. Chana sprang down and remained standing on her tiptoes, so the cracks in her soles wouldn't deepen even more. She released Boruch, and as soon as she threw his saddle on the grass, – the grass in the ravine was still thick and soft – Boruch took a few steps back and forth. Then, with resounding neighing, he lowered himself, rolled on his back to one side, then to the other, his legs stretching out to the sky, and in the next moment, stretched out on the grass. Chana watched him closely, though it was not the first time she had seen this. She let out a young-woman's primal cry, bent her knees, and rolled down from the ravine, repeating this several times. Suddenly Boruch stood up, and while Chana was still lying on the grass, he slowly approached, lowered his chin to her, and caught a hair in his opened lips, as though with a smile approving of Chana's playfulness. Chana burst out laughing because his chin was resting on her shoulder.

True, that Chana could be so playful – she was also the mother of three girls. As with all the children, they had been placed in the children's home of the commune, and she, like all the mothers, now free from the burden of child rearing, was free to do her work. Chana was the head of the stable-brigade; not a simple matter. She had enough worries about the feedings, about the placement of storage silos in the towers; she had to ensure that cattle were attended on schedule, that the pails of milk destined for the resorts at Taki be left unstrained. The kitchen must not be kept waiting for the milk going to the children's house. But with all her responsibilities, she still had to do the milking three times daily, just like all the other women milkers. She had another talent to her credit – the cows, those with hardened udders, cracked nipples, that won't stand still for a second, constantly swishing their tails – calmly allow her to milk them. She milks, and quietly beseeches: "Hogar, stay, darling, sweetie. A blessing on your hind legs." And the other stable-workers wonder that Hogar, whom they call the wild animal, has never yet kicked over the pail of milk, which Chana holds firmly with both knees.

The sun was burning. The steppe lay barren when Chana rode out from the ravine. An uneasiness suddenly came over her. It seemed to her that she was alone, all alone, not only here on the steppe, under the vast sky, but that evening in the commune she would be alone when she arrived there, shortly.

She rode out here after the first milking of the morning. Naturally she hadn't yet had a bite to eat. It was already eleven o'clock and hunger gnawed at her. She sat loosely in the saddle, her legs dangling at the horse's sides, her head swaying. Should someone have seen her, she would have appeared to be napping. But Chana was awake, and only God knows why precisely now a rush of memories washed over her. She thought about this – that no others had harmed themselves as much as she. She was in too much of a hurry, didn't listen to her parents; how right they were. But to go back – like capturing the wind in a scarf. She thought of her husband, her senior by fifteen years. Remembered, and still hadn't the slightest regret that she had left him as soon as the third girl was born. So, swinging in the saddle, Chana thought that in a certain sense, comrades from the commune were no better, no different from others.

Quite often she has to reject unsolicited attentions. For example, last week after breakfast, Chaymkeh, of the field-brigade, said to her: "Chankeh, let's talk a bit – a treasure like you is going to waste. Here in the steppe it's a joy. Stars like sheaves of wheat."

Chana didn't say what was on the tip of her tongue, because it's not acceptable for a mother of three children to be cavorting. Astonished, she looked at him sadly and in a low voice remarked: "I ask you, Chaymkeh, if I should go with you to the steppe, will the stars stop falling, or will the fallen stars rise up to the sky again?"

Chaymkeh could scarcely understand what he heard. He shrugged his shoulders, and nonchalantly retorted, "So no is no."

Even while he was speaking, Chana was striding toward the new house, where she had her room; more correctly, where she spent the night with two other comrades, Rivka and Yokheved. This wasn't the only occasion. Aside from Chaymkeh, there were other admirers. She also heard from Yisrolik, who worked in the smithy: "Chanetchkeh, when you have three children, you have nothing to lose!"

Chana heard him out and remained silent. Of all this Chana was now reminded, and was filled with remorse.

It was not fated that Chana should enjoy her meal. She understood the excuse for calling a general assembly. She saw the chairman of the commune and the secretary of the cell rise onto the stage. The chairman smacked the table several times. A strange mood reigned in the dining room. The commune members, both men and women, were smiling, while expressing a malicious curiosity. Here and there an explosive laughter erupted. The comrade from the field-brigade, who had proposed that he and Chana go for a stroll in the steppe, to "watch the stars fall," asked loudly: "Chanchkeh, what did you have against the shepherds? Are you their lord and master? Are they your dogs?"

Chana bent slightly, and as loudly as he spoke, so emphatically and seriously did her voice ring out over the entire dining room: "I care what you say as much as I care about last year's snow, and just dare to show me your teeth."

"Quiet down, quiet everyone!" The chairman again smacked the table, and soon called out: "Comrade Chana Feinberg, approach the stage. The aggrieved comrades Dovid Shapiro and Yankel Tsukerman, approach also."

Chana remained standing on the right side of the stage, the aggrieved on the left side. Dovid's face was wrapped in a red kerchief; perhaps because of this sight, the entire dining room filled with a thunderous laughter. Finally it grew quiet.

"Comrade Tsukerman" – the chairman turned to the aggrieved – "tell us exactly what happened."

In a lengthy speech, Tsukerman told how he and Dovid had driven out the herd of heifers, how they were faint from hunger. Here Chana interrupted him: "Who was faint from hunger, you or the calves?"

The ensuing laughter continued for a short while, then Dovid related that Comrade Chana Feinberg attacked him, like a real thief, and bloodied him.

Having heard out the aggrieved, the secretary of the cell directed Chana to speak.

Chana described it this way: "Fellow communard! I don't have to tell you how much we must labour, until we raise a cow. If you had seen how the heifers and the calves were wandering around the steppes, faint from thirst! At the same time, these two rabbinic labourers were sitting enjoying a banquet. I don't know if any of you would have done differently. I have no regrets, I've said all that I'm going to say."

Some other comrades approached, looking to soften the situation, while others spoke strongly and sharply.

Then the secretary of the cell spoke. "This winter we dealt with a woman who refused to nurse a small commune member, a wisp of a child, though she had sufficient milk. I'm sure you remember, comrades, how we expelled her from the commune for a full quarter. Now we have another unusual occurrence. Had this been someone other than Chana, I would be the first to vote that such a person does not belong in our commune. I say a comrade, because we all know that Chana Feinberg does the work of two, three men. But to raise a hand to a comrade! I propose she be excluded from the commune council for a quarter. I have spoken."

It was decided. The majority agreed with the secretary's proposal. There ensued a commotion in the dining room. Suddenly Dovid Shapiro – he who was wrapped with a red cloth – raised his right hand, and pronounced: "I forgot to say that Comrade Feinberg yelled at us while she was hitting us, hateful words, and said we should trade herring in Venice. I maintain that this is a grave insult."

In spite of this new information, such laughter erupted that some comrades almost choked.

"The meeting is closed," the chairman announced.

Efraim the shepherd leaped onto the stage and took his harmonica from his pocket.

He played something from Carmen, tapping with his toes, shouting: "Friends, Chanaleh, come over here, onto the stage, we have to celebrate with a dance."

Translation by Sam Blatt

TO THE GREAT WIDE WORLD

Chayele Grober

When an artist devotes her entire life to one craft and then suddenly decides to write a book, she is challenged with a variety of questions: "When?" "How come?" One elderly distant relative of mine asked me outright: "Listen, you should be well but how do you come to…?" Therefore, I would like to reply to all of these questions.

In the winter of 1941–42, I was confined to bed in my Montreal home like a prisoner, with an illness that hasn't been diagnosed to this day. I personally believe that I was sickened by the catastrophic events in Europe.

Betty Mayer, my English teacher, was then and remains today my best friend. I had begun to relate episodes of my childhood to her. She encouraged me to record these and was the inspiration behind my first English manuscript.

In 1945, when the earth of my ancestors was incinerated along with the remnants of their descendants, I had the overwhelming desire to write down what I remembered; to immortalize the names of those who bestowed upon me their love and friendship; to transmit that which I had received from my teachers and mentors; and to share the experiences I lived through along my way.

It was mid-winter of 1917–18 when I climbed the stairs of a large building and went down a narrow corridor that led to a tiny, unheated room. The atmosphere that emanated from the small group of young men and women that I encountered there was reminiscent of a political meeting. They spoke softly, earnestly, and viewed me with some suspicion. I knew no one there except Rochel Starobinyetz, my fellow Bialystoker. I felt somewhat uncomfortable, but that didn't last long. A door opened from an adjacent room and Nachum Tzemach and Y.B. Vachtangov entered. All that remains with me from my first meeting with Vachtangov is the image of his large blue-green eyes, smiling with a barely discernible irony that quickly became earnest and sharp.

I was invited to a rehearsal. My previous exposure to Yiddish theatres led me to expect high drama, emotionally charged voices, a melodramatic hand clutching the heart while the actor sinks down on his knees proclaiming true love. Instead, Vachtangov, sitting very calmly at the table, spoke softly and simply. He spoke of the great importance of the theatre to all the peoples of the world. He described the great truth illuminated by K.S. Stanislavski, the founder of the Moscow Art Theatre. He said that theatre and the artist must elevate the masses; that artists have a great responsibility to educate the youth who come to the theatre. He then explained the measures necessary to achieve this: the actor must dedicate himself to art and must withdraw from society. Art requires isolation. At the end of his speech, he demanded that each of us listen to our inner selves, examine our souls and explore whether we are prepared to make the sacrifices that theatre demanded of us. "Theatre," he said, "is difficult, and life in the theatre is often very difficult indeed." He concluded: "Theatre is the finest and most important branch of art."

That night I couldn't sleep. An unfamiliar emotion stirred in me, a haunting yearning. Hot tears covered my pillow, followed by a sweet peace and a strange happiness. I could feel the birth of a new life! From that night on I lived through ten years of suffering and joy in my one and only theatre, Habimah.

Happiness makes life colourful, tears enrich the soul. I am thankful to God for each tear that I shed throughout my life. Until that point, my cup was not yet full of tears; now it overflowed. My uncle, David Shati, had conveyed my mother's dying words to my father: "Protect my Chayele!" The only man to whom she had entrusted her entire life now turned out to be unreliable.

My father, like all the other merchants in Moscow at that time, had become a millionaire "on paper." I could never fathom why, in his time of prosperity, he informed me that I could no longer expect anything from him. It was on one of those bitter, freezing days, when Muscovites burrow deep inside their fur coats, that I ran into our house after my music lesson. The house was brightly lit and warmth radiated from within. The table was set for our midday meal. I threw off my hat and coat and entered the dining room where my father greeted me with this declaration: "Today I am informing you that I will no longer pay for your studies." I was speechless. Father continued harshly, ending with: "Nothing that you see here belongs to you. I'm working for someone else, not for you." Without a sound I left the room, put on my hat and coat, passed by the kitchen where my father's wife stood, past the frightened eyes of fourteen-year-old son Elinke, her son and past her brother-in-law, who was visiting from out of town. Nobody said a word; nobody stopped me. I left the house very slowly, and slower yet, I descended the steps. Nobody called me back. My feet carried me to the last step where they buckled under me, and I sank down into the deep snow. This was how my friend Yasha found me. He stood me up and led me to a coffee house. He wanted to know what had happened, but all I could say was: "I have been thrown out of the house I thought was mine." Yasha spoke to me all evening and offered many suggestions, but I accepted none. These words began ringing in my ears: "work for independence…work for independence…but how?" An important thought occurred to me: a young girl in this predicament is fortunate to have inherited not beauty but brains. I turned around and went home, where I remained for one more year. However, my father lost me that night, and lost me forever.

The house was enveloped in stillness, the stillness of people sleeping with a clean conscience. I went into my room and heard a trembling little murmur: "Chayele, I thought you had left me." My little sister Genya had been fearful that I wouldn't return. She was the only one who needed me now, and perhaps the only one who held me dear. I never found out what was actually in my father's heart, but I believe that we both were stubborn and strong-willed and neither one of us would give in. My father wanted me to live according to his standards: to marry with a dowry and to live a "respectable" life. I, however, marched ahead toward my goal – to work for justice and freedom through art.

Habimah's European tour started off in Riga. When we arrived at the Latvian border in the middle of the night, a tall dark young man, Orenstein, introduced himself as our new European administrator. He found the troupe sprawled out on hard benches and covered with threadbare coats. Poking out from these garments were shoes with run-down heels and woolen socks. Above and below the benches where luggage and packages were normally stowed – nothing – totally empty! We were to remain in our hotel and should under no circumstances allow the press to see us until we could be taken to some stores for suitable clothing.

We performed at the great Opera Theatre to a sold-out house. The dim lighting in the first act of *The Dybbuk* spread a wave of fear throughout the audience, and they were as silent as in a grave. In the second act, the bright lights made it possible to view the patrons – men wearing identical starched vests and black tailcoats. They sat very properly, serious and poker-faced. The ladies covered their faces with binoculars and applauded elegantly with their white-gloved hands. Every Hebrew word that sailed their way hit them in the white vest and bounced right back to us, where it remained throughout our entire sojourn in Latvia.

In Latvia, in addition to performing in Riga, we put on a show in Dvinsk. Here we appeared in the only theatre, actually situated in a train station. All eighteen actresses had to squeeze into one room to apply their makeup, and this while standing. I, however, quickly oriented myself to the surroundings and climbed into an upper berth. In a nomadic life, the ability to orient oneself quickly is a terrific advantage. The theatre here was also packed. People came in from the surrounding towns, and the crowd was warm and informal. All of the actors were as disciplined and serious as for the premier in Riga. Tzemach played the saintly man in the third act, and at the usual point he took a lengthy pause, but just at that moment, a passing train whistled *Hoot hoot.* It was our good luck that all of the actors on stage had their backs to the audience because we burst into laughter – an occurrence that happened frequently in future enactments of this scene.

In Latvia, and also in Lithuania, we gave the performances our all. Kovno was our second destination. Here we met face to face for the first time with large groups of Zionist youth. The dozens of Hebrew schools in Lithuania produced a youth eager to welcome and support our theatre. *Yeshiva* boys of the Telzher

Yeshiva, knowledgeable ones and some less so, also came to see and hear the first great Hebrew theatre. In addition to our evening performances, we added daytime shows. Because the audience understood our words, it made for a feeling of great harmony between us; the actors and the audience became a unified whole and it was truly gratifying. I will forever cherish these performances in Lithuania.

From Lithuania, we travelled to Warsaw – the mighty Warsaw! The city of the largest Jewish organizations; the best Yiddish press and the great scholars. Poland – the land of I.L. Peretz and Hasidic folk legends. Poland, the land of the greatest Yiddish theatres and the best actors, and here we were: the Hebrew theatre that originated in Moscow, under gentile direction in a non-Jewish atmosphere. We had to prepare and prepare carefully for such an encounter. Our older members were already acquainted with Warsaw, having lived or studied here. For me, Warsaw – the Jewish Warsaw – was entirely new! My background had not been Zionist, and in Moscow Zionism was considered counter-revolutionary. Zionists in Red Russia operated quietly, just as socialists had under the tsar. Habimah presented itself as a National Arts Theatre. Here in Warsaw, the mighty Zionist organizations with their great leaders were revealed to me, they not only filled the theatre, but surrounded us with hundreds of friends, including Hasidism and their followers. Here in Warsaw, culture and theatre blossomed while anti-Semitism was escalating. On Novolyepke and other main streets, hooligans were cutting off beards and ripping out sideburns; at the same time, on Oblozhne Street, famous actors such as Sigmund Turkov and Ida Kaminska played to great acclaim in the beloved Esther Rachel Kaminska Theatre. Habimah reigned in Warsaw and all Polish Jewry rejoiced.

We arrived in Bialystok at the beginning of spring and the people there opened their windows, doors, and balconies to us. From the station along the new road, Lipova, to the big hotel, The Ritz, the streets were packed with young and old. Babies were lifted out of their carriages in order to meet us; a great wonder. My uncle Kalman later told me: "This is what Bialystok used to look like when the tsar drove through." Here in Bialystok, where my father and stepmother now lived, I was once again in a homey atmosphere. When we were still in Riga, I had received a letter from my father. He admitted that he had not appreciated me; that he had not understood me. Mainly, he thanked me for honouring his name.

My impresario back then was a young man, Elinkeh Burstein. He was a student at the Krakow University and, in addition, a publicist for Yiddish theatre and actors.

At the first concert in Krakow, Elinkeh Burstein brought a short, skinny man into my dressing room, and introduced him to me: "This is my good friend Mordechai Gebirtig." I already had Gebirtig's song "Yankeleh" in my repertoire. From that night on, he attended every one of my concerts. When I completed my concert tour in Krakow, Elinkeh took me for a visit to Gebirtig.

The Gebirtig family – mother, father, and three daughters – lived in two rooms. The larger of the rooms served as both a parlour and bedroom; the room right at the entrance was the kitchen, with benches that served as beds for the children. It was the middle of winter, and Mrs. Gebirtig sat by the white-washed oven: a short, plump woman with a translucent pale face and wide, watery eyes. The three daughters were pretty, dark, charming girls. Slim like her father, the youngest was the singer amongst them. She was still very young, not yet at school, and her voice was soft and thinly vibrating. The house had already darkened, and Gebirtig asked me to listen to a new song that he wished to offer me as a present. He didn't have to beg – I'd been waiting for this, but I wasn't bold enough to ask him to sing it. He took a place near the small table, his head, as always, at a slight angle, his dreamy eyes gazing upwards. He started to sing "Three Daughters." All eyes were on him. When he came to the third verse, in which the last daughter leaves home, his eyes welled up, and as he finished I felt tears on my cheeks. Quiet reigned for a few minutes and then Gebirtig, slightly embarrassed, asked: "So, do you like it?" I couldn't utter a word. As I was leaving, I told him that I would accept the "Three Daughters," but I would include it in my repertoire only if I could sing it the way he did.

Mordechai Gebirtig was a carpenter who had never studied music, and couldn't transcribe the music to his songs. He had a whistle and, after composing a song, he would play it on his whistle, most often at night. He would sit on his bed and play until he was satisfied with the song. In the morning, before leaving for work, he'd call his good friend, the composer Hoffman, and play the song into the phone, and Hoffman would conscientiously transcribe. Professional artists sang Gebirtig's songs across the whole world, and they were incorporated into operettas. No one found it necessary to pay him, not even royalties. That any of his songs were published during his lifetime is only thanks to his good friends in Krakow. His loyal friend and agent was always Elinkeh Burstein.

The last time I was in Poland was in 1936. Already the winds from neighbouring Nazi Germany could be felt. Hitler's fascism was growing stronger, and fear was spreading. Signs appeared in the Polish stores: *Swoj Do Swojego* – Patronize Your Own. When I'd been in Czestochowa, just a few years before, I had performed at the Polish theatre. Now, in 1936, the theatre was no longer available for Yiddish concerts. I received letters from the correspondent of the Warsaw paper *Haynt*: "It's time to return to New York – and Montreal."

For an actor, every new performance is a fresh anxiety, a new experience. Our first journey into Canada caused us deep concern. The Habimah Theatre hadn't performed in Canada, and we were entering not with a play but with a new format concert. The same question kept bothering us: What do Canadian Jews expect of us, and how well will they receive us? With every approaching day I was increasingly tense. Canada loomed as a fortress that we needed to capture. As our departure date approached, I happened to bump into well-known poet Zisheh Weinper in the Real-Café. I knew that Weinper travelled often and was well acquainted with the Jewish communities. I described our tour and told him about my anxieties. With his sweet smile, Weinper said: "Don't worry! You'll meet there a wonderful Jew, H.M. Caiserman, and you can be sure, he will be expecting you."

"But we didn't let him know that we're coming, and also, we never met him."

"You'll get to know him, in fact, as soon as you arrive," Weinper reassured us.

I was skeptical.

Because of a December blizzard, our train arrived in Windsor Station, in Montreal, two-and-a-half hours late. On the train I had a bout of food poisoning. Exhausted, I barely made it to the hotel and immediately fell into bed. It was almost midnight. Loud noises and the singing of drunks emanated from all the rooms. This was during prohibition in America, and on weekends people would come from the U.S. especially to get drunk. I was worn out and soon fell into a deep sleep. The ring of a distant world wafted over me. Instinctively I lifted the telephone receiver, and heard a voice with a sharp Romanian "R."

"Good morning to you, Chayele Grober! How are you feeling? Time to get up. It's nine-thirty, and I couldn't wait any longer. Here we eat lunch at noon. I wanted to take you out for supper last night, but your friends wouldn't let us get near you. Ah, you want to know who is speaking – it's Hananiah Bar Meir Caiserman!"

After this hot stream of words, I wanted to ask my friend Zishe Weinper to forgive my skepticism.

The Caisermans lived in a modest, well-kept house on St. Viateur Street. Sarele Caiserman welcomed us with rays of joy. Immediately upon his greeting me, Hananiah Meir lifted me to the ceiling, exclaiming, "This is Chayele Grober!" Laughter resounded through the house; the black-cherry eyes of two tiny girls beheld me in wonder. These were Nina and Gita, the Caisermans' young daughters. In this house, the joyousness of a warm Jewish family prevailed. This was the start of my lifelong friendship with the Caisermans.

Hananiah had the will and the extraordinary ability to share with his friends, with all people, the best that he possessed. He took every guest up to his office in the Jewish Congress, pulling down from the bookcases important documents, older writings, anti-Semitic pamphlets, correspondence from priests, clippings from newspapers, and among all that, new works from Jewish poets – the majority, Canadian writers. His most beloved and closest friend was J.I. Segal, considered one of the most talented Jewish writers in America. Hananiah expressed his joy in the success of a Jewish artist with tears – with tears that streamed from his eyes as he read or spoke about one.

In that house on St. Viateur I set out on my path to the larger Jewish world. In those years the Caiserman living room was in the basement. The walls of that bright, warm basement were covered with books from floor to ceiling. The furniture consisted of a piano and rows of seats for guests. Since that evening, I have performed at the Gavo Hall in Paris, Palladium in London; in conservatories and theatres all over the world. But our departure concert on St. Viateur is still deeply engraved in my memory. Hananiah's wide eyes, teary with emotion, and the bright smiling face of that modest, happy Sarele, have followed me all these years.

Translation by Sam Blatt and Sarah Faerman

THE HOLY MOTHERS

Sarah Hamer-Jacklyn

As the first greyness begins to cut the night skies, shadowy figures steal by on their way to forced labour in Tshenstokhover ghetto. They walk with heads bent low, with fear in their hearts, a prayer on their lips, asking God to bring them back home in peace; that they may find those they left behind, whose number keeps shrinking, whose houses grow more empty and their streets more deserted.

Among these walking shadows with lifeless eyes is Chayele Kalke. She, her mother, and her child, a little girl of four, are the sole survivors of a family of twenty. Her young slender body is bent, as if she carried a heavy weight. She greets each passerby with a slight nod of her head, and whispers, "A meeting today of The Holy Mothers in Bunker 39, behind the old *shul*."

The women acknowledge with a simple sign, and walk on.

Chayele returns to her cellar hiding place. Her blonde little girl, Miriml, is sleeping peacefully. The child's lips break into a smile of innocent joy.

Chayele looks at her child. Her eyes fill with tears and her body breaks out in a cold sweat at the thought of what could befall her only child, as has happened to the other children from her large family.

She lies down on the mound of hay beside her child, stroking her golden locks, but won't indulge herself by kissing the small head.

"Sleep and dream, my child, of a brighter world," she whispers. "It's good that you don't understand..."

The child begins to wake and calls out, sleepily, "Mommy, *mameshy,*" as she snuggles closer to her mother.

Like a mother swallow who covers and protects her young, Chayele also covers her child, and presses her to her warm bosom, whispering quietly, "I will not part with you, my little Miriml. If we go, we will go together, together, my child."

The elderly Golde-Leye lies in a corner, buried in a pile of old clothes. Her body is covered with a large woollen shawl. On her head, she wears the black silk *shabbes* kerchief. These are the only two items that she managed to rescue from her sizeable household.

Suddenly the big pile of rags begins to move, and Golde-Leye's head emerges. In the darkness of the den, she speaks in a quiet, barely audible voice, "Chayele, were you outside again? *Vey, vey,*" she laments. "You're looking for trouble!"

"I brought half a bread, Mama."

"How many times have I told you already that you should let *me* go?" The Mother's wail comes out from the pile of rags. Then, she sits up, bent over. In the dark shadows of the lair it seems like the pile of rags takes on a shape.

"I want to prove that my life is at risk," Golde-Leye declares, her voice muted. "Only by losing my life, will I win it."

"What are you saying, Mama?" Chayele is alarmed by her mother's puzzling words.

"When these murderers take my life, as they've extinguished the lives of my family, only then will I be in the true world. I'll go where my husband and children are waiting for me, in the world to come. However, you and your child are young, and you must preserve your lives. I, on the other hand..."

"Mother, I beg you, be still. You mustn't talk this way. We must fight."

"Fight with whom?"

"With the murderers!"

"It's probably God's will," Golde-Leye answered, absorbed again into the pile of rags.

Chayele cannot understand her mother's sudden outburst because old Golde-Leye usually lay quietly for hours on that pile of rags. When frightened by the sound of spoken words, she would silently stare with strong, yearning eyes into the emptiness. Sometimes, in the middle of the night, she would start to wail and call out the names of her husband and children.

Suddenly they hear the sound of footsteps above. It seems to Chayele that she is lying buried in a covered pit and someone is stepping on her grave.

She tightly clasps her child to her bosom.

"*Sha*, my daughter, I beg you, someone will hear you." She holds her breath. The steps grow more and more faint, and eventually they vanish altogether.

"Just someone passing by," says Chayele, breathing easier.

It occurs to her that there are no more graves with family inscriptions. The Nazi murderers do not bury the bodies – no one will be able to visit a parent's gravesite.

Golde-Leye buries her head deeper into the pile of rags. Starving from lack of food, tormented by longing, she drifts into sleep.

She dreams that she is flying up to heaven. It is a long way. She presses through clouds, flying higher and higher, until she reaches Seventh Heaven, and the angel Gabriel opens the gates wide to the next world for her. Celestial singing is heard and angels fly around. Two of them descend and stand in front of Golde-Leye. She looks at them – two old women with such glowing faces. The Divine Spirit rests on them, and they are surrounded by rays of sunshine.

"Who are you?" Golde-Leye asks.

"I am Mother Rachel," says one.

"And I am Mother Sarah," says the second. "Tell us, child, what you want – you, our long-suffering daughter. What is your request?"

"I want to see my husband and children," Golde-Leye replies.

They take her arm and lead her across the celestial palaces. She steps onto clouds. It is all so beautiful. From sheer happiness, tears fall from her eyes. Mother Rachel notices the tears, raises her arms and tears off a piece of spun white silk from a small passing cloud. She wipes the tears from Golde-Leye's eyes and says, "You've wept enough, my child." And Mother Sarah concludes, "We're taking you to meet the holy spirits, so that you may celebrate together."

Mother Rachel and Mother Sarah gesture with their hands and say, "May the gates to the entrance of the Garden of Eden be opened."

Two gates of white marble open up and Golde-Leye catches sight of a garden with trees, greener than green, golden rays of sunny flowers, silver moon leaves which glitter ever so gently and delicately, and red roses which reflect the cold sparks of the setting sun. They tread on heavenly blue grasses. Over everything, birds are flying and singing songs of praise to their Creator. She has never heard such singing. It charms and soothes the tormented heart, it purifies the soul. Elevated, she feels young again, and strong.

Mother Rachel and Mother Sarah gesture with their hands and say, "May the gates of the Garden of Eden open for the holy soul of our daughter, Golde-Leye, daughter of Israel whom we escort."

Two angels open the gates wide. A soft heavenly music is heard. As she passes through the gates, the sound grows louder. Golde-Leye stands marvelling at the magic around her: Dressers and buffets are made of crystal. Entire families are seated around the long tables, with tablecloths of spun white silk. On the tables stand gleaming candelabras, their candles burning with the sun's rays. Off to one side, seated at round tables, are rebbes clothed in white sacred robes. Mother Rachel and Mother Sarah lead Golde-Leye to a large, long table. Great joy breaks out.

"Mother," cries out Shifra, Golde-Leye's youngest daughter. Her son, Simcha-Binem cries out with joy, "Children, our mother is here!" The whole family is here – Aunt Chava, Grandmother Nechele, the great-grandmother, Golde-Leye's uncles and aunts, the small children, grandchildren, the Moyshelekh, the Yoselech, the Rivkelech and everyone. Golde-Leye is happy. At last, together with the whole family.

But all at once she stops, downcast, and asks fearfully, "Where is my husband, Aaron-Wolf? Where is your father, children?"

The children break into smiles and answer with pride, "He's with the rebbe, Mother."

"With which rebbe?"

"With the Novoradomsker rebbe," says her daughter Pesye, and her son, Fishl, points to the round tables on the opposite side.

"See, Mother, the rebbes are sitting at those tables. Each rebbe is with his followers. And each rebbe has his own melody which he sings at his table. At that table, over there, sits the Alexander Rebbe with his followers, the Dzuriker Rebbe with his followers, the Roszprzer Rebbe with his. Our father is sitting at the table with our rebbe, the Novoradomsker."

Golde-Leye looks up and sees her husband at the head of the table by the side of the rebbes known as Tiferes Shlomo, Chesed Avraham, Reb Chaskele and Shloyme-Henech Rabinovitch. Those last two rebbes she knows. As for the first ones, she had only heard the wondrous tales about them.

Suddenly she sees her husband stand up and whisper something in his rebbe's ear. He comes toward her with outstretched hands. Shloyme-Chayim and his band begin to play a *freylech*, a lively, happy tune.

Golde-Leye is embarrassed, and turns red. She pulls her white, silk headscarf down over her eyes. The whole family gets up and forms a circle, clapping and dancing, Golde-Leye and her husband in the centre. They don't hold one another with bare hands, but by way of a man's red handkerchief – oh, how good – oh, how lovely! Everyone together, everyone. Then, she catches herself, stands still and asks, frightened: "Where's my daughter, Chayele, and my grandchild, Miriml?"

"*Sha, sha*," her husband calms her. "They'll all come..." But she won't be consoled and cries louder and louder, "Chayele... Miriml...Chayele...Miriml..."

"Mother, Mother, why are you shouting? I'm here, I'm right here. And here's the child. With your shouting you'll bring misfortune on us."

Confused, Golde-Leye opens her eyes and looks at her daughter. It takes her a while to grasp where she is. She recognizes their horrible reality. She is still immersed in her divine dream. Her ears still ring with the celestial singing.

What a pity that Chayele woke her up. She closes her eyes and wants to spin her golden dream again. But the dream won't continue, the thread is cut. The heavens are again closed to her.

Golde-Leye moves closer to her daughter and grandchild, who is now also awake. Speaking quietly, but with great elation, she tells them of her wondrous dream, how over there, in the Garden of Eden, she met with the entire family. She paints pictures for her daughter and granddaughter of those palaces, those gardens, those sunny roses, the divine singing. It is bliss, eternal happiness for those who are worthy of reaching that World, the true World, where one lives forever.

In the darkness of this damp hiding place lie grandmother, mother, and grandchild, and they daydream, and fantasize about a better World, a World found only in heaven, and all together they spin more of that interrupted dream.

Behind the rubble of the old synagogue, single female figures gravitate toward Bunker 39. Not far from the destroyed synagogue, Chayele stands guard. She signals to the approaching women and directs them to an open pit that stretches deep underground. There the women descend and disappear.

Once all are inside, Chayele pulls over a plank of wood covered with grass and leaves. She leaves a small opening, then squeezes in. As she lowers herself, she carefully slides the board above with her hands, and the flat board covered with green leaves blends into the surrounding green growth.

Inside the bunker a secret meeting is held by a group of Jewish women who call themselves "The Holy Mothers." Young Jewish mothers have organized themselves and sworn not to be separated from their small children. The dark hiding place is lit only by a candle. Huddling close to one another, the young women look like a flock of frightened sheep. In some there is still a gleaming fire of resistance in their eyes, in others, only sorrow – a gaze extinguished.

In the midst of this group of assembled women stands Chayele, and she stirs them up. She speaks in a firm voice but often stops mid-sentence, as if she needs to absorb strength and courage in order not to burst into tears.

"Holy Mothers, there are rumours again of an 'Action.' Those murderers will soon show up again and begin to drag away old people and young children and send them to the gas chambers. They'll let us young mothers live for now, because they still need us. But afterwards, once our strength is gone, they'll gas us too or let us die a slow death. At best, they'll shoot us like dogs.

"Holy Mothers, when they come after our little swallows, we mustn't separate from them. We have to stay with our own flesh and blood. What mother wants to continue living once her child has been ripped from her in such a murderous fashion? We would only be the living dead. If we have to die, we'll go together! Meanwhile, don't lose courage, go on with the struggle of hiding your children. In the end, justice will prevail. In the meantime, be careful, hide your children. If any of you is in doubt about your hiding place, I have a new address for you – behind the old cemetery, they've dug a deep pit. They've told me about it."

Two women approach Chayele and take the new address. Every mother gives her sacred oath that she will not be separated from her child.

Chayele pushes the board aside and climbs up. She signals that from every direction all is quiet. The women disperse one at a time, each to her hiding place and to her child.

Miriml has now been seriously ill for three days. Her eyes are closed, her little cheeks burning, her lips dry and cracked. The child is delirious with fever. She keeps asking for water. Her mother and grandmother are desperate. They want to help the sick child, but there is nothing to give, no medicine, no milk, not even a little water.

The child begs for a drink and cries without stop: "Water… water!"

The child's cries fill them with dread. Chayele scrambles for the door, but the elderly Golde-Leye won't allow it. She blocks her way and makes her daughter swear to stay with her child, letting herself out, in the hope of finding medicine and maybe a little water.

An hour later, Golde-Leye returns. From under her shawl she takes out a bundle with a bottle of water. As if it were a treasure, she pours a little water into a cup with great care, and gives it to the sick child. Little Miriml eagerly gulps the liquid. Her grandmother pulls an orange from the bundle, peels it, and gives it to the sick child. The child pounces on it with great pleasure and gulps down the pieces. Slowly, the girl's colour returns, her little face shines. She sits up and says she feels better.

Grandmother and mother look at each other, happy.

Suddenly they hear footsteps above. Mother and daughter hold their breath. The footsteps come closer. Frightened, the child cries loudly.

Chayele runs over to her and stifles the cry.

A loud bang crashes against the door and it's clear that people above have discovered the secret entrance. For a moment, all is quiet. They stand, holding their breath, but soon, there is a louder pummeling. Then the door caves in.

Grandmother, mother, and grandchild stand huddled in a corner. A statue of three. They have turned to stone.

The door makes a final rasp and falls to the ground. A streak of light from the dreary exterior flashes into the dark cave.

A man in an SS uniform stands on the threshold and looks at them with a smug, gluttonous face. He calls out sadistically, "Caught you, dogs! Hiding, eh? You want to fool the German Reich? Damned Jews! How many of you dogs are here?"

Golde-Leye and her daughter, who holds the baby in her arms, keep silent.

"Answer me!" he thunders.

The statue of startled grandmother, daughter, and granddaughter begins moving slowly. They draw back toward darkness.

But the Nazi uniform follows them.

"Don't move!"

They freeze and the child starts to cry.

"A child also! Good, good." He rubs his hands in glee. "You old witch, I saw you earlier as you were Jewishly sneaking around. So I followed you. You want to fool the Reich, to hide out! Ha!" he breaks out in a spasm of laughter. Suddenly he stops laughing and a wild look appears in his eyes.

"What is this, a sick child?" He rages as he spies the baby, tight in her mother's arms. "We don't tolerate sick Jewish children. Move it!"

The threesome walks out into the street.

"Halt!"

Golde-Leye and Chayele, with the baby in her arms, come to a stop.

The SS man scrutinizes his victims. He pauses in front of Chayele.

"You stay here, for now: we still have need of you. You're young and healthy. They go."

Chayele pales, her head spinning. With her last ounce of strength, she holds on, lest she fall. She speaks, her voice cracking, "I'm not healthy...blood...the lungs."

The SS man looks at her pale face, hesitates, waves his hand, and orders, "Then you get going. Fast, faster!" His green eyes darting, he looks around on all sides, already searching for new victims.

"We are going together," Chayele whispers to her child, pressing her more tightly to her heart. "We go together, my

Miriml…I won't be separated from you. We're together." Two tears roll down Chayele's cheeks. Suddenly she staggers. Golde-Leye steadies her, takes the child out of her arms. With one arm she carries the child, with the other she leads her daughter quickly along. She feels suddenly as if she has regained her youthful strength. She strides with light steps, holding her head high, with exaltation in her eyes as she looks toward heaven.

"Where are we going, dear Bube?" Miriml asks weakly.

"We're going up," Golde-Leye points, "up where your Papa is."

"And my cousin Moyshele is also there?"

"Also."

"And Sorale also?"

"Also."

"And my Aunt Chava and Uncle Shmuel are also there?"

"Also."

"And Grandpa?"

"All are there, the whole family."

The child smiles happily and Chayele wipes her tears. Uplifted, she looks to heaven. She presses closer to her mother who raises her head to the heavens, and walks with firm steps toward Eternity.

Translation by Ida Wynberg

SHE FOUND AN AUDIENCE

Sarah Hamer-Jacklyn

We were three: Zina, Dora, and I. We roomed together and each one of us was cut out for *something*: Zina, to be a singer; we tacked Tetra onto her name and it became Tetrazini – after the great opera singer. Dora, who dreamed of becoming a renowned actress, also studied modern dance and was a great admirer of Isadora Duncan. So we joined Isa to Dora and crowned her Isadora. I, meanwhile, busied myself late into the night with pen and ink and fantasized about becoming a great writer, and my friends did not overlook me. My name, Sarah, became Sand after the famous authoress George Sand.

The house where the three of us lived was always bustling like a country fair. Tetrazini sang, practiced, and developed her voice. Isadora would go about with a book in her hand and recite or study some role, and often she would throw herself into a dance, bending and breaking and making various poses. The telephone rang all the time. Very often the doorbell rang; sometimes flowers would arrive, sometimes a telegram, often packages of clothes, shoes, and trinkets that Dora enjoyed buying and later returning. Above all this, the air was filled with raging voices and quarrelling that would quickly turn into happy laughter. The worst troubles were because of the telephone. Each of us always expected an important call from a friend or admirer. And each of the three of us could gab for more than half an hour. The other two would stand around, as if on hot coals, and scream, "*Nu,* hurry up. Finish. How long do you need to go on with your idiotic chatter?"

Our personalities were also quite different: Isadora was like a real sister, devoted and loyal, but also distracted and nervous. She never remembered where she put things. She would often take our phone calls and mix up our rendezvous. And when you'd introduce her to a new person, she would chat with him in a very friendly manner, as if to an old acquaintance. Then suddenly it would hit her that this was a stranger, and she would extend her hand and say, "Hello" and ask to know who he was.

Tetrazini was very romantic. Her brown hair and dark fiery eyes suited her hot temperament. She was constantly entangled in love affairs. She would get passionate quickly, but would cool off even more quickly. We would listen with veiled teasing and often with open sarcasm to the amorous adventures that she freely recounted with great pathos and enchantment. At times she would become very disappointed and cry bitterly, but we knew from previous experience that before long she would suffer in the same way with a new love, and that the old one would be sidelined and forgotten. I was the one who always made peace between the singer and the actress. Those two couldn't live together. Still, a deep love and a genuine friendship bound us together.

Tetrazini was already on her way to a career. She would appear often as a solo artist at concerts. Several times she sang on the radio and at large functions for organizations where she was paid for her performance. But her big dream was the opera, and all the money she earned went for further study.

Isadora had also had a taste of recognition as an actress: her success came from amateur theatre, but she dreamed of Broadway, the Great White Way, the world stage – important roles, and she especially wanted to play the Shakespeare repertoire.

Our life rushed on turbulently. Each of us lived with her fantasies and her artistic ambitions. I used to sit in a corner of the house by my desk, totally immersed in a story that I was writing. Suddenly Isadora's clear voice would carry like a bell, ringing throughout the house, and it would carry me off to a strange faraway world. With her tall frame, and her blonde head held majestically high, she paced back and forth. Isadora was studying *Hamlet* and with her boyish haircut, her tall thin body, and her dreamy blue eyes, she really looked like the noble Prince of Denmark. I put down my pen and gave her my full attention.

"*To be, or not to be, that is the question.*
Whether 'tis nobler in the mind to suffer
the slings and arrows of outrageous fortune,
or to take arms against a sea of troubles,
and by opposing end them. To die, to sleep
no more; and by a sleep, to say we end
the heartache and the thousand natural shocks
that flesh is heir to? 'Tis a consummation
devoutly to be wished."

After this kind of monologue I would loudly applaud her, she would bow with aplomb, and would jokingly ask, "*Nu*, George Sand, what now, are you making fun of me?"

"No, Isadora. You've got the spark and with your talent, you'll go far. But I beg you, please let me write. I have to have absolute quiet. In a half an hour, I'll be done."

"But I can dance, can't I?"

"Yes. That you can do. But quietly."

I sat down again at my desk and suddenly I heard Tetrazini's loud operatic voice from the other room: *"Do re mi fa so la ti do – do ti la so....*" After a few minutes of scales, she started to sing whole arias.

Meanwhile, Isadora threw herself into her dance, beating with her feet and leaping. I would then beg them to stop and let me write, but they were so absorbed in their own practising that my words fell on deaf ears. So I would run off to the kitchen with the finished pages, with pen and ink, and close the door. Then Isadora wouldn't dance anymore, but she would work on a dramatic scene; Tetrazini would sing at a high pitch. The cotton that I always stuffed into my ears didn't help. The flashes of brilliance that had come to me vanished; I kept begging them to keep quiet for a while. Once, when my pleas were ignored, I grabbed the flowerpot and threw it; it broke and soil spilled all over the divan.

The crash roused them both and they were ready to kill me. Our screams poured out into the street. After these stormy quarrels, calm was once again restored and peace was made. In time, Isadora got a role in a play on Broadway. She was overjoyed. Knocking at the doors of agents and producers, she said triumphantly, had gotten results. True, her part consisted of just a few words. Still, she was confident that the doors that lead to an actress's success had finally opened and that the directors who were always scouting for new talent had finally noticed her.

The play, however, didn't run more than three performances and Isadora, even more stubborn and determined, kept knocking at stage doors; as soon as she heard of a new play in the works, she ran right over.

One time Isadora came in flushed. She opened up her handbag, and with trembling hands pulled out a few printed pages and shrieked, "A part! At last the long-awaited dream role! My career is taking off!"

"What type of role?" we asked with curiosity.

"Jessica in 'Shylock.' I've already read the part and it appeals to me very much. Rehearsals begin in a few days." She spoke at a fever pitch. "The famous director Sir Arthur Roy is arriving from England. Meanwhile, my friend Gavin, the young director, is getting the troupe ready for him."

Isadora studied her role day and night and we didn't disturb her. On the contrary, we walked on tiptoe. Many times we would leave the house altogether so as not to disturb her. And Tetrazini and I began to see her as the next great star. We tolerated all her whims, and excused every nervous outburst. We understood where her anxiety came from: soon she would start rehearsals with the director. She had heard that he was strict and capricious. Still, she was certain that her star was rising and that her great part would bring great opportunities. She was certain that her dream was coming true and that her life as an artist was beginning.

Finally, the day of the first rehearsal came. Isadora knew the entire role by heart. We wished her luck. Proudly, confidently, she went off to the theatre. A few hours later, she returned. Just one look at her told us that she wouldn't play the part. She could barely drag her feet. Her tall figure was bent over as if someone had given her a beating and she hardly had the strength to straighten out. She slipped down on a stool. Her eyes were sorrowful, her lips tightly shut. She stared fixedly at a single point as if she saw nothing and heard nothing.

Tetrazini brought her coffee. I served her cake, which she left untouched. The singer could not contain herself any longer and shouted, "For God's sake, Isadora, what happened there?" She shook herself as if waking up from a deep sleep, and said, "Someone else is playing my part. The director brought her from London. She has already played the role." Suddenly she picked herself up, ran into the bedroom, and slammed the door. And from the room came stifled sobbing.

For a while Isadora kept to herself. She didn't eat, went nowhere, and didn't want to speak with us. She stayed in bed and lived on black coffee and cigarettes. Weak, like after a long illness, she got up, dressed, and once again set off for Broadway. More determined than ever, Isadora knocked on agents and casting directors' doors. Always getting promised "something," she lived in a fever of anticipation that eventually she would get her long-dreamed-of role and fight her way to a place on the stage.

And at the same time, Tetrazini's star began to rise. Once, she sang at a concert where critics had been invited. They wrote about her very favourably. She came home with the newspaper in her hand, and with a great flourish showed us her picture and read us the article that predicted a great career. She nearly danced for joy.

I, too, had a surprise waiting. I took out the newspaper and showed them the announcement that in a short while a novella by a new author would be published, and my name appeared in large print. Zina put on the table a bottle of champagne that she had gotten from somewhere, poured three small glasses, and we drank to our future success. Isadora smiled, toasted us, and said, "Meanwhile, we are drinking to the success of both of you. Mine has yet to come. *Nu*, give us another drink."

We went on refilling the glasses, trying to have fun, but the celebrating ended in a quarrel and it was decided that in order to hold onto our deep friendship, we would have to live apart. That would give us peace and quiet to study and not to be disturbed.

A few weeks later, each of us had our own place, a quiet corner. But this did not diminish our friendship. Just the opposite, we missed each other a lot. Aside from frequent phone calls, we also saw each other often; there was always something happening and there was always something to talk about.

Zina often made trips to nearby towns. She was frequently in the public eye. I was very busy preparing a book for publication and settling into my new home. Isadora continued trying to break into the professional theatre, knocking on doors that were bolted shut to a young unknown actress. She would listen to us attentively, more interested in the artistic side of our lives. But she showed no interest in our private lives. She seemed to be content with the bits and pieces of success that came our way. She would often say quietly, "I, too, must become something. I'll do it."

One time, late at night while I was sunken in a deep sleep, the ringing phone woke me. In the dark, with eyes half closed, I found the receiver and angrily asked, "What is it? Who's speaking?"

"It's Tetrazini."

She was hysterical, confused, yelling, crying. I didn't catch the meaning of her words. I thought it must have something to do with a dramatic episode in her love life. "For this you wake me in the middle of the night?" I yelled angrily. "You couldn't wait till morning with your broken romance?"

"What's with you? Are you deaf? Aren't you listening? It's Isadora, our Dora."

"What's with Dora?"

I was now totally awake and began to understand the strange words, the terrible truth.

"Isadora is ill…suddenly, mentally ill. She's in an institution." She had just found out.

I didn't hear any more. A spasmodic hiccough tore out of my throat, a terrible cry resounded through the dark house. The voice on the other end was silent. Zina, it seemed, was allowing me to have a good cry. All at once, the dead receiver started speaking.

"That's enough, Sarah. There's still hope for her, she's in a private sanatorium on Long Island. Come over to my house early and we'll drive out and see her and we can find out what's happening."

And she hung up the receiver, and the phone went dead.

I went back to bed but sleep wouldn't come. Frightening images formed before my eyes. I pulled the chain on the lamp and the room lit up. It was one o'clock. I tossed anxiously in my bed; the hours dragged on like tedious days. By the time the clock showed three a.m., I felt as if I too was losing my mind. Abruptly I jumped out of bed, dressed, and found my way to Tetrazini's house.

She was not surprised by my late visit. She couldn't sleep either. We were awake the whole night speculating and trying to guess how Isadora, so clever and refined, with such a sharp intelligence, could suddenly lose her mind. We took comfort in the thought that it must be a short-term nervous breakdown which would pass, leaving her well again.

Early in the morning we phoned our friend, a doctor we knew. Like us, he was upset at the sad news. He left his office and the three of us drove to the sanatorium where our friend Isadora was. We were disappointed when they told us that we couldn't see her. She had just come out of shock treatment. Only our friend the doctor was allowed to go in. This calmed us somewhat: we would find out about Isadora's condition from him.

On the way home, the doctor told us that she was a very sick girl. She had not recognized him. But that happens frequently after "shock." Still, he said, there is great hope that she will get well. Only time would tell how long it would take before she returned to normal.

After a four-month stay in the private sanatorium, she returned home, and it looked as if she was the same Isadora as before. She resumed her activities in the theatre and, fortunately, she got a part on Broadway in one of the big theatres. The role consisted of only four words, still she was happy that the theatrical agents would see her onstage and that her dream to become "something" seemed closer. The play ran for only a week and Isadora was again left without interest and without work. Zina travelled often and we seldom saw her. I too didn't stay in one place.

During this time, Isadora got sick again. Her sisters and brothers sent her away again to a private sanatorium where she stayed for a while, then returned home, seemingly healed. But, it didn't last long. She would fall into melancholia and often succumb to wild attacks of madness. She became seriously ill again. This time, her family put her into a state institution.

During this period, I saw her in different moods, both at home and in the hospital. To my amazement, she spoke normally, calmly. Except she kept repeating the same words over and over: "I have to make something of myself."

Six years passed and Isadora remained in the state hospital for the mentally ill. For the last two years I had been traveling, but during that time I wrote letters to both Isadora and Tetrazini. The first never answered, the second one did. The singer wrote, detailing how well things were going; she was full of plans for the future. She seldom mentioned Isadora. If she did write about her, it was in a resigned tone, as one speaks of a lost soul.

At the end of the summer, I came back to New York and immediately went to see my sick friend. The institution was far from New York. The train carried many who had come to see their family and friends. The train stopped and let the passengers off. The conductor pointed me to a tall white building that, from a distance, looked like a castle. That's where Isadora was. The institution was surrounded by high mountains, tall pines, and chestnut trees. Colourful flowers spread out in a grassy carpet. Indian summer had done its magic with its yellow-brown and red leaves. From a clear sky, the sun threw its golden rays and lifted my heavy mood.

A nurse in white quietly wandered among the trees, a reminder that one was at a hospital. I approached the building and suddenly saw that the high windows were encircled with iron bars. Strange voices came from inside. I shuddered and realized clearly where I was. Nervously, and with a pounding heart, I went into the hospital. A nurse showed me where I could find Isadora Koifman. There was a large, empty hall with bare walls, just some benches where patients sat. They were of different ages and appearances, mixed races, black and white, and each of them appeared to be living in a different world. A few were pacing quickly. Others sat on the floor barefoot; one was walking quickly with an open umbrella and at the same time shaking off her dress as if from the rain. An open door led to a broad balcony that was encircled with iron bars. I looked for Isadora, but she was nowhere to be seen. I went out on the balcony; she was standing in a corner. Her tall, thin figure had become taller and thinner; she looked into space with vacant eyes; I went nearer, called her name; she didn't move and didn't hear me. Her wide eyes looked glazed. She looked as if she had been carried off to a faraway mystical world.

"Dora! Isadora!" I shook her sleeve. She became frightened, turned around and saw me.

"Oh, you. What are you doing here?"

"I came to see you and find out how you're feeling!"

"How would you feel in a crazy house?" she answered me by asking this strange question.

"*Nu*, sit down," she hospitably pointed to a bench, "and tell me what's happening in the free world, and what's doing with sane people. How is the prima donna? Is she singing opera or is she in the wine cellar?" She bombarded me with pointed questions and didn't wait for a reply.

"*Nu*, what is our great and famous George Sand doing? Have you finished writing your great and famous work, or are you in the middle of something?" She kept throwing her words as if they were heavy stones. All the while, her sarcastic smile didn't leave her lips.

"*Nu*, I have managed to get somewhere. You'll soon see…"

Suddenly she started for the big room but then stood still in the middle of the hall. She clapped her hands as a signal to the people around. Immediately she was surrounded by the patients and they began calling out: "Quickly, come here! Isadora is going to put on a show."

Isadora waited for a few minutes until everyone gathered around her. She motioned to a place for me. She held a long pose, swept her hair up, bowed majestically and started to speak – clearly, quietly – but as she went on, her rich voice rang out surer and steadier.

"To be, or not to be, that is the question."

She recited the whole monologue from *Hamlet*; received a thunderous ovation, and shouts kept coming:

"Isadora, dance!"

"The snake dance!"

"No, the dog dance!"

"The swan dance!"

She motioned to one of the patients who handed her a white sheet. Isadora wrapped half the sheet around her body, the other half she gracefully threw over her left side. She kicked her slippers off her feet, stretched her head up high, and clapped her hands, as a sign that she was beginning.

Soon her thin, bare feet let themselves go on the shiny floor. Like a butterfly, she swept around the hall and hardly touched the ground. She flew like a bird high, high into the heavens. Soon she lowered her long neck. Her body bent down to the earth, then immediately she rose up again, and again flew far far away in space. Isadora had danced the "swan dance."

I withdrew into a corner and wept quietly. All of a sudden she noticed me and came running up.

"You're crying? Why? Aha, you're jealous. You begrudge me a bit of happiness? You never thought I deserved it! Only you and Tetrazini, the singer and the writer...you and she...she and you... I didn't exist... I want to become 'something' too! And I did become something. If you have talent and patience you become something. I have won a dear and loyal audience. What difference does it make to me where I act or dance? As Shakespeare said, the world is a stage and people are actors. My stage is here. You saw how my public loves me, they long for my artistic expression, they wouldn't trade me for any other actress. Wipe away your tears and stop being envious of me. Don't begrudge me...ha? Who sent you? Get out!" she ordered imperiously. "I don't want to see you again! You and the singer won't take my public away from me." She looked at me triumphantly the whole time. And all of a sudden she left me standing there, and she threw herself into a wild fit of dancing.

Translation by Alisa Poskanzer with Judy Nisenholt

IN A MUSEUM

Sarah Hamer-Jacklyn

Infuriated, Nora grabbed her hat and coat, slammed the door, and quickly strode down the stairs.

"Wait a minute," Alex shouted after her. "One second, I'm coming too."

She didn't stop, but angrily continued farther down. With quickened steps, she distanced herself from his house, veered off onto a side street, and stopped for a while. After she had a good look around and was sure that he was no longer there, she breathed easier, and shouted into the air: "I will never look at him again!"

Nora couldn't calm herself after his wild lunge at her.

They had known each other for years. Alex was her husband's best friend and often came over to enjoy their company. It had been almost a year since her husband died suddenly, and she was unexpectedly left alone, a young widow, without friends, except for Alex.

Alex came regularly to her house, and was a comfort with his devoted friendship and innate understanding. His behaviour was always correct, and he never made her feel that he had other intentions. She became so used to Alex's visits and friendship that if he didn't come for an evening or two, she really missed him. She consulted with him over the smallest trivial details of her life, and in so doing felt she was easing her heartache with a brother.

One day, Alex invited her to his house, to show her the bachelor life he'd created. Excited to see how he lived his life, Nora accepted his invitation with pleasure. But no sooner had she crossed the threshold, when he pounced on her like a wild animal.

Now, in the street, she still couldn't compose herself, and went over it again. "How dare he! Doesn't he know who I am? What am I to him, a streetwalker? Such crudeness!"

Suddenly she realized that she was wet: the snow, falling like dense feathers, whitewashed the New York City streets, covering them like a featherbed. She stood, uncertain what to do with herself. Where to go now? It was late afternoon. Maybe to a movie? No, there were no good movies in the area. Then she remembered that she wasn't far from a museum, and decided to go there.

Once in the museum, she looked at the paintings by the old masters, amazed at their freshness, how real, how vibrant they appeared! She imagined that soon "the lady of the castle" would rise up and start talking. She examined various antiquities, and wandered to the area where the mummies were laid out in glass cases.

She found herself standing in front of a glass case, deep in thought. The mummy was wrapped in a yellow web, like an aged spider web. It was clearly a human form, and Nora felt sure that the form was female. Probably an Egyptian princess, maybe even a queen.

Maybe she was a courtesan. No! thought Nora, courtesans weren't preserved in such lavish cases. This was surely an Egyptian princess.

She was caught up by a strong desire to know about the story of the royal daughter. Did she lead an adventurous life of love and intrigues, or did she only involve herself in politics and wars?

Nora tried to visualize the figure. The princess appeared to be tall, slender, with a head of black curls interlaced with pearls. Her dark skin was as smooth as velvet. Her black, almond eyes sparkled with fire, and struck manly hearts like spears. A wild one, and she was always surrounded by royalty and courtiers and slaves. She wore the most extraordinary dresses and the most expensive jewels. She was famous over all of Egypt as a great beauty.

What did her castle look like, Nora asked herself, and in her imagination she saw, high on a hill, a marble palace with extraordinary furniture and walls of gold and silver.

Suddenly she stopped short. Was there poverty then too? And she realized that she'd been thinking out loud when she heard an answer to her question.

"There was, Miss."

Nora shuddered. She realized that those last words were indeed uttered aloud. She looked around and noticed a tall, imposing young man standing nearby.

"I've been standing here next to you for quite a while." She heard the stranger's soft voice, which, to her, rang through the museum like a voice from another world. "But you were so engrossed," he went on, "that you didn't notice me." Nora looked at him, confused.

"You probably have a vivid imagination," the stranger continued. "I noticed that in your misty eyes. You were swept away in a mystical world of ancient time."

They were both silent for a while.

"That look you have, I'd like to paint it."

"You paint?" Nora finally awoke, as from a deep sleep.

"Yes, I paint."

"Landscapes or portraits?" she mumbled, still preoccupied.

"Mostly portraits."

"Do you paint well?"

He burst out laughing.

Her heart warmed at that.

"As to that, Miss, you'll be able to judge for yourself."

It turned out that he had travelled a lot and covered the world. As an artist himself, he spoke to her with a lot of authority about the paintings.

Nora, however, still wanted to know more about the mummies. So he told her stories about ancient Egypt with its wonderful museums and mummies, embalmed for thousands of years.

She let herself be guided down storybook ways, and devoured his every word.

"How old," she asked, "could this particular mummy be?" She pointed at the glass case that held her dream princess.

"I can't know exactly, but approximately three thousand years."

"Three thousand years!" Nora marvelled.

Suddenly she felt a heaviness. A black cloud covered her face. It occurred to her that, if that's the case, man lives for a short time but death lasts forever. Yes, men's lives last for only minutes – if you count minutes – then eternity. So why make such a big fuss about each little thing? And why do people rush around so much, since ultimately they achieve nothing?

The stranger noticed that his new friend had become downhearted, so he began speaking about more recent events and cheerful stories, and Nora started to smile. Later, he talked about modern art and painting, but Nora confessed that she was not really an expert.

They walked out of the museum together. Outside, night had fallen. The white snow shimmered in their eyes and a white world unfolded.

Nora realized that she didn't want to break away from the stranger, and when he suggested that they go out for a meal, she experienced a quiet joy.

Nora insisted that they eat at her place. On their way there they bought all kinds of food, all the while talking like old friends.

He admired her apartment, including the artwork hanging on the walls, and complimented her choice in furnishings.

She set a fine table, providing all kinds of dishes. The aroma of freshly brewed coffee wafted over the rooms. Nora wanted to invite her guest to the table, but she realized that she didn't even know his name. Standing near him she said, shyly, "May I ask your name, sir?"

"Emile Tzvayg. And your name, Miss?"

"Nora Rikhter." She extended her hand, which he took, brought to his mouth, and gallantly kissed.

"And now, Mr. Tzvayg, to the table, please."

"Don't call me Mr. Tzvayg, simply Emile," he said.

"Well, come, Emile, to the table."

They sat down and all at once, Emile turned around, took Nora's hand, and asked, "Where have you been all these years of my life?"

"Here in New York," she answered, and felt good.

"Finally I know why I've wandered all around the world. I also know now why I was drawn back to New York."

"Why?" Nora asked.

"Because you're here."

He locked her in his arms and covered her with warm kisses. He kissed her eyes, stroked her hair. A pleasant shudder ran through Nora's body. She closed her eyes, and felt his strong arms carrying her off into a more vital world.

By the time Emile left Nora's house, the night was turning grey. With shining eyes, Nora, now happy, accompanied him to the door.

"When do we see each other again?" he asked, animated.

"Today, tomorrow, the day after tomorrow, forever…"

"Today, tomorrow, the day after tomorrow, forever…" Overjoyed, he repeated Nora's words and left her house.

Translation by Ida Wynberg

SHADOWS

Rachel Korn

"*L'chayim*, to Life!" Hands holding full glasses of brandy reached toward the master of the house.

"Congratulations, father, mother. *Mazel tov*, may this be a good hour!"

"Good luck to us all!"

"To life, fellow Jews. *L'chayim*."

The infant lying half asleep, lulled by the lick of brandy, was awakened by the noise and, contorting his little face, broke into a long, stubborn cry.

All who had gathered together for the circumcision at Chayim Rozenboym's were suddenly silent. Their ears perked up, as the reason for their presence here had now become clear.

Embarrassed by their own awkwardness, they averted their eyes from the cradle, their gaze straying over the walls of the room.

The apartment on Narutowicz Street in the city of Lodz – two rooms and a kitchen – which Chayim Rozenboym occupied, reflected the events of the seven years since 1939.

This "highfalutin'" house had once belonged to a Jewish manufacturer who had it built for himself and his heirs. The Gestapo had expropriated the apartment, shipping furniture, carpets, silver, and porcelain to Germany to furnish their own homes. For their use here, they had dragged in furnishings from other orphaned homes after deporting the owners to death camps and crematoria.

Though the furniture had been here a number of years, it still seemed ill-assorted. The children's room was edged in unfinished wood, on which a child's clumsy hand had carved the outline of a horse's head.

Around the wide, square table stood chairs like wedding guests gathered from far and wide. Such a jumble: a tall, threadbare, over-stuffed red plush armchair – probably once the seat of a rabbi ruling on religious matters – and richly embroidered blue silk Rococo dark wood stools, and plain white kitchen chairs.

Like the chairs, so the people: from different walks of life and from various cities, towns, and villages of Poland, Lithuania, and Galicia. Each one rescued from death tens of times, each one's life a unique miracle. They had grown accustomed to death and dying. It was difficult for them now to grasp the natural course of life. They stood around the cradle of the little soul not knowing whether to rejoice or mourn. They had lost the measure for both.

And of those who tried to laugh, their laughter sounded too shrill; of the ones who were silent, their silence grew heavy as a dense cloud on a stifling day. Two women, taking hold of the cradle on each side, brought the child to the new mother resting in her bed against high pillows.

"Give the child the breast," commanded tall, bony Soreh Gitel.

"Such a poor little lamb," Zelde wiped her eyes, "what a pity! Only eight days old and he has to suffer already – just because he's a Jewish child. I can't bear to hear a child crying."

"Don't say such foolish things, Zelde dear," Soreh Gitel interrupted her, "let it cry, scream, it's good. God forbid, nothing will happen to him. But what about us, how long since we've heard the cry of a newborn, eh?"

An old woman in a faded black jacket with a scarf on her head – the only old person in this gathering – bent over the cradle, lifted the child, and handed it to the mother. She remained by the bed, looking at the tiny, red face, turning redder and wrinkled from the strain of sucking at his mother's breast. The old woman began to rock back and forth, as though attempting to drive away a disturbing thought or memory. All at once, a smile appeared on her face and remained caught in the net of wrinkles, until Soreh Gitel cried out: "Oh my God! Why are we standing here like statues? We have to serve the refreshments!" And she was the first to head for the kitchen.

The first to be served the platters of fish and roasts were the men.

At the head of the table sat the rabbi in a broad silk hat, his head held in both his hands.

Hershel Kropeev asked his neighbour, "Where does the rabbi come from? I've never seen him here before." He answered, "These days how many real Lodzers would you meet here in the city? They come from everywhere. I heard someone say the rabbi comes from a small town in Galicia. Greyding, I think. His whole family is lost. A group of boys, partisans, hid him in a pit in a forest."

The rabbi lifted his head slowly, drops of sweat forming like pearls on his broad, yellowed forehead. He spread his hands like two witnesses on the white tablecloth, and spoke to the gathering with a strong, loud voice: "Fellow Jews, today, let us forget what is past. Let us rejoice. A new Jew is here among us today. Let it be in a good, blessed hour!"

"Amen, amen," all nodded their heads.

The blessing after the meal concluded, they began to sing Sabbath songs. And someone hummed a Hasidic melody, as if to himself. Soon all sang along, softly at first, almost restrained by hesitation and fear. Then the melody grew louder and stronger, until it engulfed them like a fire wheel.

They felt that a heavy weight had suddenly been lifted: to forget, for at least an hour or two, to forget all that had happened to them, to forget their yesterday.

Shaken by their joyousness and burst of song, everybody fell silent. Somebody's hand drew aside the curtain. Grey dusk descended beneath a cloudy sky, spreading long shadows into the brightly lit windows.

A voice was heard in the gathering: "It's time to go home."

Singly and in couples, the guests began to slip away. Already in their coats, they threw a glance at the sleeping infant, and with a tremor in their voices, wished father and mother an easy child-raising.

Velvl Honigvaks took his wife's arm. "Be careful, Fayge, there's a hole in the sidewalk."

Fayge smiled to herself, wishing with this smile to brighten the way for both of them, and for the one who lay embedded in her enlarged body awaiting its hour. No – it was she who was awaiting the hour when she would take it in her arms and, with her nostrils, with her mouth, drink in the scent of its fine little hairs.

"Velvl, you take such good care of me, you're so good. I don't know how I managed alone without you. And tell me the truth, really, the real truth – did you think about me, yearn for me, as the way I did through all the years when you were in Siberia?"

"You're such a little fool, the same foolish girl you used to be. Don't you know that you're my beloved, my dearest? Besides you, whom do I have in the whole world?"

"That's exactly what I wanted to hear. But once isn't enough. You must keep telling it to me three, four times a day. Do you hear?"

"And would ten times be enough?"

"It depends." She became more earnest. A grey cloud covered her face. "Don't laugh at me."

Velvl pressed Fayge's arm more tightly to his breast.

"You know, Velvl, I nearly went out of my mind when I was left alone without you. And I kept thinking, what if Velvl returns and doesn't find me? And even then, when they took me in a closed wagon – you know where – it was all the same to me whatever would happen. But I prayed to God that you, at least, should remain alive. All the while I whispered your name to myself. At least your name should be with me in my last hours. And see, I saved myself, one of the very few. And I can even tell you why: because I wanted to see you so much, so very much. Once more in my life. Today, when I saw everyone at the Rozenboyms', a great fear came over me. How many broken lives. Not even one unbroken family. Shards. One had his wife and children led away to be burned; another had her husband shot before her eyes. Now they marry each other quickly, just not to be alone and abandoned. Two solitudes pair themselves off forcibly. May God forgive me for talking like this. It feels like a sin, that I'm the happiest one of all."

"God has nothing to forgive you for. It's a sin to be unhappy," he answered with a smile. "And here we are, already at home." Velvl searched his pocket for the key. "I'm going to make up the bed for you right away. You have to rest. And tomorrow, right in the morning, I'll be off to look for an apartment. How long do we have to live with others!"

"Think you'll find something? It's not so easy to find a place now. You have to pay a lot of key money."

"Yes. That's why I've been saving so much lately. We now have enough for an apartment of our own."

"Remember, it should be near a park, and sunny."

As Velvl opened the door, Fayge leaned her head on his shoulder and whispered in his ear, "It will look like you, nothing else will do."

It seemed Mrs. Epstien, their landlady, had been expecting them for some time, for no sooner had she heard the creak of the door than she rushed out of the bedroom. Pointing with her finger to the room which the couple occupied, she whispered to Velvl: "Mr. Honigvaks, a strange woman with a child is waiting for you. I told her that you'd be home late. She wouldn't leave."

The first thing before their eyes as they entered their room was a basket with a kettle attached to it and, in the centre of the room, a large bundle on which a girl of three or four lay dozing. Before husband and wife could exchange astonished looks, a hand drew aside a curtain. A woman stood up, raised her head and, ignoring Fayge, ran to Velvl. Throwing both arms around his neck, she sobbed: "Volodya, Volodya, don't you recognize me? It's me, your Katya. See who I've brought you. Lida Lidachka! Here, greet your father," she grabbed the sleeping child by the hand. "You didn't even write a single word," she reproached Velvl angrily, tightening her lips. "But I found you anyway. With us you don't run away so easily from a wife and child."

With a single motion Velvl freed himself from her embracing arms, all the while looking only in Fayge's direction.

Stunned, pale, she stood tight-lipped, covering her ears with both her hands.

Velvl drew Fayge's hands away from her ears and led her to a chair: "Sit down here, you'll be more comfortable. I'll explain everything to you soon."

"You don't have to." She could barely utter the words. "Everything is already clear to me, everything."

"Fayge, dear Fayge, why are you so cruel? Why do you condemn me, even before you hear me out? I didn't stop loving you for a single moment. I just didn't know what happened to you. People told me that no one from our *shtetl* was saved."

"And you wasted no time installing a living tombstone to me," she pointed at the frightened little girl clinging to her mother.

Velvl turned toward Katya. "Why did you run after me? I never promised to marry you. Didn't I tell you that I left a wife at home, and when the war ended I would search for her, even to the ends of the earth. Don't you remember?"

Both women knew that these words were really directed to Fayge, even though he was speaking to Katya. He stated these words as witnesses that would defend him and arouse compassion from the other side.

Katya felt that it would be better to remain silent, yet despite her will, her response escaped. "So you said. But that didn't stop you from living with me as man and wife. Maybe you want to deny this? Here both of you have the evidence."

She took hold of the child by the shoulders and stood her in the centre of the room.

Velvl took a wallet out of his breast pocket and tossed ten and twenty zloty notes onto the table. "Here, here you have everything I own. You'll have enough for expenses to get home.

And choose from this room whatever your heart desires. You can take everything, everything."

Katya broke into a loud, shrill laughter, but in that laughter trembled powerfully suppressed tears: "So that's the way you want to get rid of me? You want to remain with your 'city' lady? But, if not for me, you would have dropped dead in the middle of the street, like so many of yours. You forget already how I took you into my home, sick, starving, full of lice. Now you don't want to know me, not me, not your child. But I won't move from here. Do with me what you want."

She turned her back to Velvl, undid the bundle, and began to make up a bed on the floor. Fayge took her handbag from the chair, buttoned up her jacket and, holding on to the wall like a blind person, moved unsteadily toward the door.

Velvl blocked her way. "Where are you going?"

"There is no room for two here."

"I won't let you…"

"You have no say over me anymore."

"Dear Fayge, so late at night? You know how dangerous it is on the street now. They hate us even more than in Hitler's time. Every Jew who remained alive is a thorn in their sides."

"Let me." Velvl took Fayge by the shoulder, and began to unbutton her jacket.

"Mama, I'm scared," the child broke into tears. "Take me away from here."

"Why, in all this time, didn't you tell me about that one, that other one." Fayge pointed to the corner where the Russian woman lay on the floor, a peasant scarf lowered over her eyes.

Velvl led Fayge to the bed, sat her on the edge like a small child, and began to take off her shoes. "Wait, wait until morning. It will be good again. You'll see."

"It can never be good again," she sobbed. This sobbing washed away her entire resolve. Her anxiety eased, but the feelings of isolation and forlornness strengthened and deepened. She listened closely to the being inside her. Yes, it was turning and tossing within her, seeking a way out, wishing to come to her rescue. It does not yet know that on the eve of its birth it is already homeless.

Velvl began to stroke Fayge's shoulder, hands, and feet, and murmured with dry, parched lips all the same futile words: "It'll all still be good, you'll see, you'll see." The light switch snapped as his hand turned off the lamp. Mercifully, the sudden darkness hid the anguished human faces. The room swam into the night like a ship lost on distant unknown oceans.

And it appeared that the whole world was holding its breath listening in to the silence imprisoned within these four walls.

Leon and Rita Zilber were quiet almost all the way home. Both turned their attention inward, wanting to remember something, or perhaps to forget everything.

Their steps resonated rhythmically on the half-empty street. The rising moon brushed against a tall factory chimney, appearing as if someone had cut through its centre.

Leon pointed, saying, "See, it seems like it'll break in half any minute."

"I see," Rita nodded. Not another word until they rang at their apartment door. The maid rushed over and helped Rita with her coat.

"Did anyone call?"

"No, madam."

"Agnieshka, you may go to sleep."

As he finished smoking his cigarette, Leon Zilber observed pensively, "A strange thought occurred to me today. For the first time since *that* time it's clear to me: those of us who remained alive must obey the normal laws of life."

"So that's what you think?"

"You, you alone made me think of that. When you bent over the cradle and smiled at the new citizen, your smile was – like it used to be."

"You mean to say 'like then,' when I was your friend Isaac's wife?"

Leon nodded.

"And do you know that I still love him?"

"It's possible."

"And it doesn't bother you?"

Rita walked over to the night table by her bed. There stood two framed photographs of a middle-aged man and a boy in a sailor suit. She covered them with both hands as if wishing to hide their smiling faces from the gaze of strangers.

"I understand you well, Rita. I also loved Mira and my little girl, Stefa. You have some pictures at least. For me, nothing was left."

"For the first time we're really talking about it. I thought that you'd already erased them from your memory."

"Why talk? Will talking bring them back? We have to go on with life, Rita."

"I detest those words. Don't bring them up again, do you hear? Cowards who are afraid to look at their loathsome stinking selves thought up that nice theory to hide behind like a screen. Why are you looking at me like that? I'm contemptible! No better than all the others. When they tore them away from me, I didn't go with them. I wanted to convince myself that they were really taking them to work. With tooth and nail I held on to my shabby bit of life."

"At that time no one knew where they were being taken."

"But now I know already. So what? I'm alive, I live. And do you know what it means – such a life? Prostitution, prostituting my life. And see what's become of me! Got myself a double bed with a white crocheted bedspread – in the latest style. And Isaac's place is occupied by his best friend. What a farce! I could just die of laughter."

"These last few weeks you've been more calm." Leon leaned close to Rita, stroking her throat and neck. "The sight of the child really upset you. Wait, soon we'll get away from this cursed country, far, far away; maybe to the land of Israel. As an engineer I'll find work everywhere. And in our new home – when a child comes – ours, you just won't have time anymore for all these thoughts."

Rita jumped up from her chair, and with fear and hatred she looked straight into Leon's eyes. "What did you say? A child? Never. Listen to me, I'll never have a child. No one will ever take my Zavek's place. And I'll never carry a child for nine months to deliver it to the angel of death." She came closer to Leon, so close that he felt her hot breath on his face. Like a stern judge, she measured and weighed every word separately to make it reach and hit its target. "And if something should happen to me against my will, I'll strangle it as soon as it's born. With my own hands. I want you to know that. Do you hear me?" Leon moved away from Rita. Haltingly, he lowered himself onto a low footstool, hiding his face in both his hands.

She had been drained to her very depths by these words and nothing remained, neither to say nor to hide. With her full weight she fell onto the carpet on the floor.

Her dry, burning eyes ached for the grace of a tear. "My God, what have you done with me? Is he to blame for my misfortune? But someone is guilty. Answer me, God, answer me you, you God!"

A threesome, they set off for home. From a corner near the entrance door, a shadow emerged and began to rise before them. Quick, delicate steps sounded like dried peas pouring from a cracked vessel. From the shadow a dwarf-like figure took shape. A hand slipped under Doctor Marek Bloch's arm.

"Weren't expecting to meet me here? Do you think that if you don't let me know where you're going, I won't find you? Will you introduce me to your friends?"

The glow of the streetlamp they had just approached illuminated the surrounding darkness with the harshness of a sudden light. It pointedly revealed two humps clamping together a slight, girlish figure.

And as Doctor Marek Bloch stood silent, agitated and confused by the sudden encounter, the woman stretched out her hand to Freyde and Lipe, "If you will permit me, I'll introduce myself – I am Doctor Bloch's wife."

In a strange voice Doctor Bloch intercepted, "I'll go home now. We'll continue our conversation tomorrow. Good night now."

Lipe and Freyde remained standing in the middle of the street. An odd heaviness settled in their bones.

"Can she really be Marek's wife?" they thought to themselves. Marek, the handsomest and most charming of the students, with whom all of Freyde's classmates had been in love, and probably she herself too, before she met Lipe. One of the girls had even tried to commit suicide because of him. They had been certain that Marek had perished together with his family. And just today, quite by chance, they had met him at the Rozenboyms'.

Lipe's and Freyde's disharmonious steps jarred the surrounding stillness with a clash. Husband and wife were aware that he sometimes ran ahead and then, catching up, she overtook him. As if by a secret order, hidden suppressed thoughts began to carry out their destructive work in the middle of the empty street.

In the light of the electric lamp, Freyde's blonde hair shone like ripe wheat on a summer day. "Why are you standing with your coat on like a guest who's just arrived?"

"Maybe I'm only a guest in your house." Lipe embraced Freyde in his arms and led her to the sofa. "Your hands are cold and you look really pale. Something's changed. What's the matter with you?"

"I know what you're thinking, though you keep it to yourself. I've noticed more than once that you take a pocketful of candy for the children in the street. But with me there's nothing. And nothing will ever be. I will never be able to have children. Do you hear? Never, never."

"You seem so sure. How do you know?"

"I'm very sure."

"You've talked yourself into something, my foolish girl. Tomorrow I'll take you to a doctor. No, better still, to the best specialist. And you'll see, he'll laugh at you!"

Freyde began to laugh a wild cruel laugh, as if that laugh would wrench out the hard burning knot of pain within her.

Holding her head in both hands, like a mother lulling a sick child to sleep, she stared with stony eyes at one spot. Lipe tried to slip out of the room on his tiptoes, like leaving a sick person in bed.

Freyde heard his footsteps. "Come back, sit down," she called to him.

Lipe tried to lift her lowered head, so he might look directly into her eyes; his fingers stroking her soft and curly hair.

"Don't you touch me! Do you hear? You must not touch me!"

"What happened so suddenly?"

"Sit down here right across from me."

He gave in as one does with a willful child.

"I must talk with you."

Lipe interrupted her: "Maybe we should leave it until tomorrow, when we'll be more rested? My pampered little girl can be good when she wants to."

"No, no, it has to happen now, this minute. Tomorrow – tomorrow, there's no more tomorrow. There's today – and even that is more than I can endure."

Her eyes took on their former clouded expression.

Lipe felt tightness in his throat as if invisible fingers were pressing in on him, and he began to choke. He tore off his shirt collar with one hand, and with a dry cough tried to express some sound from his blocked throat.

Only now did he realize with all his senses that this was not a nervous outburst, the residue of years of danger as he'd thought until now; nor was it the capricious coquetry of a beautiful woman, overly secure in her husband's love.

A dark, heavy cloud came over him. He hunched his back, as if to take on the new burden. What could it be?

He had carried so many dead in his thirty years. Everything that fateful, horrible time could mete out to a human being had befallen him.

Everyone, everyone lost: father, mother, brothers, and his little blond boy. Only he and his wife had survived. He didn't know how it had happened. Actually, only the will to see their child one more time drove them to take the daring risk in the game of chance with the angel of death.

He and Freyde had stolen out of the ghetto, at the time still the safest place for a Jew, hoping to see their child at least from a distance. They had entrusted a farmer they knew to hide him for the price of all their possessions, all their worldly goods.

Stealing out of the ghetto, they removed their armbands with the Star of David, knowing that any German who met a Jew outside the ghetto without that badge had the right to shoot on the spot.

Lipe and Freyde succeeded then. They saw their child asleep, and didn't want to awaken the little boy who had become used to calling the farmer "father" and his wife "mother," lest one time he blurt out a suspicious word in front of neighbours.

When Lipe's lips touched the little head, the sleeping child turned away his snubbed nose, waving his little hand as if shaking off an annoying fly.

That movement of the child's hand, more than anything else, remained etched in his memory.

At the time, he did not know – hadn't even a foreboding – that he was seeing his child for the last time. Eighteen months later, coming to pick up his little boy, he learned that the farmer had handed the child over to the Germans.

And all this time they had lulled themselves into believing that whatever might happen to them, at least their child would survive. The opposite had happened, as if the devil were playing a game with them. In the two days that they were outside the ghetto to see their child, in just those two days, the SS had carried out an action which did not leave a single Jew alive, not even the able-bodied nor the craftsmen. At the gate of the ghetto they had hung a sign: *Judenrein.* For several days, Lipe and Freyde hid in the surrounding forests until hunger twisted their intestines and drove them from there.

At night Lipe knocked on the door of a farmer, whom his father had helped more than once in the years of bad harvests. It took an eternity until a sleepy voice rasped through the half-opened window: "Who's there?"

It seemed the farmer was talking it over with his wife; it took a long while before the door opened.

The first night they slept on a bale of hay in the barn. It wasn't easy for Lipe to convince Wojtek Ziemba to hide them in his house. Lipe had already given all their money and jewellery to the farmer who had taken their child; Lipe now signed an agreement that the city house, as well as household articles and clothing buried in the cellar, now belonged to Ziemba.

"And 'yours' will have to work in the house and with the cows. My old lady is going under; the daughters married and the son isn't rushing to bring a daughter-in-law into the house. And work there is. Your wife doesn't look at all like a Jew. I'll tell everyone that she's my niece who came from the city to help out with the housekeeping."

For Lipe, the farmer had dug a deep hole in the barn, covering it – disguising it – with refuse. There Lipe lay for a year and a half.

"Why are you so lost in thought? I don't want to talk to your back, do you hear?"

Freyde's voice grew sharper, more grating with every word, as if she wanted to out-shout herself and her own uncertainty.

Lipe straightened his bent back, inhaling the air deeply several times, a drowning man whose head emerges from the water for the last time. "Speak, I'm listening."

"When you were lying there in that dark hole in the stable, and could crawl out only at night when I brought you that bit of food under my shawl, do you remember?"

"How can anyone forget? And when the cow clanged her chain or a dog barked you grabbed the pot under the shawl and I was instantly ready to drop down into my tomb. Was it a German patrol? Maybe someone spying or the farmer betraying me. I was so afraid."

Lipe pricked up his ears, turned his head toward the door as though danger still lurked on the other side of the wall.

"Once, it was Sunday, yes, I remember clearly, a Sunday night. I brought you bread and water for several days. I told you that I had to go to the nearby town to get a work permit because someone in the village was suspicious, and you shouldn't worry if I was delayed a day or two."

Bewildered, Lipe stared at his wife. What was the point of rehashing all these events which they both remembered so well, too well? And in the late-night hour at that.

Lipe caressed Freyde's pale face with a warm smile. "Know what? Let's finish the conversation tomorrow. I see that you're tired and..."

"Tomorrow? Tomorrow my strength may fail me. I must tell you now, right away – yes, where were we? Ah, you remember, I was away then for three days. And on that night, after I returned, you touched my face in the dark with your fingers and asked why my cheeks were so sunken – and when my voice changed, became hoarse, you noticed that too. I didn't tell you the truth then. I didn't go to arrange for a new document."

Lipe jumped up from his chair. "Be still, Freyde, be still, I beg you."

But Freyde did not hear what he was saying. She could not stop, like an avalanche that breaks off from a high mountain, plunges down to the deep abyss, tearing with it all in its path.

"Do you know where I was then? With an old gentile woman in Khadarobke. To rid myself of the bastard growing in me. She did it with a knitting needle. I held back from screaming with all my strength as I lay on the filthy straw mattress in her cubicle. Now you know what your wife is. Tell me, can you still speak of love to me, after all this?"

She burst into laughter, loud and harsh, as if that laugh could place a *mekhitze*, a partition between them. Let him think she is depraved and fallen. It will be easier for him to accept this, and also easier to forget her.

It seemed to Lipe that someone else, not he, was asking these questions. He himself was already dead, but her words still reached him as through a wall of cotton wadding. "Whose was it?"

"Wojtek's son, Antek."

"Do you still love him? Do you want to go back to him?"

Hatred burned in her greenish eyes, and twisted her mouth. "I would have shot him like a dog right there on the spot."

Lipe held out both hands in a gesture of helplessness. "So tell me why, why then did you do it?"

Even that he wants to know! How can she tell him? Until then, Freyde had no inkling that Lipe might ask her such a question. She knew one thing – she could no longer live like this with the lie between the two of them. Now, when she had freed herself of it, flung the truth at Lipe's feet without pity, only now did the cruelty of her naked words frighten her. If only she could close her eyes forever, not to see Lipe shrinking minute by minute under the whip of her words. Her handsome, proud husband, doubled over like a wounded animal that drags its mutilated body to some corner, hiding from all eyes. And he must not know how much she loves him, maybe even more than before. Did she have the right to wound him so? Would it not have been better to remain silent and bear it alone, however hard, however superhumanly hard it was? She put her left hand between her teeth and bit her fingers until they bled, so she wouldn't cry out in pain and sorrow.

"Now I demand an answer from you. You have no right to keep silent about what you've hidden from me."

"Lipe, better not."

"Now you can tell me everything – the worst. Nothing bothers me anymore. It's all the same. But I want to know the truth, to hear the whole truth."

"Lipe, there are things that words can't…"

"I want and I'm entitled to know what the wife whom I loved, loved so much, is capable of…"

Lipe broke into tears, a quiet soundless cry. Freyde knew he was bemoaning all the years that he had lived with her, his love and trust in her. All her previous restraint deserted her. She covered her eyes with both hands, as if afraid to look the world in the face. And she herself didn't know how the words came tearing out from her, against her will: "He – he threatened – he would hand you over to the Germans."

In the room only the merciless ticking of the clock was heard, the hands stubbornly moving over its face, as if hastening the night hour to an end.

He threw his hat and gloves on the table.

"You're following me, spying on me."

"I just want to remind you of your duty, the duty of a man to his legal wife. No more."

"I'm Mrs. Rozenboym's family doctor; I delivered her child. While she was still in the hospital, they invited me to the *bris.* Is that such a sin?"

"So, you take your wife along. But you don't want to show yourself with me among your cronies. Yet there was a time, not so long ago... Do I have to remind you how many times you assured me that you loved me?"

Doctor Bloch did not look at Aniella but at her shadow on the wall. It resembled a ghostly figure, a devilish trick drawn in charcoal. With Aniella's slightest movement, the two humped shoulders grew, stretching in divergent directions as if striving to fill the entire area; to outgrow the small, thin figure writhing under their weight.

He closed his eyes for only a while, to free himself from the nightmarish vision.

Aniella's voice cut into the stark silence with the sharpness of a slaughter knife: "You play the role of the innocent little lamb. Oh, such a good actor! But not to me! You don't fool me. You called me a spy, but what are you? You're a traitor, a mean traitor. Do you think I don't know that you secretly got yourself a foreign passport? You wanted to sneak away without me."

Marek pressed his lips tightly, holding back the word bursting from his throat. Cheekbones quivered under pale skin, greenish eyes under thick black eyebrows glared with unfettered hate.

Aniella ran to the cupboard, threw open the door, dragged out a valise. With nervous, trembling hands, she began to scatter men's shirts and underclothing onto the floor. A thin, grey-covered booklet fell out of a shirtsleeve. She grabbed it with her fingers, pushing it away from herself like a disgusting reptile, she brought it close to him: "Do you recognize it? It smells of freedom, doesn't it?"

He ran over to her and grabbed her outstretched arm.

"Give it back to me! Right now! You hear?"

She burst into a snickering little laugh. "Oh no, my dear. Not this."

The harsh sound of tearing paper grated on his ears. Aniella held the two halves of the torn booklet in her hands. Then, without hurrying, she shredded each half separately into tiny pieces, scattering them over the entire room.

"See, here is your foreign passport!"

Doctor Bloch did not move from his place, his feet rooted to the floor.

Aniella took his measure from head to foot as he stood opposite her, slim and tall, with a head of dark curly hair accentuating and intensifying her punishment. As if God had apportioned all to one at the expense of the other. And still she loved him, the unbaptized one. More than her own life, more than the One who had died for her on the cross. Even though she knew that this was a grave sin, not to be forgiven.

Aniella threw herself down on her knees. Striking her head on the floor as if possessed, she whispered to herself, "And lead us not into temptation."

Her thin hand, too long for the dwarfish body, moved from forehead to heart, from shoulder to shoulder, crossing the air with swift, feverish movements. It seemed to Marek that the bony hand was not crossing the air, but crucifying him, nailing him to her two unforgiving protruding humps.

"What do you want of me, Aniella? Let it come to an end already, let it end." She did not recognize his hoarse, stifled voice. She began to tremble like a twig in the wind. Without lifting herself from the floor, she crawled on her knees toward him. Grasping his feet, she fell upon his hard leather shoes with her parched lips. "You are mine, mine! And I'll never give you to anyone, never, never! Do you hear? Never!"

Marek bent down to Aniella and loosened her entwined hands. "Get up, Aniella, I beg you. Let's talk it over. Let's find a way out for both of us."

Aniella remained silent.

"You yourself must understand that things can't go on like this any longer. It's torture for both of us, superhuman torture. I will never forget what you've done for me, and I wish only good for you, that you should be able to live a peaceful life without worry. Everything I've saved from my work is yours. And the house I inherited from my father I registered in your name with the notary Warshavsky."

He took an official envelope out of his breast pocket and put it down on the table. "Here's a copy."

Aniella approached the table with slow, catlike steps, and with one movement pushed away the envelope. She pulled a large diamond ring from her finger, a gift from Marek, and hurled it at his feet. "Here, take this also. I don't need it. Do you think that you can buy yourself off with money?"

"Aniella, try to understand me. That's not my intention. You can no longer take on hard work. Through all these years you've suffered great hardship. Now you deserve to live in comfort and peace, together with your mother."

"I have no mother. I have no one in the world, except you."

Both fell into a deep silence which grew heavier with each moment, as if they were attempting to overpower one another through silence. Whoever could endure this deadly silence to its limit would be the victor.

Aniella was the first to give up. She burst into piercing, harsh laughter. Falling into a fit of coughing, she blurted out words like masses of clotted blood. "You, you would now lie rotting somewhere in a ditch if it weren't for me, and grass would be growing over you. Such a green, thick, furry coat. Maybe also a little tree; it shouldn't be so lonely for you down there. According to all laws, human and divine, you no longer have any right to your own life. It is mine, mine!"

"I know that myself, but you don't have to remind me at every step – so cruel! Brutal!"

Aniella raised her eyes to Marek. In her gaze was wonderment, slavish servility, and a mute plea.

"How handsome you are! As far back as I can remember, I've always dreamed of a man like you. Not one fellow in our village ever noticed me; none ever asked me to dance. I used to stand alone in a corner, watch, ashamed as the others danced and kissed. But in myself I knew that he would come, my destined one, handsomer and finer than all the village fellows. Marek, Marek, prince of my dreams, you I love. Say just one word, one loving word to me, as you did then in my mother's house."

Through clenched teeth Marek uttered, "Aniella, you must know the truth. I can't live with you any longer. I love someone else."

Aniella's pale face turned a translucent white. Only the fine, bluish veins on her high forehead stood out bold and prominent, pulsating like cut worms. She moved away from Marek as if she had suddenly seen a ghost.

"No love? No love? Did you make a fool of me then, or are you lying now?"

"I've just discovered that the girl, my betrothed, has survived. If you truly love me as you say, release me, Aniella."

She turned her back to Marek, took several steps across the room, and stood at the open window. When Marek looked up, he saw her standing on the window sill, her arms raised like a bat against the night.

"What are you doing? Are you crazy?" Marek screamed in wild terror.

"I curse you both, you and her. Let my dead body stand between the two of you. Forever!"

With a bound, Marek was beside her, grabbing her dress.

Without any resistance, Aniella allowed herself to be lowered from the window. She clung to Marek's neck and, sobbing, fell into his arms like a helpless child. "I can't help myself. Without you, I can't live."

He carried her to the bed and covered her trembling body. "I'll give you a sedative, a pill. You'll fall asleep more quickly."

"I don't need any pills. I'm afraid of medicines. Just promise me that you won't leave me for her. Never, never! Sit down, right here, closer."

Her bony fingers enclosed his hand, the tips of her fingers responding to the rhythmic pulse of the blood flowing in Marek's hand. The nervous tension in Aniella's body began to dissolve. Marek heard a sigh of relief and, soon after, her calm breathing. Aniella fell asleep.

Marek did not dare withdraw his hand from hers, lest he wake her. In his tired head two words repeated themselves: "Dance Macabre, Dance Macabre." He wished he could remember how these words had ensnared him. At that moment just this, only this was of greatest importance to him, but in no way could he arrive at any meaningful connection.

From the outskirts of town the wind carried the distant barking of a dog, soon it was echoed by a second and a third.

That was how the dogs had barked on the night he had jumped from the sealed wagon. By then, everyone knew where they were being taken. Some prayed, some wept, bade farewell to their nearest, and others were stoically silent as if no longer connected to the events of this world.

Doctor Marek Bloch had decided it was better to die by a bullet while escaping than to be asphyxiated in a gas chamber. He hurtled down a jagged slope, ending up in a deep ditch, his heart pounding.

The wheels of the rushing train resonated and the earth beneath echoed back.

He got up, looked about in all directions, and felt his body. All limbs, intact. He stretched his head to the sky, greedily inhaling the fresh air. He took up a handful of moist grass, pressed it to his nose, to his lips. It had a sharp smell of earth and of freedom. All around was quiet. Over the damp meadows and fields the neighing of horses feeding and the barking of dogs were heard. All his senses were on the alert, loyal guardians in a time of peril.

"I must not be far from a village, a human community," thought Doctor Bloch, moving in the direction of the barking dogs.

Huts stood with closed doors and darkened windows. Behind the whitewashed walls people slept. On beds, their own beds. Behind which of these darkened windows did greed lie in wait for a Jewish head? At which door should he knock? No, not this one. Also, not that one.

Scenting a stranger, the howling of dogs grew louder. A sudden terror beset him. His heart began pounding.

Get far away from here, where people live. Better to be in the forest among wild animals.

He ran past the village huts, toward the forest which loomed darkly mysterious and menacing.

In the farthest edge of the village, separated from the forest by just a path, stood a poor, little hut encircled by a small orchard. He hesitated long, a cold sweat covering his forehead and body, before he knocked on the door. The glow of a lighted lamp brightened the narrow windowpanes. Doctor Bloch heard the sleepy voice of a woman. "Who's there?"

"One of yours."

"You have some nerve waking people in the middle of the night. What do you need? Who are you?"

"My name is Doctor Marek Bloch – been to see a sick patient – lost my way in the middle of the night."

A chain lock tinkled lightly as it dropped.

"Come in."

Doctor Marek Bloch stepped over the threshold. Narrow, cunning eyes measured him from head to foot. His face and hands were scratched and bloodied by stones and twigs. His clothes were crumpled and smeared with dust and dirt. The woman soon recognized in him the hunted Jew, and no longer addressed him with the formal "you" as she had until then. "It looks like you're one of those the Germans are driving through this area in sealed wagons."

He just nodded.

"This one night I won't throw you out, but tomorrow morning very early, you have to leave. That's all I need, that I should risk my head for hiding a Jew."

She placed a small pillow on a wooden bench and threw down an old, frayed blanket. "Lie down right here to sleep."

"Matka!" A girlish voice was heard from a half-darkened corner of the house. "Oh, give the stranger, 'the gentleman,' my blanket also. One is enough for me."

"This is my daughter," the woman's stern voice softened with warm tenderness. "She's not so healthy. She's sickly. If you could only cure her for me. You mentioned something about being a doctor."

"I will do the best I can, Madame. How shall I address you?"

"Madame Maria Wojtek," she informed him, tight-lipped.

"Good, Madame Maria, we'll see tomorrow."

Each rustle of a branch, each bark of a dog tore into Doctor Bloch's ears with a hundred-fold sharpness. Every time he heard a sound outside he lifted his head trying to grasp its meaning, ready to jump up from the bench and run, run into the dark night.

Maria Wojtek rose at dawn and prepared breakfast, the quicker to rid herself of the uninvited guest. Placing a bowl of potato grits on the table, she said to the doctor, "Here, eat it up quickly and get going, before one of the neighbours sees you in my house."

"But, Madame Maria, you spoke to me yesterday about curing your daughter."

"Oh," she motioned with her hand. "I thought it over. Better go on your way."

"Even so, it can't do any harm if I examine her, since I'm already here. And it won't cost you anything."

"So, do it already. Be quick! Don't waste time. In the last few weeks, I feel, she's become weaker and paler each day. I'm just a poor widow, as you yourself see. I slave like a donkey so my daughter will lack for nothing."

After washing his hands long and thoroughly, in the manner of a doctor, Bloch made his way to the curtained corner where Maria Wojtek's daughter lay. His every movement was followed by two blue-violet eyes, shaded by long dark eyelashes. A half-undone braid, a mass of shimmering golden hair, hung over the edge of the bed. It seemed to have sucked all the blood from the small, thin face, leaving it pale and emaciated, like a pawn for the sorrow shown in the corners of her lips.

Doctor Bloch began to feel deep pity for this suffering young girl.

"What is it with you, child?"

"I'm not a child," she answered him, offended. "Next month I'll be twenty-two."

"Oh, excuse me. And what is your name, young lady?" he asked with a smile.

"Aniella," she answered, avoiding his eyes.

"Oh, what a lovely name, it really suits you. But such a pretty young lady must not waste her days in bed. I bet your admirers are out looking for you. Well, now, let's see what ails the lovely young lady."

"No, oh no! I won't let myself be examined." Wild with fear, she tossed herself about, pulling the blanket over her face with both hands.

"Don't make such a foolish fuss," her mother called out impatiently. "You know that there's no money in the house to go to the doctor in town." She strode over to the bed and with one motion pulled off the blanket. The girl covered her face with both her hands.

Doctor Bloch held his breath and closed his eyes for a moment, wishing to accustom himself by degrees to the unanticipated sight of the young crippled body.

Doctor Bloch made an effort to have his voice sound calm and natural as he turned to Maria Wojtek. "Lying in bed will only weaken your daughter. All that she needs is fresh air, good nourishment, and a little distraction."

Aniella slowly drew her face from behind her screening hands. "Mother, Mother, come closer, even closer. Bend down to me."

Doctor Bloch saw her put her arms around her mother's neck and whisper quietly into her ear. He assumed she was talking about him.

"My daughter wants you to stay for another day. She thinks you will cure her. But remember, tomorrow you must leave.

During the day you'll hide in the attic under the hay. Come with me."

At lunchtime Aniella brought him a piece of dark rye bread and cheese.

"Not in bed anymore, Miss Aniella?"

"I'm feeling better, much better, Mr. Doctor."

She did not hurry to go back down. Doctor Bloch began to ask how to get into the forest, and whether there were any Germans patrolling the area.

"Are you really leaving us?" Her timid gaze hung on to his glances.

"I must. You heard what your mother told me."

Aniella was silent, her lower lip trembled as if from a suppressed cry.

When she let herself down the ladder, the golden braid remained lying on the hay a while, like a gilded path.

At nightfall, Maria Wojtek came up to the attic. "I'll only let you to stay in my house one more night. I'm not doing it for your sake. My daughter wanted it. But remember, at dawn tomorrow you're gone."

After supper, when Maria Wojtek had extinguished the small kerosene lamp, Doctor Marek Bloch remained lying, his eyes open. Endless thoughts feverishly chased one another. Where to go? Death lay in wait at every step. He was a hunted animal with no place to hide.

Was all this worthwhile for these few hours of life?

Probably everyone who had been with him in the sealed wagon was already released from all fears. It was harder to give up now that he had felt anew the taste of freedom.

Maria Wojtek's healthy snoring, which filled the little hut, awoke in Marek a feeling of envy. At least once he wished to sleep so peacefully and soundly, assured of the coming day.

How the time flies. Only a few more hours were his, no more. What will happen to him tomorrow when he leaves this house? He saw before him scenes, one more horrifying than the next. Every torture that only German sadists could conceive was waiting for him in the folds of the coming day.

His head reeled. One thought only emerged from the chaos. He must not leave the house. Should he try to beg another day or two from Maria Wojtek? He knew that it wouldn't help. So what should he do? Maybe money would work? But the Germans had robbed him of everything. If not for Aniella, that unhappy creature who had intervened on his behalf, he would now be wandering about in a strange forest, or even... She had looked at him the whole time with such adoring eyes. And maybe this could become his salvation? On tiptoes he came to Aniella's bed. She was awake, lying with eyes closed, pretending to be asleep.

Doctor Bloch tenderly caressed her hair. "Aniella, are you asleep?" he whispered in her ear. She opened her eyes and even more quietly asked him, "Why aren't you sleeping?"

He began kissing her forehead, her eyes. "I love you, Aniella. Do you love me?"

In place of an answer, Doctor Bloch heard a choking sob.

"Aniella, are you crying? Have I offended you?"

"You are mocking me, dear Mr. Doctor."

"Aniella, it's the truth."

"I...I can't imagine it."

"You will prove it for yourself."

"Will you marry me?" she asked.

"Yes, Aniella."

"Come to me now."

Her arms encircled his neck. He felt the full bony hardness of her frontal hump pressing itself into his breast. Marek wanted to cry out loud in shame, in fury with himself, with the entire world.

Aniella's breath seared his face, his neck. Her kisses became wilder and more demanding, "I want to be yours, yours completely, I love you!"

Cold sweat covered his entire body. Doctor Bloch could exert some control over his mouth, his eyes, willing them to lie. But he could not force all his flesh and blood to affirm that lie.

What would happen to him in the morning if he couldn't overcome his repugnance, his aversion to the crippled creature who was demanding his love? He must not think about Aniella now. He will close his eyes and imagine that one of the most beautiful girls he had known in the past was lying near him.

"Genya, Genya, help me," he sobbed to himself.

He remained alive. Aniella kept him hidden in the attic under the hay for sixteen whole months.

Somewhere, in a neighbouring yard, a rooster crowed.

The first morning rays seeped through the windows and settled with ashen greyness on Doctor Marek Bloch's strained face. He tried to stand up to stretch his stiffened limbs, but with his very first movement Aniella's fingers dug themselves into his hands even more deeply, forging him into place as an eternal hostage.

Wolf Ravner stood at the gate of the house, looking about in all directions as if waiting for someone to arrive. He nodded to himself. With heavy steps he dragged himself up to his room on the third floor. He threw himself fully clothed onto the bed.

When his Zisele was born, people had also wished him and Berta much joy from their child.

His mother and mother-in-law had spent entire days teaching Berta how to care for the child, how to diaper her, feed her, so that she might grow up healthy and strong.

After work, he would come into the house on tiptoes, since she might already be asleep. And his first question to Berta was always one and the same: "How did our Zisele sleep today? Did she eat well? Did she cry?"

And when she babbled her first word, "Va-va-va," what a joy that was.

She would now have been ten years old. In fact, her birthday would fall in the next month. She always skipped, and simply could not understand how one could take a step without skipping, and on one foot at that. And her two blonde braids would fly in opposite directions. When he tried to catch her while she was running, to plant a kiss on her flaming little cheeks, her braids would whip his face.

Not one single photograph remained. Not of Zisele, not of her mother. Night after night he would lie awake for hours trying to remember some word or movement of his little daughter. He must wrest from his failing memory every precise detail.

And he didn't even know when and how they had perished. Had the murderers tortured them?

In her last hour, did Zisele call for him, her father, to protect her, to tear her out of the murderous hands?

What did they do with her braids, the two golden whips?

This morning he followed a little girl on her way to school from one street to another, and he prayed to God that her route might last as long as possible.

He would not be the first to approach, no. Let her sense that her father recognized her even from the back, and was following her.

Wouldn't she be frightened by him in that first moment? Of the facial scar that hadn't been there before? Of his twisted mouth without teeth, knocked out with one blow of a German's rifle. Caught by surprise in that first moment, she'd be a bit confused, wouldn't know what to do.

What did he mean by "she wouldn't know what to do?" What an old fool he was. His Zisele would fly upon his neck and wouldn't let go until he couldn't catch his breath. And then she'd begin to tell him how a good Polish woman had hidden them, her and her mother, from the Germans.

Their only worry had been what happened to Father. They were told that the Germans had deported him to Auschwitz. They'd have to hurry now to tell Mother the good news that Father was alive. Today she won't go to school. On this day all three must be together.

Then she would take him by the hand and they would both race about. Father would want to imitate his daughter's leap. His foot gets caught and he almost falls. And Zisele steps in front of him and laughs, laughs like in the past, like in the past.

"Little girl, why did you suddenly turn your face to me? Did you want to pet the small dog that came running from a side street? Your eyes took my measure from head to foot – foreign, ungenerous eyes."

How many ten-year-old girls such as this one, with blonde braids, with books under their arms, go through the streets of different cities every morning?

Let it be tomorrow already. Let it be morning already. To get through this night as quickly as possible, this night. To him this night was the hardest, the hardest of all nights.

In Chayim Rozenboyms' home on Narutowicz Street, the large table covered with a crocheted cloth had already been restored to its regular state. The chairs were put back in their customary place. After the day's excitement and tumult, the quiet permeated every corner even more deeply.

Chayim Rozenboym approached his wife on tiptoe. "Beyltche, I'd like to drop by the *shul* for afternoon and evening prayers. I'll call Soreh Gitel so you won't be alone in the house."

Steps were heard from the open door of the kitchen. The old woman in the faded black jacket slipped quietly into the room. Husband and wife looked at one another, surprised. They had completely forgotten that when their guests had left for home, the old woman had remained in the kitchen to help with the washing up and putting away of dishes.

"Go in good health, Reb Chayim." She wiped her mouth with her hand. "I'll stay here with your wife, God forbid, no harm will come to her."

After Chayim left, she placed her yellowed, wrinkled hand on Beyle's shoulder. "And you, listen to me and go to sleep. I'll watch the boy, you can depend on me."

"Actually, I am a little tired. I'm only now feeling it. No wonder, after such a day. If you'd be so kind, Auntie."

They all called her "aunt" although she was not related to anyone. She found a word of comfort for everyone, gave advice and took on their worries as her own. They were so accustomed to her in the city's Jewish neighbourhood that when the women met one another shopping in the morning, they would ask, "Have you seen Auntie by chance? My neighbour has to go out for an hour or two and has no one with whom to leave her sick husband."

No one knew from where she came, to whom she belonged, and out of how many she remained the sole survivor. She never spoke about herself. When anyone tried to ask her how she was able to save herself, she merely gestured with her hand and pulled her scarf more tightly around her narrow back: “Eh, not worth talking about.”

Her yellowed face was threaded with fine wrinkles so artfully spread out and woven into each other, like a net to catch and hold the tears from her half-shut eyes.

But no one had ever seen her crying.

Beyle covered herself and stretched her weary bones for sleep.

The small, pink lamp on the night table gave off a warm glow. The old woman’s head remained in the shadow as she sat at the foot of the cradle. Her soft sigh, like the rustle of fallen autumn leaves, paired itself with the child’s quiet, even breath.

Translation by Frieda Forman and Sylvia Lustgarten

THE SPRITE

Blume Lempel

Even during her lifetime, Chayale was already a legend. After her death, the legend was taken up by the survivors of the war and, like a living seed, was scattered to the four corners of the earth.

The gentile inhabitants between the Dnieper and the Dniester did not budge from that rich, blood-soaked piece of earth. In spite of themselves, they picked up the remnants of the tattered legend and wove it into their own homespun myth.

The wooden crucifix to which they had nailed Chayale still stands on the hill. The top of it still bears the girl's pale blue bonnet with the red tassel. The sheepskin in which she was wrapped has been worn away by time. Bits of fur still stick out of the rotten pole. They say that the little animals that live in the field watch over the bonnet. They take it down in the dark of night when the sprite appears, and they hang it back up when she goes away. The peasants say that the crucified girl rose from the dead just like Jesus. She lives in the forest. She is the flag-bearer, the God-sent patroness of the four-footed inhabitants of the wood. Peasant women swear that they have seen the girl wandering in the field in the middle of the night, surrounded by hordes of animals. She was wrapped in light like a crystal globe that shone in the full moon with all the colours of the rainbow. She crossed the road and came out into the open field, the animals following her. When she came near the haystack, where she would at times stay, the light-filled globe would rise up and encircle the haystack, like a halo over the head of a saint. People even saw how the straw in the haystack parted, opening a way to the burrow that she had dug out there.

Sightings of this kind spread throughout the surrounding areas. Believers came from afar, lit candles, and placed flowers. They bowed their heads near the haystack and prayed to the holy one that their alms might merit a cure for the maladies that God had visited on them.

The local priests had no idea what to do. They discussed it for a long time and came to no conclusion: to destroy the haystack and get rid of the bonnet would have meant weakening an already weakened faith. So they bit their lips, pretended not to notice, and hoped that in time the story of the crucified girl would fade, her Jewish origins forgotten. If the masses hungered for miracles, "it should at least not be a Jewish miracle." As the soldiers of the Red Army said, "the Jews have already given us one god, we don't need another."

From the time of her birth, the girl was enveloped in a mystic halo.

Her mother became pregnant after her childbearing years. With mixed feelings of joy and dread, both mother and father awaited the unexpected.

The thirteenth day of the thirteenth month of Adar, the day when all the twelve constellations of the zodiac aligned themselves above the roof, the carpenter, Reb Josef, heard the piercing, strange scream of the newborn creature. So he put away his psalm book and went into the room of the new mother.

The midwife was holding the baby by the scruff of the neck, like one holds a wet kitten.

"*Oy vey*, how can a mother have such a freak?" she lamented. When the carpenter came in, the gentile woman quieted down. Baffled, she looked first at the father, then at the mother. "You have two grown sons," she said, as if speaking to herself. "For God's sake, get rid of this freak."

The carpenter looked at the new sprout in the family. He saw a small, red creature wriggling in the midwife's hands. The little body was overgrown with long, spiky, pitch black hair, and it trembled in the air like a worm on the end of a fishing rod.

The new mother broke into a bitter cry. The carpenter stood, looked at his wife, then looked at the child. All of a sudden he turned away and started pacing the room. After he had counted out thirteen steps one way and thirteen steps back, he stood still. A broad smile spread over his face.

"By no means, wife, this is not a time for tears. What the Creator gives has to be accepted with love."

The little girl was named for both grandmothers: Brakha, after the grandmother on the father's side, and Chayale, after the mother's family. She was called Chayale Brocheh. Later, Brocheh fell away and only Chayale was left.

Chayale was in no hurry to grow up. At three she was still crawling on all fours, still nursing at her mother's breast. "Mama sit down, I'm hungry!" Chayale would say, and push the three-legged stool under her mother.

What Chayale lacked in height she made up in charm. It seemed as if nature wanted to smooth over her mistake and therefore granted the child hidden treasures. She sharpened the child's senses to the fullest; the wild black hair with which she was born gradually disappeared; her skin became clear, turned smooth and transparent over a network of little blue veins that spread out like a map of a lost world. Chayale had a head of golden curls. Her eyes lit up like flowing amber, she had a turned-up nose and a small pointed mouth like a doe.

So strange was Chayale that rumours began to spread that Reb Josef the carpenter was raising a sprite. Brides-to-be longed to hold her in their arms. A kiss from her pointed mouth meant that they would soon be married. Barren women believed that a strand from her curly hair was a remedy sure to help.

At six years old, the little sprite entered the first grade. The teacher placed her in the last row, together with the other Jewish children. One time, when the "grand lady" walked about with ruler in hand, looking for a victim on whom to vent her anger, she stopped near Chayale and told her to raise her hand. Chayale squinted her little cat's eyes and smiled with her pointed little mouth. Her face lit up with bewitching beauty, as though royal blood flowed in her veins. The teacher stood still as if in a trance. She wanted to ask something, but forgot what it was. So she stood and tapped the ruler on the palm of her own hand, searching for the thought that she had lost a moment ago. The longer she looked into the Jewish child's eyes, the farther away she drifted from the class, from her pupils. She felt as if she were standing in front of a supernatural force. The thought came upon her so unexpectedly that she made the sign of the cross.

Chayale did not know what unusual gifts nature had bestowed on her. She thought that everyone could foresee what would come to pass. She couldn't understand, for instance, why her mother didn't see how her father was already hurrying home. He was standing in Uncle Alya's yard and they were harnessing the horses. Little Yosele was already sitting in the coach box. His lacquered visor glittered in the sun.

"How can you see what's happening on the other side of the village when you're in the house just like me?" asked her mother.

"I don't know how," answered Chayale, "but I see."

The house where Chayale was born and raised stood at the foot of a high mountain at the edge of a forest, near a large fork in the road. They had no neighbours. There were no children to play with, so Chayale surrounded herself with imaginary friends. She gave each of them a name and outfitted them in special clothes. Taybele was done up in a white dress, edged with peacock feathers. She dressed Lilith according to the time of day: in the morning she was pale, bathed in dew, her hair wet and spread over her face; at midday, her braid lit up like the sun's rays while Chayale herself was wrapped in a soft shadow. Her best friend was Rochele. Chayale sewed new clothes for her. The one thing that Rochele always wore was a pale blue bonnet with a red tassel.

Her friends used to wait for her in the garden behind the house. They would spend whole days in the garden. Chayale would treat them to sweet cookies and plums from the orchard. Together they would climb the trees and throw down the fruit. In winter, Chayale would invite her friends indoors. In the quiet of her room, they would help her with her schoolwork, suggest to her what the teacher would ask, and prepare Chayale with the right answer.

Chayale was ten years old when the Germans took over her district. She sensed the danger even before the murderous news reached their village. Chayale got her big brothers to dig a hiding place in the forest. Her mother and father thought this was foolishness. "The forest is for animals, not for people," said her parents.

Behind their parents' backs, Chayale and her brothers carried clothes and food to the hideout. When it became dangerous for her brothers to be out in the street, Chayale undertook the task on her own. She took over beans, peas, flour, sugar, salt. She sneaked through all dangers, ran on her fleet little feet, low to the ground, just like a sprite. Her fantasized friends told her whom to avoid and whom to trust. She could feel the danger, whether near at hand or at a distance, and could vanish in an instant.

That is how the first winter passed. Right after Passover, new edicts were announced, among them the cruel expulsion orders. Chayale stubbornly insisted that she would not go. She would not be tricked to wait for the butcher like a goose in a cage. Her father's pleas and her mother's tears didn't help. Chayale stood her ground. She would not go with eyes open into a ready-made trap.

"Little fool, who's talking about a trap?" Her father tried to convince her. "On the contrary, God willing, the ghetto walls will protect us. At a time when Jewish lives are worthless, it is surely better to be together. You can't resist an armed power alone. Together we're a force."

On the way to town, Chayale consulted with her imaginary friends, and to the last one they decided that she had to run away. At the first opportunity she crept out of the long line of Jews and ran to her brothers in the woods.

It was the eve of *Shavuot*. In the woods, all kinds of berries and mushrooms were ripening. Thick roots pushed up out of the ground. The forest breathed a warm dampness, sweet sap oozed from the bark. Wild ducks made their nests in swampy waters, animals of all kinds found their home there. The forest welcomed the newcomers with the same open-heartedness as it did its four-footed residents. Wild growth covered the hideout, rotting leaves covered the road. For Chayale, it was the loveliest time in her life. The hideout became a centre for the runaways, for mothers with tiny children, young people with weapons in their hands. The peasants in the nearby villages trembled before them; they paid them taxes in the form of food. All at once,

Chayale became an adult. Her talents were respected, and against the wishes of her brothers, she was entrusted with important missions.

Chayale loved being independent. Under cover of night she would creep into her own garden. There, together with her friends, she would dig up carrots, beets, green peas, and sweet corn, and laughingly she would return to the forest and surprise her brothers with her great triumph. She also took her mother's jam, chicken fat, and honey and, this time, the barley that her father had prepared for his cow. It had been a long time since their cow had been in its stall. Chayale would steal into the barn of the peasant who had taken away the cow. In the dark, she would milk the cow, fill up on the warm milk, and carry the rest back to the forest. She also carried back woolen blankets, clothes, shoes, everything that her mother had hidden for later when, God willing, they would return to their home.

In the thirteenth year of Chayale's life, her friends abruptly left her. It was the night of the great fire. Their house stood in flames. From all corners of the village, peasants ran over and grabbed whatever they could gather up in their hands. One seized a pot, another a duvet, glasses, and bottles. They carried away the wood from the bedroom. Chayale stuffed a sack with her father's sheepskin coat, moldy bread, a bottle of brandy, and a garland of golden onions. She ran among the robbers and no one recognized her. Chayale was now wearing a peasant coat, high boots, and a long skirt. The golden curls that her mother loved to comb were woven into thin gentile braids and covered with a flowered kerchief.

Chayale ran with the sack on her shoulders. She looked around for her friends but couldn't find them. She wanted them to help her dig up her mother's golden chain and diamond ring that had been buried under the cherry tree. She looked for them with her eyes, with her heart she begged them, implored them. Never before had she needed them so much. Never before had she felt so alone. It seemed to Chayale that the flames encircling her home were consuming the roots of her community. And because she so wanted to hang onto something, she started to run, away from the fire, and along crooked paths into the forest.

The sun had already started to set and to paint the black trees red. Chayale saw the last sparks of her destroyed home flicker in the air. Weary and beaten, she threw the sack off her back, took a drink from the bottle, bit into the onion and felt warmth in all her limbs. But the feeling of loneliness didn't leave her. So she once again threw on the sack and went deeper into the forest. Chayale took the path to the mud hut. She stopped by the silver birch. Her friends would often wait for her there. It was a kind of island in the middle of the forest. A deeply-rooted species of silver-flecked trees had spread its domain here. From a handful of stones a living spring gushed. Chayale and her friends called this place Rachel's well, where Jacob used to come to water his sheep. While the sheep stared at the silvery wonder, Rachel and Jacob chatted with each other. The musicians in the sky drew whistles and flutes from their pockets and played a cheerful tune for the children on the earth. Now, Chayale stood and waited. The naked trees gave no answer to her questions. She raised her eyes to the celestial musicians, but their instruments were already covered by a black cloth. Never before in her life had the night been so long, so dark, so bitterly cold. A terror befell her. In her despair she chanted the *sh'mah*. In the darkness, she tramped from one marker to another. The silence in the forest grew deeper, thicker. The sky turned black, studded with stars. Chayale searched for and found her familiar star. It was neither the biggest nor the shiniest, but she knew she could depend on it. Following its direction, she came upon a sawed-off tree trunk. There she was aware of the star that lead her safely through the avenue of pine trees. Chayale counted the trees: one, two…thirty-three giant trees stood in attendance on both sides and she, with the sack over her back, strode and counted silently.

Chayale remained seated on the sawed-off tree trunk. She was still waiting for her friends and, in the meanwhile, she nuzzled into her father's sheepskin coat. She glanced at her star and closed her eyes. It seemed to her that Lilith came running up. She was wearing black. At her breast, her dress was rent in mourning. Chayale opened her eyes: Lilith wasn't there. On her lap lay Rochele's light blue bonnet with the red tassel. Chayale heard Lilith's voice but couldn't see her. Lilith told her that today was her birthday, that she was thirteen years old today: "We came with the twelve signs of the zodiac and we are pulling away with them. The present on your lap is from Rochele. She has no more authority over you. Watch over the hat like the apple of your eye. In time of need it will protect you. Go where your feet will carry you. The dug-out mud hut is empty. Your brothers are gone."

A year later, lying in a haystack, Chayale told her four-footed friends how fate had brought her here. She spoke to them half in animal talk and half in Yiddish. What she could not express in words, she completed in her mind. The field mice, the rabbits, the red-grey squirrels that lived with her, answered her in their own way: they twirled their tails, twitched their noses. In stormy weather, Chayale didn't move from the haystack. She would invite her furry neighbours to share a meal with her. Of food there was plenty. She used to go around amongst the peasant houses and throw cards and read their fortune according to the lines on their hands. Whatever she earned, she put into her sack. Chayale took whatever they gave her: bread, milk, a hard-boiled egg, sometimes even hot buckwheat soup. The peasant women gladly believed what the curious little girl read into their hands. Chayale foretold the weather, the harvest, even the outcome of the war. Whoever looked into Chayale's eyes unwillingly gave up the secrets that burdened them. She shuffled the cards and, like an echo, gave the person back his most cherished wish.

The relationship with the creatures in the haystack was easy, artless, and free of human contrivance. She did not have to look into their eyes to know what they longed for. She broke crusts of bread and spoke to the animals that danced around her.

"Things are good for you. You don't have to put on the enemy's clothing, you don't have to hang a cross on your neck or put on his damned face. There was a time when I didn't know about hiding places. I lived in a house, slept in a bed, on goose-down pillows. In winter, we would heat the big house with an iron stove. I loved to sit on the footstool looking into the fire and thinking my thoughts. Sundays, the peasants would come to drink whiskey and to sip beer. The little keg with the brass tap stood in the middle of the house. My father poured beer, my mother brewed tea. The peasants slurped the golden tea and snacked on little white rolls. Now I can no longer picture my father's face, or the sound of my name, as it would come out from my mother's mouth. Now I think, maybe I made all this up? Maybe I'm really the granny who came out of the old storybook to protect her children from the mean bear? If not for my father's sheepskin – the only proof that I belong to another species – I would gladly run about with you, grazing on grass and not thinking of what will be or what once was."

Chayale's friends became restless. They ran away and then came right back. Chayale poked her head out, the sky was black. From all sides, storm clouds were gathering. They attacked each other like Panzer tanks in no man's land. Thunder sounded and the earth trembled. A wind swept over the barren field. It picked up a gnarled branch, a windswept leaf, and danced with them in a round. Chayale buried herself in her father's sheepskin. She didn't care that the animals wouldn't sit still. She talked, told stories. Images got mixed up, events, real and imagined, looking for betterment.

"After Lilith went away," Chayale went on, "I no longer wanted to live. A thick darkness covered the sky. I saw no stars. I didn't know whether it was late or early. The animals who survive under the cover of night lay burrowed in *their* holes. It seemed as if the whole world had conspired against me. I close my eyes, I sleep, awaken, and fall into a dream again. In my sleep, I sense the smell of a skunk. I open my eyes, it's morning. A red sun breaks through the lower branches. Small creatures are hurrying among the trees; they're digging among the leaves, looking for food. A fox chases by, the animals scatter. I run too, I run in God's care. A rabbit comes out of his warren; he catches a whiff of my scent and runs away. I too detect the scent of my pursuers; I really don't want to live, but I certainly don't want to fall into their hands. So I keep on running. I don't know the way. Red berries and black mushrooms come my way. I'm aware of their message. They wink and beckon, I swallow the poison, as if it were my mother's preserves. I swallow and wait for the end. While I am waiting, I write my will. To the wolf, I leave my dead body, the bones are for the fox to gnaw on, the hair for the birds to build their nests, the eyes for the owl, and the heart for God. I crumble my last piece of bread. Birds gather around me. To whom shall I leave the sheepskin, I think, and again begin swallowing the black poison.

"A wind is blowing. It picks up the leaves, shakes the trees. My head is spinning. Someone pushes a finger down my throat, forcing me to vomit. I heave until my strength gives out. A lightness overtakes my limbs as if I might rise up and fly away. I haven't the strength to fly. The birds look at me with pity. Maybe I'm already dead? I frighten myself with my own thought. The wind whistles and I hear a voice: 'Pull the bonnet onto your head!' I know that voice. It is Rochele's voice. Her tears flood my face. I take the bonnet and put it on my head.

"The wind has subsided. A peaceful calm reigns over the forest. I look and see a white hare coming closer to me. He burrows into the sheepskin, smells my face, my eyes. I try to caress him, but he pulls away. He goes off and I go after him. When I stop, he also stops, a few feet away. He starts off on a road foreign to me, but I follow him. His snow-white coat bewitches me. He holds his tail up high like a flag. Night is already falling, but the hare is still running. He leaps out of the forest into the open field, runs up to the haystack and vanishes."

Chayale spoke to her furry companions and it seemed to her that they talked back. They brought her news from across the road. As soon as they tracked a human smell, they came running quickly. Her scent didn't frighten them anymore. In fact, they liked to hear her voice. When Chayale spoke they gathered at her feet, scrambled onto her shoulders. Every now and again they ran off to sniff the wind for possible dangers, but they came right back.

That day, when the field mice failed to come back, Chayale became restless. She was lying down and heard the far-off clang of the church bells. The clang came from the valley, travelled up to the mountain, spread out over the field, and penetrated the haystack. Chayale knew that they were calling the believers to celebrate the gentile Easter. In her sack she had baked potatoes and a couple of hard-boiled eggs that were painted in honour of the holiday. Chayale wasn't thinking about food. It was a day of great wonders. Silver birds were circling under a blue sky. White parachutes were lowered in a nearby forest. No one was shooting at them. And the church bells were ringing, blending in with the noise of the tanks: the long-awaited tanks of the liberators. Chayale wanted to share her joy. She called to Rochele, Taybele, and also the secretive Lilith. But no one answered. Also, her four-footed friends were preoccupied. They had sniffed out another joy from a misplaced trap, which entices with seductive smells.

A thought came to Chayale – to climb up onto the cross that stood by the road at the top of the mountain. Her brothers would surely see her from there. She sniffed the wind and picked up the scent of their leggings. Her heart beat loud and fast. She pulled her bonnet down over her eyes and drew the string tighter around her sheepskin. She hurried to the mountain. Her feet sank into the loose earth. On the mountain it was already spring. The earth steamed with melted snow. The silver birds circled. Church bells rang. The cuckoo bird sang.

The vision of her brothers lifted her up above the noise. She didn't see the young gentile boy blocking the way ahead of her. He grabbed her by her braids and pulled off her bonnet. He dragged her up the mountain and tied her to the cross. Chayale hung on the wooden cross, her hands splayed, her braids bound up to the cross. Believers streamed up the mountain. Someone laughed, someone cried. Someone cut off the binding rope. The sheepskin is empty.

Peasants fell to their knees. "Christ has risen! Christ has risen!" and the church bells rang. And the sun shone on the pale blue bonnet with the red tassel.

Translation by Alisa Poskanzer with Judy Nisenholt

DENAH

Ida Maze

For the Sabbath, beautiful *challahs* and buns have been baked. When Sholem makes the *kiddush,* the blessing over the wine, he likes to have all of his children sitting around the table. Near him, sit the boys. Faytl, the eldest, who is already learning at a *cheder* in a nearby town comes home for the Sabbath. With his own little *challah,* he also recites the *kiddush.* Itche sits on the other side of his father while the youngest son, Daniel, also at the table, responds "Amen." Father always keeps an eye on Denah. He notices that she recites the *kiddush* after him, word for word, and that her "Amen" is fervently expressed. When he distributes the portions of *challah* for the *hamotzi* prayer, he hands her a big piece and hears how she recites the blessing. "She should have been a boy," he says to himself. Denah takes the tiniest bite from the *hamotzi* and hides the remainder of the *challha* under the tablecloth so that no one will see it.

The next day, all the children receive buns for breakfast. Denah takes hers, puts her hand behind her back, and shuffles backwards in order to hide the bun, together with yesterday's *hamotzi*, in the closet drawer. After the noon repast on *shabbes*, when father lies down for a nap and Itche spreads himself out on the sofa with a prayer book, Denah steals quietly up to him: "Itche, are you sleeping?"

"Me, sleeping?" he answers.

"What are you doing?"

"I'm learning."

"What are you learning?"

"Would you understand? A girl mustn't know what boys learn."

Denah is discouraged. If Itche says that a girl must not know what the boys are learning, he knows what he is talking about. But, on the other hand, she simply cannot lose this opportunity to speak to him.

"Itche, would you like some *hamotzi challah*?"

"Why all of a sudden do you want to know if I want *hamotzi challah*?"

"And do you want a bun?"

"What kind of a bun?"

"Wait – you'll see."

Denah runs and quickly returns holding a big piece of *hamotzi*, a whole bun, and two little cubes of sugar.

"Where did you get these?"

"It's mine. I hid it for you."

"Why especially for me?"

"Because – because I want you to eat it."

"Well if you want me to, I will."

Denah comes closer to him, hands him the food, and lightly strokes his head with her hand. "Are you eating?"

"Yeah, I'm eating."

"Isn't it delicious?"

"Very. The bun is delicious."

"Can you tell me something?"

"What? A story?"

"No, not a story."

"What then?"

"Where is Fraydele?"

A shiver passes through Itche. "Fraydele?"

"Yes. Fraydele. Where is she?"

"Don't you know? She died."

"She died?"

"Yes. You know that she died."

"But what does that mean, 'died'? Where is she?"

"She's in heaven."

"'In heaven'?" Denah asks happily, incredulously. "How did she get up to heaven?"

"God sent an angel who took her there."

"With her cradle?"

"No. Without the cradle."

"Did you see it happen?"

"No, no one can see that."

"So where is the cradle?"

"In the attic."

"Why does mother cry?"

"Because she is lonesome for Fraydele."

Denah considers that. "I am lonesome for Fraydele too, and I also cry when no one sees. But you said that God sent for her – so does he need her?"

Itche is still, thinks for a while, and says: "Probably it has to be that way." He looks at Denah. "Here – take your sugar. Boys don't eat sugar."

Denah quietly takes the sugar. "I also don't eat sugar." She remains silent, embarrassed, then asks: "Could I become a boy?"

"What? You a boy! Are you crazy? A girl can't be a boy!"

"But I want to be a boy."

"Why?"

"I want to learn in a *cheder* like you do and know all the stories and all of the things that God does."

"Well, you're not going to know unless mother will teach you. She taught all of us before we went away to *cheder*."

"Well, Mother is not a boy, so how come she knows?"

"Oh, it was different for mother. Grandmother Gitl had a teacher living in the house for our uncles and so mother learned with them, just like a boy."

"Then I will also go to *cheder* and learn like a boy."

"You're going to learn! She thinks learning is so easy! Even for a boy it is difficult, not just for a girl – and – go away from me already. Soon father will wake up and I have to recite a page of scripture. Go away!"

Denah backs away, observing him all the while. Now she knows where Fraydele is. She quietly leaves the house, sits under a tree not far from the house, and looks up to the sky. The sky is so high and so far. Fraydele is so far away. The cold and the distance of Fraydele's new home – the sky – are reflected through the bare tree and trembling leaves. At Denah's feet, the white dog rolls in the dead leaves that broke under its spiky paws and now resemble tiny, desiccated human shards. She feels strangely lonely and cold. She draws her knees up tightly to her chest and with both elbows on her knees, holds her chin with her hands, framing her face. She sits this way, as before a mirror, gazing forlornly at the leaves near her feet.

Goldetske, the dog, bounds over to her, licking her hand and kissing her face. As if from a dream, Denah rouses herself. She can hear the melody of her father's prayers coming from the house, marking the end of the Sabbath. She recalls her talk with Itche. He knows everything, and only boys can learn in *cheder*, but Mother could teach her. By herself she can't learn anything, but still she knows by memory her father's blessing over the wine, the *kiddush*, and also *Tilim*, the Psalms. She doesn't know what the words mean, but the melody is so lovely and so sad that she senses that the words must also be sad and lovely. She picks up Goldetske and hugs her. "Are you cold, Goldetske?

You're so tiny." She releases her. "Come, Goldetske, come into the house. We'll hear how father makes *havdalah* – the Sabbath's closing prayers; we'll sing *hamavdil* and Mother…" Thinking of mother, she ponders, "And Mother will chant the prayer, 'God of Abraham.'"

One time, on a Friday evening, Itche came home unexpectedly from Slutsk. When asked "What happened?" his answer was, "Nothing." Since Uncle Shimon had been in Slutsk, he came back with him. The real reason turned up only when Itche didn't return to Slutsk but remained at home. Then his father, who was also in Slutsk, found out everything.

Chana Yashelyevitch, Itche's landlady and the owner of the ironworks, loved Itche as her own child because he was clever and well-mannered. She had no children of her own, and during the year and a half that he lived in her house and worked in her business, he became so dear to her that she often refused to let him go home for *shabbes* or holidays. When he began to chum around with his fellow students and go off with them, Chana would wait until late into the night, going to sleep only when he arrived home. Lately, however, she became very uneasy and worried about him. In Slutsk there were now many arrests and raids in search of illegal literature. Chana urged Itche to go home for a while, until matters quieted down.

Thus, Itche remained at home. At first this made Denah very happy, but it didn't take long for her to realize that this was not the same Itche as before. He no longer wished to talk about God or the *Torah*, and when she did succeed in engaging him in a discussion, his words were incomprehensible and his questions outlandish; all were strange and unfathomable to her. For example, one day he asked her if she had considered the fact that the peasants who worked for them in the fields throughout the summers and winters, drinking until they lost their last shirt, lived in privation. They can't read or write, and they don't know what is happening in the world. Didn't she think that this was an injustice?

Denah's big eyes widened in wonder and she asked, "Who is unjust?"

"Who? The landowners. Father."

Denah said, "Father is very good to them. They all love him."

"A lot they know. How is Father good to them?"

"Well, and how is he bad to them? When they work, he pays them."

"He pays them a lot?"

"As much as is needed."

"As much as is needed? If he paid them as much as they need, they would live like us and we would live like them."

Denah stood there dumbfounded and looked at Itche. Finally she stammered, "Probably that is how it's supposed to be."

Itche grimaced, "Oh really! That's how it's supposed to be."

"But you told me once that God does everything and if God wanted things to be different, things would be different."

"Oh, go on! You're a fool! What's this to do with God?" And he walked away from her.

Denah felt defeated. Now she knew nothing, and she became very sad. Her eyes filled with tears, her heart felt heavy as one who has suddenly lost something very precious. Itche had once so clearly explained to her the relationship of God to the world, and now, suddenly…

The longer Itche remained at home, the stranger his ways appeared to Denah.

It was the eve of Passover at Sholem's house. As in every year, there was the cleaning, polishing, and ritual preparation of the kitchen and ovens for the baking of the matzos. Also, the wagons in the stables were moved closer together to make room for the carts and wagons of the neighbours who would be arriving to bake their matzos.

The appearance of Sholem's courtyard had changed considerably in the last few years. Since the authorities took away his income from the sale of liquor and prohibited Jews from owning land, he had signed over his property to his good neighbour, the landowner Marco. Now everyone – owners as well as servants – stumbled about, no longer on solid ground. They feared that any day the menace that hung so ominously above them would descend. This mood in the house permeated the entire courtyard.

Not only these troubles, but other worries about his sons, spread their tentacles over Sholem's house. Faytl's life in Pesotchne with his wife Leah was grim. Pregnant, Leah wandered around tearfully wishing to die before the birth of the child. Faytl, silent and embittered, plodded about as in a strange world, working in his own store like an employee and coming home late at night.

News about Itche caused many a sleepless night for Mother and Father. The lad, not yet sixteen years, was as developed as an adult both in appearance and deportment. With his sturdy shoulders, high forehead, flashing clever eyes, and dark head of hair, Itche had grown like a tall, handsome tree.

When Sholem would return from Slutsk, he would tell stories about Itche. Rarely would they see him at home, and rarely in Slutsk itself where he was supposed to be working and studying. His landlady often complained to Sholem as if her own son's life was in danger: "What should we do with the child, Reb

Sholem? I've become old and sick because of him. What will become of him? They fill every vacant spot with him. Wherever there is a demonstration or a terrible mission – in Minsk, in Riga, in Bobrois, anywhere in the whole world – they send him! And no matter how I beg him and how much I talk to him, he looks at me as if he's the one who is right. And when I stand up to him and challenge his thinking – 'doesn't he know how this is going to end?' – he smiles: 'Somebody has to do it,' he says. 'And what if somebody else ends up with what could happen to me…' Go argue with him!"

It went so far that his mother, Peshe, wrote of her troubles to her brothers in America, and they sent a letter along with a ship ticket. As difficult as it was for Sholem and Peshe to contemplate sending such a young child off across the ocean, they nevertheless decided that, closer to the holidays, they would send him with a group from Slutsk leaving for America.

When Sholem was in Slutsk a few weeks before Passover, he told Itche that he must come home for the holiday. His mother had relayed her wish to see him, and his father also demanded that he come home. Itche, in his soft and confident manner, replied, "There is still a long time until Passover. If I can get away, I will certainly come."

In the smallest towns, even in the villages, events were brewing like before a storm. Everywhere there were secret gatherings; posters were plastered on peasants' houses: "Russian people! Free yourselves from oppression! The time is right! Do it now! We are united and on your side! Brothers, arise!"

Invisible hands were at work. People whispered secrets like bees buzzing around a beehive. As if from the sky, they came on horseback, with swords unsheathed at the sides of their blue-and-red-striped pants. Rumours flew: there was fear of rebellion – the tsar is about to make a new proclamation – all of the political prisoners will be freed. There will be freedom! In the small towns and villages all sorts of unbelievable, strange news was circulating. Echoes from the distant, large cities were transformed into outlandish rumours by the time they reached the far-flung corners.

Oheli, a city boasting many great forests, was the centre for all news of the revolution. One of the largest forests was owned by Yakov Gurevitch, an ordinary Jew who had once driven oxen but had somehow become wealthy and was now a lumber merchant. He had three sons and one daughter, and every summer he would bring his entire family to this same pine tree forest. His wife, the little dried-out Tzipke with the tiny, red eyes, would parade around in fancy Parisian-style garments and speak in half-broken Russian. Yakov himself, a tall man with a bulging stomach and broad shoulders, wore a shiny top hat and carried a walking stick, which made him look like a wealthy butcher. However, he was friendly, on good terms with everybody, and enjoyed having a *l'chayim*, a drink with any farmer that he met. This endeared him to the peasants and the local Jews as well. One could turn to him in need and he rarely spoke down to anyone. He travelled often to Zagranitze on important business related to prices, railroad ties, wood – entire forests.

His one and only daughter, Fanya – the *mezinke*, the youngest – would ride on a sleek, brown steed while her two governesses, one German and the other French, rode on two light-footed horses on either side of her. Fanya spoke both French and German and considered herself a true aristocratic child. On the other hand, the three sons, gymnasium students in Minsk, were fully committed to the socialist movement. When they were in the woods, they worked together with the lumbermen, chopping down trees and sawing the lumber. They would hand out cigarettes and brochures, making sure to inform the workers of new laws and decrees. They also visited the peasants in their homes and would spend evenings socializing with them. Nahum was already married and had a child but he behaved like a boy, committed to the ideology. His wife, a rabbi's daughter who looked like a blond boy with her close-cropped hair, helped distribute the propaganda. In Minsk, she had made a name for herself in the movement.

They all felt very much at home in Sholem's house as Yakov and Sholem, friends since childhood, did not stand on formalities. The sons were very fond of Itche and had a great influence on him. They often travelled together to the various towns and villages spreading their propaganda. They always brought regards to Sholem from Itche, adding: "He will become a great man, a born leader." They were the ones who spread the rumours of the impending liberation: "Everyone must travel to Minsk for the great celebration, to meet with the newly freed political dissidents." And whoever had the opportunity to go did not remain at home, but rather converged upon the big cities to join the festivities.

Yakov Gurevitch's three sons, with his blonde daughter-in-law, also made their way to Minsk. In the smaller towns throngs of workers advanced, singing "La Marsellaise." From the villages, they rode in wagons on their way to the towns to see the amazing sight and generosity of the *Batyushka* – the Father – who was about to free his people.

However, Jews whose children were involved in this big celebration were not joyful. Quite the opposite: their hearts trembled with the premonition of impending disaster. The old ones remained at home, sitting around the ovens or outside on the balconies, waiting for their children to come home unharmed from the big cities with the "good news."

Like an earthquake, the terrible news tore their world asunder. The workers in the cities had been deceived. They were rounded up on bridges; and in the middle of the marketplace, where speakers whipped up the crowd to the heights of passion, horsemen with artillery guns encircled the entire area. They began shooting and destroyed the bridges; thousands fell into the river and blood flowed in the streets.

A day and a night passed until all quieted down. Only a smell of blood and scorched flesh remained in the city. Then the "merciful" authorities allowed the folk to return to the marketplace to identify the dead and bring them to the cemetery so the streets could be cleaned. The crowd did not wait to be asked twice. However, instead of youth striding with rousing songs, there now appeared wailing, bent-over mothers and fathers searching for their dead children. How terrible to recognize one's child. Most, however, were beyond recognition.

Yakov Gurevitch found only his youngest son Benjamin alive. He found his other two sons and his daughter-in-law with their heads broken open.

Translation by Sarah Faerman

THE LITTLE MESSIAH

Rikudah Potash

It was hard for the neighbours of Hatabor Street to figure out what was born to Alkhasid, but judging by the greenery decorating the little alley, they figured out that it was probably a male child.

It didn't take long for two young boys with long *peyehs* sidelocks to appear. They went from door to door to announce that a male child had been born. It also didn't take long for Yemenite women, young and old, to push themselves through the low doorway where the *kimpetorin*, the woman who'd just given birth, lay on a raised bed, wrapped in a colourful Yemenite shawl. She looked like a little girl herself. She had a black pimple on the tip of her nose, and large, dark, dreamy eyes. Her hands were tawny, childlike, and they fluttered nervously. All the *cheder* boys came by to get a taste of Alkhasid's delicacy. The women coming to wish her *mazel tov* placed their hands to their lips three times and let out a strange wail: this was how news spread that a new arrival had come into this good world.

The women brought a small basket with them, in which lay needles, thread, and pieces of fabric. They sat down beside the *kimpetorin*, talking, sewing, and embroidering.

Nemah, the really old one, not a single tooth left in her mouth, tells the *kimpetorin* what she dreamt:

"To Simkhe was born a little Messiah. He came out of the womb with a tiny *Tanakh* in his hand, and this was a sign that he had studied the *Torah* for the whole nine months. He didn't even get scared when the angel came to give him a flick under the nose so that he would forget everything, a sure sign that he had brought the *Tanakh* with him."

The women stared into her mouth – how the words just spittled out of her, and how she blinked with one eye as she told about the miracle of the little Messiah.

Simkhe didn't move in her raised bed but she looked frightened as Nemah told her this. She couldn't remember what the little male child had brought with him. Maybe the midwife also saw the *Tanakh* in his hands? She should be called, because if Nemah had such a dream…

Puah, the bent-over neighbour, actually stuck her finger with the needle until blood ran when she heard that Simkhe gave birth to a little Messiah. She stood up and asked meekly: "Simkhe, you're as dear to me as my own eyes, let me see him. I've been waiting for the Messiah for so many years. Let my eyes behold the joy!"

But Simkhe didn't let her see this great joy because according to the laws of Yemen, the only one allowed to see the male child was the rabbi. He was to come and decide if the child was worthy to be circumcised according to Jewish tradition.

Meanwhile, the news spread like lightning through all the courtyards in Tabor Street, and even those women who were busy at work and couldn't take the time to sit beside the *kimpetorin* now laid aside their work and went to see the little Messiah for themselves.

On the second day after the birth, there appeared in the courtyard, which was full of green bottles and big, flowering branches, a kind of small, dark, shrunken, Yemenite Jew with a carved village flute. He played with such refined and pious tones that he could move you to tears. This Jew didn't move from his spot. He stood and played, hour after hour. The women who had been sitting indoors with the *kimpetorin* came out and warned him not to wake up the little one, the male child. So this Jew took the carved village flute out of his mouth and said:

"My dear friends, I play my songs for him. Maybe the Great Saint was just born who will do away with Jewish troubles, and maybe it's a rabbi who could lead the entire Jewish people and redeem us out of bad, goyish hands."

So the women began bringing him a variety of good things to eat. Since the *kimpetorin* is guarded day and night so that, God forbid, the evil spirits won't have power over the child, the women realized that this thin, little Jew with the flute also wouldn't allow evil spirits to come. So they didn't chase him away.

The women took turns changing the guard. Every few hours, new women came to guard the *kimpetorin*. The Yemenite flute player sat himself down and dozed. He knew that the *kimpetorin* wouldn't be left unattended.

However, Nameh, the old Yemenite woman who came to wait upon the mother of a Messiah, thought over the whole business of the old flute player very carefully; she called together the women who were guarding the *kimpetorin* and entrusted to them the secret that this was no ordinary little Jew who just goes around playing. It occurred to her that this flute player must be a distant relative of the Great Messiah, and since he, the Great Messiah is now very old and can't come himself, so a little Messiah is born and it's for him that this distant relative is playing.

Nameh, the old Yemenite woman, also told this to Khuzbeh, the mother of the *kimpetorin*, and Khuzbeh believed her. But, like a mother, she kept the secret to herself. But as the *bris milah*, the circumcision, neared, she entrusted it to the ear of her son-in-law, who became so frightened he ran off to consult the rabbi.

During the night of the *bris*, at midnight, when Jews rise to study and pray in commemoration of the destruction of Jerusalem, men arrived with their *Gemores* and seated themselves around the courtyard to study. The Jew with the flute had vanished, no one knew where to. A few hours later, the howling of an ox was heard. According to the custom of Yemen, an ox was slaughtered, the hide pulled off it, and the meat cooked for the guests attending the feast after the *bris*.

The women standing guard now thought of new answers for why the little Jew had actually brought an ox, and where he got so much money. It was a sign that the Old Messiah had given him the money to make a *bris* according to all the laws of Yemen.

Translation by Shirley Kumove

THE TENTH IS BORN IN MISHKENOT

Rikudah Potash

A tired morning dawns in the crooked alleys of Mishkenot Yakov, settling like a devout Eastern Jew in the Sfat Emet synagogue. The Sfat Emet Yemenite synagogue, which lies nestled among the tiny houses, never extinguishes the light in its ancient menorahs. Day and night a *nigun*, a song without words chanted by an arriving or departing worshipper, circulates through the synagogue. Pious Eastern Jews hold the month of Ellul more precious than all the months of the whole year. There's a coming and going from morning to night, and from the middle of the night until the breaking dawn. The prayers are chanted with fervour.

The synagogue has its own style. On the outside, etched into the wall, is a great, flattened lion that is similar to that on the inside of the *Torah* scroll. This lion has kindly eyes, like all Jewish lions from olden times, but our lion on the wall of the synagogue has strange eyes like a devout Eastern Jew. Nearby hang the signs of advocate Kozales and Doctor Breg. Opposite, hangs a sign with large letters: "The best *soyfer* in Mishkenot."

Three steps down the alley is a tiny wine shop, the wine merchant is himself very devout and dreamy. He stands near the wine barrel, tapping and tapping as if drawing the *Torah* out of there. Afterwards, he runs to the synagogue to whet his gums with a prayer.

The alley leads down to the tinsmith, the broom maker, the knife sharpener, and the pita baker. Steam and smoke, the aroma of bread and burning coals wafts about. The pita baker looks like a dried-out pita himself, with his flattened face and dots for eyes. He doesn't count the money but places it in a plaited straw basket, trusting everyone at his word. There's a hustling and a bustling. The narrow streets of the Mishkenot quarter are teeming. The Jews who live there are crowded, poor but pious.

The barber/scribe lathers up someone's beard, then dashes off into the synagogue for a moment to grab a prayer and a bit of conversation. Afterwards, he reminds himself that his customer is still sitting all lathered up in his shop. The wine merchant decants a bottle of wine, and in the middle of this, it occurs to him to utter a Jewish word, so he leaves his customer waiting and goes off to recite the lengthy prayer, the eighteen silent benedictions.

The outside steps leading into the synagogue glisten and shine. Bilhah the laundress washes them and guards them like the apple of her eye. She is highly regarded because she performs holy tasks for the worshippers. Her black braids, wrapped in a colourful kerchief, attest to her past youth. She has a masculine face, pockmarked, shifting on to brown spots along the neck. Her gold Persian earrings with the small turquoise stones dangle against her wrinkle-etched cheeks. Afterwards, she seats herself on these very same shining steps, and listens intently to the prayers that ascend like birds to the heavens.

Even though the Sfat Emet synagogue lies secluded among the little alleys, inside it's bedecked with large, multicoloured, and shimmering Persian rugs that reflect off the electric lights and the flames of the burning menorahs.

The green walls are not bare; they are hung with amulets and prayers on behalf of the sick and women in childbirth.

When the State of Israel was declared, the old scribe Reb Yishayeh wrote out a new prayer. He has a strangely ornamental script, similar to Rashi's biblical commentary, but no one knows where he learned it.

The Holy Ark is covered with a curtain of Spanish brocade, and when the light of the lamp falls on the threads, you no longer see threads but the hues of the rainbow. The several *Torah* scrolls that are kept in the ark are covered with the richest of multi-coloured mantles shot through with gold.

The worshippers, who come from all the little alleys in the Mishkenot quarter, are not the only ones here. New worshippers arrive from every corner of the world. Old Yemenite Jews in white garments, Kurds, Persians, Bukharans, Turkish Jews, Yugoslavian Jews, German, Polish, Russian, and Hungarian Jews. As many colours, that's how many countries. There's a mix of languages and dialects, a wide range of races and characteristics – some more pious, others less so. Nevertheless, everyone carries his own heartbreak, his own tears, a rupture they want to sigh about or weep over in the Sfat Emet synagogue.

The rabbi, the sage, is a Yemenite Jew. He always wears rustling black clothes and a cloth wound around his head. He delivers sermons about the Shoah, the destruction which befell the Jewish people in the Diaspora. His voice is penetrating, his speech has weight and depth.

The blowing of the shofar plays an important role here. If rain doesn't fall when needed, then they pray and blow the shofar. When rain does fall in abundance and the wells overflow, then they pray for the rain to stop and again they blow the shofar. If it snows, snow in Jerusalem is always the biggest surprise for Eastern Jews. And if the snow doesn't melt and there's a frost and the water freezes, then the worshippers become uneasy and they recite prayers that the city of Jerusalem should not, God forbid, freeze over.

Evening. The sun sets in the little alleys. The windowpanes look like they're right out of a children's story. The sun goes down in the Mishkenot quarter differently than elsewhere, because its red glow becomes more violet seen through the narrow alleys. Something weird circles the walls of the Sfat Emet synagogue. Figures emerge from the red afterglow – sweaty greengrocers, bricklayers, shoemakers, tailors – all of them hastily catching *minkhe,* the afternoon prayer.

Mishkenot has its own lunatic – a tall, shabby, elongated figure with bare feet and cracked, wounded hands. He comes to the door of the Sfat Emet synagogue, silent, melancholic, a madman. It's said that he is one of the early pioneers, that he came as a young man from Russia. Now he stands here an old man, casting a long shadow, silent with cloudy eyes and blue lips. He used to talk sometimes, long ago. He said that he came to this country together with Ben Gurion the head of state, a ship brother, literally kinfolk. He used to speak English and French perfectly, but today his soul is locked up, shut tight. Somewhere in a courtyard where children play, he sits himself down and pinches something warm, a pita which one of the bakers gave him.

She is dark-skinned like all Eastern women, wears Bukharan clothes, cooks like a Persian and the house looks Yemenite. Precisely to which ethnic group she belongs, nobody knows. She is a grandmother of six.

After him, the drunkard Sleyme comes into Sfat Emet. He has a dark, refined, cheerful face, but he's tipsy. He sits in *shul* dreamily singing in an undertone. The pious little boys pull at his legs while he spits and spews. When he's very drunk, he can stand there sobbing away, telling everyone about his one-and-only daughter, who was shot while in the old city because she was caught carrying a basketful of bombs to help the Haganah.

Now a blind person and a cripple come along. Both of them are new immigrants and they carry within themselves a world of limitless suffering. In the *shul*, they tell each other about the destruction of their families and of their children.

Among the last to arrive is Yakov Shem-Tov, the jeweler from Ohel Shem Street. This alley, among many, lies in the very centre where the main street of Mishkenot begins. In this alley you can find whole wagons full of watermelons, cantaloupes, cucumbers, and green peppers. Since the war the street has become even poorer. The abundance of watermelons has shrunk. That's why now, at the end of summer, you find peelings – leaves, rotten cabbages, squashed tomatoes, and iron filings from an iron dealer who rents space here.

Yakov Shem-Tov lives in a cellar and is always viewing the countless footsteps of the passersby, because this street is the first one leading to the market. When you stand in this street, you can count Shem-Tov's household exactly. You see the beds, the table where Shem-Tov earns his livelihood, covered with strands of silver, the chains, the filigree bracelets, the brooches with fake rubies and turquoises and coral. And you see the mother of nine children. The heart of a house is sometimes just like a human heart, and this house has a human heart. The windows don't have any curtains and they line up with the asphalt that paves the street. The daughters in this house are already married, while the five grown sons have already defended the Jewish state.

The mother of this particular house is named Khamameh. She looks like the picture of *La Gioconda* by Leonardo da Vinci.

Her giving birth to nine children didn't hurt her any and poverty didn't affect her badly either. If she would wear a white kerchief on her smoothly black hair like the Yemenite women do, you'd think that she really came out of one of Leonardo's paintings and was moving about here like a stranger – *La Gioconda*, in a cellar in Mishkenot. And perhaps…perhaps… No one ever sees her cooking…yet it's cooked. No one ever sees her sewing, washing…yet every corner of the house is white and gleaming.

Khamameh, as we've said, is the mistress of the house; she's thirty-seven years old. She worries about everybody but nobody knows when. Her daughters and her grandchildren look with hidden envy at their beautiful mother and grandmother.

The father of the household, Yakov Shem-Tov, is still quite young. He's close to forty but he has white hair, a broad beard, and dreamy eyes. He's stately in appearance as is proper for a father who rules in a cellar.

Come *shabbes*, the cellar is transformed into a holy place. The father calls together his nine children, the ones already married, the middle ones, and the youngest too.

When they're all gathered round, the daughters and the grandchildren come in. Shem-Tov smooths his moustache and white beard with a red striped towel, places a finger to his mouth, and says: "Quiet." Then he asks: "Where did we leave off last *shabbes*?"

"With the three angels," replies Khamameh, the mother of the house. Her old silk dress rustles from a secret about a new changed reality that requires she let the dress out so that the married daughters won't notice.

The father of the household again asks: "Are you ready?" Small and chubby Yigal stands up, and with laughing eyes he asks: "Am I also going to sell newspapers tomorrow?"

The father raises his thick, overgrown eyebrows, wrinkles his nose, and replies: "On *shabbes* we don't talk about foolish things that belong to the ordinary week." He continues, "The three angels drew near to Abraham's tent. They wanted to fulfill God's mission and tell Abraham that he would become well again."

"When did Abraham fall sick?" Brakha, she with the golden tooth that shines when she talks, wanted to know.

"We're not saying, God forbid, that he was sick," replies the father. "We're saying that in his older years, Abraham was circumcised and the angels came to tell him that he was healing well."

Abraham received the angels the way you receive angels, he gave them a basin of water to wash their feet and told Sarah, who was in the alcove, to make them something to eat.

Little Ezra immediately caught the words "make them something to eat," and he wanted to know why they had to make them something to eat.

"Because angels live on air. They don't need to eat but they didn't want be treated like angels," said their father.

The five little children, who were already enlightened, listened and smiled, letting the younger ones ask the questions. Still the middle one asked:

"How did they look, these angels?"

"The way angels look," answered the father.

"Did they have white wings?"

"They had dusty wings from travelling a far distance."

Shaltiel the *palmachnik*, the paratrooper, made himself important.

"Yeh *khabibi*, my dear, when we were down under the Kastel and it rained fire, we saw with our own eyes how the angels came and took away the wounded in order to save their lives."

Dvoyre, who held an infant at her breast, also threw in a word: "Why were the angels barefoot? Did shoes get more expensive in heaven?"

The mother laughed and the father of the household raised his eyebrows and wrinkled his nose: "We can't come any closer! Angels don't need to come to earth. They soar, they fly, and then let themselves come down when it's necessary."

Khamameh, who was lost in thought, asked: "Where's the chapter on Mother Rachel. We haven't got that far."

Father read on, "The angels asked Abraham, where is your wife? Where does she live? Then Sarah revealed herself – old, bent over, a hundred and twenty years old. The angels looked at her with their angel eyes, and said: 'A year from today, Sarah will bear a son.' Abraham and Sarah began to laugh. So hard that the three angels also began laughing. And it happened that a year later Sarah gave birth to a son and he was called Yitskhak."

Malka, the redheaded ten-year-old, sprang up laughing and crying: "Even in old age our mother will still have children! That's very funny! Very funny!"

"Be quiet," Brakha interrupted, "be quiet! Aren't you ashamed to speak like this about our holy bible stories?"

The father of the household blew his nose and continued reading:

"Because God granted Abraham a son, He wanted to know how valuable His gift was. So He sent a messenger, an angel, to Abraham, to bring his one and only son Yitskhak as a sacrifice to God. And Abraham brings a trembling Yitskhak to the *akeydeh* but God, blessed be He, said: 'Enough, take him back, I just wanted to test you to see how far your devotion to God goes.'"

A blue star was already peeping into Shem-Tov's house. The impatient moon rose and they all looked and saw it. Shem-Tov was already concluding the *shabbes* prayers. The tablecloth was taken off the table from which he drew his livelihood. The coming week's work was already spread out, rings and little chains, and the father was already taking out his bent scissors to cut out the filigree brooches.

The mother sits like a silent dove that doesn't coo.

"Is something hurting you? You seem so sad," the father says to the mother.

"Today my daughters scolded me and laughed at me. They say that I'm too old to bear a child at my age."

"It'll bring a whole hundred pound note!" retorts the father. "A whole Israeli hundred pound note – Ben Gurion promised. We'll buy a shop right in the centre of town and we'll put the best work in the windows and the tourists will grab. They won't stop buying."

Khamameh, with her beautiful La Gioconda face, remained sitting, silent as always.

Sophia the midwife delivers all the children in Mishkenot Yakov. She has a white sign hanging outside with big letters: "Sophia Khalmish" and *keneynehoreh*, may no evil befall, she has what she needs to keep her busy. She hardly ever goes to sleep. Soon after Israel became a country, the rate of childbirth began increasing, because every tenth child gets a hundred-pound Israeli note from the government delivered right to their poor, simple houses. It actually became an epidemic in Mishkenot because both the observant and the secular wanted to enlarge their families.

Sophia has a face like newly kneaded dough with three roots protruding on her constantly perspiring nose. The small knapsack where she keeps the instruments she brings to the winning mother is never closed. The hospitals are busy with wounded soldiers, so every expectant mother has to leave the hospital after only three days. Because of this, Sophia's livelihood improved and her hands are always busy.

This evening she's come home dead tired. The bed is waiting for her and she falls into it with her clothes still on and starts to dream. Suddenly there's a knock at the window, either it's a knocking or she's dreaming it. Sophia has sharp ears, she isn't mistaken. She's on her way again, knapsack in hand, with Yakov Shem-Tov leading the way to his house. He doesn't speak and neither does she.

A cat runs past them and Sophia stops dead in her tracks. "I'm not going any farther," she says. "When a cat crosses your path, and a black one at that, it's better to go home."

"You're not just some foolish woman," says Yakov Shem-Tov. "My wife is about to have a baby and I'm not going to look for another midwife now."

"I'll go, but I don't feel easy about the black cat. Your wife may not be to blame but I'm afraid anyway."

When Sophia entered the cellar, Khamameh was lying crumpled in pain and women from Mishkenot were wiping her with damp cloths. Sophia spread out two white hands covered with freckles like poppy seeds. She didn't realize that Khamameh, the grandmother of six, was delivering yet another child.

"Who's having the baby? The oldest, the middle one, or the youngest?"

"Ya, *khabibi*," a pious female in a white knitted headcover bent toward Sophia and whispered in her ear. Sophia tore at her white, flabby cheeks, pinching them.

"Poor one, poor one," said Sophia and pushed away the women.

"Where's the basin? Give me a basin! Get me a primus! Boil up some water!"

Soon the primus was bubbling away and the basin was steaming with boiling water. Sophia was bustling around Khamameh.

Khamameh lay in holy pain. Her *La Gioconda* face was pale and greenish. The father of the household disappeared.

The daughters were whispering secretively, looking irritably at their mother. Who needed this? The smaller children had fallen asleep in the corners.

Sophia's face flamed with weariness. One by one, the women began filing out of the house.

At the Sfat Emet *shul* it looked like it was a *yontef,* a holiday. All the menorahs were blazing with light. Yakov Shem-Tov had brought a lot of candles. He was breathless and frightened. Soon everyone in the *shul* knew that Shem-Tov would be blessed with good fortune and present to the state the newest member, the tenth child, but nobody envied him.

Shem-Tov's three married daughters ran in red-eyed and said that Sophia the midwife was asking the worshippers to say *Tilim*, to read psalms.

The Mishkenot lunatic, who was standing in a corner and watching the hubbub, suddenly opened his sealed lips and said to Yakov Shem-Tov: "I have an amulet that my mother hung round my neck when I left home. Take it, it'll help. The amulet was blessed by a rabbi, the Vorker Rebbe himself."

Shem-Tov was upset; he didn't even hear what was said to him. He didn't know what to do. Helpless, without even a thought of disbelief, he was certain that soon they would call him.

Sleyme the drunkard also came into the synagogue and went right over to Shem-Tov, slapping him on the shoulder: "*Nu*, celebrant – there'll be a drink?" He pointed to his throat to show that he was eager for a drink.

"The tenth one! The tenth one!" The worshippers called out, sighing.

Someone ran breathlessly into the *shul*, "We need a doctor."

"Maybe two," muttered a woman in fractured Spanish.

Yakov Shem-Tov hurled himself at the door.

A heavy sandstorm clouded the moon as it wound through the alleys of Mishkenot. Everyone in the quarter was standing outside, in front of Yakov Shem-Tov's cellar, whispering and weeping. Shadows, in white shirts, flitted in front of the window and impatiently peered into the interior of the house.

Khamameh lay prostrate and helpless, her smile had vanished.

The *Mogen David adom*, the Red Star of David ambulance, arrived with two doctors. Sophia, her sleeves rolled up to the elbows, moved aside. The cry of a newborn was heard.

Suddenly it grew quiet, as if before a great storm. The moon appeared to have gone to sleep. The sandstorm sky lowered itself to the cellar. Something had happened – a star fell.

Shem-Tov was the first to notice that Khamameh was no longer alive. His big shadow on the wall lowered itself to the ground, sobbing.

Professional mourners were called in – to begin their unearthly wailing.

Translation by Shirley Kumove

A COTTAGE IN THE LAURENTIANS

Chava Rosenfarb

There is almost no spring in the province of Quebec. One fine day the abundant snows of winter, which lie welded to the ground for half the year, disappear, and during the days that follow the naked trees stand ready to don their new leafy dresses. Before long, the trees welcome the world clad in flickering green, as if flocks of tiny green birds were resting on them. And so spring makes its short-lived appearance, like a lackey preceding his mistress, the Queen of Summer, in order to announce her imminent arrival. In no time at all, summer arrives and the hot days begin.

Such is the climate of Quebec which cheats on spring in order to pay back double in fall with the splendor of Indian summer. It is then that the trees, bushes, and shrubs begin to glow with the colours of sunset: a blazing array of yellow, orange, red, brown, but mainly of gold. The towns and villages with their gardens, as well as the city of Montreal with its parks, its long avenues, and narrow residential streets adorned with rows of trees, bask in the sunshine as if dipped in a painter's palette, or as if someone had hung them with garlands of gold. The falling leaves circle in the air like dancing gold coins. They accumulate on the sidewalks in golden heaps. Pedestrians stir up the gold dust with every step.

When Indian summer is at its peak, the Laurentian Mountains, which begin north of Montreal as rolling hills of moderate height, dotted with cool clear lakes and endless tracts of forest, take on the magic of a fantasy land. Nature lovers come from near and far to admire the marvellous colours of the foliage. For the inhabitants of Montreal, the Laurentians are their favourite year-round vacation spot, because during the winters the mountains assume an altogether different kind of beauty, one that is both dramatic and soothing. There is drama in the contrasting interplay of the black trees and the icy unblemished whiteness. And there is something caressing to the eye and soothing to the soul in the white stillness spreading beyond the horizon.

Sonia and Victor were born in Lodz, the Polish Manchester. Both were concentration camp survivors who had lost their families, friends, and neighbours during the war. They had arrived in Canada carrying the substantial psychic baggage of horrific nightmares and tragic recollections, but aside from these, they had – in a manner of speaking – nothing else to declare.

In their memories, the pre-war childhood vacations which they had taken in the sub-Carpathian regions of Poland stood out like the images of a paradise lost. The Laurentian Mountains reminded them of those enchanted spots, and so, even at a time when they could scarcely afford it, when their children were still small, Victor and Sonia had rented a cottage in the Laurentians when the summer heat made Montreal unbearable. They had borrowed money and renounced small luxuries so that they could rent a small cottage near *Le petit lac mirage*, which was located in a remote area, far from the bustle of the more fashionable vacation spots, an hour and a half drive from Montreal.

Later, when their financial situation improved, they bought the cottage. Victor, who was a Yiddish writer, had been offered a teaching position at the Jewish Teachers' Seminary in Montreal; Sonia, also a teacher, was hired by a Jewish high school. It was then that they began to spend not only their summer vacations, but also their weekends in the Laurentians.

During all the years that they owned the cottage they invested little money in renovating it, and it remained the same old wooden shack it had been when they first rented it. After all, how much time did they actually spend inside the cottage? Didn't they really go there to enjoy the splendors of nature? The main thing was that the roof of the cottage did not leak, the stove and the fireplace functioned well, and there was never a lack of firewood. And perhaps both Sonia and Victor harboured a subconscious wish to retain, as much as possible, the cottage's resemblance to those ramshackle huts in which they had spent their childhood holidays.

Every visit that the entire family paid to the cottage was a festive occasion. Sonia and Victor felt themselves infused with a sense of gaiety and renewal, which was largely attributable to the feeling of freedom that the generous beauty of the location gave them. The open sky, like an enormous canopy, unfurled an ongoing spectacle of colours and cloud formations, while the surrounding mountains, covered with dense needle forests, whispered of enchanting secrets buried in the womb of the crystalline lake. They kindled a craving in Sonia and Victor's hearts to fit themselves into the harmony of nature, and to come into direct contact with everything alive and present in God's magnificent world. In order to recapture their own simplicity and innocence, the couple tried to emulate the friskiness of their children, who frolicked around the cottage like young squirrels.

Of course, more often than not, both Sonia and Victor failed in their efforts. The burden of their city cares, the weight of their past, and the aftertaste of recurrent nightmares were not always easy to discard, not even in the country, not even in the company of their carefree children. And yet, despite these hindrances, the very fact of being at the cottage at *Le petit lac mirage* had a refreshing effect on them.

When Sonia and Victor's children reached their teens, they stopped accompanying their parents to the country house. They had grown tired of always spending their holidays in the same place, and so were packed off to summer camps in various locations throughout Canada and the United States.

Only the youngest son, Danny, continued to feel an attachment to the cottage. Danny had been a sickly child. But during puberty, when physical prowess is so important to boys, he had ambitiously taken up swimming and racing with a self-discipline matching that of his father. In this way he had managed to build up his strength. He grew in height and weight, and developed into a good-looking young man.

While still a child, Danny had loved music, and had talked his parents into funding violin lessons. Playing the violin became the passion of Danny's life. His love of music made his father feel an affinity with him that he shared with none of the other children. Father and son were bound to each other by a shared sensibility, a shared spirituality, and by their love of things artistic. At the age of fourteen, Danny was accepted into the Montreal Youth Orchestra.

Sonia and Victor had triumphantly maintained their love for each other through all the years of turmoil, hope, and despair after the Second World War, and they were both proud of it now.

Sonia was a charmer. She had a dark complexion and an abundance of glistening dark hair that framed her open, smiling face. Her eyes were lively, curious, even mischievous, although in their darkest depths there smoldered a barely discernible reflection of an unhealed pain. Her figure was both shapely and sturdy. She had successfully conquered the illnesses of a concentration camp inmate, like tuberculosis and typhus, and was presently in perfect health. Blessed with a sharp mind, she had both a practical sense and a fine critical taste, which went hand in hand with her great vitality and *joie de vivre*. She overflowed with such energy and zest for life that the very air about her seemed to vibrate with her restlessness. She craved compensation for the youth she had lost to the war; each day had to have the value of two, at least as far as achievement and enjoyment were concerned.

Victor, on the other hand, was a perfectionist, punctilious, a grinder, both in his teaching and in his writing. With a judicious eye he weighed and measured every step he took, both in his literary and in his day-to-day life. A skilful observer of human nature, he knew how to winnow the genuine and sincere from the pretentious and superficial. He was capable of forgiving people their weaknesses, but only up to a point. Yet he was hardest on himself.

Along with his self-imposed discipline, which seemed to have found its expression in his tall, lank figure and pale, rabbinic face, went an inborn softness of heart, which was reflected in his warm, dark, glistening, sad Jewish eyes. His orderliness and self-control were a form of armour that he had forced upon himself in order to contain his inner fire and protect it from the destructive forces of reality. Perhaps this was his way of defending his mad optimism, his faith in the redemption of the human spirit through love, a faith which the brutality of war had not had the power to destroy, a faith without which – or so he believed – he could never have been a teacher or a writer.

Sonia and Victor had five children, four boys and a girl. They had planned to have more. Victor would sometimes remark with a regretful smile, "The Jewish people need children. As a good Jew, I must satisfy that need to the best of my ability." It seemed to him that the more children he had, the more his home deserved to be called a home. He was a committed family man, the more so since neither he nor Sonia had any other surviving relatives.

Sonia, for her part, shared Victor's desire to have a large family. She was an enthusiastic mother. She felt best and looked best when she was pregnant. To her, the pregnancies, and the caring for the children and the home, had an additional significance. They expressed her own effort at self-discipline, at taming her unquenchable passion for life. She looked on her family as an exercise in harnessing her greed for experience and adventure. And so she and Victor, despite the differences in their personalities, harmonized with each other and led a life of peace and contentment.

Every day for sixteen years, Victor rose at the first light of dawn and worked for two to three hours at his desk before eating breakfast and leaving for work at the Teachers' Seminary. He often wrote in the evenings, as well as on the weekends in the Laurentians, where some of his most inspired pages were written. He was writing a novel, an epic about the Jewish tragedy in Europe during the Second World War. The backbone of the plot was the love between a man and a woman, for whom Sonia and he served as models.

When he worked on the novel – which had begun to look as though it would never come to an end – Sonia never disturbed him. On the contrary, she did all that she could to put him in the right frame of mind and to give him some peace and quiet. She watched over him like a guardian angel. She had the necessary qualities of mind to appreciate his undertaking, to grasp the vastness of the literary panorama which he was painting, and she valued his artistic achievements.

She had come to appreciate the importance of Victor's work, because she had, in a manner of speaking, sinned against him throughout all the years that he had been writing his novel. Whenever Victor was not at home, she would sneak into his room and read the chapter that he had just written. She read it with a frisson of guilty pleasure, as if she were tasting a forbidden fruit. Victor, the perfectionist, was reluctant to show the unfinished product of his labour, even to her.

But she was so overcome by curiosity that reading his chapters as they were being written became a compulsion that she could not subdue. She was particularly thrilled by the manner in which Victor described the character of his female protagonist, since she knew that this character was modeled on herself. She was fascinated by the way in which this character developed over the course of hundreds of pages into a magnificent portrait of a woman. She was flattered by the light in which Victor saw her, and adored the reflection of herself in the book – although at the same time she was also greatly ashamed of herself. Sometimes, in her enthusiasm, she was beset by an attack of spasmodic laughter that brought tears to her eyes, so ludicrous did the situation seem.

When the children grew older and left in the evenings for their various activities – Danny, for instance, to his music lessons – Sonia and Victor remained alone in the house. These were the most peaceful hours of their day, when they forgot their cares and devoted themselves to their own activities, taking delight in each other's presence. Victor sat down to work at the desk in his small office, while Sonia, still full of energy, threw herself into her housework, cleaning, sewing, and fixing whatever needed to be fixed. When she was done with that, she corrected her students' papers, and then devoted herself to reading various books related to her current interests. Sometimes these interests were in the field of zoology, at other times in the field of history, or music, or medicine, or psychology, or Buddhism, or even astrology. She wanted to know everything, to devour everything, as if she were still on the threshold of her life, ready to discover the world. Rarely did she have the patience to sit down to watch television. When her restlessness became uncontrollable, she grabbed her coat and rushed off to spend some time with a girlfriend, or she went to see a movie. Once a month she attended a ballet performance. This was an especially festive occasion for which she dressed as elegantly as if she were going to a ball.

Victor accumulated a great deal of remorse on account of his neglect of Sonia, of her being forced to go everywhere alone. Still enamored of her fiery temperament, he regretted every moment that he was not in her company, taking delight in her vitality, in her bubbling intelligence and charm. He always felt torn between Sonia and his desk, and looked forward to the day when he would complete his novel and be drawn only to her, his eternal beloved.

When she entered his room to say goodbye before leaving for the ballet, she would be dressed in her most elegant attire, her feet encased in high-heeled shoes and her purse and gloves held in a manicured hand. Enveloped by the delicate fragrance of her perfume, he would look at the black wavy hair that framed her dark radiant face, drink in her hot, dark look, and his heart would ache at the sight of her beauty. He was jealous of the many strangers' eyes that would be glancing at her, and he kissed her greedily, guiltily, and gratefully.

"Do you forgive me, Sonichka?" he whispered on one such occasion. "I have only a few more episodes to write, and I'm afraid that if I don't do it tonight, I will forget them and they will be lost forever."

Sonia's ringing laughter sounded no different than her laughter from the times after their liberation from the camps. "It's I who must ask your forgiveness, Victor, for not being able to help you in any way."

"What do you mean by not being able to help me? You help me all the time." He took her hand in his. "Can you imagine my undertaking this project without you? This is our joint endeavor, darling. That's what it is. It belongs to both of us. Just let me get this text into some kind of order…" She left. He turned back toward the desk. The dog, Lord, made himself comfortable at his feet.

When Sonia returned late in the evening and the children were already asleep, Victor forced himself to push away the piles of paper. He insisted that Sonia, tired and sleepy though she was, go out with him for a walk. They took the dog along. As they walked, they talked about their home, their children, discussed their teaching projects, and made plans for their forthcoming trip to the Laurentians.

The day of Danny's first solo performance with the Montreal Youth Orchestra was approaching and the entire family anticipated the event, making whatever arrangements were necessary to be present. Even the eldest of the children, who was studying in New York at Columbia University, came home for the occasion. Danny was everybody's darling.

But two days before the performance, Masha, the only daughter, came home with the news that she had broken up with her boyfriend, and the atmosphere of the house changed to something resembling that of *Tisha B'av*, the day of mourning over the destruction of the temple in Jerusalem. This had been the girl's first love, a great love, and Masha was devastated to the point of making herself sick. She refused to eat, and wandered about the house, clad in her housecoat, sobbing. Sometimes she stared out the window, oblivious to what was said to her, as if a wall had risen between herself and the rest of the world, so that nothing could reach her. Sonia, silent, absent-minded, looking somewhat guilty, hovered near her constantly.

There could be no talk of Masha's attending her brother's concert. Then, on the very day of the concert, Sonia declared that she too would stay home in order to keep her daughter company.

"I feel the hand of fate in this," she said to Victor and Danny. "It has not been granted to me to hear you play, Danny. But I have no doubt that, no matter what, you'll surpass yourself tonight."

Neither Victor nor Danny understood Sonia's decision. After all, Masha was not in danger. True, she was suffering the pains of a great loss, but time would heal the wound and Masha would resume her normal life. She took after her mother. She was a strong, active person, a true fighter. Moreover, Masha's closest friend had volunteered to spend the evening of the concert with her, and Masha herself believed that her mother should attend the concert – for Danny's sake.

But Sonia stubbornly persisted in her decision. Victor patted Danny on the shoulder, a half-hearted grin on his face. "How do the French say? The human heart has its reasons which the reason does not know. That's especially true when you're talking about a mother's heart."

Victor told himself that he understood the heart of this particular mother, and accepted Sonia's decision without much protest. But deep in his heart he knew that the evening was spoiled for him as well. He had been eagerly anticipating the pleasure of sitting beside Sonia in the concert hall and sharing with her his pride in the achievement of their son. As a rule, his pleasure doubled whenever she joined him at a concert, or theatre performance, or an exhibition. This would have been especially true tonight.

But his son, the artist, warm-hearted, lovable Danny, smiled at his mother and pretended that he was only slightly upset by the turn of events. "Not to worry," he said to her in an overly loud tone of voice. "Your and Masha's ticket will still be valid for my real concert, next year, at Carnegie Hall!"

Victor remarked thoughtfully, "A waste of two tickets. We could have offered them to somebody."

Sonia, busying herself at the open refrigerator, said, "That's exactly what I did. I gave our tickets to Berger."

"Why to him?" Victor asked, astonished.

"So that he could appraise Danny's playing," she answered.

Simon Berger was a musicologist, the conductor of the choir of which Sonia had been a member for many years. He was a passionate chess player, and years earlier he had been a frequent guest at Sonia and Victor's apartment. This was at the time when Sonia had set her heart on becoming an accomplished chess player, and had studied chess manuals written by the masters. Late into the evening, Berger would sit with her in the kitchen, explaining the intricacies of various strategies. When Sonia transferred her interests to anthropology and mythology, Berger stopped his visits.

Sonia was not overly fond of Berger. She considered him conceited, an arrogant boaster. Victor, although influenced by

Sonia's dislike of the man, nonetheless defended him against her criticisms, minimizing Berger's shortcomings while stressing his intellectual abilities. Had not Sonia herself raved about Berger's unusual talents both in the field of music and of chess?

Hours later Victor found himself sitting in the concert hall. Three of his children sat to his right, while Berger and his wife – a svelte, flashy middle-aged matron – sat to his left. Berger was a corpulent man with an elongated deeply creased face. Unruly strands of greying black hair stood out from his head, pointing in all directions. He had greeted Victor with a firm friendly handshake. But after they had run through the standard questions and answers – they had not seen each other for a number of years – a silence fell between them, which Berger interrupted just before the beginning of the concert.

"How is the masterpiece coming along?" he asked Victor. "Sonia told me the other day at choir rehearsal that you're about to finish the first draft. How many drafts do you intend to write?"

Victor noted the sarcasm in Berger's question. He smiled, more to himself than to his neighbour. Accustomed to the respectful disdain of non-creative people, especially the intelligent and gifted, who tried to conceal their envy with such acerbic remarks, he replied amiably, "Very soon you'll see how it is coming along."

"What do you mean?" Berger asked.

"Danny is my real masterpiece."

Berger's face flushed a sudden red. He tried to answer Victor with a smile of his own, but instead his mouth twisted into an ugly grimace. He gave Victor a strange look, then turned his head away and began to chat with his wife.

The concert began. During Danny's solo, Victor was so tense, so acutely attentive, that his ear lost its discernment, and he could no longer make out the shades of tone in Danny's playing. His heart hammered in his chest and he missed the feel of Sonia's hand in his during the moments of almost unbearable joy that overflowed his heart. When Danny's violin began to ascend to the final crescendo, Victor cast a triumphant glance at Berger and, to his amazement, noticed that the man's wide-open eyes were overflowing with tears. That moment Victor forgave Berger for everything. He felt closer to him than to a brother.

There was still a considerable amount of work to do before Victor could finish the first draft of his novel. Masha had long since been cured of her broken heart and had left for Toronto to continue her studies. Her departure had been preceded by a period of much discussion at the dinner table of the various universities and their respective merits. Victor and Sonia's other two sons were also within a year or two of applying to university. Sonia, vivacious and cheerful as ever, continued with her daily routine. She had just started on a new interest. This time it was botany. And as usual, when her enthusiasm for a new passion reached its peak, she would expound on it for hours. This time she went on and on about the development of plants, their "moods," and their sensitivity to such things as music.

The day finally came when Victor completed the first draft of his novel. In order to celebrate the end of this important phase of his work, he and Sonia decided to play hooky for a day and drive out to their cottage in the Laurentians. They took along Lord, the dog, who had grown up along with the children and had been everybody's best friend, but whose primary attachment had always been to Victor, whom he doggedly followed everywhere.

Golden autumn reigned in the mountains, and the forest surrounding the cottage was ablaze with colour. The road down to the lake, *Le petit lac mirage*, was covered with a carpet of leaves in all shades of gold. On the mirror-like lake, the fallen leaves sailed about like tiny golden gondolas in an imaginary Venice.

No sooner had they arrived at the cottage than Victor busied himself with his usual country chores, which gave him the opportunity to move his limbs and put him in a leisurely frame of mind. He chopped wood for the kitchen stove and prepared thick logs for the fireplace to be lit that evening, since he and Sonia had decided to stay overnight and return to town early in the morning. Humming a little tune to himself, he raked up the piles of leaves in front of the cottage and gathered them into large stacks. He tried not to think about his work, but to give his mind a rest, in order to fully enjoy the peaceful moments. He was also determined to concentrate his attention on Sonia. Such solitude *a deux* would strengthen their bond, contribute to their intimacy, and bring them still closer together.

Sonia too seemed to be in a cheerful frame of mind. Nevertheless, she was preoccupied, walking about absentmindedly. She was silent and her languorous smile seemed not her own. She observed every tree and shrub with a mystical tenderness bordering on piety. Victor, as he watched her, ascribed her strange behaviour to her absorption in her botanical studies. But he detected a vague nervousness in the air about her. He asked her whether there was anything troubling her.

After a moment of silence, she responded, "You know very well that I hate being completely cut off from the children. Every year we talk about installing a telephone, and we never do anything but talk."

"I give you my word of honour as an absent-minded professor," Victor playfully pounded his chest like Tarzan, "that come next summer, it shall be done. If you like," he added softly, "we could walk over to the village this evening and call the children."

"And I'll keep on reminding you..." She smiled back at him with that same nondescript smile. "Because once you set your mind to forgetting something, Victor, no amount of reminding you will have any effect. Don't we both know that?"

"When did I ever set my mind to forgetting anything having to do with a wish of yours?"

She pretended to think hard, as if she were trying to remember. They laughed. In truth, when it came to Sonia or the children, Victor was never stubborn or forgetful. If he was, it was only in matters regarding himself. But it was also true that he was not too enthusiastic about installing a telephone in their cottage. He considered the telephone a scourge, even in the city, but he had to tolerate it there. In the country, however, he preferred to be completely isolated from the rest of the world. When it was absolutely necessary to call, it was always possible to walk over to the village. What was more, the farmer who lived fifteen minutes away also had a telephone and, in an emergency, the children could always get in touch with their parents.

Sonia and Victor took their lunch on the veranda, which was draped around its borders with the climbing vines that grew over the entire cottage. This meant that on a fall day the cottage appeared to be immersed in flaming gold and red, while the veranda seemed to be surrounded by walls of fire.

The veranda was only free of vines on one side, the side facing the lake. As Victor and Sonia sat at their rustic table, consuming their lunch, they looked out on the dazzling panorama of the mountains and the lake. A light haze rose slowly from the placid surface of the lake. Sonia's eyes were just as misty as the lake. There was a strange and unfamiliar Something lurking inside her gaze as she listened to Victor talk about his feelings for her. He was capable of formulating these feelings with admirable precision. She could not detect a single banal note. His words moved her so that she stopped eating.

That day Victor's words of love were exceptionally beautiful. He was composed and satisfied with himself after the completion of his first draft, the first stage of his work. At last he had the entire novel laid out on paper. No longer was it in danger of being threatened by the vagaries of uncertain memory, no longer could any scenes fade into oblivion and slip out of his grasp. He could now visualize his work in its entirety, as a reality that had not existed before, and was now present. This gave him a great sense of relief, almost of bliss.

He considered the moment ideal to finally talk freely to Sonia about his work. He could question her about her approach to certain issues and compare her answers with the views of the most important female character in his book. He also told her which incidents in their life together had inspired some of the scenes in his book, and why and how he had transformed them in his narrative. The character of his female protagonist was not intended as a faithful reproduction of Sonia, as Sonia doubtless knew. What he was trying to do was to capture the essence of her personality.

"My purpose," he remarked, "is not to portray our lives during the war as they were, but to place them in an altogether different context. How should I say it? I wanted to come closer to the meaning of our tragedy's meaninglessness..."

They had finished eating and were now sitting at the veranda table, sipping hot coffee from their cups, as Victor continued with his monologue. He was totally absorbed in what he was saying. Her cheeks aglow, Sonia listened to him. She was aware that he was presenting her with the gift of his soul balanced on the palm of his hand, that he was offering her all that his intellect possessed, as if he were clearing out the most hidden recesses in the workshop of his mind, and revealing all the secrets he had been hiding inside.

Sonia looked up at Victor from beneath the strands of wavy black hair that dangled over her forehead and eyebrows. Her eyes were strangely troubled, and sparks of acute suffering shot up from their depths. She could not tolerate the frequent allusions to his love for her that he continued to make. They made her ache all over.

"How well I understand Hemingway," Victor continued, "when he says that he writes best when he is in love. Without my love for you, Sonichka, I would never have dared to aim so high. It was the power of my feelings for you that gave me wings."

"You're exaggerating, as usual," she frowned impatiently. "Do you realize how long we have been living together? Do you keep count? It's been ten years since I began dyeing my hair to cover the grey."

"You talk nonsense, darling." He moved closer to her. "A love such as mine for you takes no account of years. As far as I'm concerned, time has made no changes in you, and I'm not joking when I say that you are a partner in my work just as you are a partner in my life."

She sipped her coffee, and he wondered whether it was the steam from the cup that moistened her face, or whether those were tears.

In the afternoon they went for a walk around the lake, following a path carpeted with yellow leaves. Lord, the dog, ran ahead, chasing squirrels. He pounced on the heaps of leaves and barked playfully. Every few minutes he raised his leg to pay his respects to a tree trunk or to a pile of leaves that he had disturbed, and then raced on, leaping into the air with great abandon. The vacation cottages that dotted the road at a considerable distance from one another were almost all vacant.

A solitary boat sat in the middle of the lake; the person inside was catching fish. From the distance the contours of man and boat resembled the anchor of a large invisible ship. An air of something primeval and mythical hovered over the lake, as if the story of its genesis were still in the making. As if purposely disturbing the silence, Victor and Sonia held hands and trod noisily over the leaves. In their free hands, each held a walking stick which Victor had fashioned out of dry branches. They talked very little. Sonia seemed so deeply immersed in her thoughts that her dark eyebrows were arched and her forehead was wrinkled. Victor was reluctant to disturb her. He assumed that she was mulling over what he had told her at lunch.

And as a matter of fact, Sonia was thinking about what Victor had said over lunch. She was thinking about him, about herself, and their life together. She felt particularly sensitive to her surroundings this day, and found herself drawn to Victor by the secluded intimacy of the lake and the forest. She was grateful to him for the words of love which he had said to her, grateful – and, at the same time, deeply ashamed.

She had not been happy with Victor for a very long time. She was glad that he was so absorbed in his work that he had failed to notice how false her good cheer had been, how he bored her to tears, and how torn she felt. She was not really troubled by the fact that she cheated on him every now and again. Once he had ceased to touch her soul, she no longer felt any bond with him. She had lost interest in him, and she did not in the least care for what he had to say outside the framework of his novel. It had all been an act she had put on for the sake of convenience. And yet, she was constantly troubled by a sense of betrayal. It ate into her like poison. It aroused in her a feeling of guilt toward him, a guilt that had corroded her life for many years. Her natural vitality enabled her to mask it all with an air of assumed candor, but not even her vitality could erase the self-disgust from her heart. And for that she could forgive neither herself, nor Victor.

Today, however, she did not know why or how, perhaps because the magic of the autumn landscape moved her so, her heart suddenly recaptured the love she had felt for Victor during the first years of their life together, during that time after liberation, when she had been a very young woman. Now she conceived a passion for him, at the same time as she experienced a great need to merge with the atmosphere of their surroundings and partake of the innocence and honesty of nature. She had to recapture her purity of heart. She was exhausted from the effort of decorating her external self with all manner of artifice; she was even tired of her artificial hair colour and of the makeup that enhanced her false golden smile. Just as Victor had finished a phase of his work, so she longed to finish this phase of her life, and to start a new chapter along with him, her husband and lover. He would rewrite his work, while she would redo her life. She needed this remodeling in order to save herself, save her soul, and be rid of the devastating hatred that she felt for herself.

She walked on, her face lowered over the heaps of dry leaves as she punctured them with her walking stick. Then, with sudden decisiveness, she stopped and turned to him: "I must tell you something, Victor. And please forgive me for doing it today, such an important festive day for you."

"For both of us," he corrected her softly.

"First I must tell you," she continued, "that I love you..." He raised her hand to his lips to kiss, but she jerked it away. "I never loved you as much as I do now..." She was about to proceed, but suddenly she recalled a scene from a war film that she had recently seen: a Nazi aiming his rifle at a child who laughed playfully while it gamboled through a pasture full of field flowers. Sonia recoiled from the memory. Her head still lowered, she moved slightly away from Victor and neglected to take the hand which he held out to her. "But I must tell you this..." she broke off for a moment to catch her breath. Her heart pounded violently.

"Go ahead," he smiled encouragingly.

She flung up her head and stared straight into his eyes. His smile pierced her heart, but she held straight to her course. "This is going to hurt," she warned him. "I hope you're strong enough. I hope you'll forgive me."

"Shoot!" He spread his arms theatrically.

She waited for him to drop his arms. "Danny is not your son!"

The smile did not leave his face. "What do you mean, not my son?"

"I mean to say that you are not his father."

"Then who is?"

"Berger is."

"You're crazy."

"This is my first moment of sanity, Victor. I've been leading a double life for the last fifteen years. You were so deeply buried in your mountains of paper that no suspicion ever entered your mind. What did you expect me to do? I needed some intimacy, a soulmate, or even just a companion. I wanted to live, to enjoy myself, to go places after the daily drudgery at work and at home. You were always at your desk, always scribbling away, day in and day out, week after week, year after year. What did you expect? I'm not an angel. I wanted a little happiness for myself, just as you got yours for yourself. You found your thrills in your work, while I found mine in other men. You made love to paper people, and I made love to people of flesh and blood. Yes, you deceived me too. You forgot that I really existed outside the confines of your imagination, as a living woman who loves life – real life, Victor!" She had not intended to hurl reproaches at him. She was not certain that even if her reproaches were not true, she might not still have deceived him. Yet the only way that she could defend herself was to make an attack.

His face had grown grey. He looked helplessly in all directions, then leaned his shoulder against the nearest tree. She hovered near him. They stood face to face. She continued talking as she observed her victim wince and writhe against the tree trunk like a snake in agony. Soon she would revive him with all the loving words that overflowed her heart. Soon she would tell him how powerfully her love for him had returned to repossess her soul. Soon she would throw herself into his arms and kiss the despair from his pale face, kiss the protruding eyes which stared at her blindly, full of despair. Soon she would smother him with the most transporting caresses, and reinstate herself in his heart where she would reign forever. She could achieve this so easily. He would never be able to live without her. But first, she had to drain the last drops of venom that had accumulated in her heart over the years. She had to mitigate her own guilt by accusing him. They had sinned, both of them. They were partners. He had said that she was a partner to his work, then let him be a partner to her guilt.

"I could have gotten rid of the pregnancy, Victor," she continued in her hard metallic voice, while struggling to dam the tears that welled up behind her eyes. "But then you would have found out everything, and I was not yet prepared to let you know. I wanted to protect our home and the children, and that's how it happened. Now I don't regret it at all. I have Danny. You have Danny. You are his father. Can you imagine our life without Danny? And, Victor, later on..." The tears finally overflowed her eyes, but her voice remained clear and sharp. "In later times, when the children were grown, and I felt so unhappy in our relationship, I did not leave you – not because of the children, and not because I did not want to break up our home, but because of you. I wanted to spare you; I wanted you to continue with your work, your great work. I wanted you to succeed, to become famous. I sacrificed myself for you more than you can imagine."

"But..." he mumbled. "How could you have found...have found..."

"How could I have found the time to have affairs? Is that what you want to know? Ask the blood in my veins. My compulsion was so strong, my craving was so powerful..." She ran out of breath and she, too, failed to complete her sentence.

Victor said nothing more. He slumped down to the foot of the tree. After a long silence, he said to her, "Go back to the cottage. Let me sit here for a while." The dog snuggled up beside him and Victor patted him with rapid mechanical strokes. His dull gaze followed Sonia's figure as it edged away from him through the sea of golden leaves.

"My beautiful Sonia, my beloved, my only one," he muttered aloud, his voice hoarse. "You are so powerful, more powerful than the Nazis. They tortured my body, but they could never reach my soul. You alone managed that. You have destroyed me, and destroyed the image of yourself within me... Danny!" He let out a prolonged howl and burst into sobs.

As he followed Sonia's receding figure through misty eyes, he suddenly recalled how they had met for the first time. He saw vividly the infirmary of the Neuengamme concentration camp. It was a grey rainy afternoon. A salty sea wind danced between the infirmary walls, penetrating his bones to the marrow. That day he had been assigned to scrub the floor in the corridor of the infirmary. There he noticed a young female inmate sitting on a bench, shivering in her striped camp outfit – a scrawny, ugly creature whose skeletal face, twisted with cold and suffering, seemed to consist only of a pair of fierce black eyes overflowing with tears of pain and rage. She had been brought to the infirmary from another smaller camp that had no infirmary. Her feet were wrapped in wet rags and she held a pair of wooden clogs on her lap. She had stubbed her toes so badly during the marches to and from her workplace that her toes had become infected and covered with boils.

As he knelt with the scrubbing brush in hand, Victor felt that the girl's eyes were calling to him in desperation from her corner. He glanced at the SS guard who stood at the door, his rifle at the ready. Moving his scrubbing brush vigorously back and forth over the floor, he managed to surreptitiously move closer to the girl. As a member of the inmates' underground at the camp, he was used to doing forbidden things under the noses of the SS men.

The moment he was within an arm's length of the girl, he heard her rasp out between chattering teeth, "Have you got anything to eat?"

Yes, he did. He had on him the second half of his daily bread ration, which he had put aside to eat in his bunk that night, so that the pangs of hunger would not keep him from falling asleep. He carried the small chunk of bread around with him so that nobody would steal it from him. He kept it inside his striped pants, wrapped in a rag, tied with a string, and attached to the cord of the pants. He got it out and placed it quickly in her palm. Saliva dripped from her mouth onto his hand like a kiss, like a hot seal. As soon as the SS guard turned away, Victor managed to tell her that he came from Lodz. She said, "So do I." He told her his name, she told him hers. He asked whether she had met any women inmates with his name. She asked the same about her male relatives. That moment they knew everything there was to know about one another; their bond was sealed.

The next time that they met was after the liberation, in the DP camp in Feldafing in Bavaria. She recognized him among a crowd of survivors. From then on they were inseparable. Both of them were alone; they had no one in the world but each other. They moved in together into a tiny cubicle in a mansion that had formerly housed the SS brass. The mansion was crowded with DPs. Victor and Sonia slept on the same cot, since there were no extra cots available. It was not a question of love at that time. It was fate.

It did not take long before Sonia recovered from her various illnesses and blossomed into a beautiful, life-loving charmer, bubbling with energy and greedy for pleasure. Victor's demeanor changed in the opposite direction. In the concentration camp he had been sociable, active, involved with his comrades in various dangerous activities. Now as he began to write, a distance sprang up between himself and his comrades. Sonia would often run off alone to meet her friends, while he stayed in their tiny room whose window faced the Ebensee, the most beautiful lake in Bavaria. It was during this time, surrounded by the most beautiful landscape imaginable, that Victor and Sonia's passion for each other took root.

It was Sonia who supplied them both with food. She organized escapades into the countryside, sneaked into German farmhouses, making off with delicious freshly-baked bread, rolls, and succulent chunks of ham. She would bring them back to their cubicle for their mutual delectation. It was she who had also organized their illegal crossing of the border into France, and from there, assisted by the UNRRA, arranged their departure for Canada. They were married just a few days prior to boarding a cargo ship called Patagonia, and setting out on the long, stormy sea voyage across the Atlantic.

As he slumped against the tree, Victor could not tear his eyes from Sonia's disappearing form. As he looked at her, he had the impression that the cottage, whose roof was visible in the distance, was receding, floating away from him like a boat that he had failed to board. He knew that when he saw Sonia's face again, it would no longer be the same face that he had loved.

A few hours later, they returned to the city.

Victor lacked the capacity to forgive Sonia, although he tried to understand her. Sonia was right: he must have been a terrible bore. He made an effort to justify her in his mind. He had been wrung dry, devoid of liveliness. He had nothing to offer her. All the riches of his soul had been invested in his work. Whatever sense of adventure, whatever flights of fancy and sparks of humor were left in him, he had kneaded into his text in order to render more digestible the essential morbidity of his story.

But despite his best intentions, he found himself unable to live with Sonia any longer. What was more, he felt himself incapable of going on with his life at all. All the scaffolding that had supported his existence seemed to have collapsed. Like an automaton he went about his daily routine. When he was at home, he no longer sat down at his desk. He wandered about the house, chatted with the children, or even with Sonia, but did not really see them. A dull pain nagged at him, as if he had taken too weak a dose of chloroform. When he felt himself choking in the apartment, he went out into the street. Several times he considered visiting a brothel, or just calling up one of his literary women friends, but he had no taste for women. He loathed the very idea of touching them. He desired no one, desired nothing. Every impulse within him was dead. He walked about like a sleepwalker.

Danny was the first of the children to notice the strangeness in his father's behaviour. He tried to strike up a conversation with him; he volunteered to play Victor's favourite pieces of music on his violin. He proposed that they go somewhere together. But Victor was unable to look at Danny without tears coming to his eyes. The sight of the boy made him feel weak. He avoided him even more than he avoided Sonia.

As for Sonia, he talked to her about practical matters, about the children, the home and expenses, but he looked at her as if she were a stranger, and treated her as if she were a neighbour with whom he was obliged to discuss certain necessary housekeeping details.

Sonia comported herself with no particular pride. Nor was she more humble or servile than before. She could not change what had happened, but she was willing to change what she could in the future. She was tormented by the suffering she had caused Victor, but knew that she could not alleviate it. She too suffered. She came to realize that as much as she wanted to, she could not shake off her feelings of guilt toward Victor, and she began to think that she was doomed to carry them to the end of her days. But if it was not given her to win Victor back, she still preferred the present situation to continuing with a life of lies.

It never entered her mind that Victor might leave her. She knew him too well, and knew the power of his love for her, even if he never again acknowledged it. She also knew how strong his sense of responsibility to his family was, and how attached and devoted he was to their home.

So she kept herself composed and patiently waited for a change in Victor's attitude. In the meantime, she abandoned her scientific pursuits. She lost interest in them, but promised herself to take them up as soon as Victor came back to her. Every once in a while, when she and Victor happened to be alone, she would softly say to him, "Remember, Victor, that I love you." Or she would reprimand him, "For heaven's sake, Victor, cheer up. You're exaggerating the whole thing, as usual. Times have changed. Your rigid puritanical approach toward infidelity was outdated even at home, before the war."

He did not react to her words, as if he had not heard them. He continued to sleep with her in the same bed. After all, during the war, he had slept in the same bed with total strangers. He was as unresponsive as a rock. Nothing mattered to him. Whatever he did was transitory, temporary – he was certain about that. Not that he intended to commit suicide, although he thought of it quite often. But these thoughts of suicide, detached and logical though they were, brought him always to the conclusion that he must not grant the Nazis such a victory.

Finally, the day came when Victor knew clearly what he had to do. He told Sonia that she should prepare to live her life without him, that he would not stay in the house any longer, that they ought to make certain practical decisions. The main thing was not to upset the children any more than was necessary.

"When?" she asked.

"I don't know yet," he answered woodenly.

Sonia did not believe him. She was convinced that he would not have the courage to go through with his plan. She could not imagine him packing a valise and walking out of the house, never to return. Even if he were capable of such an act on her account, he would never have the strength to walk out on the children. His conscience, the severe and rigorous demands he made on himself, would never permit this to happen. His home was something very sacred to him. This was not a pose, nor a pretense.

She was, however, convinced of another thing as well: that he would not go back to work on his great book, of which their mutual love had been the backbone. This she regretted profoundly. She regretted it, not only because she knew that his work was a masterpiece in the making, but also because she loved his work just as sincerely as she had hated his continual absorption in it, and she loved herself in the image that he had created of her. She wanted to have his work at her side, for herself alone, to admire at will as she would when looking into a mirror, regardless of the outcome of their marital upheaval. She wanted to be able to refresh her heart for the rest of her life with the image of the magnificent Sonia of the book. She so detested the real Sonia.

And so, gradually, without Victor's knowledge, Sonia took each chapter to be copied. When it was all done, she put the huge manuscript into a cardboard box, put the box into the car, and drove alone up to the cottage at *Le petit lac mirage* in the Laurentians. There, she wrapped the copy of Victor's work in many layers of silver foil, put them in cellophane bags, and stacked them in a metal safe which she had bought for that purpose. She hid the safe in the cellar between the piles of firewood that were stacked in a corner. She intended to come up to the cabin whenever she felt like reading the book.

Sonia was correct in her assumption that Victor would never resume his work on the novel. Coming home from work one afternoon, she was confronted on the landing by a disheveled Victor, his shirt unbuttoned, throwing the last of his manuscript into the incinerator.

"What are you doing?" she cried, pretending to be both angry and desperate. Inwardly, she congratulated herself on her foresight in predicting Victor's behaviour. This strengthened her conviction that he would never leave her. Moreover, she was glad that she had saved his work, and she was convinced that Victor himself would thank her for it one day.

"It's gone! Burned! Burned!" he exclaimed in a frenzy. Instead of returning to the apartment, he ran down the stairs and out the door. He stayed away for many hours. Soon after this incident, Victor rented a room, packed a trunk of his personal belongings, and went to live on his own.

The first sleepless night that he spent in his rented room, he told himself that this was the beginning of a new long night in his life. Thereafter he went to work as usual, and as usual contributed to the support of Sonia and the children, but he never again set foot in the apartment. He met with the children, but after the initial shock of their parents' separation had worn off, they concealed their confusion and resentment, claiming to be too busy with their lives and with their plans for the future to devote much time to their father. At length, Victor remained close only to Danny, who was very attached to him. The two of them maintained the same affectionate contact that they had always had, although Victor could hardly look at Danny without tears coming to his eyes.

When Danny learned from his mother that Victor was not his real father, their relationship, despite their genuine love for each other, underwent a change, caused by the uneasiness of diverging emotions and thoughts. Danny, the gifted young musician, was the most innocent victim of his parents' frailties. His soul was forever scarred by the sins of the two adults who were responsible for his well being. This truth peered out from his bewildered, questioning eyes. Victor felt that he should sink to his knees before Danny and beg his forgiveness for not being his father.

Fortunately Danny had his violin. This was his salvation. Before long, he was accepted at the Juilliard School in New York, and with the beginning of the school year he left Montreal.

Victor's physical and emotional disintegration continued. He sank deeper into depression, became lackadaisical in his professional work, negligent in his appearance, and ever more eccentric in his habits. Neither his students, nor his colleagues at the Jewish Teachers' Seminary could restrain the inclination to make jokes at his expense by recounting anecdotes of his absent-mindedness. Victor knew that he was being mocked behind his back, but he did not care.

He regarded his experience with Sonia as the pivotal point in the dark night that engulfed him. There was now a total absence of light, of hope, in his outlook on life. One day, when he found himself in the very depths of despair, on the verge of a complete breakdown, he had a sudden impulse to leave for the cottage in the Laurentians. He and Sonia each had a key to the cottage. It was the beginning of winter. The first heavy snow had fallen.

When he got to the cottage, he went for a walk. Thick snowflakes dotted the air between the trees. The snow descending on the lake brought to mind the image of a continuous fall of white curtains sprinkled with small, white cotton balls. The stillness was occasionally broken by a bird's cry. In the whirling whiteness, Victor watched the flapping wings of birds, black as ink blots, sawing through the air.

As he ploughed through the snow, he felt as if he himself were a black rock frozen in one spot, while the snow whirling through the air seemed to be moving slowly ahead. He smiled at himself. A black rock? And why not a black bird about to rise into the air? He was only weary and exhausted. All he needed was to rest for a while before soaring into the flight which Destiny had decreed was his.

All of a sudden a craving began to stir in his heart. He wanted to write! "In spite of yourself, you must write!" he called out in the white stillness.

Writing was his destiny, his assigned function in life. This was how he was meant to contribute to the singing of the birds, to the slashing hum of waterfalls, to the howl of the wind, and to the soundless fall of the snowflakes. It must be so! It was for the sake of his calling that he had needed this tremendous crash in his life. What a wealth of suffering he had discovered in the dark abyss of his soul! Too soon had he forgotten the suffering that he had endured in the depths of a former horror. He had abused the entire supply of knowledge which he had gleaned from his former trials. He had squandered it almost entirely with a naïveté of heart that bordered on stupidity! Only now, enriched by a completely new kind of torment, did he see himself standing one rung higher on the ladder of experience. Now he had a better view of the panorama of human fate, of the human comedy. During the time between that other storm and this new one, he had become fossilized, stagnant in his fool's paradise; he had lost contact with reality.

He was spoiled. Writing had become a game for him. True, it was a serious game, but it was a game nonetheless. Having described people starving from hunger, he had sat down to a feast at his dinner table. Having described a character's terrifying loneliness, he had gone to bed with his wife. Having describing executions by firing squad, he had plunged into the lake to frolic with his children. Only now did he have his finger on the pulse of life's mystery. Only now did he taste the sting of its simultaneous banality and brutality. Now was the time to sit down and write his book. He must! This was his calling!

Although there were no particular ideas forming in his mind, he was overcome by the longing to write – just to sit down and write. He felt himself possessed by this passion. He forgot that he had barely any strength left as he marched through the forest at a quick heavy pace in order to catch up with the swiftly running currents of his mood. Suddenly he turned back.

Two hours later he was sitting at his small writing table in his little room in Montreal. On top of the table he had placed a sheaf of clean, white, lined writing paper. Each sheet was a field waiting to be sown. The perfectly straight parallel lines were furrows; they were elongated mouths ready to swallow the seeds. The pen in Victor's trembling hand swept forward toward the top line on the first sheet of paper, and before long he was racing along the lines like a farmer rushing to sow his field before the sun set behind the horizon.

From that day on, Victor worked feverishly in his room, writing with a quick hand. He wrote in the grey hours of dawn, and during the late evening until long after midnight. He went to work as usual, but hurried home every day like a mother racing home to nurse her baby. He ate while writing, drank while writing. He clung frantically to his pen. The first draft of the novel that he had burned had had a well-organized plot as its backbone. How ludicrous and false! Life was devoid of backbone. It resembled a coiled snake, rings collapsed inside rings. This being the case, he would represent life in these pages in just such a haphazard form. As far as Victor was concerned, the disjointedness of life was none of his business. His business was to allow the ink to flow from under his pen in time to the flow of blood in his veins, to let words, like leeches, suck the pain from his soul. That was all that he had to do.

Occasionally he stopped to check himself. What about his pain? Was it gone, or was he still drowning in it? What did it matter, as long as he was himself again. He had his dignity.

And so he continued to write, not rereading what he had written, not knowing what he was writing about, not once glancing back. The crooked mirror in his mind had to remain crooked. His memory had to be cleared of the refuse of words, in order to be refilled with new clutter, with new mountains of words. He had to pile them higher and higher. They would divide themselves into paragraphs on their own, according to the tempos, to the tides and ebbs of his passion. Let the words fall where they would. The only thing he would permit himself was to number the pages, number the chapters, and divide them into sub-headings. This was the only concession he would make to conventional form.

His pen sped on. Eight hundred pages lay in front of him, densely covered with the black pepper-grains of his handwriting. He put a clean sheet on top of the pages and wrote: "Volume One." He pushed away the pile and reached for a new sheet of paper. The second volume had begun.

He still had not read what he had written. He would read it later. Now he had to grab his inspiration by the hair. It was enough for him to know that he was writing a work of art. He was an artist. He felt it in his bones, felt it in the intoxicating intensity of his moods, in the ferocity of the blaze which roared within him – an all-consuming fire, the rage of a tormented creative spirit. He was not conceited. He had never suffered from any megalomanic tendencies. But he ought not to be overly modest, either. He was fully aware that what he was now creating breathed the breath of eternity. Only now, after he had found the strength to destroy his previous work with its deceitful construction, had he reached true greatness.

"Hemingway was a dwarf of a writer. That's why he needed to be in love in order to write at his best," Victor mumbled to himself. "But I'm not like that. I write best when my soul is sick, just as the world is sick. I write best when my soul hurts, just as life hurts."

Onward he galloped with his pen. He must not stop. He had a routine to which he must submit. Every free moment of his time must be crammed with words. He must pile them up, allow them to speak, to sing, scream, mumble, and groan, so that the knottiness of existence should find its reflection, not within them, but between them, around them, in the chaos that they create as they hit against each other. James Joyce wanted to achieve this with his *Ulysses*, with his *Finnegans Wake*. But he did not go far enough. He lacked the courage, lacked the experience, lacked the trials of horror.

"I," Victor mumbled to himself, "I have survived the camps. I have faced the unspeakable, the unutterable...and I've got the courage. I certainly have!"

A year went by. Sonia and Victor had not seen each other for a very long time. The cottage in the Laurentians was their only point of contact. But they never met there. Sonia drove out mostly during the week, when she had a morning free from work, while Victor drove up for the weekend. She knew that he had been there by the mess that he left behind. He, however, knew nothing of her visits, never noticing the order she restored to the cottage. But he sensed her presence nevertheless. It permeated the air.

They still had not made any formal arrangements with regard to their separation. He refused to bother about it. He did not care about such matters. He fulfilled his financial obligations as usual. Sonia, for her part, did not abandon hope that he might come back to her. She continued with her free way of life, just as she had always done, and derived even less pleasure from her adventures than before. She yearned for the warm and intellectually stimulating atmosphere that Victor had created in their home, despite his constant preoccupation with his work. She would gladly have reverted to the life which she had led before she told Victor the truth about Danny. Obviously, in life, just as in art, the truth was not always the best choice.

Time went on. One winter's day, Victor found to his amazement that the thread of his narrative was running out. He took it as a sign that he was about to finish the last volume of his work. A dybbuk seemed to have entered his mind in order to tease him. "You're coming to the end of the line," it squeaked. "The thread is breaking. Soon you'll have nothing to hold on to!"

He stopped writing. Glancing at the tabletop, he saw that it was covered with piles of paper filled with his handwriting. There was only a small space left for his arm, for the hand holding the pen, and a sheet of paper. He could not understand how he had come to fill all these sheets of paper. Here were the completed volumes arranged all in one row, paginated in perfect order. The drive to make order is no doubt innate in human nature. It cannot be avoided. That was why he had to make the meaningless concession of paginating. Now all that was left was to add the conclusion, and number that as well. Perhaps there was something intrinsically positive about numbering?

The little devil sitting in his head teased him. "Soon you'll have nothing to number but blank pages...blank days."

Victor chuckled wisely, "But I have to start writing all over again – from the beginning! I must rewrite! There is no writing without rewriting! That is the writer's duty and his privilege! It is only life that happens once and cannot be repeated. You cannot restart it from the beginning. But the work about life can be started over and over again. That's why the Romans said, *ars longa, vita brevis*. Art is eternal, life is short."

Once again he was zealous. He wanted to keep his mind fresh for the conclusion of his book and forced himself to get up from the table. It was the end of the week. A thick snow had fallen outside. Never mind, one way or the other he would make it out to the cottage in the Laurentians. There he always rested best.

He looked at the table once again. His entire work lay there unprotected. He turned down the heating, checked if the burners on the gas stove were turned off, and unplugged all the electrical appliances so that no spark could chance to fall on his work. At the foot of the bed lay a heap of newspapers. He never read newspapers, but bought one every day in order to glance at the headlines. Now he clipped those articles which he thought might help him relax in the country. He carried the remainder down to the garbage dump. Once back in his room, he put on his winter jacket and boots. He was still worried, fussing like a mother who was forced to leave her child alone for a little time. After he locked the door, he checked to make certain that it was well locked.

He drove as quickly as he could through the snow-covered highway. Soon the mountains loomed ahead, the snow on their peaks undulating like puffed-up blankets of white eiderdown. He began to feel calmer. What a peaceful world!

The countryside was hushed, quiet. A wall of snow covering half of the window had transformed the cottage at *Le petit lac mirage* into a small fortress. Victor began to dig a passage for himself to the front steps. Exhausted, he climbed onto the snow-covered veranda and shook the clumps of snow off his clothes and boots. He kicked away the snow from the door and entered the cottage. The first thing he did was light a fire in the fireplace. Then he took off his heavy wet winter jacket and hung it up to dry on the back of a chair, so that it faced the fire. He threw himself on the cot which stood nearby. It was already late afternoon. Soon night would fall and trap the world in darkness. Tomorrow morning he would go for a long walk on the frozen lake. There it was the easiest to walk. He stared at the snowshoes which hung on the wall near the door. He would put them on tomorrow.

He lay on the cot with his eyes open and saw the night slowly creeping down the frozen windowpanes. Soon the melting panes would begin to weep. The fireplace was loaded with wood. The room was warming up quickly. Before long the panes, completely cleared of frost, would let the darkness of the night invade the entire room. Victor did not think of his work. It was enough for him to know that he would not stop writing it. The flights of his imagination would never cease. It did not matter that at that very moment he was too tired to do any work. It occurred to him that it must already be late. The wind howled inside the chimney. The wolves howled outside. Or perhaps this was the sound of Danny's violin wafting through the room? Victor wondered how it would feel to write to the accompaniment of the wind's laughter, to the accompaniment of the howls of the wolves, and the sobbing of Danny's violin?

But he had no energy to get up from the cot and sit down at the table. In any case, he had to have his entire work beside him when he wrote. There had been a time when he had worked well in this cottage, no matter what. Then he had been surrounded and supported by his family, by Sonia and the children – at least he had thought that they supported him. Now the piles of paper filled with his own handwriting had become his family. Their presence strengthened him. They supplied him with spiritual fortitude. But he had left them in his small room in Montreal. So now he had no option but to lie on the cot and dream – just dream.

He drifted off to sleep. His winter jacket hung on the back of the chair very close to the fire in the fireplace. The rolled-up newspaper clippings that he had brought along to read poked out from the pocket.

He snored heavily. Outside, the wind's fierceness increased. The wolves howled. The storm peaked in its rage. The fire in the fireplace gorged on the wind and gagged, its flames flailing as if they were arms. A long, red tongue shot out to the chair and licked it avidly. Another tongue reached the jacket pocket, and wound itself around the protruding roll of newspaper. At first it licked the paper, as if to get a taste of it, then the flaming mouth clamped down until it had got the entire jacket in its craw. Crackling triumphantly, it swallowed chair and jacket in one fiery gulp.

That was the last night of Victor's life and of his and Sonia's cottage in the Laurentians. The fire burned the cottage to the ground. It also entered the cellar, and through the cracks between the stacks of wood, slipped into the place where Sonia had negligently hidden the metal safe containing the copy of Victor's manuscript. She had often come out to the cottage. She felt that this cottage and Victor's work complemented each other in some way. More than once she had become so immersed in her reading of the novel, and wept for so long over it, that it had grown late and she had had to hurriedly hide the safe.

The flames had a difficult job with the metal safe. But eventually they broke through. Fortified by their consumption of the cottage, the fire melted the thin metal of the safe until it yielded, causing a crack that permitted access to the stacks of papers hidden within. In a wink the flames swallowed them all, down to the last white page, which had held only two words written in Victor's hand: "The Epilogue." And so Victor, their creator, shared the fate of his characters.

When, for the first time after his death, Sonia entered Victor's small room, she was struck by the sight of the stacked sheets of paper covered with Victor's handwriting, which were piled on the table in neatly arranged numbered volumes. The first thing that occurred to her was that Victor – whose death had devastated her – had played a trick on her; that he had discovered the copy of the manuscript negligently hidden in the cellar of the cottage in the Laurentians, and had made a second copy of it without letting her know. This would have been an indication that he still loved her, and that he had begun the definitive version of his novel.

Everything had happened as she had foreseen it. He had not been able to stop loving her. She had known it all along. In his heart he had never left her. This awareness alleviated Sonia's sorrow at the same time as it deepened the pain of her loss. She congratulated herself for her foresight in saving his masterpiece for posterity by copying it. She noticed that there was no title on the cover page of the first volume, and thought that Victor had probably wanted the two of them to think up a title together. Now she would have to do it alone. Now more than ever was she a partner to his work, and she would remain his partner forever. This work would become their joint offering to the world. She now had a purpose to live for; it might perhaps awaken in her a renewed zest for life.

A number of times Sonia felt an impulse to glance at Victor's work. But she did not dare do it so soon. She feared that this might lead to her complete breakdown. So, with trembling hands, she tied all the volumes of the manuscript with string, packed them into a large cardboard box, and took it home. Before long the box assumed a presence of its own in the apartment. It seemed to be calling her, tempting her to open it. Immersed in her mourning as she was, it occurred to her that the soul of the living Victor was to be found inside the box, between the lines of his novel; that inside, in that box, she could also rediscover her own soul, the soul of the real Sonia, the beautiful and innocent.

One autumn day, nearly a year after Victor's death, when Danny was home on vacation, Sonia proposed to him that they drive out to the ruins of their cottage in the Laurentians. She wanted to take Victor's manuscript along and there introduce Danny to Victor's work. But Danny would not hear of it. Ever since Victor's death, a change had come over him. He was his own man now. He answered her with such a categorical "No!" that it sounded like a clap of thunder. Sonia did not dare to broach the subject again. So, after Danny's return to New York, she carried the box with Victor's manuscript down to the car by herself. For a moment she thought how good it would have been to take along the dog, Lord. But Lord had died not long after Victor.

And so Sonia left alone for the Laurentians. After she had arrived at the ruins of the cottage, she spread a blanket on the grass amidst the nearby pine trees, facing *Le petit lac mirage*. She removed the box from the trunk of the car, placed it on the blanket, and laid out all the volumes stacked inside, arranging them neatly in front of her. She had the feeling that this was the most suitable place for her first thorough reading of Victor's work.

With a reverential tremor, she reached for the first sheets of the first volume. She was stunned by their strange appearance. The handwriting was unrecognizable and barely legible. It took her a while before she realized that the thousands of handwritten pages were full of thousands of nonsensical disjointed paragraphs – a meaningless scribbling without beginning or end, a hodgepodge, a mess, a diarrhea of phrases, a disgorging of words ...words...words... a heap of garbage.

She wondered if Victor had gone mad. This provided a logical explanation for his suicide at the cottage. His insanity had prompted him to destroy himself along with the sole copy of his earlier work, and the cottage where he, Sonia, and the children had spent the happiest moments of their lives.

In the distance, the contours of the mountains resembled a chain of question marks hooked into each other, seeming to guard a mystery locked in their midst. A curtain of haze fell over the mirror of *Le petit lac mirage*. Golden leaves of autumn soundlessly detached themselves from the trees and slowly circled in the air before they touched the ground. There was stillness in the air, such a stillness!

Translation by Goldie Morgentaler

MILTCHIN

Dora Schulner

Miltchin was a small town in the province of Volhynia, in the district of Novogrod-Volynsk, near the Polish border. At one time it was a comfortable little *shtetl* that looked more like a village. It belonged to Sergei Avarov, the local aristocrat who lived in a palace that was subsequently confiscated by the Soviets and transformed into a school for children. Sergei Avarov was friendly to the Jews, permitting them to build their own houses. The Jews of Miltchin were primarily involved in business. Sixty Jewish shops were scattered around the marketplace. Although the Jews were far from wealthy, at night the moon would look down lovingly from the luminous sky, and on clear nights the stars twinkled fondly at the Jewish sons and daughters out for a stroll, speaking Hebrew, the holy tongue, and longing for Eretz Israel.

Fate intended that I remain in that little town for several weeks and record my experiences of the very hospitable Jewish community there. Its members used to help out homeless Jews who were fleeing the pogroms and trying to cross the border into Poland on their way to America. The Jews of Miltchin will remain in my memory forever.

We arrived in Miltchin in September of 1922, after having left our birthplace, Radomyshl. We were on our way to America. A bright moon accompanied our wagon and the stars shone like diamonds. As the coachman, from his high perch, gently urged on the horses, I could hear the sounds of the wheels turning and horses neighing. My sister Rokhl was asleep. Snuggling up beside her was her young daughter Frumele. My children were huddled together like little kittens, one on top of the other.

Travelling through the forest, I was listening to the rustling of the trees when suddenly the wagon shook, and Rokhl woke up with a start. She looked around, half-asleep, and asked me where we were. The children woke up and wanted something to eat. Rokhl told them to go back to sleep: "No one eats at night, and besides, if you want to eat at night as well as during the day, we won't have any food left." This excuse did not convince them, so Rokhl shoved little pieces of bread into their hands, which they devoured with gusto. My Khanele wanted to show how grown-up she was by refusing to eat. We offered the coachman some bread, but he said, "Wait. When we're out of the forest, we'll eat." He added that we still had to cross a mountain. Upon hearing the word "mountain" Rokhl became frightened, and began asking how far it was to the mountain. We were all anxious to know, but coachman did not answer.

I noticed that Rokhl could not sit still. She told the children to move closer together inside the wagon, and repeatedly asked when we would come to the mountain. Finally, the wagon climbed up a hill and down the hill, and the coachman informed us that, thank God, we had gone over the mountain. Rokhl gave him a piece of her mind, and we all burst out laughing.

By morning we were all in a more relaxed mood. The horses sped up their pace as the coachman informed us that we were almost in Miltchin. By now we were wide awake. Suddenly I heard the coachman announcing our arrival and asking where to take us. Stopping in the middle of the marketplace, we were met by a beautiful day but no people, because we knew no one. Before we had the chance to worry, however, an impressive looking woman approached us and asked whether we had a place to stay. When Rokhl said no, she seemed pleased, and welcomed us as though we were her relatives. She directed the coachman to her house, which was not far from the marketplace. After helping us take the children and our baggage into her house, she informed us that we would have to sleep on the floor, as she had no beds. The coachman bade us farewell, but I followed him out for one last look. He was, after all, returning to my birthplace, which I would most certainly never see again. Off went the wagon, and sadly I returned to the house.

The house had actually become a hostel for emigrants who were leaving for America that year. In Radomyshl my sister Rokhl had met a Jewish agent from Miltchin who had advised her to come here to cross into Poland. Miltchin had been transformed into an emigration hub, not unlike a port city. Because it was illegal to cross the border, whoever wanted to reach Poland had to spend at least one night in Miltchin. The Soviet authorities kept the border heavily guarded, but during the changing of the guards, agents took the opportunity to smuggle people across.

As soon as we were in the house, Rokhl began preparing a meal for all of us, including the landlady and her children. She cooked a big pot of potatoes, fried an onion, and soon the house was filled with a delicious aroma. The children, playing outside, already felt completely at home. For them, the entire journey to join their father in America was one big holiday.

Russian currency was in use there, but even more desirable were American dollars. The landlady began asking how many dollars we had. Rokhl asked her why she needed to know. First of all, the landlady explained, she wanted a few dollars for herself, and secondly, the agent would accept no other currency. "This is how I earn a living. How else could I manage? Every morning I go to the market to find emigrants, preferably women going to their husbands." I gave her the bad news that not only did we have no dollars, but aside from the five hundred *katerinas* to pay for crossing the border, we had very little money at all. I saw Rokhl's face grow as white as the walls, and realized I had made a mistake. "Please, don't talk to my sister," she said. "You're better off talking to me. But first, let's eat. The potatoes are ready. The children are hungry, and later God will take care of us. You won't lose money on us."

The children were pleased with the meal. We all drank black chicory and the children went out to play again. Rokhl and the landlady had come to an understanding. The woman was an honest widow who needed to feed her children. Her husband had died a few years earlier, but the house belonged to her. Rokhl confided to her that the seven of us were on our way to America, and that dollars would only reach us once we were in Poland. She begged the widow to help us find a wagon to take us across the border. The landlady promised to assist us, but first she had to run out to the marketplace to find some wealthier emigrants who would be able to pay her. "I would really prefer to have you here, but I'm quite certain that from you I won't have enough money to prepare the Sabbath meal."

When we were alone in the house, I asked Rokhl why she looked so frightened when I had mentioned how little money we had. She did not answer but untied her little bag of money and tied it to me, saying: "Be quiet. Don't get involved. You just stay here in the house with the children and I'll go and see what's in town." Rokhl left the house. Through the window I watched my children playing as though they were meant to stay here. Khanele's face beamed with joy, her black curls tumbling out of her kerchief. Frumele, Beylke, Itsikl, and Motele ran happily toward my sister.

It did not take long before our landlady reappeared with some newly arrived emigrants – a father, a mother, a daughter, and a grandchild. At first glance it was evident that these people had dollars. They had come with an agent who was to take them across the border the next day. The daughter was happy to be travelling to her husband in America. I saw the mother and the landlady huddled together talking. They were also preparing a meal, an entirely different kind of meal. With money one can buy the best.

Rokhl returned dejected. Seeing the other family with the agent sitting comfortably at the table enjoying themselves, she went over and introduced herself. They asked her whether she was travelling to her husband in America. "No," she answered, "my sister is joining her husband. I'm going with her to America, and then I'll return to my hometown Radomyshl." She discovered that the family was from Avritch, and that they would be happy to travel with us across the border. Then I heard Rokhl propose to the agent that he take us as well. He asked her how many dollars she had. Rokhl laughed, saying she would give him the dollars in America. Here he could take her *katerinas*. She and the agent came to an agreement: he would take us, and the children, but on condition that if we were caught, he would not act as a guarantor. A deal was struck, and we made plans to cross the border the next day.

That night we hardly slept. The family from Avritch slept in the landlady's beds while she lay on the floor with us. The agent woke us before dawn, and soon we were on the road to the border. Our baggage was on the wagon with the elderly couple, their daughter, and grandchild, while we, along with a few other people who had no dollars, went by foot. On that quiet morning on the Miltchin road, we could hear only the noise of the wagon wheels. Those of us who had not paid – my four children and I, Rokhl and her daughter, and another woman with three children – ran after the wagon.

Suddenly there was a loud whistle and a pistol shot. We stopped in our tracks. Where had the commissar on a motorcycle suddenly come from? Shooting into the air, he ordered us to stand still. Rokhl disappeared into a nearby courtyard. I remained with our five children, the woman with the three children, and some people who had tried to be more clever than we were by attempting to cross the border on their own. We stood terrified as he demanded to know where we were going. The mother of three smiled and said: "What do you mean, where are we going? We're hurrying to a wedding." Angrily the commissar said to us: "You'll soon have plenty to laugh at! Back to town, you saboteurs. March!"

Our heads bowed, we returned to the town. The children wept quietly, but I did not cry. On the contrary, it was as if I had awoken from a deep sleep. The jail we were brought to was suffocating. Since there were no benches, everyone sat on the floor despite the fact that it was damp with spit and worse. This was not like a real jail, as it consisted of one room with a chicken coop. When Motele or Khanele had to relieve themselves, they were taken outside under guard.

I was waiting to be interrogated when suddenly I saw my sister Rokhl standing near the door attempting to get into the jail. She was overjoyed when she finally discovered where we were. Having decided she would rather be with us because she had nowhere else to go to, she begged the guard to let her in. The guard made fun of her: "Go away." he said. "We don't provide free lodging here. You were not arrested. Get away from here!"

Rokhl looked at him as though he were crazy, and waited for an opportunity to slip in unnoticed.

Kustenko was the name of the commissar who arrested us. We were in jail for two weeks. Townspeople brought us food, but how long would we be kept there? There was no interrogation. All the emigrants arrested with us had been released, and Kustenko wanted to release us as well, but he wanted money. The entire time I spent in jail I saw other emigrants arrive on a daily basis, but when their agent appeared and slipped the guard an envelope, he let them go. How long would we have to sit here and wait? After we had been sleeping on a filthy floor with the chickens from the chicken coop roosting on our heads for three weeks, they allowed Rokhl in to visit us, but she had to sleep at the landlady's house.

The town was buzzing. Everyone was talking about the woman with the five children in the jail under arrest. Kind people brought us meals every day. Among them was a lovely girl who had taken an interest in my predicament. She was a Zionist, and had a brother living in Philadelphia whom she intended to visit before travelling to Palestine. She was certain that I would be released and that she would travel with me to Poland. Endless days and nights passed without a trial. Finally, the day came when they sent me to the city of Novogrod-Volynsk, with other people who had been jailed. Rokhl remained in the prison with the children. I was already on the wagon, trying to make myself comfortable, when a beautiful blonde curly-haired young Polish girl accused of espionage was placed with us. The coachman nudged the horses, and drove away from Miltchin.

On the way to Novogrod-Volynsk, known in Yiddish as Zvhil, we stopped in a village for the night. We had no food with us, and there was no food in the hut where we spent the night. A small lamp lit up the large room with an earthen floor and an oven opposite the door. The landlady went back to the cot where her husband and children were sleeping. We lay on the ground covered with sackcloth. The Chekist, as the members of the Soviet secret police were called, was lying beside us, and next to him was his revolver, ready in case we tried to escape.

To me, this was the height of irony. Just recently I had been a Communist big shot, and here I was lying on the cold, hard earth like a political prisoner. Sleep eluded me, and through the small windows I stared at the dark night. I will remember that night forever because it was followed by a bright day.

In the morning we continued our journey. We had started out on a Thursday and on Friday at noon we arrived in Novogrod-Volynsk. To me, it looked exactly like my birthplace, Radomyshl, with the same Jews rushing here and there, probably shopping for the Sabbath. As we rode through the town, we were very conspicuous because the Chekist was guarding us closely. I looked around and spotted the marketplace in the distance.

It was not long before the Polish girl and I found ourselves in jail, but this jail was not like the one in Miltchin. It was housed in a large walled building intended for bandits and criminals that deserved to be there. Among them, however, were innocent people. They herded us into a dark cell. The Chekist told them our names and took away my money, my twenty-five *katerinas*. In the meantime, I saw that I was in a long, narrow cell with one large cot, and near the ceiling was a tiny window with iron bars. There were already four women in the cell and we made six. The four women were Russian, all quite young, and had been going to Rovno in Poland every week to buy various items to sell illegally in Zhitomir, and had made millions. They had been in prison for a few weeks now, with no end in sight. When I asked them why it was taking so long, they repeated the usual refrain: "Damn the Jews who brought the revolution! Because of the Jews we have to suffer!" I looked at their faces, yellow as wax. They knew I was Jewish, but continued to vent their anger at all Jews. The young Polish woman asked them for something to eat. One of the girls took a piece of bread from the window sill, saying: "Here. Have some bread with lice." I thought she was just trying to scare us, but when I saw the bread crawling with filth, I felt sick.

Suddenly the warden appeared and told me to clean the office. I could not even speak; for two days I had eaten nothing. He began swearing at me. I answered back and found myself in a narrower cell where I couldn't move, let alone sit down. With all my strength I banged on the door, and began screaming. I do not remember how long it took but I must have fainted, because when I regained consciousness I found myself in the office with the warden pouring water over me. As soon as I opened my eyes, he threw me back into the cell with the other women.

Completely exhausted, I fell into a deep sleep. I don't know how long I slept but when I awoke, it was dark. The Polish girl was lying beside me, but I could hear the deep voice of a man. Why was a man here? It occurred to me that this was the voice of the warden. I sat on the cot and asked in Russian: "Who's there?" The answer was immediate: "Keep your mouth shut or I'll throw you back in the dungeon." I flew off my bed and began to yell. The warden hissed: "You dirty Jew! I'm not bothering you." Loudly I shouted back, "You scoundrel, you bandit, you think these are the old days? Get out of here!" It did not take long before banging came from the men's section. The warden disappeared. After I had calmed down somewhat I asked the women why they permitted this. They told me that if they did not give in to him, he wouldn't release them. He had been tormenting them for two months now without arranging for a trial.

That night none of us slept. They asked me who I was. I believed in justice, I told them, and assured them that I would not spend another night there with them. The women did not believe me, unless, they said, I was planning to run away. I insisted, however, that I would not run away because I was not a criminal. I did not want to betray the Soviet Union.

Very early the next morning, on a Saturday, as the sun shone through the window, the door opened noisily and someone in the uniform of the Soviet secret police, the Cheka, appeared. He was a refined-looking man with kind, black eyes and a friendly smile that revealed a mouth full of healthy teeth. He wore the cap of a Red Army soldier, and held a revolver in his right hand. Perhaps he had been told that a dangerous criminal had been brought here. In a strong and commanding voice he asked me who I was. I was so engrossed in studying his appearance that I did not hear his question. He asked me whether I understood Russian. I realized that this young man was a Jew. I asked him whether he could speak to me in Yiddish. A smile spread across his face and he replied, "If it is easier for you in Yiddish, go ahead. Explain why you made such a commotion last night that none of the prisoners could sleep."

While the Chekist was talking to me, the warden was busy in the men's section. Before answering, I asked him his name. He laughed and said, "Avrom Goldshteyn. But I'm not the one required to give a report. I'm asking you why you caused such a disturbance."

Angrily I began to tell him about my experience with Kustenko in Miltchin who kept me under arrest for three weeks, about the warden here who molested women during the night, threatening that if they did not comply, he would not release them. I described the journey from Miltchin to Zvhil where the handsome Chekist tormented us. "Comrade Goldshteyn, is this the kind of revolution we wanted? So that bandits like these would have important jobs and torture people to death? If I myself had not experienced this hell last night, I wouldn't have believed it," I said, showing him the lice-infested bread and pointing to the women. "Is this the way it should be?" Goldshteyn's face darkened, and at that moment he saw the warden trying to unlock the cell door. Goldshteyn spun around and grabbed the lock from the man's hand, opened the door, and the clumsy warden fell into the cell with the prisoners who broke into laughter. Goldshteyn locked the door, turned to me, and in a friendly tone informed me that a car would come for me tomorrow at noon. I remember this as though it were a dream.

When Goldshteyn left, the women bombarded me with questions: "First of all, who are you? What were you talking to him about?" When I told them that someone would come to get me tomorrow at noon, they laughed. I was not laughing. I honestly believed that someone would come, and I was not disappointed. At exactly twelve noon the bell sounded at the gate, and my name was called. Soon I was out on the street accompanied by two armed Chekists. The voices of the women were still ringing in my ears: "Tonight you will sleep here." My answer had been "No," and so it was.

In the Cheka headquarters everyone was very pleasant to me. They spoke to Yatsevsky of the Radomyshl Provisional Executive Committee, who told them who I was, and that they could allow me to cross the Soviet border. As for the Polish border, they could not be responsible. They were also to return my money, since it was only a small amount and might be of use to me in Poland.

In a word, Radomyshl and Zvhil understood one another. The comrades shook my hand and said what a pity it was that I wanted to go to America. "You should stay with us for a few months." Goldshteyn humorously recounted how I had treated him as if he were the guilty party, but finally asked: "Comrade Schulner, are you hungry?" What a question! It had been two days since I had eaten. I was immediately released.

The Secretary from Miltchin, who happened to be in Zvhil on an assignment, was designated to be the one to take me to a good restaurant, and after that to Miltchin. It turned out that he had enough room for me in his coach to give me a ride back to my children. And so, before the sun had set, the coach was on its way to Miltchin and to my family.

Translation by Sarah Faerman

AUNT MINDL, UNCLE YOYNE, AND MEIR YONTEF

Mirl Erdberg Shatan

Of all my aunts in the old country, the one most strongly etched in my memory is my Aunt Mindl. Actually, she was my great-aunt – my grandfather Reb Fishl's sister. A series of unforgettable events revolved around her. Had I not personally witnessed a number of these incidents, I, along with many others in our *shtetl*, would have said they sounded like fairy tales.

She had already become a wealthy woman while still with her first husband Uncle Yoyne – may he rest in peace. In the *shtetl* people said that her wealth had come to her through a bizarre miracle. Uncle Yoyne was in the synagogue as usual, either studying or at prayer, and Aunt Mindl was in her leather shop reorganizing her merchandise. She was always very well dressed and wore a great deal of jewellery – long gold earrings, a large brooch. From under her wide-brimmed bonnet, pulled down over her high white forehead and adorned with a variety of ribbons and bows, peered a pair of clever blue eyes.

One day, as she was putting her merchandise in order, a blustery autumn wind burst through the open door of her shop, and in flew bundles of paper banknotes. No one other than Aunt Mindl had actually ever seen the money – or counted it. That is what they said in our *shtetl*.

Mindl had no children. She was – may we be spared such a fate – barren. Therefore she did many good deeds, but whether she did them out of goodness or piety, I do not know. From what I remember, she was not a kind person, and rather stingy. When children came to her home on Saturday afternoons for fruit, as was the custom in those days in the old country, the fruit was rather meagre. However, doing good deeds was straightforward. One had to arrive in heaven with a clean slate, and by doing good deeds one could redeem one's soul from each sin. And who of us has not sinned? Even the most righteous are not free of sin.

Uncle Yoyne hardly ever involved himself in business matters. Even when it came to giving charity, he relied on Aunt Mindl. Most of the time, he sat and studied. Only on market days, when peasants would come into town to do their shopping, did he help her out in her shop. He did everything exactly as Aunt Mindl commanded.

Her first important good deed, one she continued to perform for many years, was paying the wedding expenses for poor brides. The rent from a single room in her house, about forty rubles a year, went to a poor bride. She also paid for a *Torah* scroll to be written after Uncle Yoyne's death. The *Torah* scroll was brought into the synagogue with musical accompaniment, and Aunt Mindl was dressed like an empress. She did many more good deeds, without forgetting to leave six thousand rubles in her will for her brothers and sisters and their children.

Two years after Uncle Yoyne's death, she married Meir Yontef. He was called Reb Meir Yontef (*yontef* meaning holiday) because he always wore a *kapote*, a long, black silk coat with a fine sash tied around it, and a *shtrayml*, a hat in the manner of the Hasidism with a large fur brim. His cheeks were always the colour of a fresh apple, and his full beard made him look very dignified.

Having married a wealthy widow with no children, he immediately considered himself the head of the household. Through flattery and deception, he cheated her out of a great deal of money and jewellery, as though he expected to outlive her. He promised her that when she passed away, his son-in-law, the rabbi, would come from the town of L. and deliver the eulogy. "Little fool," he would say to her with a false smile, "do you know what it means to have a rabbi deliver a eulogy? Not everyone is worthy of that, but when you die, I want you to have a resplendent place in paradise." With these and other fine words, he cajoled her into giving him everything he wanted. On his way home from the synagogue, he would always make a quick visit to one of Mindl's relatives, and with small talk and compliments, he endeared himself to all her nearest and dearest to ensure that they would suspect nothing. This is how he gained control of all her property. He emptied several sacks of gold coins which lay hidden in the cellar of her large house, and filled them with copper kopeks and groschen. Neither Aunt Mindl nor her relatives had the slightest qualm about him. The relatives, most of whom were poor, had never been preoccupied with money. Hence it never occurred to them that Meir Yontef, with the long silk *kapote* and the large *shtrayml*, was capable of doing such a thing.

One day, upon entering her house, I found Aunt Mindl lying in bed. The smooth white skin on her noble face was yellow, her lively eyes somewhat lifeless, her white bonnet pulled down over her forehead. Around her neck hung a long, gold chain that reached almost down to her waist. She called me to her bed and said quietly: "Look, Mirele. This chain will be a wedding present for your brother Avram's fiancée." A few days later the chain had disappeared from around her neck. When her relatives came to pay a sick call, they had not even noticed. They also failed to notice that every day something else was missing from the house. When they did make a timid attempt to ask Meir Yontef about it, his reply was terse and abrupt: "I had to pawn everything to pay for doctors and medicines."

With each passing day Aunt Mindl's condition worsened. Once, when my mother went to see her, I went along. Aunt Mindl called me to her bed, and in a quiet raspy voice, said to me, "Mirele, go to Malka. Tell her to come."

Malka, Hersh-Ber's wife, was an old friend of hers from childhood. A devoted friend and dear person, an honest and pious woman, Malka arrived almost at once, greatly distressed. Aunt Mindl pointed to the book cabinet, and Malka understood at once. She took out a prayer book and recited the confessional prayer with Aunt Mindl. Both women were crying. Tears were running down my aunt's hollow cheeks and falling onto her snow-white pillows. My mother also cried, and my eyes welled with tears.

The woman who had been taking care of her wiped her tears, gave her something to drink, and left with a sigh. Soon afterward, Meir Yontef came home in his long, silk *kapote* with his *shtrayml* on his head. In his hand he had a white piece of paper for her to sign giving him permission to sell the house. Aunt Mindl was already teetering between life and death. He took her hand in his and directed it onto the paper. The very next day the house had been sold. I was not even ten years old yet, so it was hard for me to understand what was happening. Yet, my young heart told me that some very unsavoury things had taken place here. My grandfather, Reb Fishl, and my great-uncle, Meir Erdberg, who lived in Kutno to the age of 104, went into the cellar to see what had happened to the property. However, they did not touch anything until after the burial and the seven days of mourning. As Aunt Mindl lay on the floor in a black kerchief with a lamp beside her head, Meir Yontef summoned the whole family and revealed that he was selling the bedding because there was no money for the burial. The burial society wanted a large sum of money, and he did not have even half the amount. "Also, I have sent a telegram to my son-in-law the rabbi, and to bring him here costs a pretty penny. Since I promised her while she was alive, that my son-in-law the rabbi would deliver the eulogy after her death, I will not break my promise. With medicine, doctors..." he had raised his voice, "nothing will remain of the house, nothing at all."

Almost all the members of our family were people with little experience in financial matters, and they thought that everything he said was true. One of the brothers, however, did speak up. "And what has become of the sacks of gold that were in the cellar?"

"Sacks of gold? Kopeks and groschen. You can have them. They're lying in the cellar."

To this day, I remember how the rabbi arrived that same day in a coach hired expressly for the purpose, just as the funeral had begun. He was forty-one years old and looked very distinguished with his impressive black beard, a pair of clever eyes, and a fine sonorous voice. Of his entire eulogy I remember only a few words which he repeated several times in a rabbinic chant: "This world is only a vestibule leading to the eternal world."

This rabbi was also at the centre of a complicated story. Rumour had it that he was a foundling, and no one knew who his parents were. He was less than eight days old when he was found wrapped in swaddling clothes, behind the steps of a wealthy man's house, with a note attached to him that read: "Circumcise him. He is a Jewish child." Although many attempts were made to find out who his parents were, no trace of them was ever found. The community took charge of the infant, circumcised him, and gave him to a poor woman to raise him. With her scant breast milk she managed to nurse her own child and feed him as well. Kind women would always bring the woman a pot of cooked food so that she could nurse better. When he grew older, he was sent to Talmud Torah. He happened to have a good head, and was the best student of all. At thirteen years of age, he was sent to a *yeshiva* in another town.

Menashe – that was the name he was given – studied diligently and turned out to be the best student in the *yeshiva*. The head of the *yeshiva* boasted about him, and often trotted him out before great scholars to be examined. After he had been ordained as a rabbi, not one of the town's upstanding citizens wanted him for a son-in-law. That is a shortened version of the story that I heard whispered about Meir Yontef's son-in-law.

After the seven days of mourning for Aunt Mindl, my grandfather and Uncle Meir came into our house, each with a sack of copper coins and two chairs. That was the inheritance they brought home from their wealthy sister. A third brother, who was less naïve, succeeded in obtaining a pair of silver candlesticks that had been hidden, and a coveted seat for his wife near the eastern wall of the large synagogue.

Aunt Mindl's death did not put an end to the bizarre stories. The six thousand rubles that she had wanted to leave as an inheritance for her family, she had entrusted to her relative, Nokhem Erdmann's wife. It so happened that she was the richest woman in our town. I never knew her husband, Nokhem. He was already in heaven. But I remember his widow to this day. To me she looked like an empress. She was always decked out in silk and satin, covered from head to toe in jewels. All the buttons sewn on her blouses were made of precious stones. She looked like a queen without a crown.

Suddenly, in her old age, she got the idea that she had to move to Warsaw where she had even wealthier relatives, and could display her wealth more freely. Why live here among lowly tradesmen? It had been a different story when her husband was alive. So one fine day she took all her possessions, and the Polish servant woman who had worked for her for two decades, and left for Warsaw. There, the servant made herself at home in her house, and invited her gentile friends, both male and female. The widow did not object, and made everyone feel comfortable.

We in Kutno, the poor relations, were unconcerned about the six thousand rubles, trusting that after the widow's death, it would be divided up, if not among ourselves, then among our children or grandchildren.

Early one morning, my sister and I were leaving for school. We left the house with my father, may he rest in peace, who was carrying a *talles* bag under his arm. In the street we saw groups of people talking among themselves with horrified expressions. We understood right away that something bad must have happened. My father went over to one of these small groups to find out what had happened. Like a thunderbolt came the news that the widow's servant woman had murdered her. The servant and her friends had chopped off her head, and fled with all her possessions. It is not hard to imagine the reaction in our town. Everyone kept saying: "She moved to Warsaw to suffer such a terrible death! Here in Kutno she probably would have enjoyed a long life. To meet such an end, and only two years after having moved there to Warsaw!"

Later on we heard that the murderers had been arrested, but what happened to her wealth and the six thousand rubles, we never ascertained. No one in the family had the courage, or the energy, to undertake the journey to Warsaw to ask her relatives what became of the six thousand rubles. That was the end of the rich aristocratic wife of Nokhem Erdberg.

Translation by Vivian Felsen

THE BAGEL BAKER

Mirl Erdberg Shatan

In Memory of Her Birthplace, Kutno

Early each morning, just before dawn when the sky was still half grey and the town deep in slumber, Meyer the bagel baker would get out of bed. He would perform the ritual hand washing and immediately go to light the oven. Once the oven was properly fired up, he took his *talles* and *tefilin* and walked to the *beys medresh* to pray in the first *minyan.*

Once he had left his cellar apartment, his wife, Necha, would get up and sigh over her difficult lot in life – spending her days peddling bagels door-to-door, while her only daughter, Dinele, had to work as a servant in the home of strangers. Still half-asleep, she would wash, recite the required blessing, and drink a glass of hot tea. Feeling more awake, she would begin preparing the bagels so that when her husband returned from his prayers, they would be ready to bake.

The whole week they baked bagels. On Thursdays and Fridays women would come to bake *challahs* for the Sabbath. In the town everyone called him "the Bagel Baker." Almost no one used his real name. In fact, it was his wife who was the real bagel baker, and worked much harder than he did. She kneaded the dough, formed the bagels, fried them, placed them on pans, and prepared them for the oven. Her husband heated the oven, put in the bagels, made sure that they did not burn, and took them out of the oven when they were baked. Then both husband and wife very carefully placed the bagels, still warm, in baskets. The wife would take two full baskets to peddle to wealthy houses.

After she had gone, the bagel baker would walk around idle for almost the entire day with nothing to do. On beautiful summer days he opened the tiny windows and the door of his two lonely rooms to air out the cellar after the long, dreary winter, when everything had been hammered shut. Letting in as much light and air as possible, he enjoyed basking in the sunlight.

Sometimes he said to himself: "What a pleasure, these summer days!" and his pointed beard grew longer and fuller, his eyes opened wider, and his vision became clearer. He would stand at the entrance to his cellar abode, his mouth wide open, as though wanting to breathe in all of the summer air. Sometimes he would visit the neighbours who lived in the cellar room next to his, and with a joke or a clever word, or by clowning around, he made them burst into laughter. It seemed that he was always in good spirits and satisfied with his lot. It absolutely did not bother him that on the floor above lived wealthy people who possessed so many good things: bright rooms, wide windows facing the sun, flowing silk curtains bathed in a sea of light, and more food than they could eat. To the bagel baker, this seemed to be God's will. It was preordained in heaven that he should live underground in dark cellar rooms while those above him lived in bright sunshine, and that his wife should have to peddle her bagels to wealthy customers, and his daughter Dinele should be a servant.

On winter days, when the town lay blanketed in thick white snow, it was lonely in the cellar. The windows were covered with frost which made the greyness even greyer. The baker would lie for hours on the large oven with his face turned to the smoke-stained ceiling, and snore. The sound of his snoring mingled with the sound of crickets chirping between the walls day and night without interruption, and the bagel baker was warm and cozy.

When twilight peered through the tiny windows, thrusting grey shadows on the walls, the bagel baker crawled down from the oven, said the evening prayer, lit the small kerosene lamp, and hung it over the door between the two rooms of his home in the cellar. Then he waited impatiently for his wife to return with her empty baskets to cook his supper. Hearing her footsteps approaching, he would run quickly to open the door wide and announce: "The rascal is coming." His wife, tired from a whole day of walking around with her baskets, was not at all amused by his greeting. She would answer him with a sigh: "I barely managed to sell the last two bagels at Madame Zhelikhovky's in the large mill." "A long way," answered the baker in a more serious tone. His wife put away her baskets and began to cook their modest supper. He stood next to her, watching her cook. To make her tired face a little happier, he told her some jokes. Sometimes she would become angry at his cheerfulness, but at other times she would laugh at one of his jokes. And so the bagel baker's life dragged on, slowly and monotonously, for weeks, for months, and for years, in his lonely home in the cellar.

Only on Thursdays did the winter nights in the cellar acquire an entirely different appearance. The rooms became warmer, lighter, and more spacious. A bright lamp was suspended over the large baking table, and the small kerosene lamp that hung each night between the two rooms was placed above the oven. The bagel baker was even more cheerful than usual. He would walk around with a high, white paper hat on his head, looking like someone preparing for a great celebration.

On those Thursday winter evenings women would come to bake *challahs* for the Sabbath. Here at the baker's they kneaded the dough and scoured the troughs while telling stories about husbands, children, financial worries, weddings, divorces – everything under the sun. When the dough was ready, they would "tithe the *challah*" by tearing off a piece and piously reciting the proper blessing. Mothers or grandmothers who had brought along their daughters or granddaughters made sure they heard these blessings.

Cakes were placed on pans greased with oil. The *challahs* were braided, and again left to rise. Thus the hours passed until late in the night. By the time the *challahs* were completely baked it would be midnight. The women were fully absorbed in their baking. They did each step with so much reverence, treating the *challah* like a holy object. When the *challahs* came out well, they were very happy and considered it a double *mitzvah* to be baking so late at night.

While the *challahs* were baking, the women would sit around the oven and listen eagerly to the strange tales of the bagel baker. In his flour-covered clothes, and his white hat on his head, he would sit with his feet by the oven, feeling like a king on his throne. With a pleased expression on his lively face, he would tell them stories of demons, spirits, and ghosts, and his half-grey pointed beard would swell with pride. The women would sit around the oven terrified. They listened quietly and attentively, afraid to move, like statues. They were even afraid to turn around. They would draw closer to one another as he recounted in an earnest tone: "Every night after twelve o'clock someone bangs with a hammer on Brokha-Tsirl's window. This is the tall Vigder coming to demand his bride Esther, and little Esther holds on to her mother in bed, and cries in her sleep. She knows that Vigder left this world because of her parents. They did not approve of her marrying the young tailor. One Friday evening he went to the river and never came back. Night after night he bangs on the window." Fear would grip the women as they listened with solemn faces. They thought they could hear banging, as well as someone weeping in the stillness. The bagel baker would then tell them about the goat with the long, white beard that roamed around the synagogue after midnight. The women become even more fearful. The sound of the crickets and the snoring of the baker's wife in the next room added to their anxiety.

When the *challahs* were finally baked, they were left to cool before being placed in the baskets that the women brought with them from home. The women would do everything slowly, as though wanting to remain here until daybreak. The bagel baker understood what they were thinking. He would put on his old fur coat and fur hat, take the large lantern and a stick, and walk the frightened women home. They would hurry past the synagogue terrified, afraid to lift their heads. They thought they could hear Vigder banging with his hammer on Esther's window. They heard her quiet weeping. In the dark of night, the synagogue looked like a high mountain, and in the darkness they thought they could see demons dancing around it. The women felt their waists to make sure that they were wearing their aprons, which warded off demons and prevented them from having any power. With a silent prayer on their lips – "Hear O Israel" – one by one they fell into their houses where their families were already fast asleep.

Each time there would be one woman less, until the bagel baker remained alone in the darkness. Walking over the frozen snow he sighed deeply, and his sigh echoed in the hollow night. It bothered him that his only daughter, Dinele, still had not found a husband. True, an extremely attractive girl she was not. Since the age of ten she had been working as a servant in the homes of strangers, and her hard-earned money, several hundred rubles, had not yet been paid to her by Moshe Bromberg with the fat belly. Who knows? Perhaps he would also declare bankruptcy. He could do what Ya'akov Gavinsky the moneylender did, taking several thousands from the hard-earned dowries of young women. Bankruptcy! One could protest in vain, and his wife could stand with other women under the window of the rich man's house, and cry and beg: "Hand over my daughter's hard-earned dowry! Hand it over!" His non-Jewish bookkeeper would come out and calmly declare: "The honoured gentleman is not here. He has gone abroad for a rest." The moneylender would stay with his wife in luxurious spas until the paupers here were paid off with groschens instead of rubles, and when things settled down, they would come back. The baker's only daughter Dinele – Heaven forbid! – could be waiting until she turned grey. And his wife? If God let her live, she would have to continue delivering bagels to wealthy houses. He would make his way through the deep snow and, with these sad thoughts, arrive at his cellar. Quietly and slowly he would open the door, and extinguish the large lamp. He would remove the small lamp from above the oven, hang it up on the door between the two cellar rooms, and turn it down low. All the while he would hum a quiet melody as if trying to forget the worries that were just on his mind. Quietly he would read the bedtime prayer, the *krias shma,* and go to sleep.

Translation by Vivian Felsen

AFTERWORDS ~ THREE INSIGHTS

ON MIRL ERDBERG SHATAN

Miriam Krant

Mirl Erdberg Shatan is one of a number of poets with whom our city of Montreal is blessed. Her subject matter is a varied, deeply felt echo of our time.

She was born in Kutnk, Poland, where she received both a Jewish and secular education. Upon her graduation from a teacher's seminary, she became a kindergarten teacher.

Mirl's father, a learned "old-new" Jew, was both deeply immersed in the works of the great Talmudists, and also interested in the modern Hebrew writers. Her devout mother, a lustrous figure, read not only the *Tchines,* the prayer book for women, but also the great modern Yiddish writers like Peretz and Frug.

Interestingly, the writer tells us that her family had collected a large number of Yiddish books, and since the city had no library, they opened the first library in their own home. Anyone could borrow a book for a *grosh*, a penny a week. Her mother, who was familiar with all the books, advised readers on their selection of appropriate ones. In time a large library was established, and they donated all their books to it.

Mirl Shatan's first book, *Nit Fun Kein Freid* (*Not from Any Joy*), published in 1950, consists of a large number of Holocaust poems which are crafted in powerful, expressive lines. The deep tragedy of the Holocaust, says the poet, is part of the long chain of suffering endured by generations of Jews. It seems to her that we can see traces of the massacred everywhere:

On every page
I see your last tremor.
On every blade of grass
The trace
Of your last steps
On each drop of dew
Your last tear.

She feels an acute longing for her home city, which had been "as full as a pomegranate" with Jews, but was now hollow and empty:

Without Berl the porter, without Yankl the smithy,
Without Jewish stores, without Dzhelokov's mill,
Without clusters of Jews at dusk by the mill.

And so the poet lives again in the past, in the homey atmosphere of the *shtetl* that is so dear to her.

After a long break between books, *Regenboign* (*Rainbow*), her selected works, appeared in 1975. This radiant volume, with an introduction by her son, Chaim, includes poetry, essays, stories, and memoir pieces, and a chapter about her husband's (Moishe Yechiel) years in the Bund. However, we will focus primarily on her poetry.

A broad social thematic is dominant in this volume. Despite the optimistic title *Rainbow*, the poet states that she will never sing of joy until the world is free from hunger and war.

In the innovative and melodic lullaby, "Dzsum," she asks the child not to fall asleep. A harsh sound of airplanes above, soon the enemy will come and they will have to flee again. Father has not gone off to deal in raisins and almonds, but to do battle with the enemy, she tells him. A particularly striking poem, "Saint Joseph Boulevard," describes a street completely, irrevocably changed when four rows of thickly branched, leafy trees are cut down. How aptly she compares the street to an empty house without windows, without a door.

Shatan is happy and thankful to find herself in this land of abundance, but with bitter sarcasm she berates Canada for keeping her gates firmly closed to the unfortunate of the world. Her poems are filled with unrest and longing, yet there are bright moments. The establishment of Israel evokes joy in her, and she certainly finds joy in her own family, whom she portrays in their individual talents.

She sees her poetry as the tower of light in her life and regrets the "unsung," the unwritten. It seems to her that she has not yet created a truly artistic poem, and she asks:

When will I cut loose the seed?
And little time is left
And to whom shall I mete out the bread
When it is ready to be eaten,
Who will be the guardian
That my toil not come to naught?

Here in this poem, with its fine metaphors, the poet expresses her sadness about the younger generation's estrangement from Yiddish culture.

Her poetry is distinguished by its content, rhythm, and language. In this small prayerful poem, she asks the Creator to give her the joy of faith.

How long it still is destined for me
To walk upon the earth
Eat bread, drink water,

Let me not sink into despair
Give me, Creator, the joy of belief
That man will raise himself
And I will yet with my own eyes
See the light of the rainbow.

From *Entwined Branches: Essays and Poems*.

Translation by Sylvia Lustgarten

LOVE AND TRANSLATION

Goldie Morgentaler

My mother and I used to fight about translation. These were not genteel disagreements but passionate, intemperate shouting matches. She would say: "That's not what I meant! You twisted my words. Why can't you just translate what I wrote?" I would say: "Because it's not English; you can't say that in English!" Or: "It's too sentimental, too much mush, too many adjectives." She would say: "What a cold language English is!"

My mother was the Yiddish writer Chava Rosenfarb; she died in January 2011, at the age of eighty-seven. I tell you about our quarrels not to suggest that my mother and I had a quarrelsome relationship. On the contrary, we seldom fought about anything non-literary. Nor do I tell you this because I want to demonstrate that she and I were a team, a translating team, although that is exactly what we were. I tell you this because I want to emphasize just how important writing was to my mother's life and how much emotion, passion, and energy she devoted to it.

The first thing journalists and reviewers usually say when they refer to my mother is that she was a Holocaust survivor, as if this one event defined her for all time. Well, she *was* a Holocaust survivor, but it was not the essence of her life. When asked what she did, she always replied, "I am a writer." And she bristled if anyone implied that because she did not leave her house and go to work every day, she had no job. Writing *was* her job; more than that, writing was her life. She was never more miserable than when she had a writer's block, and never happier than when she had a great idea for a story. When she was elderly and could not write much anymore, she would shake her head and say with regret, "I was happiest when I was writing."

But writing is a lonely business, and it was especially lonely for someone writing in Yiddish. When her great work, *The Tree of Life*, was first published in Yiddish in 1972, she received letters from readers from all over the world and glowing reviews in the Yiddish press, which acclaimed it as one of the superior literary depictions of the Holocaust. But she could not convince an English-language publisher to take a chance on the novel until 2000.

In the wider world – that is, the English-speaking world – she was unknown, merely another obscure housewife who thought she could write. As she put it in her essay, "Confessions of a Yiddish Writer":

"If writing is a lonely profession, then the Yiddish writer's loneliness has an added dimension. Her readership has perished. Her language has gone up with the smoke of the crematoria. She creates in a vacuum, almost without a readership, out of fidelity to a vanished language; as if to prove that Nazism did not extinguish its last breath, that it is still alive."

She felt, she said, "like an anachronism, wandering across a page of history."

Like most Yiddish writers, she required a translator, and so she gave birth to one – she gave birth to me. We began collaborating on translations of her works when I was thirteen years old, and we never really stopped. Sometimes, she did most of the translating and I was merely an editor, as with her novels *Bociany* and *Of Lodz and Love*, for which she won the John

Glassco Prize for Literary Translation. Sometimes, I did most of the work. This was especially true of the short story collection *Survivors*, and of *Letters to Abrasha*, her last novel, on which I am still at work. But mostly, we worked together and fought about words and meanings and transmutations of sentences.

In a sense, the tragedy of Yiddish – the fact that it went so quickly from being the *lingua franca* of the majority of the world's Jews to being a language spoken by the very few – brought us together. We became more than simply mother and daughter; we became partners and collaborators in a great literary enterprise.

Literature was the all-in-all for my mother. When she was not writing it, she was reading it. She read novels and books of poetry. She read in Yiddish, in English, in French, in Polish. Her favourite non-fiction books were the biographies of other writers. My mother loved her children; she loved her garden; she loved my dogs. She loved flowers and magnificent landscapes like the open skies of the Canadian Prairies, where she spent her last years. But it was in the literary world that she found her true joy, her sense of purpose, her redemption from suffering and terrible memories. It was only while writing about the Holocaust that she could come to terms with it – and the same was true for the tragedy of her failed marriage.

My mother was sensitive to a fault, but she had the warmest heart and the sharpest mind. She believed in the value of the everyday, in the holiness of mundane things, because she had lived too much in interesting times. She had desperately wanted a happy, sedate family life without tension or betrayal or cruelty. She did not get it.

As you may imagine, I have many memories of my mother; some of the sweetest are very ordinary, such as shopping trips we made together, or going for walks with the dog, or of her wonderful chicken soup, which was the only thing she ever cooked that conformed to the stereotype of the Jewish mother. But my favourite memory is of the sight of my mother, sitting at her desk, so immersed in what she was writing that she did not hear what was said to her. When I saw her there, with her beautiful hazel eyes fixed dreamily on the distance – or, more accurately, fixed on the inner landscape of her imagination – I knew that all was well with the world and that life was good.

Goldie Morgentaler

MRS. MAZA'S SALON

Miriam Waddington

In the fall of 1930, when I was twelve, my family moved to Ottawa from Winnipeg. The reason was this: my father had lost his small sausage-making and meat-curing factory to a partner in a lawsuit. The world was then in the grip of the Great Depression, and the west had been especially hard hit. My father had the idea of starting a small sausage factory in Ottawa, and since there seemed nothing else to do, my parents rented out our Winnipeg house, sold the piano, packed us children into the car, and set out.

The whole family was unhappy about the move. My parents had come to Canada before the First World War. They had met and married in Winnipeg and, once there, became firmly integrated in the circle of secular Jews who had founded a Yiddish day school and named it after the famous Yiddish writer I.L. Peretz. They had many close friends and led a busy social life of meetings, lectures, and family friend dinners in winter, and picnics or camping with other families in summer.

In Ottawa it was a different story. There were very few non-observant Jews and even fewer Jews who had, like my parents, made Yiddish language and culture their home and community. It took them some months to find congenial friends, especially since their energies were absorbed by the task of finding a place to live and sending us four children – all under the age of fourteen – into a new school environment.

Their problems adjusting to this strange and unfamiliar Ottawa community must have affected us children. I knew that I mourned the loss of my two best friends until I found a new one with whom I could walk to school, go to the movies, and share my innermost thoughts and feelings. Also, Ottawa in 1930 was still a small city which, with its population of eighty thousand, seemed like a village compared to Winnipeg. There was some compensation in the fact that Montreal was so close – only 120 miles away, with frequent two-dollar weekend train excursions. After a year or so, my parents discovered the Jewish community in Montreal, and we came to know a number of families whom we could visit.

Among them was a Yiddish poet, Ida Maza. She had published several volumes of poetry and knew all the Yiddish writers and painters in Montreal and New York. Her husband was an agent who represented several manufacturers of men's haberdashery – mostly shirts and ties. His route took him through the small towns between Ottawa and Montreal, and also past Lachute up into the Laurentians. Whenever he was in Ottawa he stayed with us, and he often took me back with him at times when I had no school.

It is hard to describe Mrs. Maza and what I have come to think of as her salon without placing her in the social context that I remember from my childhood. For example, my parents and their friends spoke Yiddish among themselves and regularly addressed one another by their surnames. If it was a man, he would be addressed simply as "Maza," and if it was a woman, it would be "Mrs. Maza." First names were rare and reserved for close relatives. Similarly, when speaking Yiddish – which is an inflected language – they used the polite form of "you," never the intimate "thou."

Mrs. Maza was what is called a *jolie laide.* She looked Japanese and emphasized her oriental exoticism with her carriage, her way of walking and dressing, and her hairdo. She had thick black hair which she piled up around her face in interesting twists and turns like doughnuts and buns. Her colouring was that of the native girls in Gauguin's paintings, and like theirs, her cheekbones were wide apart and prominent. Her eyes were large and dark and Mongolian in feeling. She was short in stature and slight in build, and always wore long kimono-like dresses with sashes and wide sleeves into which she would tuck her hands. Her shoes were simple low-heeled slipper affairs, and she walked with small shuffling steps, for all the world as if her feet had been bound. She had a beautiful low voice, full of dark rich tones, and a chanting, trance-like way of talking. Most of the time she was serious and melancholy in mood, but every now and again she would break into short little bursts of soft chuckling laughter. This was usually when she was with her husband, whom she always treated with tender affection. She liked to tease and jolly him because he took everything to heart with a childlike seriousness.

Looking back, I realize she was not only a very intelligent woman, but full of cleverness and wisdom. She had been born in a village in White Russia and been brought to Montreal while she was still a child. Since she had lived most of her life in Montreal, she spoke English with only a slight accent.

I met Mrs. Maza when I was fourteen. I had been writing poetry for about four years, and my mother must have mentioned it, because Mrs. Maza at once offered to read my work. I showed it to her hesitatingly, and with fear, because she was not just a teacher but a real writer. She praised it and at once took charge of my reading, urging me to Emily Dickinson, Edna St. Vincent Millay, Sara Teasdale, Vachel Lindsay, Conrad

Aiken, and Yeats. Occasionally she would read me one of her own Yiddish poems. I listened, but confess that I didn't give her poems my fullest attention. Most of them were children's poems, playful and tender; or else they dealt with the relationship between mothers and children, not a subject of great interest to an adolescent girl. I have since gone back to read Ida Maza's poems with an adult eye, and find them full of warmth and a lyrical charm that manages to shine through even a rough translation.

In the next two or three years I often stayed with the Mazas during my Christmas and Easter holidays. They lived in a third-floor walk-up on Esplanade. The building was old and resembled a tenement. It contained a buzzing hive of small apartments that you entered through an enclosed courtyard. It faced east and looked across a small park to the Jewish Old People's Home, and just down the street, also on Esplanade, was the Jewish People's Library, which served as a lively community centre for lectures and educational programs.

The staircase leading up to the Maza apartment was narrow and dark. Once inside, however, the front room was bright and colourful, the walls covered with paintings and the furniture draped in Eastern European embroideries and weavings. The furniture consisted of a small sofa and two mission-style oak chairs sternly upholstered in brown leather. There was a matching oak library table loaded with books, and more books were encased in glass on the shelves of an oak bookcase. A long, skinny hallway led from the front room to the kitchen, past two bedrooms that branched off to one side. On the way to the kitchen, and before you reached it, there was a dining room with a round table in the middle, surrounded by chairs. There was also a sideboard, and what was probably the most important and most used piece of furniture in the house, something called a Winnipeg couch – but by Mrs. Maza and her friends it was referred to as a lounge, and pronounced "lontch." On this couch her husband took his Sunday afternoon naps, and in the evenings visiting poets and painters sat on it two or three abreast, listening to poetry being read aloud by one of them or, on occasion, trying out new ideas for publishing a magazine or a manifesto. Or else they discussed new books and gossiped. The reason they sat in the dining room instead of the front sitting room, I now realize, was that it was close to the kitchen, that universal, nonpareil source of food.

To these artists, most of them middle-aged and impecunious, and all of them immigrants, Mrs. Maza was the eternal mother – the food-giver and nourisher, the listener and solacer, the mediator between them and the world. There she would sit with hands folded into her sleeves, her face brooding and meditative, listening intently with all her body. As she listened she rocked back and forth and, as it then seemed to me, she did so in time to the rhythm of the poem being read.

She gave herself entirely and attentively to the poem; she fed the spiritual hunger and yearning of these oddly assorted Yiddish writers whenever they needed her; but not only that. She also fed them real food, and not just once a week, but every day. She served endless cups of tea with lemon, jam, and sugar lumps, plates of fresh fruit, Jewish egg-cookies, homemade walnut strudel, and delicately veined marble cake. And for the really hungry there were bowls of barley soup, slices of rye bread thickly buttered, and eggs – countless eggs – boiled, omeletted, and scrambled. I never knew her to serve anyone, including her family, a conventional meal from beginning to end, but she was always making someone an egg or opening a can of salmon or slicing a tomato to go with a plate of pickled herring.

Who were these Yiddish writers and painters? Some were occasional visitors brought from New York or Israel to give a lecture in Montreal. If I ever knew their names I have forgotten most of them, but there is one writer I remember well. She was Kadya Molodovsky, a Yiddish poet from Warsaw living in New York. One of her poems, "Der Mantel" ("The Coat"), was read and loved by Jewish children everywhere. She had a mild European face that shone with blessedness.

One occasion I remember is Louis Muhlstock's coming to Mrs. Maza's apartment to draw Kadya's portrait. He was very tall and thin, with a mop of dark hair and an animated rosy face. He was a well-known painter even then, although he couldn't have been more than twenty-three or four. He set up his easel in the front room, unrolled his paper, tacked it up, and in the most relaxed way began to draw and talk, talk and draw. Kadya talked too, and laughed, and told funny stories – and neither of them minded the awkward fifteen-year-old girl who sat there watching.

Of the poets who lived in Montreal and frequented Mrs. Maza's salon, J.I. Segal was the most outstanding. He was a prolific writer, well known in the Yiddish literary world, and had already published many books. At the time I stayed with the Mazas, Segal was on the staff of the Yiddish newspaper *Der Keneder Adler* (*The Jewish Daily Eagle*) and was also giving Yiddish lessons to children. A number of other poets also frequented Mrs. Maza's: Moshe Shaffir, Shabsi Perl, Esther Segal – the sister of J.I. Segal – N.I. Gottlieb, Yudika (Judith Tzik), and one or two other women poets. Some of the writers worked in factories and lived lonely lives in rooming houses. One of them wrote a poem with an image that has stayed with me to this day. He likened his heart to the jumbled untidiness of an unmade bed. At the time I thought the metaphor with its image of the unmade bed was so weird that I remembered it for its absurdity. But since it has stayed in my mind for more than fifty years, it can't really have been so absurd. The more I think about it, the more it seems to epitomize and sum up the essence of poverty with all its disorder and loneliness.

The image must have also touched a sensitive spot in my own unconscious, and that was my ambivalence about my parents' generation of immigrant Jews. At that time I bitterly resented my difference from my Canadian friends whose parents had been born in Canada of English background, and who spoke without an accent. How could it have been otherwise? Canadian society during the twenties and thirties brainwashed every schoolchild with British Empire slogans, and promoted a negative stereotype of all Eastern European immigrants, but especially of Jews. Moreover, during all my primary school years, the phrase "dirty Jew" had regularly been hurled at me from the street corners and back alleys of North Winnipeg. Later, when I attended Lisgar Collegiate in Ottawa, I also sensed a certain disdain directed toward Jews, a disdain equalled only by that felt for French Canadians in those days. Perhaps it was no accident that the girl who became my bosom friend was French. She was also from a minority within her social group because her parents were that rare thing, French-speaking Protestants. Her mother came from an old clerical Huguenot family in France, and her father was the son of a well-to-do converted Catholic who had quarreled with the priest in his small Quebec village.

I was not very conscious in those adolescent years of the nature and source of my ambivalence and conflicts – but they manifested themselves in vague feelings of uneasiness and guilt and an awkward sense of always being a stranger in both worlds and not belonging fully to either. Ambivalence, I now realize, also tinged my admiration and fondness for Mrs. Maza and her circle. I often felt uneasy at what I thought of as their exaggerated feelings, or at any rate, their exaggerated expression of those feelings.

I didn't see Mrs. Maza only when I visited Montreal on school holidays. For several years our families spent part of each summer together near St. Sauveur in the Laurentians. The Mazas would rent an old farmhouse, and my parents would camp somewhere not far away. Mrs. Maza loved the gentle contours of the mountains and the way the changing light continually moved up and down their slopes. And there was always a little river – hardly more than a creek – in the neighbourhood of her house. It was good for wading in the shallows, but we children wanted to be near a lake where we could swim. Failing that, we had to amuse ourselves by hunting for mushroom puffballs in the farmer's pasture, or climbing up the mountain to pick raspberries.

Sometimes I would wander over to the Maza's house at four o'clock when the humming heat hung over the afternoon, and would find Mrs. Maza sitting alone on the veranda, her hands folded into her sleeves – she always wore long sleeves, even in summer – rocking back and forth and looking sad. I remember asking her once why she was so sad. She answered in her slow, musical voice, making every word count, that today was the anniversary of Jacob Wasserman's death. Thanks to her I already knew who he was, and under her tutelage had read *The Maurizius Case*, *The Goose Girl*, and *Dr. Kerkhoven's Third Existence*. There wasn't much I could say, so I sat there dumb as a stone, watching the bees alight on the blue chicory flowers beside the veranda, listening to her as she dramatized Wasserman's unhappy life and mourned for him in sad funereal tones.

And he wasn't the only writer whose anniversary of death she observed; there was Edna St. Vincent Millay, Elinor Wylie, Sara Teasdale, and a long roll call of dead Yiddish writers. She mourned them all, and recounted their tragic lives as well as their artistic triumphs in spite of adversity. She would often read me passages from their work, and sometimes she would ask to see my poems and read them back to me, analyzing and praising and prophesying a good future.

My parents, in spite of their unquestionable identification with Jewishness, were not observant of rituals and never went to synagogue. When it came time for the high holidays, Rosh Hashonah and Yom Kippur, my parents, the Mazas, and two or three other families all converged upon a farmer's house near St. Sauveur – the Lamoureux place. There we stayed for a week or ten days enjoying continual harvest pleasures. Mme. Lamoureux set a long table with huge bowls of food: soup, chicken, beef, vegetables – raw and cooked – apple and blueberry pies, and home-grown Lamoureux pears, apples, and plums. Everyone heaped his or her own plate at these country feasts. And I have no doubt that the grown-ups, as they strolled along the gravel roads, gave thought in their own way to the year past and the year still to come.

The Lamoureux are long dead and their farm is no longer a landmark. It was long ago absorbed by modernism and the auto route to the Laurentians. And Mrs. Maza is no longer alive to mark and mourn the anniversaries of the death of her favourite writers, or the loss of the Lamoureux farm, with its harvest bounties that were so happily shared by a group of friends. But they are still alive and present in my mind, and they keep me company whenever I watch the light change on mountains or pick wild raspberries in some overgrown ditch. Somewhere, Mrs. Maza is still urging hungry poets to have a bite to eat, and turning on the light in her dining room to illuminate a crowd of displaced Yiddish writers. And behind them stretches a larger crowd, the long procession of every writer who ever wrote in whatever language. No matter. Each one paid his individual tribute to the love of language and to its inexhaustible resources. And their traces still linger, marking out the path for all writers still to come.

GLOSSARY

In general, we have tried to transliterate Yiddish words according to the standard devised by the YIVO Institute for Jewish Research. However, for commonly used words such as Hasidism, or *cheder*, we have retained the spelling in customary use, rather than *Khasidizm* or *kheder*. Where the Hebrew pronunciation of certain words is in common use, we have transliterated the words accordingly.

beys medresh – from the Hebrew *beit midrash*: literally "house of study." A small Orthodox synagogue.

bris – from the Hebrew *brit milah*: the Jewish ritual circumcision ceremony performed on eight-day-old boys.

Bund – Jewish Labour Bund, abbreviation of "General Jewish Workers' Union in Lithuania, Poland, and Russia": Jewish socialist political party committed to Yiddish and secular Jewish nationalism.

challah – traditional Sabbath bread.

cheder – religious elementary school for boys.

Cheka – Soviet secret police, predecessor of the KGB.

Chesed Avraham – Avraham Yissachar Dov Rabinowicz (1843–1892), the second rebbe of the Radomsk Hasidim, named after his book of teachings entitled *Chesed Avraham.*

Eretz Israel – the land of Israel: the name used by Jews when referring to Palestine prior to the establishment of the State of Israel.

Gemore – from the Hebrew *Gemara*. The *Gemara* and the *Mishnah* together make up the Talmud, the book which is the basis of Jewish law.

Gerer Hasid – a Hasid from the town of Ger (Gora Kalwaria). Before the Holocaust, Ger was the largest and most influential Hasidic group in Poland.

Habimah – Hebrew, literally "the stage": Hebrew-language theatre founded in Russia in 1905 which eventually became the national theatre of Israel.

hamavdil – the prayer recited during *havdalah*. See below.

hamotzi – Hebrew, literally "who brings forth": the blessing recited over bread.

Hasid pl. *Hasidim* – adherent of the religious revival movement that began in Eastern Europe in the latter part of the eighteenth century emphasizing pious devotion, joyful worship, and the individual's relationship with God.

havdalah – Hebrew. A Jewish religious ceremony marking the close of the Sabbath and holidays.

kapote – long black coat in the style of the Hasidim.

kibbutz – communal farming settlement in Israel.

kiddush – Hebrew, literally "sanctification": blessing recited over wine or grape juice to sanctify the Sabbath and Jewish holidays.

kimpetorin – woman in childbirth.

krias shma – from the Hebrew *kriat shema*: bedtime prayer.

l'chayim –To life. A Jewish toast.

mekhitze – from the Hebrew *mekhitsa*: a partition separating men and women during religious services.

mentsh – literally, "human being." In Yiddish used to describe a person of integrity.

mezinke – the youngest daughter.

minyan – quorum of ten men required for certain religious services.

mitzvah – a good deed.

Pesach – Passover.

Reb – Mister.

rebbe – Hasidic rabbi.

seder – festive Passover meal at which the story of the exodus is recited.

sha – Be quiet.

shabbes – Sabbath.

Shavuot – the holiday known in English as the Feast of Weeks, commemorating the giving of the Ten Commandments to the people of Israel.

shiva – week-long period of mourning.

shlemazl – an unlucky person.

shtetl – Prior to World War II, a small Eastern European town populated mostly by Jews.

shtrayml – fur-brimmed hat worn by Hasidim.

shul – synagogue.

soyfer – from the Hebrew *sofer*, meaning scribe.

sukkah – Hebrew. A temporary hut used during the week-long Jewish festival of Sukkoth, the Feast of Tabernacles.

talles – from the Hebrew *talit*: the shawl worn by Jewish men during morning prayers.

Tanakh – the Hebrew Bible.

Tefilin – phylacteries consisting of two small black boxes with straps attached to them that Jewish men are required to wear during prayer on weekday mornings.

Tiferes Shlomo – the name given to Shlomo Hakohen Rabinowicz (1801–1866), the first rebbe of Radomsk, after his classic Hasidic book of teachings entitled *Tiferes Shlomo*.

Tilim – from the Hebrew *tehilim*: Book of Psalms.

Tsena-Urena – early seventeenth-century Yiddish-language religious book for women containing Biblical commentary and folklore.

yeshiva – educational institution for Jewish religious studies.

yontef – from the Hebrew *yomtov*, meaning holiday.

zloty – unit of Polish currency.

zogerin – female prayer leader who would read prayers aloud for the other women in the women's section of some pre-Holocaust Eastern European synagogues.

Publication Data

A Note of Explanation: The careful reader will notice some inconsistency in the transliterations of the Yiddish titles. Some writers and publishers chose to follow their own paths rather than the accepted conventions. These include Rachel Korn, Sheindl Franzus-Garfinkle, Shira Gorshman, among others.

Lili Berger

"The Teacher Zaminski and his Student RifKele" - *Ekhos fun a Vayten Nekhten: Dertseylungen, Eseyen un Skitsn* (Echoes of a Distant Past) Farlag Yisroel Bukh, Tel Aviv, 1993.

"Jewish Children on the Aryan Side" - *Fun Vayt un Noent* (From Far and Near), Imprimerie S.I.P.E. Paris, 1978.

Rokhl Brokhes

"The Shop" - "*Der Tsukunft*", vols 10 -12, 1922-24.

"The Neighbor" - *A Zamlung Dertzeylungen*, Vilner Farlag, Vilna, 1922.

Sheindl Franzus-Garfinkle

"Rokhl and the World of Ideas" excerpt - *Rokhl,* Montreal, 1941.

Shira Gorshman

"Chana's Sheep and Cattle" excerpt - *Chanas Shof un Rinden* (Chana's Sheep and Cattle), Israel-Book Publishing House, 1986.

Chayele Grober

"To the Great World" excerpts - Tsu *Der Groyser Velt* (To the Great Wide World), Farlag Bialystoker Vegen, Buenos Aires and *in Mayn Veg Aleyn,* Peretz Publishing House, Tel Aviv. 1968.

Hammer-Jacklyn, Sarah

"The Holy Mothers" - *Lebens Un Geshtalten: Dertzeylunge* (Lives and Portraits), Novoradomsker Association, New York, 1946.

"She Found an Audience" - *Shtamen Un Tzweigen* (Stumps and Branches), Novoradomsker Association, New york, 1954.

"In a Museum" - ibid.

Rachel Korn

"Shadows" excerpt - 9 *Dertsaylungen* (Nine Stories), Montreal Committee, 1957, (5438).

Miriam Krant

"On Mirl Erdberg Shatan" excerpt - *Geflecht Fun Zweigen: Eseyen un Lider* (Entwined Branches: Essays and Poems), Montreal. 1995.

Blume Lempel

"The Sprite" - A *Rege Fun Emes* (A Moment of Truth), I.L.Peretz Publishing House, Tel Aviv, 1981.

Ida Maze

"Denah" - *Denah* (Denah: Autobiographical Novel), The Ida Maze Book Committee, Montreal.1970.

Rikudah Potash

"The Tenth is Born in Mishkenot" - "*Der Tsukunft*" April, 1950 Vol. 55.

"The Little Messiah" - *Geslekh fun Yerushalayim* (In the Alleys of Jerusalem), Israel Book Publishing House, Tel Aviv, 1968.

Chava Rosenfarb

"A Cottage in the Laurentians", "*Dos Maysterverk*" - "*Di Goldene Keyt*", no. 112, 1984.

Dora Schulner

"Miltchin" excerpt - *Miltchin,* published by a Group of Friends, Chicago 1946.

Mirl Erdberg Shatan

"Aunt Mindl, Uncle Yoyne, and Meir Yontef" - *Regnboigen: Lider, Eseyen, un zikhroyne* (Rainbow: Poems, Essays and Memoirs), published by Chaim F Shatan, New York, 1975.

"The Bagel Maker" - ibid.

Biographies of the Yiddish Women Writers

Lili Berger (1916–1995)
Born in Malkin, Bialystok region, Poland, Lili Berger was a prolific novelist, short story writer, literary critic, and journalist whose works have been published in major Yiddish and some Polish publications on several continents. Her award-winning fiction, including *Fun haynt un nekhten* (*Of Today and Yesterday*), reflects the Polish Jewish experience in the twentieth century. In 1936 she settled in Paris, and during the Nazi occupation of France was active in the Resistance. After the war she lived in Warsaw until 1968, then again in Paris where she resumed her literary activity and lived until her death in 1995.

Rokhl Brokhes (1880–1942)
Born in Minsk, Russia, Rokhl Brokhes made her writing debut at nineteen, followed by publications in distinguished Russian and American Yiddish periodicals. Her novellas and short stories included in *A zamlung dertseylungen* (*A Collection of Stories*) poignantly depict life among Russia's impoverished and powerless, women in particular. Her collected works, over two hundred of them short stories, were at the publishers when the Nazi invasion put an end to the project. Brokhes was murdered by the Nazis in the Minsk Ghetto.

Sheindl Franzus-Garfinkle (1899–1957)
Born in Bershad, Ukraine, Sheindl Franzus-Garfinkle migrated to Montreal in 1922. In the 1930s she began her writing career in the Yiddish daily *Der Keneder Adler*, with short stories that received a great deal of attention and critical praise. She published a few books, including *Rochl* and *Erev Oktober* (*On the Eve of October*), which describe the lives of idealistic young people during the Russian revolutionary period in Odessa and in Jewish towns and villages. She died prematurely in Montreal.

Shira Gorshman (1906–2001)
Born near Kovno, Lithuania, Shira Gorshman's life was characterized by continuous wandering. In Odessa and Moscow she began her writing career with short stories and novellas – largely autobiographical – about life in the *shtetl* as well as in the Jewish collectives of the Crimea, which she depicted in the novel *Khanes shof un rinden* (*Chana's Sheep and Cattle*). Her language was traditional Yiddish, ironic yet gentle, visually

rich and poetic. Her last home was in Israel where she continued to write well into old age.

Chayele Grober (1896–1978)
Born in Bialystok, Poland. During World War I Chayele Grober began her acting career in Moscow in the Jewish national theatre, the Habimah, which she helped found. In 1928 she arrived in Montreal, the city which became her home. While in Montreal she wrote articles about the Yiddish and Hebrew theatre for the Canadian Yiddish dailies and other periodicals. Her memoirs *Tsu der groyser velt* (*To the Great Wide World*) and *Mayn veg aleyn* (*My Own Way*) recount her experiences and encounters with Jewish artistic life in Montreal. At the end of her life she lived in Tel Aviv.

Sarah Hamer-Jacklyn (1905–1975)
Born in Novoradomsk, Poland, Sarah Hamer-Jacklyn immigrated to Canada in 1914. Captivated by the Yiddish theatre in Toronto, she began her career as an actress and singer at sixteen. Retaining her love of Yiddish as well as her dramatic connection with the theatre, her short stories serialized in the Canadian Yiddish daily *Der Keneder Adler*, as well as in major literary journals, depict a wide range of subjects spanning *shtetl* life, Holocaust narratives, and women's search for creative expression in America. Her collection of short stories, including *Lebens un gestalten* (*Lives and Portraits*) and *Shtamen un tsveygn* (*Stumps and Branches*), published in the 1940s and 1950s, were received with critical acclaim.

Rachel Korn (1895–1982)
Born near Pokliski in East Galicia, Rachel Korn spent the war years in Uzbekistan and Moscow. In 1948 she immigrated to Montreal. In the course of her literary career she published nine volumes of poetry and a collection of stories and novellas, including the major *Nayn Dertselungen* (*Nine Stories*). Her work, drawing heavily on Holocaust experience, has been translated in a number of languages including English, French, Hebrew, and German. She received many literary awards, including the prestigious Manger Prize for Yiddish Literature.

Blume Lempel (1910–1998)
Born in Khorostov, Galicia, Blume Lempel immigrated to Paris in 1929. In 1939, on the eve of World War II, she immigrated to New York. In the 1940s she made her literary debut in Yiddish-American periodicals with short stories and a serialized novel. She is the author of widely rang-

ing volumes of fiction including *A rege fun emes* (*A Moment of Truth*) and *Balade fun a kholem* (*Ballad of a Dream*), published in the 1980s in Israel.

Ida Maze (1893–1962)
Born near Minsk, White Russia, Ida Maze lived from 1908 to the end of her life in Canada, first in Toronto and later in Montreal. Called "the mother to Yiddish poets," Maze helped writers and intellectuals (among others) in DP camps obtain visas to Canada. Widely published in Canadian Yiddish periodicals, her works, especially her poetry for children and young people, appeared worldwide in numerous anthologies of Yiddish verse. Some were translated into Hebrew, Russian, French, and English. Her only novel, *Denah*, describing the small-town Jewish life of her childhood, was published posthumously in 1970.

Rikudah Potash (1903–1965)
Born in Tshenstokhov, Poland, Rikudah Potash became a poet at sixteen. Stirred up by the Lemberg pogrom of 1918, she turned to Yiddish; her stories, novellas, essays, and theatre pieces appeared in literary journals worldwide. In 1934 she left Poland and settled in Jerusalem, where she lived for the next thirty years and continued her multi-faceted literary life. Her last prose writings, *In geslekh fun Yerusholoyim* (*In the Alleyways of Jerusalem*), were devoted to the Eastern Jews from Yemen, Bukhara, and Salonika facing the challenging realities in the newly established state of Israel.

Chava Rosenfarb (1923–2011)
Born in Lodz, Poland, Chava Rosenfarb was one of the most important Yiddish writers of the second half of the twentieth century, and received most of her schooling in Yiddish. During World War II she was incarcerated in the Lodz Ghetto, sent to Auschwitz, and then to Bergen-Belsen, where she was liberated. After the war, Rosenfarb settled in Montreal and commenced a prolific six-decade literary career, strongly informed by her Holocaust experiences. One of the few female novelists writing in Yiddish, her novels include *The Tree of Life: A Trilogy of Life in the Lodz Ghetto*, *Bociany*, and *Survivors*. Awards for her work include Israel's highest award for Yiddish literature, the Manger Prize; the Award of the American Professors of Yiddish; the John Glassco Prize for Literary Translation; the Canadian Jewish Book Award; and an honorary degree from the University of Lethbridge.

Dora Schulner (1889–1962)

Born in Radomysl, Kiev province, Dora Schulner immigrated to America in 1914. Her writing career began in 1940 with the publication of short stories in Yiddish journals in the United States, Canada, and Mexico. Her novels and short stories expressed Jewish life in its full range: from the religiously observant life in the shtetl, to the idealism and exuberance of the early revolutionary period, to the immigrant experience in America. Her publications include *Miltchin* and *Ester*, recognized for their frank portrayal of Jewish women in the Russian Pale of Settlement before, during, and after the Russian Revolution and Civil War.

Mirl Erdberg Shatan (1894–1982)

Born in Kutno, Poland, Mirl Erdberg Shatan arrived in Montreal in 1926. A longtime staff writer for *Der Keneder Adler* (*The Jewish Daily Eagle*), she also published oft-anthologized poems, short stories, book reviews, as well as translations from Polish literature. *Regenboign, lider, esayn un zikhroynes* (*Poems, Essays and Memoirs*) was published in Montreal in 1975.

Biographies of the Translators

Frieda Johles Forman

Born in Vienna into a Yiddish-speaking family. After the war, she and her parents migrated to the United States where she later taught Hebrew and Jewish Studies. Years later, she founded Kids Can Press, the children's book publishing house, and directed the Women's Educational Resources Centre of the University of Toronto. She is the author of *Jewish Refugees in Switzerland During the Holocaust: A Memoir of Childhood and History* (2009) and the researcher, an editor, and translator of *Found Treasures: Stories by Yiddish Women Writers* (1994). She also edited *Taking Our Time: Feminist Perspectives on Temporality* (1994). Articles by Forman have appeared in *Jewish Women: A Comprehensive Historical Encyclopedia* (2006) and *Jewish Women in America: An Historical Encyclopedia* (2001).

Sam Blatt

Born in Montreal into a Yiddish-speaking home, studied Yiddish and Hebrew in Yiddishe Folks Shule, Montreal. Blatt was a founding member of and performer in the Dora Wasserman Yiddish Drama Group. He is a member of several Yiddish groups including Yiddish Women Writers. He is also the editor of *Seizing Control of Space in East Jerusalem* by Dr. Meir Margolit.

Sarah Faerman

A retired teacher and social worker, grew up in the "Yiddish *shtetl*": north-end Winnipeg. She was the founder and editor of *If Not Now*, a newsletter addressing Holocaust survivor issues. Her translations include the *Yizker bukh* (*Memorial Book*); *Dubossary*; and a story of her father's in *Tracing Our Roots, Telling Our Stories*, published by the Jewish Genealogical Society of Canada (Toronto).

Vivian Felsen

With her background in languages and history, has been translating French into English professionally for more than three decades. Long involved in Yiddish circles, her translations from Yiddish have received the Canadian Jewish Book Award for *Montreal of Yesterday: Jewish Life in Montreal 1900-1920* (2000) and the J.I. Segal Award for *Between the Wars: Canadian Jews in Transition* (2003). Both volumes are translated from the works of Yiddish journalist Israel Medres. She includes in her translations *Memoirs of the Lodz Ghetto* by Yankl Nirenberg (2003). Felsen is a highly respected visual artist in Toronto.

Shirley Kumove

Born and educated in Toronto, considers Yiddish her mother tongue. She is a frequent lecturer on Yiddish language and literature and on the art of translation both in Canada and abroad. The translator and editor of *Ordinary Jews* by Yehoshue Perle (2011); *Drunk from the Bitter Truth: The Poems of Anna Margolin* (2005); *Words Like Arrows: A Collection of Yiddish Folk Sayings* (1984); and *More Words, More Arrows: A Further Collection of Yiddish Folk Sayings* (1999), Kumove also contributed to *Found Treasures: Stories By Yiddish Women Writers* (1994) and numerous other publications.

Sylvia Lustgarten

Born in Montreal in 1926, is the daughter of J.I. Segal, noted Yiddish poet. She grew up in the rich, dynamic Yiddish cultural world of early twentieth-century Montreal. In her adopted city of Toronto, during her ten years as director of the Yiddish Committee of the United Jewish Appeal, she established several significant cultural organizations including Friends of Yiddish and The Yiddish Women Writers Group, which resulted in the publication of *Found Treasures: Stories by Yiddish Women Writers.*

Goldie Morgentaler

A professor of nineteenth-century British and American literature at the University of Lethbridge, is the French-to-Yiddish translator of numerous works. She translated Michel Tremblay's *Les Belles-Soeurs*, which was performed by the Yiddish Theatre of Montreal in 1992. Her translations from Yiddish to English include several short stories by I.L. Peretz, which appeared in the *I.L. Peretz Reader* (1990). She is the translator of much of Chava Rosenfarb's work, including the play *The Bird of the Ghetto,* and the three volumes of Rosenfarb's *The Tree of Life: A Trilogy of Life in the Lodz Ghetto* (1985). Her translation of Rosenfarb's book of short stories, *Survivors: Seven Short Stories* won the Helen and Stan Vine Canadian Jewish Book Award in 2005 and the MLA's Fenia and Yaakov Leviant Memorial Prize in Yiddish Studies in 2006. She is the editor of Rosenfarb's book of poems in English translation, entitled *Exile At Last: The Poems of Chava Rosenfarb* (2013). She also contributed an Afterword.

Alisa Poskanzer

Born in Poland, and grew up in Winnipeg, and was educated at New York University and the Hebrew University in Jerusalem. She worked as a family therapist in Canada and Israel. Her publications include *Ethiopian Exodus* (2000) and "Matryoshka: Three Generations of Russian Immigrant Women."

Ida Wynberg

Born at the end of World War II to Yiddish-speaking parents en route to a DP camp in Germany. She emigrated with her family first to Norway in 1946, then to Israel in 1948, and finally to Toronto in 1952. A graduate of the University of Toronto, she worked as a psychologist and later in the field of architecture. For the past eight years, she has devoted much of her time to the study of Yiddish language and literature: at the University of Toronto, The Florence Melton Jewish Studies program, as well as in Yiddish reading groups.

Biographies of the Authors of Afterwords

Miriam Krant (1914–2004)

Born in Pabianice near Lodz, Poland, Miriam Krant arrived in Montreal in 1922. Recognized by the literary critics of her day for her talent, she published poetry, essays, short fiction, and children's stories in *Der Keneder Adler* and other periodicals across the world. Her book *Lider un essayn* (*Poems and Essays*), containing literary and personal portraits of women poets, was published in 1979 in Montreal.

Miriam Waddington (1917–2004)

Born in Winnipeg, Miriam Waddington is a much published, translated, and acclaimed author of poetry, stories, and essays. She herself has translated both poetry and prose from Yiddish and German. Waddington was the editor of *Canadian Jewish Short Stories* and *The Collected Poems of A.M. Klein*. *Apartment Seven*, her autobiographic pieces and essays, from which "Mrs. Maza's Salon" is here excerpted, provides a unique contribution to Canadian Jewish culture and in particular a vivid picture of Yiddish writers.

Permissions

Every effort has been made to contact the copyright holders of the Yiddish works included in this anthology, some of which are in the public domain. Since many of the original Yiddish texts were published privately or by publishing houses no longer in existence, it has not been possible to clear permissions in every case. In the case of any omissions, rights holders should contact the publisher for corrections in future editions.

"Shadows" (*"Shotens"*) by Rachel Korn translated with the kind permission of her grandson, Dr. Allan Coopersmith.

"On Mirl Erdberg Shatan" ("*Mirl Erdberg Shatan*") by Miriam Krant translated with the kind permission of her son, Shloime Perel.

"The Sprite" ("*Dos shretele*") by Blume Lempel translated with the kind permission of her son, Paul Lempel.

"Love and Translation" copyright Goldie Morgentaler, by permission of the author.

"A Cottage in the Laurentians" ("*Dos maysterverk*") by Chava Rosenfarb translated with the kind permission of Goldie Morgentaler.

"Mrs. Maza's Salon" by Miriam Waddington reprinted with the kind permission of her son, Marcus Waddington.

Acknowledgements

Often left to the last, acknowledgements actually reflect vital aspects in the process of bringing a book to light. Our collection, involving thirteen authors, eight translators, several editors, and a copy editor under one cover, provides the opportunity for many thanks and much gratitude.

To Richard Teleky, who by his vision for the book converted a loosely structured reading group into a fierce army of Yiddish translators. His unstinting efforts and generative guidance on behalf of the collection will certainly earn him a place among the enablers of this world.

To Sam Blatt, who undertook with good humour, imagination, and tenacity the unenviable task of formatting a manuscript of many fonts, formats, sizes, and spacing that came to him from members enthusiastic but uninitiated in the ways of computers.

To Vivian Felsen, who took great initiative and intellectual rigour in editing and researching the countless details intrinsic to a work of such complexity.

To Ida Wynberg, who brought order out of chaos, creating files and documents for a desperate editor.

To Sarah Faerman, Shirley Kumove, Sylvia Lustgarten, Alisa Poskanzer: wonderful partners and colleagues in a shared labour of love.

To Simcha Simchovitch for his generosity in sharing his exceptional knowledge of Yiddish, Hebrew, and Jewish history and culture, both secular and religious.

To Nessa Olshansky-Ashtar for making available to us her excellent research skills.

To Chris Doda, who stepped in at a crucial moment and helped with careful computer entries.

To Dana Snell for careful, tactful, and reliable copyediting: winding her way through the maze of unfamiliar Yiddish transliteration rules and conventions.

To Matt Shaw for his superb contribution to the final editing of a difficult and often bewildering text.

To Michael Callaghan for his enthusiastic efforts on behalf of the book.

To Nina Callaghan for her sharp eye for details.

For their generous support to the publication of *The Exile Book of Yiddish Women Writers* we thank the following: The Miransky Fund at the Jewish Foundation of Greater Toronto, the Committee for Yiddish UJA Federation, and Friends of Yiddish in Toronto.

To Anna Moransky for her welcoming hand to the project.

To Shannon Hodge at the Jewish Public Library Archives, Montreal, for her kind assistance in locating rights holders.

To Rhea Tregebov for her warm response to the book and her help in locating rights holders.

To Faith Jones for her help in locating rights holders.

Friends played a vital role during the years of shepherding the collection (of people and texts) from conception to completion. Their countless acts of true friendship, encouragement, and prodding sustained the often frustrating, lonely work of giving life to a project as complex as this.

Thanks, appreciation, gratitude to:

Sharon Kirsh, who listened critically and lovingly to the early translations and inspired continuity.

Eva Cohen, for the pleasure of reading the Yiddish stories together and for providing the right words when needed.

Pat Mills, for her deep understanding of the significance of this literature and never letting me forget it.

Paula Doress Worters, for being a loyal advocate for our shared vision of giving a voice to the silenced.

Leora Freedman, for the joy of integrating friendship and study.

Esther Israelski, for the weekly stimulus of Yiddish as our parents spoke it.

Rusty Shteir, for heartening wise words and exhortations to stay with the task.

Ann Pappart, for her inimitable spirit in supporting the work at hand.

Nora Gold, for her unflagging work in giving Jewish literature its due.

Leah Bacon, who remembered always to express her engagement, even at a distance.